More THAN
MEETS THE *Eye*

Books by Karen Witemeyer

More THAN MEETS THE Eye

KAREN WITEMEYER

BETHANYHOUSE
a division of Baker Publishing Group
Minneapolis, Minnesota

© 2018 by Karen Witemeyer

Published by Bethany House Publishers
11400 Hampshire Avenue South
Bloomington, Minnesota 55438
www.bethanyhouse.com

Bethany House Publishers is a division of
Baker Publishing Group, Grand Rapids, Michigan

Printed in the United States of America

ISBN 978-0-7642-1283-3 (trade paper)
ISBN 978-0-7642-3191-9 (cloth)

Library of Congress Cataloging-in-Publication Control Number: 2017963586

Scripture quotations are from the King James Version of the Bible.

This is a work of fiction. Names, characters, incidents, and dialogues are products of the author's imagination and are not to be construed as real. Any resemblance to actual events or persons, living or dead, is entirely coincidental.

Cover design by Dan Thornberg, Design Source Creative Services

Author is represented by Books & Such Literary Management

18 19 20 21 22 23 24   7 6 5 4 3 2 1

To Jeff and Kristie Gilliam

Some might call it coincidence, but I call it providence. Only God could cross our paths at just the right moment to bring such blessing to all concerned. Your appearance in that Lubbock bookstore two years ago brought me genuine joy. I hope to return the favor with this long-awaited story. May the love reflected in these characters be reflected in your lives until Christ calls us home.

Let all bitterness, and wrath, and anger, and clamor, and evil speaking, be put away from you, with all malice: And be ye kind one to another, tenderhearted, forgiving one another, even as God for Christ's sake hath forgiven you.

—Ephesians 4:31–32

Prologue

1879 — FANNIN COUNTY, TX

"Don't lose heart, children. We have several strong families lined up in Bonham. I'm sure we'll find good homes for each of you."

Four-year-old Evangeline Pearson smiled at the sponsor from the Children's Aid Society as the lady made her way down the train car aisle, bracing her hand for balance against one empty seat after another. Seats that had been filled with children when they'd left New York.

Miss Woodson always made Evie feel better. Even after seven . . . eight. . . . Evie scrunched her nose and unfolded her fingers one at a time as she tried to count. How many stops had they made? When she ran out of fingers, she gave up, huffed out a breath, and flopped back against the wooden bench seat. It didn't matter. No one had wanted her at any of them. But Miss Woodson had promised to find her and Hamilton a home, and Evie believed her. She was such a nice person, after all. Nothing like the lizard lady sitting stiff and straight at the front of the train car.

As if Mrs. Dougal had heard Evie's thoughts, she twisted her neck around and scowled, her bulging eyes and pursed lips making Evie shudder. She buried her face in her brother's shoulder.

"Don't let her scare you," Hamilton whispered as he gently lifted his arm and wrapped it around her. At nine, Hamilton was ever so much bigger and stronger, and not afraid of anything. Even when Mama and Papa died. Or when Children's Haven had decided the Pearson siblings would be riding the orphan train west. Never once did he cry or fret. He just hugged her tight and promised that everything would be all right. He was the bravest boy who ever lived.

"She doesn't like me." Evie snuck a peek at the lizard lady, found her still scowling at her, and burrowed deeper into her brother's side. "It's 'cause of my eyes, isn't it?"

Hamilton slid his hands under her arms and lifted her onto his lap. He tipped her chin up and looked straight into her face. "There is nothing wrong with your eyes, Evie. They're beautiful. God's gift. Remember what Mama used to say?"

Evie's chin trembled slightly. Thinking of Mama always made her sad. Made her wish everything would go back to the way it had been. Mama holding her in the rocking chair and singing lullabies. Papa swinging her high into the air and laughing with that deep belly laugh that always made her giggle. Her room with rose paper on the wall. Her bed with the pink quilt and soft pillow. But it was gone. *They* were gone. Forever.

"What did Mama say?" Hamilton insisted.

"That only special little girls get eyes with two colors," Evie mumbled. She wanted to believe it was true. She really did. But if having two different eyes made her so special, why did no one want her?

Hamilton nodded. "That's right. And you know what?"

Evie glanced at her brother, envying his normal, matching brown eyes. "What?"

"I wish my eyes were the same."

"As mine?" Evie leaned back, her forehead wrinkling. "Why? Then no one would want you, either."

Hamilton smiled and bopped a finger on the tip of her nose. "Every time you look in a mirror, you see both Mama and Papa looking back at you. Mama from your blue eye, and Papa from your brown one. And you know how much they both loved you. It's kind of like getting one of those hugs where they sandwiched us between them. Remember those?"

Evie nodded slowly. Oh yes, she remembered. So warm. So safe. Her in her nightdress in Mama's arms, her legs wrapped around Mama's middle. Mama smelling sweet, her long braid tickling Evie's bare toes. Papa growling like a hungry bear, saying he needed an Evie sandwich, before he grabbed Mama and squished Evie between them. Their three heads jostled together. And their eyes . . . Mama's bright blue ones to Evie's left and Papa's twinkling brown ones on her right. Just like hers!

A smile broke out across Evie's face. "Oh, Ham-ton, you're right! I have the bestest eyes ever!"

He folded her into a hug—not quite as bearish as Papa's, but still warm and safe and full of love. "Don't ever forget it," he said as he squeezed her tight.

As Evie rested in her brother's arms, voices drifted to her from the front of the railcar.

"Bonham's the last stop," Lizard Lady grumbled as Miss Woodson slid into the seat next to her, "though I don't know why we should bother with it. No one's going to take these misfits. Zacharias scares the women and angers the men with his hostile, defiant manner. Seth is so sickly, most families assume he'll not make it through the winter. And Evangeline. She behaves well enough, but those unnatural eyes of hers unsettle decent folk. Heavens. They unsettle *me*."

"Lower your voice, Delphinia," Miss Woodson urged. "The children can hear you." She twisted in her seat to smile an apology at Evie. The smile didn't take away the sting of Lizard Lady's mean comment, but it gave Evie just enough gumption to ignore it while considering for the first time what the other leftover children must be feeling.

Evie straightened away from her brother and turned around in her seat to look at the two boys behind her. Three rows back sat a boy close to Hamilton's age. He looked nothing like her brother, though. He was so pale and skinny. The new coat the Children's Aid Society had given him hung on him like it would a scarecrow. He stared out the window, his shoulders slumped, chest caved. And every time a puff of soot found its way into the railcar, he coughed.

The other boy sat in the very back of the car on the opposite side. His back was pressed sideways into the corner, one long leg drawn up onto the bench, his hat pulled low on his face. Not so low she couldn't see his eyes, though. They were dark, just like the rest of him. Dark clothes. Dark hair. Darkly tanned skin. He even had dark whiskers growing on his cheeks. But those dark blue eyes made her shiver. Especially when he stared straight at her. Like he was doing now.

She didn't think Zach had any friends. He was always by himself, even when the train had been filled with children. She had Hamilton. Zach didn't have anyone. That was sad. Everyone needed a friend.

Evie smiled and wiggled her fingers in a timid wave.

Zach glared at her and showed his teeth like a growling dog.

Evie snatched her fingers back and spun around in her seat. Maybe some people didn't need friends after all.

"I've had great success placing children in Bonham before," Miss Woodson said. "I'm sure everything will work out."

Mrs. Dougal harrumphed. "The only kid you might place is the Pearson boy. Several have offered for him already. All you have to do is separate him from his sister."

Separate her from Hamilton? Evie's heart pattered so hard it felt like it might break out of her chest. She grabbed her brother's hand and held on for all she was worth.

"But it's so hard on the children when we split them up," Miss Woodson protested.

"It'll be harder on them if they end up on the streets in New York. If we can save one, I say we do it. Sometimes the hard decisions are the right ones." Mrs. Dougal tossed a quick look over her shoulder at Evie and Hamilton before sniffing and turning back to Miss Woodson. "There's no reason to kill the boy's chance at a promising future just to stave off a few tears. They'll recover."

Evie stared hard at Miss Woodson, begging inside her head for her champion to tell Lizard Lady she was wrong. But she didn't. Instead, Miss Woodson bit her lip and nodded.

"You can't let them split us up, Ham-ton!" Evie wailed in a desperate undertone, careful not to let Lizard Lady hear. "You can't!"

Hamilton squeezed her hand, his chin jutting out. "Don't worry. I won't." Keeping hold of her hand, he slid off the seat and made his way into the aisle. "Come on. I need to talk to Zach."

The scary boy in the back of the railcar who'd just snarled at her? Evie dragged her heels. "I don't wanna—"

Hamilton huffed out a breath and gave her one of his don't-be-such-a-baby looks. "He's just a kid like the rest of us, Evie. And he can help."

He was most certainly *not* like the rest of them. She wasn't even fully convinced Zach was a kid. Not with whiskers and legs nearly as long as Papa's had been. But she wasn't about to let her brother think she was scared, so she pressed her lips together and let Hamilton drag her along.

"What d'ya want?" Zach lowered his leg from the bench to sprawl across the opening between his seat and the rear-facing one across the way, barring Hamilton from getting close.

But that didn't stop her brother. He just climbed over the barrier and sat in the seat facing the other boy, leaving Evie to clamber up beside him.

"I need advice," Hamilton said, his voice firm like Papa's used to be whenever he was instructing them on proper behavior. "The sponsors think to split us up at the next stop, and I can't let that happen. So I need to know how you get people not to claim you."

Slowly, Zach sat up and leaned across the open space between the two seats. His dark blue eyes narrowed, and the edge of his mouth lifted in a smile that looked downright scary. Evie's stomach clenched.

"I tell them that I'll kill them in their sleep."

Evie gasped. How could someone say such a terrible thing? Surely he didn't mean it. Did he?

Zach smirked at her. Evie whimpered.

Hamilton, on the other hand, nodded. "Right. Threaten to kill them. Got it."

What? Evie's gaze jerked to her brother. He couldn't!

Zach must have thought the idea outrageous as well, because he shook his head and sighed. "Look, kid, just because it works for me doesn't mean it'll work for you. You got one of them angel faces. No one will believe you capable of murder."

"Maybe he can cough, like me." Seth wandered down the aisle, a sudden hacking making everyone turn to look at him. "Act"—he coughed into the handkerchief the sponsors insisted he carry—"sick."

Zach shook his head. "Nah. He looks too healthy. They'll assume he'll get better." The older boy lifted his hat and scratched at a spot on his head, the meanness leaking away from his face. "We gotta find something else."

Evie looked from one boy to the next. Was Zach actually *helping* them? Maybe Hamilton was right. Maybe he just *pretended* to be awful. Though why someone would want everyone to hate him, Evie couldn't understand, not when she tried so hard to get people to like her.

Zach eyed Hamilton up and down, then crossed his arms over his chest and leaned back in his seat. "Spoiled rich kid. That's your angle."

Hamilton frowned. "But I'm not rich. All I have are one spare set of clothes and the cardboard suitcase the Children's Aid Society gave me. Same as everyone else."

Zach unfolded his arms, a devious light twinkling in his dark blue eyes. "Yeah, but with names like *Hamilton* and *Evangeline*, it'd be easy as pie to get people to think you come from money. Farm folk resent rich folk. Think they're spoiled and have no work ethic."

Evie had no idea what a work ethic was, so she probably didn't have one. Maybe *that* was why no one wanted to take her home. Hamilton must have one, though, since people liked him. He'd have to find a way to hide it.

"Start throwing demands around. Then throw a fit. Yell. Scream. Flail around." Zach was grinning now. A smile that actually looked happy instead of scary.

"And if all else fails, bite 'em." Seth offered that bit of advice once his cough settled. "Whenever I wanted the nurses to leave me alone, I bit 'em. They stayed away for a good long while after that."

Zach slapped the frail boy on the back, nearly sending him to the floor. "Good idea! May have to try that one myself someday." He started chuckling, and the other boys joined in.

Evie laughed, too, even though she didn't think biting was particularly funny. A kitten had bitten her finger once, and it hurt for two days afterward. But if biting would keep her and Hamilton together, she'd bite someone, too.

"Get back to your seats, children," Miss Woodson called from the front of the car. "We're almost to Bonham. You'll need to gather your belongings."

Evie shared a look with Hamilton, then climbed off the seat and headed back to where they'd been sitting. Her tummy twisted and pinched at the thought of what might happen when the train stopped, but she remembered what Mama had always told her to do when she felt afraid.

Once in her seat, she folded her hands in her lap, bowed her head, and closed her eyes.

Don't let them take Hamilton away from me. Please. I need somebody down here who loves me.

An hour later, Evie stood on a raised platform in the local courthouse with Hamilton, Seth, and Zach, waiting for the families to come in and look them over.

"Stand tall, don't fidget, and speak only when spoken to." Miss Woodson gave the same instructions she did at every stop as she walked the line to inspect them one last time. She paused to tug Seth's coat sleeves down over his wrists, then ran a smoothing hand over Evie's hair. When she moved toward Zach, he gave her such a mean look that she backed away without touching him. "Smile," she said as she shot a chiding look at the boy slouching in the corner, "and mind your manners."

The families started coming in, and Evie's heart raced. *Please let someone want me. And Hamilton. Together. Please.*

She did everything Miss Woodson had told her. She didn't fidget. Stood tall as she could manage. Smiled. All while hiding her eyes. She kept her face downcast, watching feet instead of faces move through the courthouse lobby.

Hamilton stood a few feet away, talking with a man and his wife.

"We really only want a boy, one who can help in the fields," the man was saying.

"Remember the agreement you signed, Mr. Potter." Miss Woodson joined the group. "Any child you receive must be treated as a member of your family. And if you expect a farmhand's labor from him, you must offer a farmhand's wages."

"I know. But he's talkin' about me takin' on his sister as well. She's too young to be much help on the farm, and if I'm payin' wages, I won't have the funds to feed and clothe another child."

"Let's just look at her, John. Please? She's got the same reddish-brown hair Nellie did. Maybe if I had another girl around the kitchen, I wouldn't miss our daughter so." A gray skirt swished in Evie's direction.

Evie smiled as wide as she could stretch her lips. *Please want me. Please want me.*

The lady in gray stopped in front of Evie, then hunkered down. Determined to hide her eyes, Evie kept her gaze focused on the lady's skirt.

"What's your name, child?"

Evie swung back and forth, then remembered she wasn't supposed to fidget and stopped. "Evangeline."

"That's a pretty name. You remind me of my daughter, Nellie. She's grown now. Married a man from two counties over, so

I don't get to see her very often. I miss having a little girl around. I could teach you how to cook and sew. Would you like that?"

Evie nodded, her excitement building. "Yes, ma'am."

A pair of rough boots plodded up beside the gray skirt. "Look at a person when you speak to them, girl." The hard, manly voice made Evie jump.

What should she do? If she showed her eyes, they might not want her anymore. But if she didn't look up, they'd think her defiant.

"Maybe she's just shy, John," the gray lady said. Her hand came up to cup Evie's chin. "My Nellie had such lovely brown eyes. Are your eyes brown?"

Evie nodded. It wasn't a lie. She did have a brown eye.

"Let me see." The lady pushed Evie's chin up.

Maybe she could just show one eye. Evie tried to open her right eye while squeezing her left eye shut, screwing up her mouth in concentration.

"Quit making faces, girl," the man barked.

The sharp tone startled Evie, and she forgot to keep her left eye shut.

The lady gasped and pulled her hand away. "Her . . . eyes. Miss Woodson, what's wrong with her eyes?"

Evie immediately shuttered her gaze, blinking back the tears that rose.

"Nothing's wrong with her eyes!" Hamilton rushed to Evie's side and grabbed her hand. "She can see just fine. That's all that matters, isn't it? That they work. My sister's smart, cheerful, and strong for her size. You'd be getting a deal if you take us both on. You wouldn't even have to pay me any wages. I'll work for free if you take Evie, too."

"So her eyes won't ever . . . fix themselves?" The lady in gray stood, backed up a step, then rubbed her arms against a shudder.

Miss Woodson's familiar blue skirt came into view. "Hamilton is correct. Evangeline's vision is not impaired, and she truly is a darling child."

"But those eyes are so . . . peculiar." The woman backed away another step. "They give me the shivers."

"That decides it," Mr. Potter said. "We'll take the boy. Not the girl. One extra mouth to feed is all I can afford anyway."

"Very well." Miss Woodson sighed. "Mrs. Dougal can assist you with the paper—"

"No!" Hamilton stomped his foot. "I'll not go without my sister."

Evie stared at him. That fierce voice didn't sound anything like the kind brother she knew.

"Don't sass your betters, boy." The man pointed a finger in Hamilton's face.

"You're not my better!" Hamilton shoved his nose in the air. "I'm a Pearson. My papa used to hire people like you to work in his factory. People too stupid to do anything more than simple tasks, like planting seeds and watching them grow."

"Hamilton!" Miss Woodson's shocked voice echoed Evie's disbelief.

The man glowered, his face turning bright red. "You better watch your mouth, boy."

"Or what?" Hamilton challenged. "You'll whip me? Beat me? Chain me up in your barn? I'd expect nothing less from a man who probably can't even read."

Mr. Potter shook with rage, and Evie worried that her brother had gone too far.

"He doesn't mean it." Miss Woodson placed her hands on Hamilton's shoulders and pulled him away from the man, who looked like he was about to strike. "He's just afraid of being separated from his sister."

"I do too mean it." Hamilton jerked away from Miss Woodson's grip and stepped straight up to the farmer and his wife. "And it's not just him who's ignorant. His wife is, too. Why else would she be scared of something as trifling as eyes that are two different colors?"

The man's hand fisted.

Evie lunged for her brother and wrapped her arms around his middle. "Stop, Ham-ton. Stop!"

"He's a child, John." The lady in gray had stepped in front of her husband as well and stared up into his face as she placed a staying hand on his arm.

"I'll not tolerate anyone speaking about you that way, Georgia. No matter his age." He set his wife aside and jabbed his finger into Hamilton's face. "If you ever speak ill of my wife again, I'll—"

Hamilton lurched forward and bit down on the man's pointed finger.

The farmer howled, then cuffed Hamilton across the head with his other hand. Hamilton toppled. Evie fell with him. Women screeched. Men yelled. And all Evie could do was hang on to her brother and pray that everything else would go away.

"Well, that was a disaster." Lizard Lady's pronouncement bounced around the interior of the railcar as it rattled down the tracks, taking them back the way they had come. There'd be no more stops. No more chances at finding families.

"That weren't no disaster," Zach said with a grin as he punched Hamilton lightly in the shoulder. "That was brilliant! Well done, Ham-bone. I'm impressed."

Hamilton grinned as if he'd just been named king of the mountain. The boys had all chosen to sit together in the back of the railcar, Zach actually making room for Seth on the seat next to him as Hamilton and Evie sat in the rear-facing seat in front of them.

Evie thought them all crazy to be so proud of themselves for such awful behavior, but she and Hamilton were still together, so she wouldn't scold them. Lizard Lady had done that enough already.

The boys recounted the event over and over until Evie grew bored. And sleepy. Being scared wore a girl out, and she'd been more scared today than any day she could remember. The rocking of the train made her eyelids heavy, and her head started to loll toward her chest.

"Here, Evie." Hamilton set his back against the window like Zach had done earlier and made room for her to nestle up against his chest.

She curled up against her big brother and slept until a harsh jolt tossed her onto the floor. Her head bumped against someone's bony knee, and she cried out as the terrifying sound of braking train wheels screeching against the rails pierced the air.

Luggage fell from the overhead racks. The sponsors screamed. Hamilton called Evie's name before he dropped down over her and wrapped his body around hers.

"Crawl under the seat, Evie, and hold on to the chair legs."

She did what he said, hugging the ornate iron leg that connected the bench to the floor with all her might. Then the train slammed into something. Hard. So hard, the force tore Hamilton away from her.

"Ham-ton!"

A loud groan rumbled, and the railcar started to tip. Evie wailed her brother's name.

"Hold on, Evie! Don't let go!"

She did. Until the railcar tipped on its side, throwing her

against one of the windowpanes. Metal ripped. Glass shattered. The train tore itself apart as it slid sideways down an embankment. Evie cried, trying to find something to hold on to. The train slid over a rock, the jagged surface knocking out the glass of the window next to Evie's and bouncing her into the air. Something hard stabbed against her side. She whimpered but grabbed for the hat hook, her little fingers clinging desperately to the metal hanger.

It seemed to take days for the train to stop its slide. When it did, Evie called for her brother and waited for him to come for her.

He didn't come.

"Ham-ton!" Where was he? Was he hurt? Evie started to cry. He couldn't be hurt. She needed him. "Ham-ton!"

Letting go of the hat hook, she got to her hands and knees, then slowly pushed to her feet. "Ham-ton!" She took one step. Then another. Broken glass crunched beneath her shoes. Her legs shook. Her head ached where she'd banged it against the luggage rack. Her eyes searched through tears that wouldn't stop flowing.

Suddenly a pair of arms wrapped around her.

She turned, ready to hug her brother tight. Only it wasn't Hamilton. It was Seth. His chest made a funny noise as he breathed, almost like it was squeaking.

"You're hurt." Evie touched his head where blood matted his hair.

"It's all right," Seth said, holding her close. "Stay here . . . with me . . . Evangeline." His chest heaved as he gasped between words.

"I have to find Ham-ton." She tried to pull away. His skinny arms were surprisingly strong, though, and he held her fast.

"Not yet. You . . . need to wait."

He was scaring her. The way his eyes looked at her. Sad. Sorry. The way people had looked at her after Mama and Papa had gone to heaven.

Evie struggled. "Ham-ton! I want Ham-ton!"

She stomped Seth's toes and broke free. She stumbled forward, tripping on a window frame, but grabbed the edge of a sideways bench to keep from falling. Everything was sideways. Crumpled. Broken.

She spotted Zach hunched over, a giant plate of glass in his hands that he yanked upward and tossed aside.

"Zach?"

She was going to ask if he knew where Hamilton was, but when he turned to look at her, his face made her forget her words. He didn't look mean or tough now. He looked . . . lost.

"He saved my life," he mumbled, his stare blank. "Pushed me out of the way and saved my life." Zach blinked, then seemed to recognize her. He jumped to his feet and tore at his coat as if it had suddenly caught fire. Finally, he flung it from his back and tossed it on top of a pile of something behind him.

Seth joined them. "We need to get . . . her out. Shouldn't . . . see this."

Shouldn't see what? Evie looked from one boy to the other. What were they hiding from her, and where was her brother?

"She needs to say good-bye," Zach argued.

Say good-bye? To who?

"Evie?" A weak voice cut through the argument, stilling everyone.

Hamilton!

Evie pushed past Zach and found her brother at last. He lay on his back, not moving. Zach's coat covered him up. She stumbled up to where his head lay and wrapped her arms around his neck. But he didn't hug her back. Didn't rub her hair and tell her everything would be all right. He just lay there. Still. Too still.

"Ham-ton? You gotta get up." She grabbed his shoulder and tried to pull him into a sitting position. "Get up, Ham-ton!"

"Easy, princess. You don't want to hurt him." Zach crouched beside her and patted her back. It felt awkward and stiff, but it was warm, too. And Evie felt so cold, as if her heart had turned to ice.

"Zach's gonna . . . take care of you now," Hamilton said, struggling to open his eyes. "He made me a promise, and I trust him . . . to keep it. You can trust him . . . too."

"I don't want Zach to take care of me. I want you, Ham-ton!"

Her brother smiled, or tried to. "I know, Evie, but I can't stay. I have to . . . go see Mama . . . and Papa." He coughed, and something red came out of his mouth.

Terror seized Evie, shaking her from top to bottom. Hamilton couldn't leave her. He couldn't!

Zach helped Hamilton turn his head and wiped away the blood, the tenderness so strange from the rough boy. Once he was done, Hamilton looked at Evie again.

"I love you, sis. Always . . . and forever."

"Don't leave me, Ham-ton." Her voice broke as she collapsed on his chest and cried out her heartache. "Don't leave me."

Something gurgled in his lungs; she could hear it beneath the coat. But she also heard voices. Seth and Zach arguing.

"They'll never let you stay with her," Seth was saying. "As soon as we get back to New York, they'll divide us up again."

"That's why we're not going to New York."

"What?"

"We're making a run for it."

"But we're just kids. How can we—?"

"If you don't want to come, don't come. But I made the kid

a promise, and I never go back on my word. I'm gettin' the girl out of here. If I can survive on the streets of New York, I can survive in Texas. We'll make do."

"But they'll search for us."

"So we change our names. Become our own family with our own name."

The boys quieted, leaving nothing but the shallow gurgles of her brother's chest to echo around Evie. Then even that stopped. "Ham-ton," she moaned, knowing he'd left her.

"Hamilton's a good name," Seth said.

"Yeah," Zach answered. "Hamilton it is."

CHAPTER

1

Logan Fowler dismounted outside the Lucky Lady Saloon, anticipation thrumming in his veins. Seven years. That was how long he'd been waiting to enact justice. Seven years of loss, sacrifice, and preparation. And today represented the beginning of the end—for Zacharias Hamilton.

"I'll make it right, Ma," Logan vowed beneath his breath. He patted his chestnut's neck before wrapping the reins around the hitching post. "For Pop."

Logan tugged his hat brim a little lower on his forehead. The long white scar that slashed diagonally across his left eye from halfway up his brow to a spot close to the top of his ear tended to draw attention, and he'd rather be inconspicuous while gathering information. Not that the scar didn't have its advantages. Especially in saloons. Looking dangerous gave a man an edge. Demanded respect.

At only twenty-three, Logan had worked hard to cultivate a stony bearing to match the hard heart he'd spent seven years callousing. He wore a beard to disguise his youth and a gun to keep folks at a distance.

He squinted toward the west, where the sun still hovered well above the horizon. A mite early for a crowd to have gathered in the saloon, but then, he'd timed his arrival for precisely that outcome. An inveterate gambler like Hamilton wouldn't bother to put in an appearance until the whiskey had been flowing for a couple hours, softening the brains and the inhibitions of his marks. Which made now the perfect time to collect intelligence.

With slow, swagger-heavy steps, Logan strode up to the bat-wing doors and pushed through. He moved just inside the entrance and stood with his back to the wall as his eyes adjusted to the dim interior.

A woman with henna-red hair and a bodice that left little to the imagination stood with her hands on her hips atop the small stage at the front of the room, haranguing the piano player about rushing the tempo of her song. A group of four men—farmers, judging by their overalls and serious expressions—sat around a corner table, discussing the necessity of getting a Populist elected to Congress. But it was the man behind the long, polished counter that Logan found most intriguing.

"Thirsty, mister?" the barkeep asked as Logan approached. He finished drying a tall glass, then used the dish towel to shine up the counter in front of the stool closest to Logan. "Delta County is dry, I'm afraid, but I've an assortment of switchels and shrubs, ginger water, sarsaparilla, coffee, or tea. Also got a full menu of food options if you're in need of a meal."

The barrel-chested fellow smiled warmly enough, if cautiously, as he took in Logan's appearance, but when Logan pushed his hat back and fully exposed his scar, the disgust that registered in the barkeep's face before he could hide it stirred Logan's ire.

"Coffee's fine." Logan leaned an elbow on the bar, keeping his body angled so he could see both the barkeep and the door.

The Lucky Lady was a tame watering hole compared to the dives he'd frequented over the last four years, a necessary training ground for one who wanted to master not only cards but faces—learning to read tells and ferret out cheats. Consorting with the worst scoundrels humanity had to offer also taught a man a thing or two about survival. The recollection of the broken bottle that had been used to decorate his face kept Logan from underestimating anyone in the room. Even the flame-haired songbird making eyes at him as she conspicuously adjusted the scarlet garter holding up her black stocking. Women could be just as treacherous as men.

The barkeep set a brown ceramic mug on the counter in front of Logan, then retrieved a pot from the stove behind him. As he poured the brew, he peered up at Logan with a questioning arch of his brows. "So, you passin' through?"

"Nope. Bought a spread up by the North Sulphur River. Plan to stay a spell." At least until Zacharias Hamilton got his comeuppance.

His host eyed him with skepticism as he plopped a tin cup onto the counter. A small set of tongs rattled against the rim of the makeshift sugar bowl. "Ya don't exactly strike me as the farmin' type." His gaze darted to the men at the corner table and back.

Logan shrugged and dropped two cubes of sugar into his coffee. "You got a spoon . . . ?" He drew out the pause, waiting for the barkeep to supply his name.

"Dunn. Arnold Dunn." He wiped his hand on his pant leg, then extended it across the bar.

Logan shook it. "Logan Fowler."

Dunn showed no recognition of the name. Not surprising.

Seven years ago, the town had been brand-new, barely a post office to its name. Dunn probably hadn't even been around. It wasn't until the railroad came through in 1888 that people started flocking to the area. Which made Hamilton's crime all the more severe. Logan's father's land would have tripled in value with the railroad's arrival, but Hamilton had stolen it from him before that could happen. Had stolen his father's *life* as well.

The barkeep extracted his hand, then found a spoon and set it on the counter next to the mug. As Logan stirred the dissolved sugar into his coffee, he cast a quick glance around the room to ensure no one was paying him any particular attention. Then he casually brought up the topic he most wanted to discuss.

"You get many high-stakes games in here?"

Dunn chuckled. "Didn't call her the Lucky Lady for nuthin', did I? Highest stakes in town. You a gamblin' man?"

Logan took a sip of his coffee, studying the other man. "When properly motivated."

"Only go for the rich pots, huh?" Dunn's mouth curved in a sly grin.

Logan just sipped his coffee, letting the barkeep think what he would. In truth, Logan despised gambling. Hated the greed that accompanied it, the unnecessary risk, the completely irrational belief that one could actually control fate. He'd learned to count cards, to run probabilities in his head, to read the faces of those sitting at the table around him, but he still lost. Not as often as most, and not more often than he won, but often enough to remind him that control was an illusion. No man controlled fate. God alone claimed that honor.

He eyed Dunn over the brim of his mug. "You got any big players around here?"

Dunn shrugged. "Most of the folks in these parts don't have

much ready cash. The boys from the mill will get up a good game when they've got wages burning a hole in their pockets, but the rest play friendly games as a way to pass the time. Play runs deeper here than at L. A. Campbell's place, though. I don't put no limits on the stakes or kick people out if things get a little rowdy. Unless someone starts breakin' up the place. That's just bad for business."

"A fellow by the name of Hamilton ever play here?" Logan's gut clenched even as he forced his expression to remain cool. He wouldn't want the man to think him *too* interested in the answer.

"*Zach* Hamilton?" Dunn's eyebrows arched.

Logan lifted the coffee to his mouth in a carefully measured display of nonchalance. "Man has the reputation of a player, and I heard he lived around here."

"Oh, he lives around here, all right. Probably'll be your neighbor, seein' as how his spread backs up to the river, too. But a player?" Dunn shook his head. "I can't picture it. Oh, I've heard the rumors that he might have gambled in his younger days, but I ain't never seen him so much as touch a deck in my place. Nowhere else in town neither, as far as I know."

Logan froze, the cup halfway between his mouth and the counter. *Never touched a deck?* That couldn't be right. The cardsharp his father had described would never just hang it up. The thrill of the game? The addicting rush of power that came with each win? Logan himself battled the pull, and he despised the pastime. It made no sense for a gamester like Hamilton to simply retire.

"Maybe he rides over to Ben Franklin to play," Logan gritted out as he slowly lowered his cup. It would make sense. If Hamilton had set up permanent residence in Pecan Gap, he'd not want to stir up trouble amongst his neighbors. Beggaring them with his underhanded gameplay would make any aboveboard business dealings next to impossible. It'd be wiser to conduct his confidence games elsewhere, and Ben Franklin was only a few miles' ride farther from the homestead than Pecan Gap. Or he could even ride to Cooper. Bigger city. More anonymity. The fact that he didn't gamble here didn't mean he didn't gamble at all. It didn't mean Logan's scheme would fail. It just meant Logan would have to be patient. Learn Hamilton's habits. Get under his skin. Hamilton was smart. Cagey smart. Logan would have to be smarter.

"I wouldn't know anything about what Hamilton does over in Ben Franklin," Dunn was saying, "but he don't exactly seem the socializin' type. All them Hamiltons keep to themselves."

"*All* the Hamiltons?" The question jumped out of Logan's mouth before he could mask his surprise. He quickly swigged another mouthful of coffee and forced his spine to soften back into a more casual position after springing to attention at Dunn's statement.

"There's three of 'em." Dunn glanced around, then placed an elbow on the bar and leaned close, lowering his voice to a raspy half-whisper. "Odd bunch. Claim to be siblings, but if you ask me, there's no way they're related. Not by blood. None of 'em look a thing alike. And that girl?" He turned and spat at the floor.

Hoping there was a spittoon back there somewhere, Logan hid his repulsion at the barkeep's abysmal manners and lowered his mug to the counter. Somehow, the coffee seemed a lot less appetizing after that display.

Dunn swiped the back of his hand beneath his lower lip, then eyed Logan with a grim expression. "I ain't the superstitious sort, mind you, but if I were, I'd swear that gal was a witch. A freak of nature, she is. Eyes that don't match. And I'm not just talkin' about eyes that are slightly different shades. No, this gal has one eye as brown as chocolate and another so bright blue, it pierces a man's soul." He shivered. "I can feel that blue eye of hers following me whenever she's around. Cursing me." He turned his head and spat again.

Logan arched a sardonic brow. "And here I thought you weren't the superstitious sort."

"Scoff if you like, mister, but you'll see what I mean if you stick around long enough. Get those eyes trained on you, and you'll change your tune. See if you don't."

Logan didn't care about some girl with mismatched eyes. He cared about Zacharias Hamilton. Although, if Hamilton was claiming this girl as his sister, Logan might be able to use that to his advantage somehow. His honor wouldn't permit him to threaten her in any physical way, but if Hamilton had an emotional tie to the female, she might be a weakness Logan could exploit.

A good card player used every weapon at his disposal to win, only two of which were the actual cards and the chips in the pot. Rattling one's opponent with a few well-placed barbs, using the hint of a grin to sell a bluff, complimenting a player who took a round through sheer luck on his exceptional skill in order to elicit overconfidence on the next hand—they were all strategies of emotional warfare. Strategies Logan had honed to a razor's edge.

He pulled a coin from his trouser pocket and tossed it onto the bar. "Thanks for the coffee and the conversation."

"Leavin' already?" Dunn bristled. "Ya ain't even finished your brew."

"I'll be back." Logan winked. The barkeep might have the manners of a cockroach, but his information was solid. Best to keep him an ally for now. "I got a bit of a ride ahead of me. Time to get after it. But I hope to sample some of your other entertainments before too long."

"Ah." Dunn gave him a knowing grin. He nodded toward the redhead on stage. "Like what you see in Arabelle, huh? She may not have the best set of pipes in the county, but her set of—"

"I was thinking of the tables," Logan interrupted. Good grief. The last thing he needed was a female in his way, complicating his mission and causing trouble. Unfortunately, the scantily clad Arabelle must have had ears like an owl, for she was clambering off the stage and heading his way with disconcerting haste.

Tugging his hat back down over his scarred eye, Logan straightened away from the bar. "Catch up with you later, Dunn." He offered a wave in parting as he stretched his stride, choosing speed over swagger. At this juncture, self-preservation outranked image.

Once the saloon doors safely swung closed behind him, Logan relaxed. But only for a moment. His mind cranked through the new information he'd gained and what it might mean.

He unhitched his horse and mounted in a smooth motion while his brain churned. Hamilton wasn't acting as Logan had expected. He'd need to modify his timetable, adjust his plans. Learn the man's habits and ferret out his weaknesses.

So be it. Logan wouldn't blow his chance to achieve justice for his father by getting in a hurry. He was willing to play the long game.

He clicked his tongue at Shamgar and headed off at a trot. Time to investigate the homestead. He might have bought the property as bait to lure Hamilton into a high-stakes game, but it would serve equally well as a place to conduct reconnaissance.

Hamilton wouldn't remain a mystery for long.

CHAPTER

2

"Don't you dare bring that pig into this house!"

Evangeline Hamilton halted her arm mid-pull, leaving the back door halfway open. Busted. She swore Seth had eyes in the back of his head and ears everywhere else. Zach might be the Hamilton sibling who intimidated everyone outside of the family, but Seth was the dictator at home.

"He's clean," Evangeline cajoled. She'd bathed the mud off Hezekiah just a few minutes ago. He loved cool baths in the summer, and even *she* wouldn't dare bring him inside covered in mud. Mainly because she would be the one cleaning up whatever mess Hezzy made.

"I don't care." Seth's singsong voice was deceptively pleasant, but it carried a steel undertone.

She could usually sweet-talk Zach into giving her what she wanted, but Seth was a harder sell. Probably because Seth had been the one left behind to watch her while Zach took whatever odd jobs he could find to keep them fed in those lean years after the train wreck. That meant Seth knew all her tricks.

Evangeline quirked her lips. Well, not *all* her tricks.

"I just need to grab Hezzy's bow. I left it in my room." She never took Hezekiah out without his bow. The bright red ribbon was the hog's only defense against would-be hunters.

After Zach had nearly shot Hezzy last fall, her elder brother had demanded that she either find a way to label the critter or keep him penned full-time. The bow had been the best compromise she'd been able to conceive. Not the most masculine of attire, but Hezekiah didn't seem to mind. Not if it meant accompanying her on her afternoon jaunts. The hog hated to be left behind. He'd holler and ram the fence, breaking Evangeline's heart with his desperation to be free.

"Here." A bright red bow suddenly appeared around the edge of the door. Attached to Seth's arm.

The scalawag. He'd snuck up on her.

Laughing, she snatched the bow from his hand. "You must have had this on the kitchen table, waiting for me."

Seth stepped into the half-open doorway and grinned. "After fifteen years of your shenanigans, I've learned a thing or two about getting the upper hand. It's my only defense."

"As if you need one." She punched him playfully in the arm.

"Ow!" He grabbed his shoulder and staggered back a step.

Evangeline rolled her eyes. Really. He was six inches taller than her and carried an extra fifty pounds of muscle. To actually hurt him, she would have to go for the eyes like Zach had taught her. Or the groin. But she loved Seth to death and would never willingly cause him pain. Besides, he was the most normal of their gang, and therefore their best chance for begetting a future generation of Hamiltons. And she wanted nieces and nephews someday.

"Did you finish weeding the sweet potatoes?" Seth asked.

"Yep. Picked up where you left off and worked down the last three rows." As indicated by her mud-encrusted hem. She'd cleaned the soil from beneath her fingernails and rinsed off her face during Hezzy's bath, ensuring no dirt smudged her cheeks or nose. She might have a pet pig, but that didn't mean she wanted to look like him.

Seth nodded. "Thanks. I didn't get quite as far as I hoped this morning."

Evangeline shrugged off his comment. "No problem. I didn't mind the extra time. It's a pretty day."

Years ago they had worked out a system. Seth would start and she would finish whatever outdoor chores were required for the day while Zach tackled the larger projects. Seth's asthma made it difficult for him to work when the wind stirred up the dust, yet he refused to remain indoors like an invalid, so he went out first thing in the morning when things were relatively still and the air clean. He'd work until he felt tightness build in his chest, then pass the job off to her.

"I heard your caterwauling all the way in the house." Seth grinned as he leaned against the doorframe.

Brothers. Critics, the both of them. As if either one of *them* could sing. Seth's voice wobbled like a sick cat, and Zach—well, Zach never sang. Not even in church. So who knew what his voice sounded like? But to Evangeline, music was like sunshine. It brought things to life and made chores whiz by in a happy blur. She loved singing. The louder, the better. Hymns, popular tunes, even little ditties she made up on the spot. Didn't matter. She'd chirp out whatever came into her heart. Sometimes in praise to God, sometimes for pure fun, and sometimes in self-defense to keep the loneliness at bay.

"The potatoes didn't seem to mind," she quipped instead of following her first instinct of sticking her tongue out at him. At nineteen, she was too mature for such antics. At least in theory.

Seth rolled his eyes. "The potatoes don't have ears."

"Well, the corn plants do, and they didn't complain, either," she sassed.

"Probably because their ears are still covered." He raised a brow waiting for her comeback.

"*Shucks*, Seth. You know those stalks are experts in *hominy*. They adore my singing."

He groaned.

"Really?" She shoved his shoulder. Not that it moved much. "Come on. That was a good one. Hominy—harmony?"

"Weak, sis." He tried to hold a straight face, but a chuckle broke through. "Weak."

"Yeah? Let's see how weak I am."

She hooked Hezekiah's ribbon over her wrist, then poked Seth in the chest. Not just with one finger. She never did things by half measure. She got both pointers out and drilled him in alternating staccato motions until he backed away from the attack, throwing his hands up in surrender.

She felt victorious until a strong force butted her from behind and knocked her sideways into the wall.

She yelped. Seth grabbed for her. And Hezekiah found his opening. He barreled his way inside, snorting in glee as his hooves clicked across the floorboards of the kitchen in his race to the stove. He flopped down in front of the cast iron box and released a contented grunt.

Evangeline shot her brother an apologetic glance.

"Evie . . ." Seth's voice lost its playful tone. "If you don't want pork chops for supper, I suggest you get that beast out of my kitchen before I find my rifle."

"It's not his fault he likes that spot so well," she pled on her pet's behalf.

"No, it's yours. Who in their right mind brings a feral piglet into the house and bottle feeds the thing? As if we don't have a big enough wild pig problem around here, you go and bring one of the ugly things home."

"Hezekiah is *not* ugly. Besides, you know I couldn't leave him out there on his own with no mama to protect him. His little baby squeals broke my heart."

Seth rubbed a hand along the back of his neck. "Well, he's no baby now. He must weigh a hundred pounds or more. Barges into the house like he's the family dog," he grumbled. "It's ridiculous."

"It's charming," she countered, ignoring Seth's snort of disagreement.

After being abandoned and rejected time after time in her childhood, Evangeline couldn't bear to see any creature suffer the same fate. Her adopted brothers had taken her in, fed her, raised her, *loved* her. She could do no less for anyone or any*thing* in need. Even a slightly less than handsome hog.

"Come, Hezzy." She tapped the side of her leg, and good boy that he was, Hezekiah got up and trotted over.

Seth shook his head. "Even comes when you call him. Crazy."

Evangeline bent slightly and patted the hog's bristly black hide. "That's because he knows his mama loves him. Don't you, Hezzy? Such a good boy."

"Please." Thick sarcasm flavored Seth's tone as he pushed past her, grabbed a wet dish towel, and immediately mopped the section of floor where the hog had lain.

Evangeline wasn't offended by his need to wipe away any residue Hezzy might have left behind. After years of experimenting, they'd finally figured out that keeping the house free of as much dust and dirt as possible helped keep Seth's lungs from getting inflamed. So they had no rugs in any of the main rooms and no bric-a-brac to collect dust, just flat surfaces they could run a rag over every morning.

"Hezzy and I are going to explore the east woods again today over by the creek bed," she said as she fastened the wide red bow to the leather strap Zach had fashioned as a collar for the hog.

There was a strict family rule—she never went anywhere without first telling either Zach or Seth where she was headed. The boys didn't think it necessary to keep her informed of *their* every move, so it was a bit of a double standard, but there *had* been that one time she'd snuck away from school during recess and gotten lost for two days after Mary Lou Edison had pulled her hair and called her a freak. Some stranger had eventually found her huddled by an oak tree and taken her to the local church to wait to be claimed. Never had Evie been so frightened. Or seen Zach so angry. If she hadn't caught him secretly wiping his eyes while Seth hugged her, she might've thought he didn't love her anymore, with all the yelling and lecturing he did. But then she realized he'd been scared, too. Scared he'd let his family down.

That was why she didn't fight the family rule even now that she was a woman grown. She wanted to spare her brothers the worry. It was the least she could do after all they'd done for her over the last fifteen years.

What she didn't tell them was exactly what she planned to do when she went out on one of her excursions. A woman of nineteen deserved a few secrets, after all. And lately there had been evidence of suspicious goings-on near the eastern property line. Evidence of human activity. An extinguished campfire. Boot prints. Horse tracks.

It was a mystery that needed sorting out, and she loved a good mystery. Truth be told, she loved anything that broke up the monotony of her usual routine. If she were a normal girl, she'd simply stroll to town to meet up with friends. Maybe do a little shopping. Buy some penny candy or a ribbon for her hair. Laugh and play and talk about how to gain the favor of a handsome young man.

But she wasn't normal. And going to town brought only heartache.

Stares. Whispers. Not from everyone, but from enough to make her want to fold in on herself. Some of the bolder ones even spat when she walked by or crossed the street to avoid coming too close, as if her eyes might be catching. Of course, none of that happened when her brothers accompanied her. No one would dare treat her disrespectfully when Zach was around. His black stare could inspire more fear than her mixed-colored one. But when children dared each other to hit the witch with a slingshot missile or look her in the eyes to see if they'd turn to stone, a gal learned to avoid town. Her heart could only take so many hits before the bruises became permanent.

So she sang songs to sweet potatoes, rambled with pigs, and made her own happiness wherever she could find it. And today, finding it entailed an adventure to ascertain the identity of a mysterious visitor.

Was he friend or foe? Only one way to find out.

Spying.

Her pulse raced a bit at the prospect. Stealth. Danger. The risk of discovery. Oh, she'd take precautions. She wasn't one of those heedless dime-novel ninnies who ran headlong into trouble without once considering the consequences, then fainted at the first sign of trouble. No wonder those damsels needed a man to swoop in and save the day. They failed to utilize the brains the good Lord had given them.

Evangeline, on the other hand, treasured her fully functioning cerebellum and planned to use it. She'd scout from a distance.

Stay hidden in the trees. Collect clues, yet not directly engage anyone she might find.

Whoever this interloper was, he wouldn't know the terrain like she did. That gave her an edge. One she intended to use to full advantage.

CHAPTER

3

Seven years might have passed, but Logan remembered every detail of this terrain. His youthful explorations had left indelible marks in his mind, as if printed there by a mapmaker. Rather handy when one wanted to get around unseen.

He wound down a sloping creek bed, using an elm tree to steady his descent. Low ground made the best cover due to the dense vegetation of the area, and since the prickle that had been shivering against his nape for the last ten minutes warned he wasn't alone out here, cover seemed a wise idea.

At the base of the hill, a set of tracks caught Logan's eye. He squatted near a bramble that had grown up in the dry creek bed. The dual ovals imprinted in the damp soil indicated a four-legged critter instead of a two-legged one. Could be a deer, but the more likely culprit was a pig.

Feral hogs. He shivered. Nasty creatures. Logan had gotten between a sow and her piglets once. He still bore a scar on his right calf where the enraged female had slashed him open with her tusks. There only seemed to be one set of tracks here, though, so he probably wasn't about to stumble upon a sounder again. Thank the Lord for small favors.

Logan brushed his hand against his thigh to wipe away the dirt as he stood. A single boar posed no problem. Loners were more apt to run away from people than attack.

As he followed the creek bed east, a noise caught his ear. A horse whinny. Logan dropped into a crouch. Shamgar. He'd left his mount secured inside a corral fashioned by tying rope around a set of trees on the outskirts of his camp. An ex-cavalry horse, Shamgar had been trained for silence. He only whinnied when someone approached with a treat. Apples and carrots in particular. But who would be out in the wild armed with a treat for his horse?

Reaching across his body, he eased his revolver from its holster and crept toward his campsite. It couldn't be Zacharias. Logan had left his nemesis slaving away in a sorghum field less than an hour ago. And from what he'd observed this past week, the other Hamilton male didn't venture far from the house. Some kind of namby-pamby who preferred woman's work to a man's labor. That left the female. She was harder to monitor. Always flitting about. Inside. Outside. He only seemed to find her when she started singing.

Arabelle at the Lucky Lady had nothing on the Hamilton gal. The saloon singer's husky tones were probably supposed to pass for sultry, though the little Logan had overheard brought a mournful hound dog to mind more than an enticing siren. Zacharias's sister, on the other hand, spewed tunes like a geyser, full tilt, with no care as to who might be listening. Even a trespassing scoundrel determined to rain justice down on her family.

Logan rolled his shoulders against the tightening in his neck as he climbed the slope leading to his camp. What happened to the girl as a result of the coming confrontation was not his concern. Hamilton hadn't cared about repercussions to his opponent's wife and son when he'd lured Logan's father into deep play, then cheated him out of his home. Logan could be equally callous. He had to be. It was the only way to set things right.

His head inched above the embankment near his camp, and his gaze immediately sought out Shamgar.

Logan blinked. Twice. *What in the world?*

His highly trained cavalry mount was prancing around like a colt. Tossing his head and showing off like an adolescent youth trying to impress a pretty girl. And the girl *was* pretty. At least from what Logan could see from this distance. Rich, auburn hair glinting red in the sunlight. Slim figure. And a smile that punched him in the gut even from here. She laughed at Shamgar's antics, then held her hand out to the horse. An empty hand.

Logan frowned at the old boy's susceptibility to the female's wiles. Apparently no treat had been needed. Fool critter. Did he remember none of his cavalry training?

Shamgar raced to the girl's side, nuzzled her hand, then preened as she cupped his cheeks and pressed her forehead to his face. She had him completely enthralled.

Snap!

Logan jerked, then dropped his chin to spy the dry twig beneath his boot. Of all the careless, idiotic—

A whistle pierced the air, bringing his head back up. His self-castigation would have to wait. The little filly was on the move.

Logan scrambled the rest of the way out of the creek bed and positioned himself behind a pair of oaks as he debated whether or not to go after her. She'd found his camp and would no doubt tell her brothers. Was it worth the risk of exposing himself to try to convince her to keep quiet?

The girl was fast.

And heading in his direction.

Shoot.

Logan holstered his revolver and ducked to the far side of the tree. She ran past and whistled a second time. He winced at the sharp sound. No fingers had been required for the shrill call. Impressive.

Then a rumbling started downstream in the creek bed. From the direction Logan had just come. Snorting. Charging. The vegetation shook in a path leading straight for the Hamilton gal.

Logan's mouth went dry.

Double shoot.

He leapt away from the tree and set off after the girl. His boots slipped on the loose soil of the embankment, but he kept his balance. He took his eyes off her long enough to plot his course out of the dry wash, then panicked when he couldn't find her green skirt amid the vegetation. Sensing she'd head west toward home, he veered left.

There. A flash of white. Her blouse. Logan churned up the earth. Earth that rumbled with the approach of a rogue boar. The grunting grew louder. Closer. Sweat dripped down Logan's temple. He had to get between the girl and the hog.

He stretched his stride. Caught a glimpse of her between the trees. Heard the grunt of the boar. Spied its black hide barreling down on the girl from the right. Only one chance to get between them.

Logan sprinted over a lip of higher ground and launched himself into the air.

Before his feet hit the ground, his chest hit her back. His arms cocooned her as he twisted to the right in order to absorb the impact and use his body as her shield.

The girl squealed, not unlike the pig. He released his hold on her, intending to draw his pistol. That was a mistake. The female turned on him. She flipped around and brought her knee up into his groin. Air whooshed from his lungs as pain radiated through his lower half. He would have thrown her off him except he was too busy dodging the fingers jabbing at his eyes.

Good gravy. She fought dirtier than a saloon brawler. If he hadn't spent so much time in disreputable establishments learning how to stay alive, he'd no doubt be down at least one eye by now.

When the heel of her hand narrowly missed the bridge of his nose, Logan decided the time for chivalry had passed. He grabbed her wrists, wrapped a leg around her hips, and rolled her onto her back, taking extra care to pin her legs with his weight. He had no intention of joining the soprano section of the church choir.

She writhed beneath him, terror etching her face.

"Be still, would ya?" he growled, rearing back as she tried to butt him with her head. "Land sakes, woman. I'm not tryin' to hurt you. I'm trying to protect you."

"From what?" she demanded.

"From the—"

Boar! A black shadow caught the corner of his vision a heartbeat before the beast's head plowed into Logan's side, bowling him off the girl. Fearing she'd be trampled, he snaked an arm around her midsection and dragged her back under him as he pulled up on all fours. Using his body as a barrier, he gritted his teeth against the force of the hog's shove, bracing his arms and digging the toes of his boots into the soft earth.

At least his damsel had the good sense to cease her attacks. In this position, all his tender parts were at her mercy. She did keep shouting "No" at him, though, in the same stern voice his mother had used when scolding him as a boy.

The boar backed away—probably to get a running start at

him again—and Logan snatched the opening. He sat back on his haunches, drew his revolver, and swiveled to face the feral hog.

"No!" the girl screamed, panic more than scolding resonating in her voice now.

Logan tuned it out as best he could, concentrating on lining up the head shot. A hog's skin was so tough, a miss would just anger the beast and put them in more danger.

Time slowed as he fit his finger to the trigger. Then the crazy female lurched upward and grabbed his gun arm.

"Don't shoot!"

He tore free from her grip and shoved her back to the ground none too gently.

"Look at the bow," she cried as she scrambled back to her feet.

Logan took aim, his focus glued to the area between the animal's eyes.

She launched herself onto his back and tackled him to the ground. "He's not wild," she insisted even as Logan bucked her off and rolled her to the side. "Please!"

The desperate plea and tremulous voice tugged at a heart he'd thought long ago hardened past all sentimentality.

Logan paused. Took in his adversary. Snorting, ugly, black creature. Yet not charging. And a ridiculous, gargantuan red bow hung wilted against its right shoulder.

Maybe he *should* shoot the creature. Out of pity. The shame of being subjected to such a prissy accessory would mortally wound any male's pride. The boar would probably thank him for putting an end to his suffering.

The girl lunged to her feet and rushed to the boar's side. She dropped to her knees and wrapped her arms around the beast's neck. "Hezekiah's no threat to you, mister. Please, just let him be."

Logan lowered his gun as he shook his head. "Hezekiah?" He pushed to his feet and tucked his pistol into its holster. "Doesn't exactly strike me as the kingly type."

She grinned, and her face lit up with what could only be called joy. The purity of it took Logan aback. One didn't see expressions like that in saloons or lumber camps, and he'd spent little time elsewhere these past years.

Then she ruined it by turning that glorious smile on her pet and putting her face disastrously close to the boar's teeth.

"Whoa, now." Logan jumped forward, grabbed the girl's elbow, and yanked her away from the hog. "Those things have nasty teeth. I don't care how tame he is, he's still a creature with animal instincts. And tusks."

"Not Hezzy," she said as he pulled her to her feet and twirled her toward him. She brought up her hands to catch herself before she rammed into his chest. Her palms flattened against the cotton of his shirt, and his heart did an odd little hiccup at the contact. "My brother removed his cutters when he was a few months old. Zach wouldn't let me keep him otherwise."

Smart man. Logan had long respected Hamilton's intelligence. It was his character Logan despised.

All thought of Zacharias fled Logan's mind when the girl finally tilted her chin back and hit him with the full impact of her eyes.

One blue. One brown. Just like Dunn had said. Startling in their difference, yet so vibrant that he couldn't describe them as anything other than stunning.

She stared back at him, unblinking. Until, that is, her gaze fluttered to his scar. He steeled himself for her reaction. He knew the blemish was unsightly, leaving a slashing void in his eyebrow and puckering the skin along his cheekbone.

Something soft flashed in her eyes, just for a moment. Not

disgust, nor even discomfort. Something that felt oddly like . . . kinship.

He shook his head to rid his mind of the disturbing sensation and said the first thing that popped into his mind. "Why'd you name your pig Hezekiah? Kind of insulting to the king who served God so faithfully, don't you think?"

Her mouth quirked up on one side. "You saying my Hezzy doesn't have a regal bearing?"

The pig in question grunted and set about rooting in the dirt near the base of the closest tree, covering its snout with a thick layer of muck and leaves before turning his side into the trunk to rub against the bark. The beast had all the manners of a drunken oaf scratching an indiscriminate itch with no care as to who was watching. All that was missing was a loud belch to complete the picture.

Logan raised a questioning brow. The girl glanced at her pet, then burst into laughter. The sound tinkled like the crystal chandelier he'd rammed his head into once in a fancy hotel lobby.

"I suppose you have me there," she finally admitted. "Hezzy's not exactly cut from the royal cloth, but when I found him alone and abandoned in the woods, half dead, I knew he needed a reason to live. A reason not to give up hope. So I called him Hezekiah."

A memory clicked into place in Logan's mind. "Because Hezekiah became ill and was supposed to die until God granted him an extra fifteen years."

Her eyes glowed as if proud of his answer. Like he was some ragamuffin pupil in a classroom. He should be insulted. So why did his chest expand under her unvoiced praise?

"That's it exactly." There was that smile again. All sunshine and rainbows. As if this girl had never known a single hardship in her life.

Logan scowled.

Her smile dimmed. Just a bit, but enough to make him feel more in control. All this frivolous laughing and grinning was bad for his digestion.

Her eyes found his again, and the playfulness vanished from her gaze. "Everyone deserves to be treated like a king, even if they're only a humble pig."

The bald statement stunned him momentarily. Then opened a Machiavellian door in his mind. This girl had a bleeding heart, an undeniable drive to right wrongs and champion the cause of the downtrodden.

The perfect ace to hide in his sleeve.

The stranger's mouth lifted at one corner, and a little spurt of elation shot through Evangeline's belly. She'd made him smile. She probably shouldn't count that as such an accomplishment when she knew so little about him, but she couldn't help it. He reminded her too much of Zach. All stern and gruff. Shoulders that seemed to bear the weight of the world. Men like that needed to be reminded how to smile. How to laugh. How to bask in sunshine instead of lurking in shadows.

Besides, he *had* been trying to save her, albeit from a non-existent threat. Still, she appreciated his misguided heroism. It wasn't every day a young maiden ran across a gentleman willing to put himself between her and a wild boar. Then spared the boar at the maiden's request. A more fanciful woman's head might be turned.

Evangeline kept hers facing him straight on while trying not to notice how close he was standing or how her palms were flattened against his very firm chest. There was no ignoring *that*. She cleared her throat and stepped back. His arms fell away.

"I'm Evangeline Hamilton," she blurted, extending her hand into the space she'd just vacated. "You new to these parts?"

His hand closed around hers. Firm yet gentle. No more grabbing and hauling her around. Just a sincere shake and release.

"I've been here about a week."

She waited for him to elaborate. He didn't.

Yep. A lot like Zach.

Well, she had fifteen years of experience pulling information from reticent males. She'd not let him put her off.

"Since you're new to the area, you might not be aware that you're on Hamilton land." She crossed her arms over her chest. Lifted her chin. Widened her stance. "My brothers won't begrudge you snaring a rabbit or even taking down a deer if you're in need of nourishment, but we don't take kindly to squatters."

His lips quirked again. What was it about her trying to act mean that made men grin? It was so annoying. Evangeline frowned at him.

His smile widened. "I'm aware of the boundaries. My camp is east of your property line."

"But *you're* not." She unfolded her arms and poked him in the chest.

He stared at her finger then nudged his own against her shoulder. "Because I was trying to save *you* from being gored by a wild boar."

"One that wouldn't have actually hurt me."

"That's debatable." He folded his arms and looked down his nose at her. "Even without tusks, that thing could do serious damage if riled."

"Then you best not rile him." Evangeline gave a sassy wave of her head, as if she could order Hezzy to attack at any moment. The only damage her pet would likely render involved pig slobber and a head butt that might manage to knock a fellow off-balance. But something told her this man wouldn't be bowled over too easily.

"What about riling *you*?" He rubbed the scar that traversed his left eye. Subconsciously? Or was he trying to intimidate her with evidence of his dangerous character? As if such a puny mark would frighten her away. He had just tried to save her life. No matter how crotchety he was acting, he wasn't dangerous.

"I don't rile easily." To prove her point, she smiled. If Zach were the one on the other end of this near-lecture, she'd jump forward, hug him, and plant a loud, smacking kiss on his cheek. Unanticipated affection always threw him off his game and spared her from unpleasant harangues. Too bad she couldn't use that stratagem with a stranger.

Nevertheless, the old adage about catching more flies with honey hadn't survived this long without holding a measure of truth.

"Thank you, by the way." Evangeline smiled even more broadly when he blinked in confusion. "For your heroic rescue." She dipped her chin. "Just because your actions were unnecessary doesn't mean they're not appreciated."

He cleared his throat and shifted his weight. "You're welcome." His voice tapered up at the end, making the statement sound more like a question, but Evangeline chose to interpret it as a successful change of direction anyhow.

"You have a lovely horse." She stepped to the side and twisted, letting her skirt twirl about her just a little. She'd never been good at standing still. The rhythmic twisting, even in small doses, calmed her growing nerves.

Now that the initial excitement of the discovery, chase, and tackle had subsided, she was becoming acutely aware of the fact that she was alone with a man. A man who actually treated her like a woman. Not a sister, not a freak of nature with unnatural eyes. But an ordinary, *normal* woman.

"He's very handsome," she said. "Your horse." The horse's owner qualified for that descriptor, too. That wavy dark brown hair curling over his collar. Gray eyes that had softened from steel to the color of fluffy storm clouds. Tall. Strong. A little rough around the edges. "And friendly, too."

He mumbled something beneath his breath about horse sense not being what it used to be, but Evangeline chose to let that bit of cynicism go without comment.

"What's his name?" she asked.

"Shamgar."

Evangeline tilted her head. "Is that from the Bible?"

"Yep."

Heavens. He hoarded words like a squirrel did nuts. "Which part?"

"Judges."

"Was Shamgar a judge?"

"Yep."

Now he was being deliberately reticent. She could tell by the slight crinkling around his eyes. Zach did the same thing when he was trying to get a rise out of her. Well, after all the years she and the boys had grown sorghum, she knew one had to mill a lot of cane to extract enough juice to make even a single crock of syrup. She might not be the most patient person in the world, but no one could say she wasn't persistent. If this was to be a battle of wills, she fully intended to be the victor.

Her gentle twirling became a little more forceful. "I don't remember that one. Who was he?"

Her would-be rescuer shrugged. "All the Good Book says is that he saved Israel by striking down six hundred Philistines with an oxgoad."

"What's an oxgoad?" Not that she really cared, but he'd actually given her a response longer than a single word, and she wanted to keep the syllables flowing while the pump was primed.

Unfortunately, all he did was shrug again, killing her hard-gained momentum.

"Well, at least we know we have something in common, now," she said.

He raised a brow in question. Apparently the pump handle had seized up completely.

Evangeline laughed. Really, he was stoic to the point of being ridiculous. "We both have pets named for characters from the Bible."

"I suppose we do."

"And speaking of names," she said, keeping her voice deliberately light and teasing, "you seem to be holding yours hostage." She smiled, expecting him to apologize and rectify the oversight.

He didn't.

Instead, he just stared at her—his gaze frosting slightly, his features dulling, his expression becoming as still as a shallow pond in a breezeless summer. It was as if the fire within the vibrant man who'd selflessly attempted to save her life had been snuffed. And all because she'd asked him for his name.

Who was this stranger, and what was his true purpose for being here?

"I've given you mine," she said, gently pressing for the answers she sought. "Now it's your turn. The trust train runs both ways, you know."

A veteran poker player should have more self-control, but Logan couldn't stop his lips from twitching. "The *trust train*?"

She raised her brows to comical height. "What? Would you prefer a trust wagon?"

He shook his head at her inanity. She grinned, her mismatched eyes dancing.

What kind of girl was this? So ready to choose laughter over taking offense. It had been a long time since someone surprised him. He read people for a living, but this slip of a girl had done nothing but surprise him since he'd tackled her. First with her wild fighting style, then her pet boar. Who in their right mind wanted a pig for a pet? Then the barrage of little girl innocence and determined cheerfulness that made his skin itch with irritation even as it created a senseless craving for more. And just when he thought he could dismiss her as some kind of rainbow-loving idealist who had no true understanding of reality, she zinged him with a challenge, proving her sunny disposition hid a keen mind.

If the girl ever took to the tables, she'd be able to bluff her way into a fortune.

Logan peered at her earnest face, finally detecting a hint of suspicion in the line of her brow. "Train, wagon, whatever you want to call it, I don't travel that road easily," he admitted. "In my experience, trust is something people exploit."

There. She'd been warned. What happened from here on out was on her head.

"That's a pretty cynical view." Her brow softened, her suspicion melting under the bleeding-heart compassion he'd noted earlier. "I'm sorry you feel that way, but I can understand. People can be cruel. Hurtful. For no good reason."

There she went surprising him again. Real pain flashed in her eyes. Logan's jaw clenched. Who would hurt this sparkling delight of a woman? Then he remembered the saloon owner in Pecan Gap and that superstitious claptrap about her eyes.

And what of his own intentions? Logan tried to ignore the twist in his gut. He meant no harm to her personally, he rationalized, yet if he harmed her family, it would affect her. Just like Hamilton's harm of Logan's father had devastated him and his mother.

Enacting justice sometimes led to casualties. An unfortunate ramification, but not one that merited forfeiting his path. If he kept Evangeline close, maybe he could minimize the damage. Protect her from the worst of the aftermath even as he used her to advance his own ends.

A gentle touch to his arm made Logan jolt out of his thoughts.

"No matter how many people reject or betray you," she said, her voice soft yet intense, "if you have even one person in your life that you can count on—really, truly count on—you can overcome any obstacle." She stepped closer to him. "Trusting the wrong person might lead to temporary heartache, but trusting the right one provides a strength that can fuel you for a lifetime."

Spoken by anyone else, that sentiment would ring hollow, but this girl's eyes shone with such sincerity, such . . . belief that Logan's cynicism found no foothold. "You are a remarkable woman, Evangeline Hamilton."

Pink colored her cheeks. Her lashes dipped over her eyes. "I know what it's like to be hurt by others." Her lashes lifted, and the vivid contrast of her eyes struck him anew. "And I've learned to be careful—guarded, even—around people who aren't family. But I've also learned how to recognize those with good hearts."

Her eyebrows drew together as she stared up at him, and Logan had to fight not to squirm.

"You're a stranger who won't tell me your name nor reveal your purpose for camping on the border of my land. You're reticent, stubborn, and have an obvious dislike of pigs." She grinned momentarily before firming the line of her lips into a sober expression. "All marks against you. Yet you ran to my rescue when you believed me to be in danger, you're familiar with obscure biblical characters wielding oxgoads, and you haven't made a single comment about my eyes." She glanced away. That last observation, tacked onto the end of the list, apparently carried the most weight.

Logan swallowed, an unwanted wave of protectiveness surging inside him.

"All marks in your favor." She cleared her throat and turned her face back to him, those rare eyes probing beneath his carefully crafted mask of detachment—a detachment that seemed harder and harder to hold on to the longer he was in her presence. "I haven't yet decided which column to lean toward. Any recommendations?"

Run away from me and never look back. The thought screamed through Logan's brain, but the words never touched his lips. He would undoubtedly cause her pain by the time his game ended, but he didn't want to send her away. She afforded him an advantage over his opponent. And beyond that, he actually *liked* her.

He'd spent such a large portion of the last seven years hanging around people he merely tolerated that he'd forgotten the pleasure that could be found in the presence of someone whose company he enjoyed. The men at the lumber camp were rough and crude, and when they weren't swinging axes, they were swilling beer and swinging fists. And in the gambling halls, men were either weak-willed fools unworthy of his respect or sharps looking to steal his coin at the tables or at the point of a knife in the alleyway afterward.

So even though a true gentleman would send her away, he extended a hand and breathed easier when she clasped it.

"I'm Logan," he said. "Your new neighbor."

Warm tingles shot up Evangeline's arm as Logan's hand tightened around hers. His long fingers nearly pinched her smaller ones in the firmness of his grip, but the expression on his face made the discomfort inconsequential. There was something there. An old hurt, maybe? Bitterness? Fear? Whatever drove him, the desperation for connection she sensed was palpable. It throbbed in her heart, tugging on her sympathies until she felt a physical ache. He'd told her straight out that he didn't trust easily, but she could feel that he wanted to. Deep down inside, he yearned for more than a solitary existence.

He was wounded. Lonely. Her stomach clenched. She couldn't ignore his pain any more than she could ignore her own. Because it *mirrored* her own. She rubbed the pad of her thumb over the skin on the back of his hand in silent comradery.

He jerked at her touch, dropped her hand, and stepped back. His face went blank, all hint of vulnerability vanishing.

Well, all *visible* vulnerability, at least. She, better than anyone, knew that a soul's sore spots didn't really disappear. They could be buried, defended, and denied, but until they were loved, they wreaked havoc with a person's peace. She still had a few tender places that ached when prodded, but Zach and Seth had loved and accepted her into a place where past hurts mattered less than present blessings.

Maybe God had brought her into this stranger's life to do the same for him.

Evangeline smiled. "So, by *neighbor* do you mean you own the property next door?"

"Yep. Bought it a couple weeks back as an investment."

"An investment? So you don't plan to stay?" The disappointment twinging in her chest had no business twinging. For heaven's sake, she'd only just met him. Sensing a kindred spirit didn't mean she should feel a loss at the thought of him leaving.

"I haven't decided." He eyed her in a decidedly masculine way, one that made her itch to check her hair. Not that she could repair the damage with a few tucks and pats. Thanks to her sprint through the woods and subsequent tumble and skirmish with her rescuer, she'd need a brush, a mirror, and about a dozen new hairpins to tame the bird's nest she felt drooping lopsidedly behind her left ear.

She'd finally met a man who didn't seem to care about her contradictory eyes, and now her hoydenish behavior would probably run him off.

Evangeline straightened her posture and brushed away a few dead leaves still clinging to the front of her forest-green skirt. As if that would help. She felt slightly better when Logan ran a hand through his own hair and dislodged some leftover pieces of grass. Of course, all he had to do was flick the debris away from his shoulder to completely put himself to rights.

She sighed, missing the days when she had run around in Seth's cast-off trousers with short hair and no thought for her appearance. Life had been much simpler before Charlotte Clem, wife of the local Baptist preacher, decided to interfere and teach her the art of being a young lady. Mrs. Clem was a dear woman with a big heart—and really, it would've been worse to meet Logan while running around in britches and shorn locks—but knowing the standard of womanhood he was probably accustomed to and realizing she fell woefully short at the moment did little for Evangeline's confidence.

"I can't be sure how long I'll be around," Logan finally said, breaking the silence that was growing increasingly awkward. "Depends on how long it takes to wrap up my business." .

"Selling your land?"

He gave her a look that warned her questions were veering into the realm of too personal.

She knew it was rude to quiz a man about his personal business, but how was she supposed to get to know him otherwise? A niggle of unease stirred in her stomach. If he didn't have anything to hide, wouldn't he be more forthcoming?

Then again, how many times had she and her brothers ducked questions about their past, needing to keep their secrets in order to keep their family intact? Nobody really believed they were blood kin, though some claimed they all came from the same mother but different fathers. That particular rumor was far from complimentary of their hypothetical mother, so Evangeline fiercely refuted it whenever it arose. She didn't remember much about her true parents, but what she did recall filled her with warmth and love and happiness. She'd let no one speak ill of her mother, even a pretend version that hadn't actually existed.

Perhaps she should grant Logan the same courtesy she wished to receive from others and stop prying.

"You know," she said, backing the conversation up to a place where her footing had been more solid, "if you want to make the most of your investment, you should improve your acreage.

Build a cabin. Clear some land. That sort of thing." She'd vowed not to pry about his business, *not* to cease interfering. Besides, if she convinced him to linger, she'd have a better chance of getting to know him. A prospect that grew more tantalizing by the minute. "You'll fetch a better price that way."

His eyes crinkled just a bit, as if he knew exactly what she was thinking.

Heat crept up Evangeline's neck, but she brazened it out, keeping her smile in place and only twisting a smidgen from side to side as she waited for his response.

A response that took an eternity to arrive. He just kept staring at her, saying nothing. Nothing with his mouth, anyway. His eyes were a different story. They seemed to ask a hundred questions, peering at her with an intensity that made her believe he could excavate his answers without her uttering a word.

"You might be right," he finally said. "I'll give it some thought."

Elation surged through Evangeline's veins and lifted her up onto her toes in a happy little bounce. "If you decide to build, I could ask my brothers to help you frame out the walls. They built the smokehouse we use for—"

"No."

The forceful interruption smacked her back down onto her heels.

A muscle ticked in Logan's jaw as he jerked his gaze to the right, away from her. "Sorry." He fingered the scar by his eye again, then turned back to face her. "I didn't mean to snap at you. But I don't want to be beholden to your brother. To anyone, actually. This is my project, and I'll see to whatever needs to be done."

"All right." Her enthusiasm quickly buoyed. No help meant it would take him longer. Which meant he would stay longer. Which meant she had more time to forge a friendship.

Or something more.

She slammed the door closed on that thought. It was much too soon, and she still had too many questions about her new neighbor. Like why he had set up his camp in the thick of the woods right next to her property line when there were surely dozens of better sites across the rest of his land. And why the mere mention of her brothers had him snapping like a turtle going for a fish.

Come to think of it, being snappish wasn't the only similarity between Logan and the crusty old turtle she used to play with down by the pond behind the smokehouse. Solitary creature. Hard shell to protect all vulnerable areas. Adept at camouflage.

That last one made her uneasy. The turtle used to cover itself with mud at the bottom of the pond until only its eyes would show, then strike whenever an unsuspecting fish swam within reach.

Logan wasn't doing that, was he? Hiding his true purposes in order to hunt prey? Evangeline swallowed. If so, who was his prey?

Don't jump to conclusions, Evie. Snapping turtles only became aggressive when threatened. They were shy by nature, avoiding human interaction. Yet many considered them vicious creatures and went out of their way to destroy them. Rash decisions based on assumptions instead of facts too often led to needless suffering. How many times had she been judged based on appearances and not on her true nature? More than she could count. She'd not judge Logan until she understood him. And to understand him, she'd have to spend time in his company.

That scaly old turtle at the pond eventually allowed her to pet its shell and even the top of its head. After weeks of patience and kindness and a few dead minnows tossed its way, it eventually learned to trust her. Logan would too.

Hopefully.

Evangeline smiled up at him. "So . . . do you need anything?"

Confusion creased his forehead. "Need anything?"

"You know, like supplies and things." Goodness. Could she sound any less intelligent? She pinched the edges of her skirt on both sides and twisted with a little more vigor. "When I was snooping around your camp, I didn't notice much in the way of food."

He raised a brow. "So you admit to snooping around my camp?"

"Of course." His eyebrows disappeared into his hairline at her blunt answer, and her twisting stilled as her confidence reasserted itself. "Do you admit to trespassing on my land?"

He grinned—an actual, both-corners-turning-up grin—then shook his head.

She rolled her eyes at him. "Figures. Your species is a stubborn breed."

"My species?"

She was dearly tempted to respond with *snapping turtles* but decided to stick with a safer, yet no less truthful, reply. "Men."

He chuckled, and the warm, low sound did odd things to her belly. "That's not stubbornness, Miss Hamilton. It's determination. Stubbornness is what affects the female strain."

Evangeline clucked her tongue even as she secretly delighted in the teasing exchange. If this kept up, she'd be winning her turtle's trust in no time. "Stubborn *and* deluded. It's a miracle your kind has survived this long."

"Deluded? I beg to differ." Logan crossed his arms over his chest and smirked with an impressive level of haughtiness. "I travel with a horse, the most useful animal known to mankind. You travel with a hog."

"A very kingly hog," Evangeline defended loyally.

"Who destroys garden plots, weakens trees, and roots up the soil."

"Not Hezzy." Unless he managed to get out of his pen. But that hadn't happened since Zach fortified the fence last month. "He's a devoted companion."

Logan uncrossed his arms, took a step closer to her, and leaned down until his face was uncomfortably close to hers. "And that, my dear, is the core of the feminine delusion. You allow sentiment to overrule logic." All playfulness drained from his expression. He stared at her, hard. "Leading with your heart instead of your head leaves you susceptible to exploitation, hurt, and disappointment."

Evangeline narrowed her eyes and stiffened her spine. "It also leaves you susceptible to love, joy, and hope. And I'm not willing to give those up, so go peddle your pessimism somewhere else, mister. I'm not buying."

His mouth tightened slightly, but he didn't continue the argument. He just glared at her. Evangeline held his gaze without backing down. Something had hurt him. Hardened him. Yet there was still softness hidden in his crevices. He'd run to her rescue when he thought her in danger. Even now he seemed more intent on warning her to guard her heart than on proving himself right.

Well, she was no stranger to loss, to hurt feelings, to prejudice. But she'd decided long ago not to let pain dictate her life. *For ye have not received the spirit of bondage again to fear; but ye have received the Spirit of adoption, whereby we cry, Abba, Father.* That was what she chose. To let her Father lead her down a brighter path, a path where the joy of the Lord became her strength. A shell, no matter how fortified, was not impenetrable. Pain always found a way inside. The only way to truly overcome was to dissolve the darkness with light.

"Take your pig and scurry on home to your brothers, Miss Hamilton," Logan growled as he turned his back on her and bent to reclaim the hat he'd lost during their tussle earlier. "It'd be safer for you to mind your own business and leave the strange men you encounter in the woods alone."

Evangeline smiled at his grumpy protectiveness as he brushed the dust from his hat's crown. "Oh, come now. You're not *that* strange, Mr. . . ." She paused, her forehead crinkling as she realized he'd never told her his surname.

He turned to face her, his brows raised in mocking confirmation that he was, indeed, strange after all.

Oh, for pity's sake. Was he really going to make her ask?

He said nothing, just reshaped the brim of his black hat.

Fine. "I don't think you told me your last name."

"That's right." The hat temporarily blocked his face as he lifted it to his head. He took a moment to fit it into the precise spot he preferred, then finally lowered his arm and met her eyes. "Better you not know."

"Why?"

His mouth twitched with impatience. "Must you question *everything?*"

She shrugged. "Usually."

His eyes widened slightly, then he blew out a breath that carried a hint of exasperation. "I'm starting to learn that about you." He glanced away for a moment, and when he turned back, his eyes sought hers. "Look, I didn't choose property in Pecan Gap at random. My family has history in this area. A history I'd rather keep private for now. If you knew, it would . . ." He looked at the ground. "It would change the way you see me."

Sharp memories pricked at Evangeline. A little girl staring at the ground to hide her eyes, afraid to reveal her flaw, knowing it would change everything. People would see her differently. They'd no longer want her.

Her throat thickened with sympathy. She reached out and touched Logan's arm. His head jerked up; his gaze collided with hers.

"Once you get to know me better," she said, "you'll learn that I don't let rumors or superficial traits dictate my opinion of people. But for now, I'll stop pressing you for answers you're not ready to give." She smiled at him and gave his arm a friendly pat before pulling her hand away. As she sauntered over to where Hezzy dozed in the shade, she glanced back to wave at the man who seemed to be frozen in place. "I'll come by tomorrow with some bread and other goodies to welcome you to the area."

He frowned. "You don't—"

"It's only neighborly," she insisted cheerfully, subverting any further protests he might feel compelled to voice by whistling to her hog. Hezzy lumbered to his feet as she passed by, and the two of them set off for the house. "See you tomorrow!" she called after she'd put enough distance between them to ensure Logan couldn't argue.

Her new neighbor might be determined to protect her from herself, but she was equally determined to return the favor.

CHAPTER

6

That evening, a lengthy, spirited, completely internal debate waged in Evangeline's head throughout supper and continued into the clearing of the dishes. She never kept secrets from her brothers. It was a family rule. Hamiltons watched each others' backs. Always. A tradition that required openness and honesty so that nothing could sneak up on them without warning.

On the other hand, Zach and Seth's protective natures tended to overreact where she was concerned. To the point where watching her back meant restricting her movements so that her back was always within sight. Such confinement was stifling. And rather inconvenient if she planned to continue visiting Logan. Which she did.

She nibbled her lower lip as she made the rounds, filling a coffee cup first for Zach, then for Seth, before fetching the teakettle for herself.

"Sorghum's growing a little slow. Probably ought to rotate it with oats next year," Zach said as he lifted his cup to his mouth and leaned back in the wooden kitchen chair.

"Cotton's a better cash crop," Seth ventured.

Zach's jaw clenched, and tension immediately filled the room.

Evangeline shot Seth a sharp look. If she were closer, she'd smack the back of his head. Not that it would make much difference. He'd just ignore it, like he was currently ignoring her glare. Her grip on the kettle handle tightened. Of all the nights to bring up this old argument. She already had one minefield to maneuver. She didn't need a second.

"Everyone around here already grows cotton." Evangeline purposely kept her voice light as she slid back into her seat at the table and poured steaming water from the kettle through the tea strainer and into her cup. "When have we ever followed the crowd? We Hamiltons forge our own path. Besides, with everyone else planting cotton, there will be more local demand for oats."

Her cup filled, she set the kettle on the metal trivet in the center of the table, then looked at her eldest brother and smiled. "I trust your instincts, Zach. If you think oats are the way to go, then we'll plant oats. You haven't steered us wrong yet. Just recall that remarkable yield of syrup we had last year. We sold nearly a thousand gallons of molasses! Even if the yield is smaller this time, we'll still have enough to get by, thanks to your capable management."

"Laying it on a little thick, aren't you, Evie?" Zach smiled around the brim of his coffee cup, and the tension gripping the room eased a fraction. "You don't have to play peacemaker. We're big boys. We can handle a little disagreement now and again."

"Of course you can." If one counted icy silence and grumpy stomping for the next two days as *handling* things. She needed them in a good mood right now. She winked at Zach, then turned to smile at Seth as well, adding a silent plea to her expression, begging him to let the matter drop. At least for tonight.

Seth managed the family funds—kept the books, studied the agriculture market, researched trends and innovations, monitored the accounts. He was the brains behind Zach's brawn. Seth's well-timed investments had slowly padded their income over the years, taking what Zach had scraped together through odd jobs and back-breaking toil and growing it into something substantial. Having gone to bed hungry more nights than not during the lean years after the train wreck, security was something they all craved. Yet lines still existed that could not be crossed.

Cotton was one of those lines.

Evangeline didn't know all the details. Zach never spoke about his past, but she knew he despised farming. Cotton in particular. The fact that he had purchased a farm seven years ago and started raising sorghum and corn of his own free will testified to his love for his siblings. She was convinced that nothing else would have ever compelled him to work the land again. He'd proven countless times over the years that he'd do whatever it took to provide for her and Seth. And if farming was what it took, that was what he'd do. Even if he hated every minute of it.

Seth used to be content to let Zach make all the decisions, but the older he got, the more driven he seemed to assert himself. And judging by the stubborn tilt of his chin, this was fixing to be one of those times.

"Cotton fetches twice the price of oats, and you know it," Seth challenged. "I don't understand why we can't plant a few acres just to try it out."

Zach slowly set his coffee cup on the table, his whitening knuckles the only outward show of strain. "Be my guest," he said with a wave of his hand. "You want to plant cotton, plant cotton. But I ain't working it."

Seth leaned forward, eyes narrowing. "Why not? You work the sorghum, the corn, the oats when they're rotated in. Why not cotton?"

"I got my reasons."

"You got your reasons." Seth's voice rose, his temper slipping. He scraped his chair back and pushed to his feet.

"Please, Seth. Leave it alone." Evangeline reached a hand toward her brother, but he pulled away from her.

"I'm not going to leave it alone. Not this time." He stormed around the table to face Zach without a barrier between them. "All these years, he's been the one deciding what's right for us. What's best. But we aren't kids anymore. And this is not a dictatorship."

Zach lifted his coffee cup and sipped, ignoring the rant, which only angered Seth more. Evangeline's stomach cramped. She hated when her brothers fought. It didn't happen often, but when it did, it brought long-buried fears surging back to the surface. Fears of being abandoned again. Fears that they'd decide this little patchwork family of theirs wasn't worth the effort any longer and leave.

Evangeline hurried around the table and placed herself between the two men she loved more than anything on this earth. She placed one hand on Zach's shoulder, the other on Seth's elbow.

"Zach provided for us when we couldn't provide for ourselves. He kept us together. Kept us alive. He's always put us first. Always." She squeezed Seth's arm, praying he would relent. "If he doesn't want to work cotton, we don't work cotton. We owe him that much."

Seth turned hard eyes on her, eyes that shone with . . . hurt? "And what about what he owes us?"

That got Zach's attention. He turned toward his brother, his face a blank mask that reminded Evangeline of another man she'd gone toe-to-toe with earlier in the day. "And what exactly do I owe you, *little* brother?"

Seth jerked his arm away from Evangeline's hold. "Respect."

Zach blinked. Twice. Then hardened the line of his mouth.

Seth continued, undaunted. "I'm a man, same as you, Zach. Not a boy. Just because I can't work the same as you doesn't mean my opinions hold no weight."

Zach twisted in his seat and rested an arm on the chair back. "And here I thought you were the smart one of the family. I heed your opinions all the time. You have full control over the family finances. Wherever you say to invest, we invest. I hand my money over to you every time we bring in a harvest or butcher a hog. I wouldn't do that if I didn't respect you, Seth."

"Yet you don't respect me enough to treat me like an equal. I'm not your *little* brother. I'm your partner. Yet you still keep secrets as if we're children who can't handle a few rocks in our road."

Evangeline looked from one to the other, sensing they weren't talking about cotton any longer. If they ever had been.

Zach slowly rose to his feet, taking full advantage of his greater height as he looked down at Seth. "Some things are better left hidden."

"Better for who?" Seth pressed closer, nearly squishing Evangeline between the two men.

Why wouldn't he just let it go? But in her heart, she knew. Those secrets were poisoning Zach's soul. She could feel it, and apparently Seth could, too. Zach had been closing himself off from them a little more each year. Withdrawing emotionally. Not that he'd ever been the demonstrative sort to begin with, but it was almost as if he was trying to protect them from himself. Though that didn't make any sense. He *was* their protector. Always had been.

"You really want that cotton fluff growing around here, Seth? Might stir up your asthma."

"Still sidestepping the real issue, aren't you, Zach?"

Fists began to clench. Chins jutted. Good heavens! They might actually come to blows.

Evangeline thrust herself more forcefully between the two, planting one hand on each brother's chest. Then she blurted the first thing that came to mind.

"I met a man in the woods today."

Both faces bent toward her, redirecting their antagonism squarely in her direction. "What?"

Well, at least she'd managed to unite them, even if it was at her own expense. They had chorused their demand in perfect synchronicity.

Evangeline smiled. Now she just had to find a way to extricate herself without giving away too many details about her secret project. "I met a man," she repeated, "in the woods."

Zach's eyebrows arched sharply. "What man?" He was in full-on protective mode now. Big brother impulses trumped personal issues every time. He really was a sweetheart under that lone wolf exterior. "Evangeline . . ." he growled.

All right, so he also had fangs, but she could deal with those.

"Don't get your dander up, Zach. It was all perfectly innocent."

Seth glowered, taking a stance beside Zach, his arms crossed. "Nothing is ever perfectly innocent with you, Evie."

Really? That was just uncalled for. She cast a glare at her middle brother. Just because in this instance it *wasn't* perfectly innocent—she'd been rummaging through Logan's camp, after all, and he was probably involved in some sort of clandestine, better-if-you-don't-know-my-full-name kind of activities of his own—didn't mean she *always* behaved in a such a manner.

"How'd you meet him?" Zach, of course, was still focused on the man.

"He rescued me," Evangeline said, hoping to reassure her brother that Logan meant her no harm. Yet instead of soothing him, her remark seemed to increase his agitation. He grabbed her upper arms in a controlled grip. It wasn't painful, but it demanded answers.

"Was someone threatening you?" He looked her up and down, frowning at the small bruise she knew was forming over her right cheek where she'd collided with the ground when Logan tackled her. It hadn't darkened much yet, so she'd hoped it would escape their notice, but apparently that was no longer an option. At least they couldn't see the other sore places along her hip and ribs. "Are you all right?"

"I'm fine. And truly I was never in any danger. It was just a silly misunderstanding."

Zach eyed her skeptically. "A misunderstanding that led a man you'd never met to believe you in need of rescue?"

Evangeline shrugged, a rather neat trick, considering Zach still had hold of her arms. "He might have reached the erroneous conclusion that I was in the path of a wild boar's charge."

"Hezzy." There was that synchronicity again, as both her brothers chorused her pet's name with equal levels of exasperation. But at least they were no longer glowering at her. Zach even released her arms, freeing her to punch his shoulder lightly.

"Don't say his name like he's the bane of your existence," she scolded. "Hezekiah is a fine hog and a faithful companion."

"He's a nuisance and a plague."

Evangeline would have been offended had all the heat not drained from Zach's voice and his lips not curved into a hint of a smile.

She threw her arms around her brother's neck and kissed his cheek. "You love him and you know it."

His arms came around her back for a light squeeze before he disengaged himself. "I tolerate him."

She grinned up at him. "Because you love me."

He never actually said the words, but his actions and countless sacrifices proved them true. So a few years ago, she'd decided to start saying them for him.

Zach rolled his eyes. "Brat."

She wrinkled her nose at him. "Tyrant."

They shared a smile, and Evangeline's heart filled with the warmth of family. She headed to the washtub to start cleaning the dishes, her step light and bouncing until Seth's determined voice echoed from behind her.

"I think you left a few details out of your story, Evie. Time to tell us more about this man in the woods."

CHAPTER

7

Logan leaned an elbow on his knee as he bent forward to place the eight of clubs he'd just drawn atop the nine of diamonds lying among the rest of his solitaire stacks. He chanced a glance at the sun dipping ever lower in the afternoon sky, then drew another card from the shrinking pile in his hand.

Queen of hearts. Useless. She didn't play anywhere. No black kings were hanging out, waiting for her. Unlike the foolish knave sitting on his bedroll with a deck of cards, twitching at every leaf rustle or twig snap.

Logan tossed the feckless queen atop his solitaire offerings with enough force to scatter the center stacks.

She wasn't coming. Of course she wasn't. Why would she? He'd all but run her off with his abrupt manner and dark conjectures. Stupid conscience. Why had he felt the need to warn her away? Evangeline Hamilton was the perfect pawn. Naïve. Soft-hearted. Trusted by the enemy.

Fate dealt him an ace, and like an idiot, he'd discarded it.

Maybe he should be glad that she'd failed to follow through on her impulsive promise to return. She might make a great pawn, but she was certain to be a distraction. One he couldn't afford. He had to stay focused on the end game, on enacting justice. He didn't need a spunky wood sprite showering him with happy-sappy fairy dust at every turn. Spouting ridiculous adages about joy and hope and telling him to peddle his pessimism elsewhere.

Logan's mouth quirked into a reluctant smile at the memory. She might be a romantic idealist, but she had the gumption of a military general when it came to standing her ground and advancing her position. No wonder his horse had taken to her.

A quiet nicker sounded behind him.

Speaking of his horse. . . .

Logan pushed to his feet, his eyes scanning the wooded area in front of him. His heart pounded in moronic anticipation as his neck craned in an effort to peer deeper into the trees. Having maintained a grasp on at least a few of his faculties, he kept a hand on the butt of his revolver as his ears finally picked up the soft treads that had alerted Shamgar to their approaching company.

A flash of red caught his eye. Dark red, like wine. His gut tightened. His chest throbbed. Then she cleared the trees. Her red skirt snapped in time to her purposeful strides. An ivory blouse with thin, matching red stripes outlined subtle curves he couldn't seem to look away from. The high collar and upswept hairstyle accentuated a graceful neck that he'd failed to notice yesterday during their tackling and sparring session.

Good gravy, but she was a beauty. Not that he hadn't figured that out during their first encounter, but today she wasn't covered in dirt and debris from an unneeded rescue. Today she looked . . . fresh. Bright. Like she'd purposely taken care with her appearance. For him.

A touch of male swagger loosened his limbs as he strutted forward to meet her.

Dropping his hand from his weapon, he reached forward to relieve her of the basket she carried. "No pig today?"

Evangeline shook her head, her mysterious eyes twinkling. "I didn't think it wise with food involved."

He lifted the towel covering the basket, and the aroma hit him. Bread. *Fresh* bread. Fresh, *still warm* bread.

Logan's mouth watered and his stomach rumbled with embarrassing volume. He hadn't eaten fresh bread since . . . he couldn't remember when. The last time he'd visited his mother at his aunt's house, he supposed. How long had that been? Five months? Six?

The cook at the logging camp in east Texas where he'd worked for the past three years tended to serve dry, crumbly biscuits that were only palatable under gravy. And the saloons he'd frequented to keep his card skills honed focused more on catering to the male appetite for whiskey, women, and winnings than food. Suddenly coming nose-to-basket with what he'd been missing stirred a surprising hunger inside him.

His companion giggled. "I can hear you salivating from here. Don't worry, I won't make you wait. There are few pleasures more delightful than warm bread with butter."

Logan jerked his gaze up to her face. "You brought butter, too?"

The little minx grinned. "Of course. A small crock you can keep cool in the stream that runs past your corral."

Logan held a hand out to her when they reached a rough patch of terrain. Pink tinged her cheeks, but she laid her fingers in his palm and allowed him to help her over a tiny ravine breaking apart the ground in their path. Not that she needed his help—her adroitness yesterday proved her surefootedness—but he'd not completely forgotten the manners his ma had taught him.

Picnic basket, pretty gal in nicer-than-usual clothes, fella with an empty belly and an appreciation for rosy blushes and teasing conversation—this outing had all the markers of a legitimate social engagement. Well, maybe not legitimate. His intentions were not entirely honorable, after all. He'd never harm the lady or her reputation, but he fully intended to seduce information from her—learning how Hamilton's thought processes worked, what he valued, what secrets might be hanging about that could be exploited. Logan planned to mine Evangeline for every nugget of insight he could extract.

All while trying not to hurt her in the process.

Probably not completely possible, but he'd give it his best effort. If his luck held, her soft heart would bleed enough over his own sad tale that he'd win her to his side. Then she'd actually *help* him take her brother down.

Allying himself with the cheerful little sprite proved a rather attractive prospect when he thought about it. Too bad the odds of a troll beguiling a fairy were slimmer than a playing card's edge. But slim odds were better than no odds, and he'd never throw in a hand before all the cards were dealt. He had time to maneuver, to cultivate advantages, and bluff his way into her good graces. He knew how to win and wasn't afraid to raise the stakes.

"I wasn't sure your brothers would let you come," he ventured. "Meeting a strange man out in the woods and all." He chanced a glance at her profile. "The way you described them yesterday made them seem like the protective sort."

"Oh, they are," she assured him, her eyes twinkling. "But after I told them about your gallant attempt to save me from a rampaging boar, they relented when I proposed I bring you a basket to welcome you to Pecan Gap." She grinned at him, a sideways, mischievous twist of the lips that made him think they were sharing a secret. "They're not terribly fond of my keeping a hog as a pet, so the fact that you tried to shoot Hezzy actually raised you in their estimation."

This woman defined delightful. With her dancing eyes and teasing smile numbing his brain, it took Logan several seconds to remember why he'd started this line of questioning in the first place. Oh, yes. Find out what she'd told her brothers about him. They knew of his presence. What else?

"I'm still surprised one of them didn't escort you out here."

Her chin came up a fraction. "Women pay neighborly calls in town all the time without a male escort. Why should this be any different?" She slowed her step and eyed him with sudden suspicion. "Unless you're not the gentleman you led me to believe yesterday." She leaned away from him, her smile vanishing. "Just so you know, I never travel this country unarmed. I carry a knife in my boot, and Zach made sure I knew how to use it."

Great. Now he was scaring her off. *Way to go, Logan.* He backed off and tried for charm instead of answers. He placed his right hand over his heart and thickened his southern accent. "I swear, ma'am, that you are safe in my company. My mama raised me to guard a woman's person and her virtue with equal vigor. I only wondered at your brothers' faith in a man they had not yet met. If you were in my keeping, I'd not be so trusting."

Some of the sparkle came back into her eyes. "If I were in your keeping, I'd escape your smothering vigilance just as often as I escape theirs."

He chuckled. "I don't doubt it."

Evangeline Hamilton craved freedom and had a mild rebellious streak. He could use that.

"Besides," she said, her shoulders lifting in a shrug, "I told them precisely where I'd be, so if I'm not home in an hour, Zach will come looking and probably shoot you for causing him worry. He does tend to fret where I'm concerned. It's sweet but a tad constricting."

She worded the threat in such a matter-of-fact fashion, Logan couldn't tell if she was kidding or not. Hamilton had already proven himself capable of hurting others without conscience. Cards, pistols—simply a different choice of weapon. But now Logan knew the man had a weakness. His sister.

"I guess we better get on with our visit, then, shouldn't we?" He steered her to his campsite and steadied her while she seated herself atop his bedroll. "So what else is in here? It feels heavier than a loaf of bread." He lifted the basket cover to peek inside, then placed it between them and settled on the opposite side.

"Go ahead and unpack it," she said, her voice a teasing lilt. "I wasn't sure what you'd like, so I brought an assortment."

An assortment of treasures. Stunned by her generosity, Logan inwardly gaped at each new item he pulled from the basket, though outwardly he kept his expression limited to polite interest. In addition to the bread and crock of butter, she'd also included a pint of red jam. Strawberry? Boy, he hoped so. It was his favorite. A thick slab of smoked ham wrapped in brown paper. A quart of string beans.

One jar remained. He reached for it, then stilled. Reverently, he brought the fruit jar out of the basket. Peaches. Sweet, juicy, yellow peaches.

He glanced sideways at his companion. "You're giving these to me?" Peaches were a luxury. A treat for special occasions.

Evangeline shrugged and turned her attention to her lap. "We have a pair of trees by the house. I put up a half-dozen quarts every summer. We can spare one to welcome our new neighbor."

Trees by the house? Logan cradled the glass jar in his arm as he struggled to contain the emotion that swelled inside him without warning. His mother had planted a pair of saplings by their front porch. He'd forgotten those little trees. The ones she'd watered with such care to ensure the roots wound deep into the soil. He'd not paid them much attention at the time, more interested in romping about the countryside than pampering baby trees. He didn't even know what type they had been, since they hadn't produced any fruit before he and his mother had been forced to leave. But if they were his mother's trees. . . .

Thickness clogged his throat. He cleared it away and forced himself to set the peaches aside as if they weren't the most valuable gift he'd received in the last seven years, then pasted a generic smile on his face. "Thanks."

She smiled in return, but her eyes probed his, and he sensed she'd not been fooled by his manufactured nonchalance.

Logan turned away, using the near-empty basket as his excuse. *Keep your guard up, man.* It wouldn't do for her to learn his tells, ferret out his weaknesses. She could turn against him, ally herself with his enemy. He had to maintain control of their interactions. Reveal only what was advantageous to his end game. Nothing more.

He found two utensils in the bottom of the basket. Knives— one for slicing the bread, the other for spreading butter. He drew them out, placed them across his bent leg, then reached for the loaf and gently removed its cloth wrapper.

"Join me?" he asked as he lifted the serrated blade above the golden brown offering. He peered at her. "This bounty is far too great for me to indulge in alone."

She leaned forward as if to impart a secret. Cupping her hand around the side of her mouth, she whispered, "Why do you think I packed the knives?"

He chuckled. "A conspirator, I see." He winked. "A woman after my own heart."

Evangeline grinned at his devilish quip, but she filed the odd word choice away. Conspirator. Was that how Logan saw himself, or was he just being flirtatious?

She dipped her chin. Heavens, but she wanted him to be flirting. She'd never been on the receiving end of such attention before, and her belly fluttered with delightful little spasms at the thought that this heroic rescuer of women from imagined boar attacks might actually find her attractive. Might truly enjoy her company.

As the edge of the knife sawed through the crusty outer layer of bread, Evangeline looked up, greedy for the opportunity to study Logan while he concentrated on his task.

He'd trimmed his beard. Her heart stuttered at the observation. Yesterday it had been a mite unkempt. Scraggly. A tad fluffy, even.

The fluff had disappeared. Cropped close, the beard outlined the squareness of his jaw without the scraggly bits trailing down his neck that had been there yesterday. Had he done that for her? Because he'd wanted to look his best when she brought the supplies? His shirt was clean, too. And while his boots were just as worn as they'd been yesterday, less dust clung to the cracked leather.

Evangeline sat a little straighter and smoothed a hand over the skirt draped across her bent legs.

Of course, his efforts might have absolutely nothing to do with her. Perhaps it was simply his day to clean up. Like laundry day.

But he *might* have done it for her. To make a favorable impression. She nibbled the inside of her lip. No harm in assuming the best until proven wrong.

Logan glanced up from the loaf as if he'd sensed her attention. Evangeline looked away. Spying the crock of butter, she pounced. "If you'll hand me a piece, I'll start buttering it for you."

"Thanks." His eyes radiated nothing but warmth as she accepted the first raggedly uneven slice from his hand.

She slathered it with a generous portion of butter, then proffered it to him. "Here. I'll slice the rest while you eat."

"Probably a good idea," he said, shaking his head over the four slices lying on the bread cloth. The heel was half an inch thick at the top, but thin as a toothpick at the bottom. "I seem to be making a hash of it."

He handed her the knife, handle first, and her fingers rubbed against his in the exchange. Her skin tingled where she'd touched him, and her breath caught slightly. He didn't seem in any hurry to release his grip. Even with the prize of warm buttered bread in her other hand, right below his nose.

Evangeline tightened her grip on the utensil's handle and tugged it from his grasp. Logan might make her head spin and her insides dance around like popping corn in a hot skillet, but she knew better than to let a few frilly feelings turn her mind to mush. He was a mystery that needed solving before anything personal could develop between them.

Thankfully, he received her less-than-subtle message and removed the bread from her other hand with barely more than a brush of his little finger. Nothing more than what she'd expect from one of her brothers taking something from her, but the impact of that barely-there touch was magnified a hundred times compared to anything she'd felt from Zach or Seth. She could feel it still, even several heartbeats after Logan moved away.

Determined to focus on something other than the man consuming every thought currently running through her head,

Evangeline set to work on the bread, fully intending to prove her womanhood by slicing the remainder of the loaf with geometric precision that would make an architect proud. Unfortunately, two slices in, Logan bit into his bread and started making the most disruptive sounds. Moans, really. Transported, elated moans that no baker with an ounce of pride could ignore. Apparently she had more than an ounce.

She glanced up and was immediately struck by the rapture on his face. Eyes closed, head tilted slightly toward the sky, he chewed and savored as if she'd fed him a fancy French pastry instead of a slice of ordinary bread.

"Oh . . . mmm . . ." he managed to get out when his mouth opened to take a second bite that ended up engulfing the entire remaining portion. "This is so tasty!"

At least that was what she thought he said. It was hard to tell for certain with his overstuffed mouth muffling the words. It could as easily have been "Thick as goo, pasty," but he seemed to be enjoying what he was eating, so she assumed the first interpretation was correct.

She hurried to butter him a second slice. His enjoyment was such a delight to behold, she probably would have fed him the entire loaf if he hadn't slowed after three pieces to insist that she take the fourth.

He held up a hand and shook his head, though he had to swallow before he could actually speak the apology his eyes were signaling. "You must think me raised by wolves." He cupped his palm beneath the hand holding out the next slice and gently steered the offering back toward her. "Please. You take this one."

"Are you sure?" she teased, even while her insides rioted at the touch of his hand on hers. "I don't think I could enjoy it half as much as you seem to. It'd be a shame to waste it on such an unappreciative palate."

"I insist." He finally drew his hand away from hers in order to thud his fist against his chest in a gesture of fervency. "I swear I'll not eat another bite unless you join me in the feast."

"Well, we can't let that atrocity occur. This was meant to be a gift, after all. I'd hate to have to take it back and feed it to Hezekiah."

Logan's stricken gaze darted from her face to the bread as if he actually feared she would do such a thing.

Evangeline laughed. "Here." She pushed the crock of butter toward him, then lifted the bread to her lips and took a healthy bite off one corner.

"That's my girl." Logan grinned and immediately set about buttering a fifth slice, unaware of the impact of his casually spoken words.

My girl.

They tapped into every dream she'd hidden in her heart since childhood. The dream of belonging.

At first it had just been about family, but over the last few years, as she witnessed girls her age and younger pairing off with beaus, then marrying and having children, she'd started dreaming of belonging to someone in particular. A man. A special man. One who would see past her oddities and love the woman inside. Who would accept her patchwork family and rejoice in becoming a part of it. Who would give her the chance to be a mother like the one she barely remembered, to raise children who would know without doubt that they were loved and accepted, that they belonged.

Her whirling thoughts slowed her eating pace so that she barely finished her single slice in the time Logan ate two more. With a joking comment about how he'd eat every slice if he didn't remove the temptation, Logan wrapped the remaining bread back inside the cloth.

As he tied a knot across the top of the half-loaf by pulling two corners tight, he searched out her eyes. "That was the finest bread I have ever tasted, Evangeline Hamilton." His sincerity washed over her and seeped into every dry crevice that hungered for approval, for acceptance. "You've made me feel welcome in a place that has offered me little kindness in the past."

"I'm glad." Whatever he'd suffered, she wanted nothing more than to be the balm that soothed his wounds and helped him heal.

Evangeline made a decision. No, a vow. She'd pray for this man with no last name. This man who carried heavy secrets and mysterious intent. She'd pray every night as she fell asleep and every morning when she awoke. She'd pray for healing of old wounds, for an abundance of new blessings, and for godly direction to guide his steps.

As Logan jumped nimbly to his feet and held out his hand to assist her in rising, she realized she'd better add another prayer to her list. One that involved an extra helping of discernment for her own heart. She was walking a tightrope with this one, and she very much feared there would not be a net to catch her if she fell.

CHAPTER

8

Things were getting out of hand.

Logan hung back and watched Evangeline twirl like an autumn leaf caught in a whirlwind over the patch of ground he'd spent the last week clearing. His chest tightened as joy bloomed on her face.

"It's perfect!" She stopped spinning and turned the full force of her smile on him. "Oh, Logan. It's beautiful. A view of the river to the north, woods to the south and west. The creek out back for water until a well can be dug. You couldn't have picked a better spot."

And that was exactly why things were so out of hand. He'd spent two days riding back and forth across his acreage, searching for the location she would find most pleasing. Then he'd spent the last five days clearing brush, pulling stumps, and leveling the ground so it would support a cabin. Not because he cared about improving his land in order to make it a more attractive lure for Zacharias, but because he'd wanted this: Her reaction. Her pleasure in his efforts. Her pride in his accomplishment.

He'd done it simply to make her happy.

Well, and to have an excuse to see her for an extended period of time instead of the few stolen moments he managed to wrangle for himself when she took Hezekiah for his afternoon jaunt. Apparently her brothers weren't all that keen on her spending time alone with the new male neighbor—shocking!—and she felt the need to limit her visits with him to no more than a quarter hour to avoid arousing her siblings' suspicions.

Logan hadn't argued, but he'd plotted a way to carve out a healthier dose of time to spend with her. He told himself it was all part of his plan to cultivate a relationship so she'd open up to him and share information he could use against her brother. Yet watching her just now, he wasn't calculating his next move or revising strategies. He was simply enjoying the show.

"You should build a porch," she declared as she traipsed up to the edge of the cleared area and spread her arms wide. "Right here." Her eyes brimmed with excitement. "Just think how lovely it would be to sit on the porch in the evening and watch the sun go down." She wrapped her arms around her middle as she lifted her face to look at the sky. "A cup of tea in your hand. Perhaps a dog sitting beside you, his head in your lap."

Why'd she have to go and paint a picture? Especially with that dreamy voice of hers, as if she could see into the future. He didn't have a dog. And tea? He rolled his eyes. A man drank coffee. Tea was a woman's drink.

At the thought of women, his mental picture shifted. The porch stretched in his mind, widening to accommodate a second chair. No, a swing. One long enough for two. A man *and* a woman. And there weren't no dog's head in his lap. Instead, there was a woman's head on his shoulder, his arm around her back, his fingers caressing her side as they watched the red and orange sky slowly fade to gray. A woman with fire in her hair and love in her eyes.

"Logan?"

He startled, and the image vanished. "Sorry." He cleared his throat and straightened his posture. "Did you say something?"

A peculiar look crossed her face, but then her smile resurfaced to brighten her features. "I asked if you liked the idea of a porch for your cabin."

"It's not *my* cabin, Eva. Remember?" *His* house was currently occupied. By Hamiltons. "This property's just an investment."

He expected her to argue or tease or shrug off his gloomy pronouncement as she so often did and continue laying claim to the rest of the floorplan, outlining where the kitchen should be, along with the parlor and bedrooms. Instead she simply stood at the edge of his imaginary porch and stared at him.

"Did you just call me Eva?"

Logan winced. "Don't like it, huh?"

"It's not that. I've just . . . never been called by that name." She lifted her chin as if coming to a decision. "I like it. Much more sophisticated than Evie."

"That what your brothers call you?" He closed the distance between them. If he could get her talking about her brothers, they might make real progress today. And all that brush-clearing and land-leveling would be worth the sore back and blisters.

She smiled with true fondness. "Yes. Unless they're vexed with me." She scrunched up her face to demonstrate, but she looked about as angry as a pouting kitten. "Then they call me, 'E-van-gel-ine.'"

He chuckled. She might not be able to pull off the vexed face, but she nailed the annoyed brother voice.

She laughed along with him as she took the arm he offered and allowed him to lead her toward the creek. "In truth, I wouldn't know how to react if they started calling me something other than Evie. That's been their name for me since childhood." She peeked shyly over at him. "But *you* can call me Eva."

His pulse did an idiotic little dance at the idea of sharing a special intimacy with her, but before he could lecture himself out of the reaction, his companion did a little dance of her own. She flounced ahead a couple paces, her hand on his arm barely tethering her as she spun back around to beam a smile at him.

"Maybe I can call you Gan. Or Lo."

He pulled an aghast face and was rewarded with an infectious giggle.

"Oh, I know!" she exclaimed, planting her feet and bringing them both to a halt. "Log. Very strong and manly, don't you think?"

He rolled his eyes. "Get a few of us together, chink us, and you'd have yourself a cabin."

She laughed deep and loud at his quip until she was forced to wipe a tear from the corner of her eye. The blue one. The vibrant, glistening blue one that seemed to project joy to the same extent her brown one projected warmth. Together they were an addicting combination. One he found himself craving more and more of late.

"Perhaps we ought to stick with Logan." He made that dour pronouncement, then resumed their trek toward the creek, staring at the ground in front of them rather than the spritely wood nymph by his side.

"I suppose that would be best," she agreed, residual laughter coloring her voice. "Though it's rather unsporting of you to have a name that fails to lend itself to shortening when mine has so many options. Zacharias has Zach. Hezekiah has Hezzy. Although, Seth is just Seth, so I suppose we *do* have precedent."

A gentle silence fell between them as the trees thickened and the trickle of creek water drew them closer to their destination.

Logan had searched out the ideal conversation spot earlier this morning. Secluded, perhaps even a touch romantic. A place to put a woman at ease and lower her intellectual guard. This bend in the creek had everything he'd required. A picturesque view where the water bottlenecked between two stones, then tripped over a ledge to form a miniature falls. Oak and pecan trees for shade. A fallen limb that he'd dragged close to the water's edge to provide a bench.

When they rounded the bend, Eva's indrawn breath sent satisfaction spiraling through him as they slowed to a halt. "I hoped you'd like it."

"It's beautiful." She turned her radiant face toward him, and his chest constricted with pleasure at her obvious appreciation of his gift. "We don't have anything half as lovely on our land. There's a little pond that's quite nice," she said as she twisted back toward the creek bed, "but nothing like this. I could sit here for hours."

"Well, we might not have hours," Logan said as he gestured toward the large limb to their left, "but I can offer you a hand-selected seat and slightly questionable company if you care to take a small respite before returning home."

"Oh, dear. I'm not sure about that *slightly questionable company*." Her eyes danced as she teased him. "I do have my reputation to consider."

Logan played along. Just to flatter her, of course. All part of the seduction process. Not because it actually made his heart feel lighter when they bantered.

"I misspoke. I meant to say question*ing* company." He leaned close and gave her his best rogue's smile. Though he hadn't had much opportunity to practice it when all his training had been devoted to erasing as much expression from his face as possible to succeed at the poker tables. Nevertheless, the blush tinting her cheeks proved he wasn't quite as inept as he'd feared. "I plan to question you mercilessly, my lady."

"Question me? For what purpose, sir?" The smile didn't slip from her face, but a hint of caution clouded her gaze.

"So that I might get to know you better, of course." He waggled his brows at her. "You are the most intriguing neighbor I've ever met."

Eva's glance darted toward the water before shyly returning to his face. "I doubt that."

"It's true." And it was. She fascinated him. He drew close and lowered his voice to a raspy whisper. "At my last residence, a drugstore clerk with thinning hair and a nose resembling a hawk's beak lived to my left and harped at my mother for allowing her flowers to wander into his yard. Apparently he suffered from sneezing attacks during the growing season."

Eva raised a suspicious brow, but he nodded and held up his right hand to attest to his veracity. Mr. Pickwick had been a decidedly unpleasant, yet very real neighbor. As was Mrs. Abernathy. "On my right lived a sixty-year-old widow who shouted every word she spoke as if unaware that she was the deaf one and not the rest of us."

Eva chuckled softly, and the caution in her eyes faded.

Logan maneuvered her toward the improvised bench. "So you see, you far outshine any of my previous neighbors."

"Well, in that case, how can I refuse?" She adjusted her dark green skirt, the same one she'd worn the first day they'd met, and took a seat. His tree-limb bench sat quite a bit lower to the ground than one of the normal variety, so he cupped her elbow and counterbalanced her descent. She smiled her thanks and waited for him join her.

"So tell me more about your family," he prodded. "Despite the fact that you've returned unharmed from each of our visits,

I'm rather surprised neither of your brothers has come out to threaten me about staying away from their sister."

"Zach thought about it." She grinned. "But after our first meeting and the welcome goodies I delivered, I've been pretty closed-lipped about our interactions, so he probably doesn't suspect there's a need." She turned her attention to the creek and circled her arms around her knees. "He's used to men keeping their distance from me. And me from them."

If Arnold Dunn from the Lucky Lady was an accurate sample of the reactions of most local men to Miss Evangeline Hamilton, their lack of interest proved Pecan Gap was a town filled with idiots.

"What about Seth?" Logan asked, wanting to steer the conversation back toward her brothers. If he thought too long about the hurt feelings the beautiful woman next to him was trying so hard to hide, he was liable to get riled, and that wouldn't aid him in wooing information from her. "Is he not the protective type?"

"He's more the scolding type." One would expect a beleaguered sigh after a statement like that, but Eva's voice rang with fondness. "After we were orphaned at such a young age, Zach and Seth took over my raising. Zach was the oldest, so he carried the burden of providing for us. He'd be gone for long hours, scrounging up any odd job he could find in order to bring home enough food to fill our bellies for the night. A heavy responsibility for one so young."

Logan's jaw clenched. It was hard to hear her glowing account of her brother's deeds. Maybe they *had* gone through hard times, but that didn't excuse what Hamilton had done to Logan's family once he'd grown. If he'd had enough money to play in a high-stakes game, he'd had enough to provide for his siblings without stealing another man's livelihood.

Eva fell silent for a moment, gazing at the creek. "He might have looked like a man with his height and beard scruff, but he was only thirteen when he made the choice to keep our little family together instead of letting the Children's Aid Society split us up."

The corners of her mouth tightened slightly, and a pair of tiny lines crept across her brow. When she continued, her voice held a fierceness that hadn't been there before. "He didn't have to do that. Keep us together." She flashed a glance at Logan before turning away again. The connection only lasted for a heartbeat, but she seared him with her fervor. "He could have taken a position with a family and worked for a field hand's wages. He could have had a home. Security. But he made a vow to keep us together, and he did." Her voice softened. "Sometimes I worry about what he had to do to keep us fed, how he might have been mistreated or abused. But he never complained. He just did what had to be done. Kept us together and kept us alive."

Logan knew *exactly* what Hamilton had done to keep them together. He'd become a con man and a thief.

An uncomfortable stirring tugged on Logan's conscience. What had *he* become to restore what rightfully belonged to his family? Many considered gamblers no better than thieves. Hadn't he modeled his retribution after the very man who'd done the damage in the first place?

He ground his molars. It wasn't the same. *He* wasn't the same. He never cheated. Never took from men who couldn't afford to lose what they placed in the pot. Well, at least none that he'd known of. Another ache poked at his chest. He might be able to read faces, but he couldn't read minds. It wasn't his fault if players wagered more than they could afford to lose.

Something heavy sank into the base of Logan's gut. Zacharias Hamilton had probably justified his gain of the Fowler land with the same argument.

He didn't want to see himself in his enemy. Didn't want to

picture the coldhearted man who'd stolen his father's life as a hardscrabble youth doing anything he could to provide for his family. He'd wanted insight into his nemesis, not sympathy.

"Sounds like your brother is a good man." Logan forced the words out even though they threatened to choke him. He needed to win Eva's trust, after all.

"He is," she said with unwavering conviction. Poor deluded woman.

"And Seth?" Logan shifted the topic, afraid that if he pressed too much for information on Zacharias, she might suspect his interest in her family stemmed from something other than his interest in her.

Eva leaned back a little. "Seth has weak lungs. Asthma, the doctors call it. Which means that when we were kids, he got stuck tending me while Zach hunted for work." She laughed softly. "Poor fella. Just what every young boy wants—to be saddled with a whiny little sister."

Logan scoffed. "I can't believe you were ever whiny."

The smile he'd been missing blossomed anew across her face. "Oh, I had my moments. I could be a downright terror when I set my mind to it."

"*That* I can believe." He rubbed a hand over his jaw. "I remember the wallop you pack when you get your dander up."

"Well, in all fairness, you started it by tackling me." She nudged his shoulder with hers, her eyes twinkling with humor.

Who knew making a gal smile could leave a man feeling so accomplished?

"Seth is my best friend," Eva said, her eyes growing more serious. "He's the smartest person I know. Reads all the time. Works miracles with numbers. Zach might have been the provider, but Seth was the one who ensured we survived on what Zach brought home."

How wrong he'd been to think Eva's cheerful nature sprang from an easy life. This girl had suffered. Perhaps even more than he had. Lost her parents. Lived in poverty. Yet the darkness of hardship hadn't tarnished her soul. It still shone with a brilliance that stole his breath.

"It took years for us to learn how to control Seth's condition. Every time Zach managed to scrape together a few extra coins, he dragged Seth to another doctor. He tried burning ozone papers, smoking asthma cigarettes, and about every restorative potion the drugstores offered. Nothing helped. So Zach declared them all quackery and had Seth start keeping a written record of his daily activities—what he ate, where he went, what he did—noting when he had a flare up and when he didn't. Eventually patterns emerged. It was brilliant really. Very scientific. It took years, and in truth Seth still makes notes every day, but we eventually discovered that the presence of dust, smoke, and cats increases the likelihood of attacks. Drinking coffee, mild exercise, and eating fish seems to prevent them."

Logan fought a scowl. Again with Hamilton being the champion. The defender of sickly children and lost little girls. It wasn't right for the villain in Logan's story to be the hero in hers. Hamilton didn't deserve her loyalty, her praise. He was a thief. A killer.

Eva shrugged, oblivious to Logan's thoughts, his poker training paying steep dividends at the moment. "I can't see how what you eat affects your lungs," she said, "but I can't argue with it. Seth fishes every day and rarely has an attack anymore unless he overexerts himself outside. We have a system, though. He works the garden first thing in the morning when the wind tends to blow less, and I take over when he feels his lungs tighten. He spends most of the day in the house where he can control his environment, then ventures down to the river for a short while every afternoon to catch his supper."

Finally. Something Logan could use. He filed away the information. It was always handy to know where people were and when. Made snooping around without getting caught that much easier.

"I owe my life to my brothers," Eva declared, twisting slowly until her gaze jutted squarely up against Logan's. "Zach especially. He sacrificed his future to ensure mine. There's nothing I wouldn't do for him."

Logan bobbed his head in friendly agreement even as he registered the warning hidden in her words. Her allegiance lay with her brothers first and foremost. And though he hated to see any redeeming value in Zacharias Hamilton, Logan had to admit the man had done right by his sister. Perhaps one who wasn't even related by blood, if the town suppositions and his own deductions were correct.

Winning Eva to his side was going to be an uphill battle. Exposing Hamilton's perfidy might not be enough. But he had to take the chance. He'd sit here and let her sing more of Zacharias Hamilton's praises, even if it made his stomach churn. She was too big an asset to forfeit this early in the game.

CHAPTER

9

Evangeline stole a peek at the man sitting next to her. Something seemed different. The easiness between them had grown tight and uncomfortable. Yet nothing untoward showed on Logan's face. He nodded at her, his features bland and polite.

Maybe that was the problem. The spark had been doused.

She'd probably rambled on too long about her brothers. She'd wanted Logan to understand how important they were to her, but it seemed all she'd accomplished was creating distance between them.

"I'm sorry. I'm boring you, aren't I?" She smiled an apology.

Logan leaned backward, his eyes widening. "Boring me? Not at all." He found her hand and cupped it between both of his. "Forgive me if I gave you the impression that I wasn't interested. Nothing could be further from the truth."

He rubbed his thumbs over the back of her hand, and delightful little shivers danced across her skin.

Logan shook his head, his gray eyes filling with regret. "I have a confession to make." He peered at her, and her heart instantly softened like whipped cream on hot apple pie. "One that might make you decide I'm not worthy of your company."

He tightened his grip on her hand as if worried she'd pull away. But she wasn't like that. She didn't turn away from a friend just because he might or might not have done something of which society did not approve. She didn't give two figs for society's approval. Closed-minded people with nothing better to do than sit in judgment of others would not be dictating her opinions. She decided those for herself.

He must have seen the truth in her face, for his eyes brightened a bit. "The method I used to gain the funds to invest in this property was not particularly . . . traditional. For the last several years, I've worked at a lumber camp to support my mother and myself, but when I decided to invest, I needed extra capital, so I . . . padded my income at the poker tables. It's why you thought me uninterested just now. I've trained myself to conceal my reactions. Perhaps too well." He met her eyes, waiting for her condemnation, no doubt.

While she wasn't particularly thrilled that the man she found herself increasingly attracted to had chosen a less-than-honorable method to supplement his income, she wouldn't paint him with a black brush just yet. Everyone could be reformed, after all.

Before she could say as much, though, he rushed on.

"I know it's a despicable pastime." The pressure on her hand increased again. "I only took it up out of desperation, and when it turned out I had a talent for it, well, I decided a short-term suspension of my more high-minded principles would be acceptable if it produced a long-term benefit to my family. In all honesty, though, I despise gambling. I've seen too many lives ruined by it."

Well, that sounded encouraging. Evangeline's spirits rebounded. He was half reformed already.

"My father was one of them. Several years ago, he was lured into deep play and lost everything. Unable to face what he'd done, he took his own life."

"Logan." His name leaked from her like a moan. Tears clouded her vision as an unbearable ache radiated through her chest.

She knew the pain of losing a parent, but her parents had died from illness. They hadn't left her intentionally. What agony Logan must have endured to lose his father in such a sudden, violent way. She couldn't imagine the devastation. The helplessness. The anger.

Evangeline touched his knee with her free hand, driven to comfort him somehow. "I'm so sorry." The words were too small, too inadequate, but she couldn't think of anything else to say. Nothing could make that situation better. Nothing but time and God's grace.

Logan turned toward her, and for once, he made no effort to mask his feelings. Raw agony lined his face. "Every year, my mother slips further and further into melancholia, and I'm helpless to stop it." Something fierce lit his eyes. "I'm not just investing in this land for financial gain, Eva. This investment serves a greater purpose. It's a step toward justice and recompense against the man who cheated my father and destroyed our family. It's all I have left to offer my mother, to free her from the dark place inside that is swallowing her up little by little every day." His voice resonated with righteousness and an intensity that almost frightened her. Light flashed in his eyes for an instant before he dropped his gaze to his lap and softened his tone. "What must you think of me?"

She thought him incredibly courageous to share such a piece of his soul with her. What this man had endured! She tugged her hand free of his hold just far enough to clasp his hands in both of hers. "Justice is important, Logan. Too many suffer because people are afraid to take a stand or too consumed with their own problems to get involved. I admire you for wanting to make things right, but . . ."

No, she shouldn't say it. He didn't need her interference. He needed her compassion.

He raised his brows in challenge. "But?"

She shook her head. "Nothing."

"It's not nothing, Eva." He gripped her fingers and shook her arms lightly. "Tell me."

She nibbled her bottom lip.

"Eva?"

"What about your mother?" she blurted. "Don't you think she needs *you* more than she needs vengeance?"

"It's not vengeance, it's justice." His jaw clenched, and he pulled his hands away from hers.

Eva slumped. She knew she should have kept her mouth shut.

"And I was with her. For years. I've only worked in the logging camps for the past three. She lives with my aunt, and I make regular visits. But my presence doesn't seem to help. She spends long hours in her room, sewing or reading or just lying in bed. We only see each other at meals, and even then, she rarely engages me in conversation." He paused. Swallowed. "I think she sees my father when she looks at me."

He ran a hand over his face. "She was the one who found him. In the barn. After." He sighed, and the sound was so mournful, it broke Evangeline's heart. "I was out gallivanting like usual. Didn't even hear the shot. By the time I came home for supper, she had washed away the blood and covered my father's body with her best tablecloth. She sent me to fetch the undertaker. Wouldn't let me see more than the good side of his face so I'd know it was really him. I've tried to imagine what it must have been like for her. . . ." He shook his head then bent forward, planting his elbows on his thighs and burying his face in his hands.

Evangeline rubbed his back, tears rolling freely down her cheeks. "Don't torture yourself, Logan. She spared you that burden intentionally. Out of love. A mother protecting her son."

His shoulders quavered, but he sucked in a breath and turned his attention to the sky in a bid for control. "She lost everything that day. Her husband. Her home. Her future. Now she lives off the charity of her sister in a house that doesn't belong to her, with a weight on her that grows heavier by the day. She never smiles. Never laughs. And nothing I do helps."

And that was the crux of the matter. Evangeline leaned her head against his shoulder. Flashes of the train wreck passed through her mind. She didn't recall many details. She'd been too young, and Zach had kept her away from Hamilton as best he could, but she remembered how helpless she'd felt, how bereft, how she'd blamed herself. After all, if it hadn't been for her and her stupid eyes, Hamilton would have found a home with a family long before the train derailed.

Fortunately, she'd had good memories to cling to and new brothers to care for her. Smiles and laughter eventually returned, thanks to a little divine intervention, and the world became a place of beauty and hope once again. Unfortunately, Logan's poor mother seemed stuck in the dark, chained by the past, unable to move forward.

Logan surged to his feet, leaving Evangeline awkwardly attempting to catch her balance. "My mother deserves recompense," he declared. "She deserves justice. Maybe then she can find peace."

"Peace doesn't come from outside a person," Evangeline murmured softly. "You can't give it to her, Logan. She has to find it within."

He didn't turn, just stood stiff and straight with his back facing her, so she didn't know if he'd heard her or not. But she couldn't leave the rest unsaid.

"There is only One who can provide peace. He's knocking on her heart even now, but it's up to her to answer."

Silence. Tense, charged silence. But he hadn't stormed off. Hadn't snapped at her to mind her own business. Hadn't demanded she get off his property. Things could be worse.

"I had another brother," she said, shocking herself with the admission as she rose to stand behind Logan.

She never spoke of Hamilton. At least not to anyone outside of Zach and Seth. They'd trained her to leave the past behind when they created their new family. It had been a necessity. However, they were all adults now. No one could separate them. And the time felt right. The situation felt right.

"He and I were close," she said, the words stiff at first. "Inseparable, really, after Mama and Papa died. He had such a kind nature and always seemed to know exactly what to say to make a person feel better. Everyone loved him. *I* loved him." She inhaled a shaky breath. "He died when the orphan train we were riding ran off the rails. I was only four, but I remember the devastation of that loss. Remember blaming myself. I should have done something different. *Been* something different. A girl with matching eyes who didn't scare potential families away. Then he wouldn't have died."

"Eva, that's not tru—" Logan started to turn, but she stopped him with a hand to his back, pressing him around again. She didn't think she could keep the tears at bay if he looked at her.

"Zach and Seth helped me through the worst of my grief with their patience, their protection, and sometimes even their swats on my behind when I needed to be jarred back into the land of the living. Yet that's not what opened my heart to joy again. God did that."

"How?" Logan's voice rasped like gravel against glass.

Evangeline smiled. "He sent me a flower."

Logan twisted toward her, and this time she didn't stop him. Furrows etched his brow so deeply that she could've planted potatoes in the ridges. "A . . . flower?"

"I know it sounds silly to an adult, but to a five-year-old girl, it was a miracle. And my heart still believes it was a gift from God planted specifically for me to find."

His head tilted at a skeptical angle, but he held his tongue, waiting for her to continue.

"We were living in a storage shed out behind the livery where Zach had found work as a stable hand," she recounted, her gaze drifting back to the creek. "I used to sit and watch the horses in the paddock and make mud pies near the trough. I never spoke to anyone, scared that someone might take me away from my brothers, and anytime someone entered the corral, I'd scamper back to the shed and close myself inside. Until the day a young boy came to collect the horse his father had bought him for his birthday.

"The boy's hair was the same color as Ha—as my brother's. The one who died. He was about the same height. He smiled and laughed and clapped his hands as he watched the livery owner put the horse through its paces. He was so happy, so full of life. Everything my brother had been. Everything *I* had been before the train wreck.

"Suddenly, I wanted that life again. I didn't like being sad all the time, being scared. I wanted to laugh, to clap, to dance around in a circle like that boy at the paddock. But I'd forgotten how. I felt heavy inside. Dark."

Evangeline turned and focused her attention on Logan.

"That's when I saw the flower." She smiled at the precious memory. "A bright yellow sunflower. Growing straight out of the crack where the side of the shed met the hard-packed ground. The only color in the entire area. So many horses and men trampled the ground around the livery and corral that not even grass grew there. Just dirt. And mud. And weathered wood. Brown and gray everywhere. Except for that flower. A flower that hadn't been there earlier in the day."

Logan's mouth curved upward in a slightly patronizing way. Not that she blamed him. This was the memory of a child, after all. Yet her heart knew the truth of what happened that day.

"Looking back, logic tells me that flower was probably a quick-growing weed that I hadn't noticed because it hadn't bloomed until later in the day. But it doesn't really matter how it came to be there, because in the depths of my five-year-old soul, I *knew* that God had put it there for me to find at that precise moment. As soon as my eyes locked on that flower, warmth spread through my heart like a fire lit in a room that had sat cold for too long. God saw me. He cared about me. And he was showing me how to leave the darkness behind and enjoy beauty once again."

Evangeline looked down at her shoes, her throat suddenly thick and her voice quivering. "I know I probably sound like a fanciful child, but the impact of that day still lives within me." Gathering her courage, she lifted her chin until she met Logan's eyes. His kind, thankfully nonjudgmental eyes. "If God can make a fleece wet when there is no dew on the ground, and replenish a widow's store of oil until it fills every jar her neighbors bring, and if he can make the sun stand still in the sky, who am I to doubt that he can make a flower bloom to show a grieving child how to live again?"

Slowly she lifted her hand and cupped Logan's cheek. His eyes widened a bit in surprise, but he didn't pull away. "He can do that for your mother, too. I'll pray that he does. I'll pray for you, as well, Logan, that you won't lay burdens on yourself that only God is meant to carry."

CHAPTER

10

Two days later, Eva's words still lingered in Logan's mind as he sat atop Shamgar and stared at the white clapboard church at the edge of town. A score of wagons stood in the yard, along with drowsy horses at the hitching rails beneath the trees. An occasional tail flicked, shooing away a fly. Singing drifted through the open windows, and he swore he could pick out Eva's soprano. He grinned as he shifted in the saddle. Purely a fanciful notion. From this distance, all the sound blended together. Yet every once in a while, someone hit a high note that rang above the rest, and he imagined it was her. No doubt she sang with the same vigor at church that she did while working her chores at home.

Eva was so open with her opinions, with her faith. She exuded confidence. That was why her declaration to pray for his mother, for *him,* had struck such a deep chord. Some well-intentioned folks might make a similar pledge, then get busy with their own lives and forget. Not Eva. He wasn't sure how he knew, but he felt certain she actually prayed for him and his mother on a regular basis. Her genuine, compassionate nature wouldn't allow anything less.

Logan shook his head. He couldn't remember the last time someone had promised to pray for him. Or the last time he had promised to pray for another. Truth be told, he hadn't prayed much at all since his father's death. Oh, he asked God to grant him justice on a fairly regular basis, but after his conversation with Eva, he'd actually prayed for the well-being of his mother for the first time in . . . well, he couldn't remember how long.

Shame had hit him hard when Eva made that promise. Shame and guilt. He wired money to his aunt every month to pay for his mother's expenses, even though Mama refused to touch his *ill-gotten gains,* as she referred to money won at the card tables. It didn't matter that most of what he sent came from his logging pay. Because he gambled, she judged all his money as tainted. Aunt Bess had a much more practical bent, thankfully, but that didn't absolve him of his other failings. He hadn't prayed for his mother. Hadn't asked God to relieve her grief or help her find forgiveness for the husband who had left her and the son who had done much the same. Evangeline had hit too close to the truth with that observation.

It was as if she could see directly into his soul. Unnerving, yet he craved more of that connection. He'd spent so many years hiding his true self from others that no one knew him. Not even his mother. It made a man solitary. Lonely. Hard. But Eva saw past the mask to the man beneath. Even the bits of darkness he'd allowed her to glimpse hadn't scared her off. It made the prospect of pursuing her for more than information mighty tempting.

That was why he was here. Staring at the church. Longing to join in the worship, to join *her,* to become the better version of himself her words had challenged him to be.

Yet he worried about what would happen when Eva's brother saw him. Would Hamilton realize who he was? Logan couldn't afford to jeopardize his plan. He hadn't intended to meet his nemesis face-to-face until Hamilton agreed to meet him at the poker table.

A prospect that was turning out to be more of a challenge than Logan had anticipated. Arnold Dunn's impression seemed to be correct: Hamilton had hung up his cards. Logan had ridden over to Ben Franklin after Eva's visit, determined to find out where Zacharias Hamilton plied his swindling trade, yet no one at the Seven Ponies Saloon recalled ever playing him. The one fellow he'd found who even recognized Hamilton's name only knew him from the sorghum syrup he bought from them every fall.

Then yesterday Logan had made the longer trek down to Cooper, only to encounter the same results. No one at any of the saloons in town recalled playing poker with a man named Zacharias Hamilton. So either he played under a false name, or he really had given up the game. A turn of events that made luring him into a high-stakes revenge match more difficult than Logan had initially projected.

Which was why he'd decided to continue improving the property to sweeten the incentive when he finally challenged Hamilton, and why he'd continue meeting with Eva to learn all he could about the man who refused to conform to expected patterns. Meeting Hamilton face-to-face would help in that endeavor as well, and Eva provided Logan's way in. It would be risky to get so close to his target, but every gambler knew the potential reward a skillful bluff could produce.

Logan nudged Shamgar into motion and steered his mount toward the churchyard. After finding a place to tether his gelding, he slowly climbed the four steps leading to the entrance. He tugged off his hat, ran a hand over his hair to make sure it wasn't sticking up like some wet-behind-the-ears kid's, then inhaled a deep breath. Squaring his shoulders, he pulled the door open.

The singing instantly increased in volume. Individual voices became more distinguishable, especially those of the less melodious variety. Careful to keep his footfalls quiet, Logan crept through the vestibule toward the doorway to the main sanctuary. Once there, he stopped, his gaze glued on the three people sitting in the last pew on the left by themselves. An empty row stood between them and the next family.

Flanked protectively on both sides by her brothers, a subdued young woman with auburn hair sat with her head bowed, mouth barely moving as she sang. Logan strained to hear her voice—the bold, unrestrained notes that carried across fields and echoed in barn rafters—but he couldn't make it out. He stood less than five feet away and couldn't hear a sound from her lips.

His vibrant, effervescent Eva had been muted into someone he barely recognized. What was going on?

Logan slid into the back pew on the right side. The blond brother—Seth—turned and offered a friendly nod of welcome. Eva, however, kept her head bowed and her eyes fixed firmly on the hymnal in her lap.

But it was the man to Eva's left that hardened Logan's gut. Rigid posture. Arms crossed. Lips closed in a tight line. A sinner in a room of saints. Uncomfortable. Almost belligerent. No singing at all fell from his lips. Zacharias Hamilton might have made an outward show of giving up his old ways—avoiding saloons, packing up his cards, attending church—but Logan read the disconnect in his posture. He hadn't changed. Not really. Given the proper incentive, he'd pick up those cards again. Logan just had to find the right button to push.

Distracted by his scheming, Logan simply went through the

motions of the service, bowing his head during prayers, singing softly with the hymns he remembered from childhood, and listening with half an ear to the preacher recount the story of Jesus feeding the five thousand. He tossed a subtle glance across the aisle, but instead of landing on the Hamilton who'd been dominating his thoughts, Logan's gaze snagged on Eva. She still hadn't looked up. Just traded her hymnal for her Bible, her lowered head never lifting.

Logan frowned. What was wrong with her?

The preacher kept on, his deep voice booming through the sanctuary, emphasizing Jesus's power, the disciples' duty to deliver even in the face of their doubt, and the amazement of the crowd as the miraculous feast unfolded. Logan had heard it all before. He'd grown up on the stories of Jesus. Yet when the preacher started talking about things from the boy's perspective, something changed. It seemed new somehow, and Logan found himself drawn in.

"If we want the Lord to accomplish mighty deeds in our own lives, the first step is to put what we have in his hands," the man declared. "This boy had a lunch, enough food to get him through the day. He'd planned ahead. Had everything under control. He'd not go hungry. He had every right to hold on to those loaves and fishes. They were his. But then he looked around at the suffering of his neighbors, heard hungry little ones crying out to their mamas, and he made a decision. He found one of the disciples, showed him his provisions, and offered to give them to Jesus."

The parson left the pulpit to pace across the stage, and when his eyes scanned the crowd, they found Logan in the back row, hovered for a brief moment, then moved off to another section of parishioners.

Had that been a flash of recognition? The Clems had arrived in Pecan Gap two years before the Fowlers had left. John Clem and Logan's father had been acquainted—not well, since Pop hadn't been much of a churchgoing man, but enough that a family resemblance might be noted. Clem hadn't been preaching in those years, so it had been a surprise to see a familiar face in the pulpit. Thankfully, Logan's beard kept most people from recognizing him as the smooth-cheeked boy who used to romp about the countryside, but he'd need to take care that Parson Clem didn't make the connection.

"Most of us like to solve our own problems," the preacher intoned, "to control the direction our lives take."

Logan shifted in the pew, the wooden bench suddenly rubbing roughly against his spine.

"But think what would have happened if this boy had chosen that path." The parson paced back to the middle and raised a single finger. "*One* would have been fed instead of five thousand. Only God can miraculously multiply our loaves and fishes. Yet just as he asked the disciples to handle the problem, he asks us the same. Unfortunately, we tend to scramble around like the Twelve did, trying to solve the problem on our own, when what he really desires is for us to surrender our plans, our control, and place our loaves and fishes into his hands so he can accomplish the impossible."

Logan frowned. He didn't need the impossible. He didn't seek restitution from a multitude, just from one man.

He pulled his pocket Bible out of his coat and used the ribbon marker to open the pages to the verse that had given him purpose and direction during the past seven years. Proverbs 21:3. *To do justice and judgment is more acceptable to the Lord than sacrifice.* The Lord approved of justice, of righteous judgment. Validation rose to soothe the prodded places of Logan's conscience until his eyes drifted upward and read the verse immediately preceding the one he had underlined.

Every way of a man is right in his own eyes: but the Lord pondereth the hearts.

The sore spots on his conscience started aching again.

This was ridiculous. Of course his plan seemed right to him— it *was* right. The Lord could ponder Logan's heart all he wanted. His motives were pure: To see justice done. To restore what had been stolen.

His finger scraped down the page to the next set of verses he'd underlined, verses six and seven: *The getting of treasures by a lying tongue is a vanity tossed to and fro of them that seek death. The robbery of the wicked shall destroy them; because they refuse to do judgment.*

Zacharias Hamilton had gained his treasure through deceit. He'd refused to deal justly with Logan's father, so the way to destroy him, to see justice done, was to rob the wicked, to steal back what had been wrongfully taken from Logan's family.

The final underlined verse called to him from the next column, verse 15: *It is joy to the just to do judgment: but destruction shall be to the workers of iniquity.*

Joy would come with justice. To him. To his mother. His cause was righteous, and nothing was going to keep him from that path.

The parson offered an invitation to sinners wishing to repent and saints desiring prayers as the congregation stood to sing a hymn. Logan fell into neither category, so instead of moving forward down the aisle, he retreated straight out of the sanctuary and into the churchyard. He knew how preachers were—always positioning themselves at the back so no one could escape without facing them after service. Well, Logan didn't plan to give John Clem a chance to inspect him more closely. Yet neither was he ready to leave.

He didn't mind being a mystery to others, but he was less

fond of people being a mystery to him. Something was off with Eva. Her meek demeanor inside the church didn't sit well. Not for a bold woman who tied bright red bows around her pet hog's neck, faced down trespassing strangers with nothing more than gumption and a contagious smile, and charmed fractious neighbors with homemade goodies and thought-provoking conversation.

Logan slapped his hat back on his head and strode to the rail where Shamgar stood hitched. Patting the horse's neck and giving the tack a cursory inspection as camouflage, he waited for the service to let out. He didn't have to wait long—just the length of a hymn and a prayer—before the parson swung the doors wide and took his place, shaking hands with the congregants as they exited.

The Hamilton siblings emerged first—not surprising, given their preference for the back row. What *was* surprising was the way Eva skittered past the minister while Seth shook Clem's hand. She kept her chin down until she'd navigated the steps, then lifted her face and looked around. As soon as she found him, she lit up, becoming the vibrant woman he remembered so well, and dashed straight toward him.

"You came! Oh, I'm so glad." She skirted the wagon and team in front of the hitching rail and came around to face him.

Logan grinned, exercising cheek muscles that had been woefully out of shape before Eva tumbled into his life. "Didn't think you'd seen me." He didn't think she'd seen anything with her neck bent like a shepherd's crook.

She slapped his arm lightly. "Of course I did. Well, to be honest, I didn't know it was you at first. Not until you got up after the sermon and I caught a glimpse of your face. But all through the service, I was hoping it was you."

Logan smirked. "Missed me that much, did you?"

Pink stained her cheeks, but mischief danced in her eyes. "You? No. But I'd been getting awful lonesome for Shamgar." She sidled around the edge of the rail and took the chestnut's cheeks in her hands, reaching up on tiptoes to place her forehead against his white blaze. "You missed me too, didn't you, sweetheart? All alone with that grouchy ol' man. It must have been terrible."

Shamgar snuffled, then bounced his head up and down as if in agreement. Eva laughed, the sound so delightful, Logan couldn't help but grin. Though he quickly squelched the expression into a parody of an offended frown.

He swatted Shamgar's flank with the flat of his hand. "Traitor. No oats for you tonight."

"There you are, Evangeline."

Logan flinched at the unexpected feminine voice. He'd grown accustomed to having Eva all to himself. For a moment, he had forgotten where they were.

Mrs. Clem, the parson's wife, scuttled over to them, her smile wide in welcome and her eyes alight with curiosity. "I see our newcomer is not as much a stranger as I supposed."

Logan's heart seized for a moment until she held out her hand and began an introduction.

"Charlotte Clem."

Logan took her fingers and bent politely over her hand.

"I'm the minister's wife." She glanced behind her to indicate the preacher still standing guard at the church door. "We're so glad to have you visiting this morning. Will you be staying in Pecan Gap long? If so, you must meet my John. He's not just the preacher, though that is his true spiritual calling." She paused just long enough to draw in a breath and turn a pious glance toward heaven before turning back to Logan. "He also runs the sawmill."

"I imagine he's quite a busy man, then." Logan made a mental note to go to Ben Franklin to purchase the lumber for framing his cabin.

"Oh my, yes." Mrs. Clem fanned herself with a hand. "He used to be the postmaster as well until Mr. Wood took over. Fine man, Mr. Wood. Owns the newest general store in town. If you need supplies, I would highly recommend his establishment."

She was something of a whirlwind, jumping from one subject to the next with the speed and adroitness of a thoroughbred leaping fences in a steeplechase. Fortunately, that quality made it easier to avoid answering her questions. He'd just hang on and wait for the next fence.

"Do you have a family, sir?" Mrs. Clem's sharp gaze darted from Logan to Eva and back again, and suddenly Logan wanted to back the horse up to take another run at the Mr. Wood-and-his-new-store fence. "Pecan Gap might be small, but we have a fine school. We even have a music teacher, Mrs. Miller. She gives piano lessons to many of the town's children."

Logan fought the urge to run a finger under his collar. Mrs. Clem might be a jolly sort, but he knew a matchmaker when he saw one, and all his bachelor instincts were screaming at him to run.

"I'm sure she does a fine job, ma'am." He shot a pleading look at Eva, who seemed unsportingly delighted over his predicament.

"Oh, indeed she does. As do all our teachers here in Pecan Gap, Mr. . . . What did you say your name was?"

Eva finally took pity on him and interrupted, drawing Mrs. Clem's attention. "Is that Mabel Edwards?" She pointed to a pinched-faced woman in a dark blue dress who seemed to have planted herself in front of the parson, causing a bottleneck at the church exit. "She seems quite upset about something."

"Oh dear." Charlotte Clem's face fell slightly, and she let out a sigh. "Poor John. I best rescue him. Mabel can be a bit . . . opinionated when it comes to biblical interpretation. She must not have cared for the sermon." Mrs. Clem dashed away, only pausing long enough to throw a cheerful, "Hope to see you next Sunday," at Logan before turning her full attention to the harried preacher in need of a little wifely salvation.

"Thank you." Logan let out a breath and smiled at his own rescuing angel.

Eva shrugged. "Charlotte means well. She's a bit . . . fluttery but as kindhearted as they come. Always chases me down after services to make sure I don't get away without someone speaking to me."

That was a comment begging for exploration. "Do you often—?"

"Ready to go, Evie?" A husky voice growled directly behind Logan, startling him into silence.

He stepped sideways and pivoted to face the man who'd successfully snuck up on him, though he already knew who he'd find. Mentally bracing himself, he ignored the clenching of his gut and the harsh thumping of his heart and relaxed his features into a bland façade.

Zacharias Hamilton glared at Logan with all the ferociousness of a coyote protecting its young. "Who . . ." His eyes narrowed as he took in Logan's face. " . . . are *you?*"

CHAPTER

11

Logan forced an amiable smile to his lips as he stuck out his hand. "Name's Logan," he said, "and if you're one of Miss Hamilton's brothers, I suppose that makes us neighbors."

Zacharias Hamilton's fingers circled Logan's palm and squeezed with more than customary vigor. His eyes were cold, assessing. Logan firmed his own grip, needing Hamilton to know he wasn't easily intimidated. Then, deciding to take a card from the deck Mrs. Clem had been dealing, he continued rambling, hoping to disguise the fact that he hadn't given a complete name.

"Your sister was kind enough to bring me a few foodstuffs last week. That strawberry jam of hers is delicious. You're a lucky man to benefit from such sweet treats on a regular basis."

"Evie's the one who likes things sweet." Having exerted his manhood enough to make the bones in Logan's hand ache, Hamilton released his grip and folded his arms across his chest. "Me? I don't like to sugarcoat things. I prefer my food and my conversation straightforward."

"Yeah, you look like a black coffee kind of guy." Logan

purposely ignored the implication that his conversation was less than straight. He wouldn't take that bait. Hamilton could glower and insult Logan all he wanted, but he wouldn't dance to the other man's tune. *He* was the one doing the leading, and if he wanted to swirl around the dance floor in circuitous patterns, then by George, that was what he'd do.

"Zach, don't be rude to our new neighbor." Eva swatted her bear of a brother on the arm.

Logan watched the sibling byplay with interest. Hamilton turned his hostile glare to Eva after she tapped him, but the daggers shooting from his eyes had no apparent effect on her.

What did have an effect was the crowd slowly milling in their direction. When Eva turned to smile reassuringly at Logan, her gaze shifted behind him, where an increasing amount of hoof stomping and harness jangling indicated that families were starting to collect their buggies and wagons for the ride home. Her smile faltered and her chin dipped, hiding her beautiful eyes from him as she stared at her feet.

Logan wasn't the only one to notice.

Hamilton immediately unfolded his arms and touched Eva's shoulder in a manner so gentle that Logan would not have thought it possible from such a hard man.

In a low voice, Hamilton murmured, "I'll get the buckboard."

Eva nibbled her bottom lip and nodded.

"Actually," Logan interjected, earning a glare that rivaled the heat of molten iron from the brother who had taken two steps away from them, "I was hoping that since we live in the same direction, I might be permitted to walk your sister home."

"No." After voicing that single syllable, Hamilton turned to resume his stride.

Well, he hadn't been lying about not liking to sugarcoat things.

"Yes."

Logan's heart drummed a victory cadence at the soft feminine rebuttal. He knew better than to read too much into the situation—walking with him was a minor matter, after all—but that didn't change the fact that Eva had just chosen *his* wishes over those of her brother.

Which left Zacharias Hamilton less than pleased.

He spun around to face her, a growl reverberating in his throat. "You don't know this man, Evangeline. *I* don't know this man." He leveled another glare at Logan. "I'm not about to leave you alone with him."

"I know him well enough to accept his escort." She lifted her chin, her inner fire overriding her desire to hide herself away. "We'll be on a public road in full view of anyone passing by. There's nothing improper about a man seeing a lady home."

Hamilton's face hardened, another denial surely about to spring forth. Until Eva touched his arm and turned pleading eyes on him. A less-trained observer probably wouldn't have noticed much change in his features, but Logan swore he saw Hamilton's resolve crumble that very instant. His features softened just a hair, his posture went from ramrod straight to slightly pliable, and his eyes glanced away, as if unable to withstand the pressure of her entreaty.

Her quiet words only made it worse. "Please, Zach." Her voice lowered even more. Logan had to strain to hear as he fiddled with Shamgar's saddle and pretended he wasn't listening. "He looks and speaks to me as if I'm normal." His chest tightened at that admission. She *was* normal. Better than normal, in his opinion. "Never once has he made me feel self-conscious or uncomfortable. I trust him."

She trusted him? A con man would rejoice at those words, but Logan simply felt awe and a deep sense of responsibility not to let her down. The ache in the region of his heart intensified, and an odd swirling sensation afflicted his gut.

"If it will make you feel better," she said, a tiny smile playing at the corners of her lips, "you and Seth can follow us in the wagon."

Hamilton harrumphed. "While you walk? For three miles?" He shook his head. "Watching paint dry would be a better use of my time."

Logan kept his body language neutral even as he pumped a victorious mental fist. Getting Eva to open up about her odd behavior would be difficult enough without her overprotective brothers watching their every move.

Hamilton prowled over to Logan and glared at him across Shamgar's back. "If my sister's not home in an hour, I'll come looking." He eyed Logan up and down. Logan jutted out his chin and accepted the perusal, silently praying Hamilton wouldn't see his father reflected in his features. Hamilton frowned, and his eyes narrowed, as if not particularly impressed by what he'd seen. "I promise it won't be pleasant if I have to come find you."

Logan accepted the threat as his due and nodded. "You have my word that I'll see her safely home."

"Emphasis on the *safely*, mister. She so much as stubs her toe, and you'll answer to me."

"Oh, for heaven's sake." Eva shoved Hamilton's shoulder. He swayed slightly but gave up no ground. "I traipse all over the countryside by myself seven days a week. I think I can manage to walk the road from here to home without endangering my health."

"It ain't your capability I'm questioning." Hamilton's stare never left Logan's eyes. Logan knew exactly what he was questioning. His honor. But the way Eva's forehead wrinkled proved her too innocent to fully comprehend the implication.

"Sure sounded like it," she grumbled. "As if I need a man's arm to keep from stumbling over my own two feet. You make me sound like an invalid."

Logan finally broke Hamilton's stare to smile at Eva. "You are far from an invalid, Miss Hamilton. I find you delightfully . . . robust."

A strangled noise gurgled out of her brother's throat, but Eva's giggle banished the sound. "Robust, am I? I do believe that is the most unique compliment I've ever received."

"Oh, for pity's sake." Hamilton turned his back with a grunt and waved them off. "Take your walk already and spare me this idiotic conversation."

Eva grabbed her brother's arm and lifted on tiptoe to plant a kiss on his cheek. "Thank you, Zach."

Hamilton wrapped a rather awkward arm around her shoulders before releasing her and stepping away. "Be careful, Evie." He glanced over her shoulder at Logan. The warning was evident, but so was the worry. "People aren't always what they seem to be on the surface."

"I know." She glanced at Logan, too. "But unless I get past the surface, I'll never know the truth, will I?"

Logan held her gaze for a heartbeat before looking away and setting his jaw. She'd discover the truth soon enough. *All* of it. Including her brother's sins.

Logan flipped his wrist and freed Shamgar from the hitching rail as the blond Hamilton brother joined their group, a frown marring his brow. Before he could verbalize the questions written on his face, Logan moved the lead line to his left hand and offered his right arm to Eva.

"Shall we?"

She smiled and fit her slender hand into the crook of his elbow. "We shall."

"What—?" the blond brother sputtered, his head swiveling to follow their progress as they swept past.

"Neighbor," Hamilton huffed in explanation before grabbing Seth by the shoulder and directing him toward the wagons.

Unfortunately, Hamilton couldn't manhandle the rest of the gawking crowd. Eva's smile dimmed under the weight of their stares. Conversations hushed and eyes prodded—some with simple curiosity, others with something more akin to the look one would give a bearded lady when gaping at circus oddities. It took only a few steps for the heaviness to bend Eva's head back into the shepherd's crook she'd sported in the pew.

"Who's that man with Eerie Evie?" A pair of girls near Eva's age pointed at them as they walked past, their voices hushed yet projecting loudly enough to ensure the couple would hear.

"I don't know," her companion sneered, "but look at that scar. He's probably as wicked as she is."

"Maybe she hexed him with one of her spells, and he's trapped in some kind of trance."

"Probably. It's the only way a girl like her could get a man to walk out with her."

Indignation flared in Logan's chest. The *good* people of Pecan Gap needed a lesson in manners and common decency. He glared at the insufferable girls, wishing he could give them the dressing down their cruel words deserved, but lashing out at them wouldn't help the woman at his side. He'd no doubt embarrass her and cause her to retreat further into herself. This called for a different tactic.

He leaned close. "Ashamed to be seen with the guy with the scar?"

Her head snapped up, just as he'd bet it would. "No! Never. I—" Her eyes darted away from his face to the smirking girls, then to the rest of the crowd standing in little clusters around the churchyard. She started shrinking again, her posture going lax, her neck bending.

"Good," he said. "Had me worried when your head went all droopy."

His words had the desired effect. Her chin jutted forward, and determination straightened her neck. "You don't understand," she whispered. "It's me they're staring at. I've never had a . . . man walk me home before."

That hesitation. She'd been about to call him something else before she thought better of it. Suitor? Beau? His limbs loosened into a stride with a bit more swagger, though he worried a bit over why his mind had leapt to fill in the blank with *those* particular terms.

He wanted her to think of him fondly, he assured himself. Romantically, even. The closer they became, the more information he could glean. Yet when her striking eyes met his, a shy blush rising to her cheeks, it wasn't information he found himself wanting.

Logan hugged her hand to his side and gave her his best roguish grin. "They'll get used to it." He winked. "I plan to walk you home next week, too. And the week after. Pretty soon, seeing us together will be so ordinary that no one will even think twice about it."

Her eyes softened. Grew dewy. For a heartbeat he panicked, afraid he'd made her cry, but then a tender smile blossomed, and her expression took on a glow of such dreamy adoration, he felt as if he'd single-handedly slayed a den full of dragons. He tried to shake off the feeling, leery of its addictive properties, but it lingered despite his efforts, warming his insides.

They walked in silence through the remainder of the church-yard, Eva with her head up and her steps in time with his. Taking the road that led away from town, Logan waited until her brothers' wagon rolled by—one dark face scowling at him while the other sported concern—before broaching the topic most on his mind.

"Why do you hide yourself from them?"

Eva turned startled eyes on him. "What?"

"In church. You never looked up. Not at me when I came in late. Not at the preacher. Not even during the singing. It was as if you were a different person. Timid and afraid, not the warrior sprite I remember from the woods."

She grinned. "Warrior sprite? I like that. Even more than *robust*."

He chuckled. "I aim to please."

She held his gaze for a moment before her smile slipped away and her attention floated down to the road in front of her. "I . . . disturb them."

"What do you mean, *disturb*?" He kept his voice deliberately neutral even as anger rose inside him at the cruelty of people who should know better.

"You heard those girls. *Eerie Evie*." Her voice clogged as she struggled to get the awful name past her lips. "They've called me that since school. They'd throw rocks at me during recess when the teacher wasn't looking and threaten to tie me to a tree and burn me at the stake if I looked them in the eyes. So I stopped looking at them.

"Not everyone is as heartless as Ethel and Hortense, though," she rushed to explain, as if she could feel the tension radiating up his arm beneath her fingertips. "I've been here long enough now that most people are used to my strange eyes and pay me no heed. There are even a few I consider friends, like Charlotte Clem and Mrs. Bishop. She was my teacher for a couple years before she married." A small grin tugged the corners of Eva's mouth upward. "She made Hortense stand in the corner for a full afternoon one day when she overheard her awful taunts." The twinkle returned to her beautiful, mismatched eyes. "Best school day ever."

Logan smiled even as he inwardly railed. This kindhearted woman was defending the townsfolk with pitiful evidence. Two friends. Two. Both older than her. Both in mentoring roles. People who were *supposed* to make those in their care feel welcome. Did Eva not have any friends her own age?

The truth hit him hard in the gut. She didn't. The Hamiltons kept to themselves, just as the saloon owner had told him. No visits to town. No shopping excursions. No social calls. Eva's closest companion was an ugly black boar with a ridiculous red bow.

"It's usually better in church," she said, "but I hide my eyes there, too, because it's easier for everyone to worship if they don't have to worry about certain . . . distractions."

He wasn't going to let that one slide. "People deal with distractions all the time during worship, Eva. Random thunderclaps. A cricket hopping across the floorboards. A baby fussing. If they can't handle a beautiful woman smiling at them from the back pew, they should contemplate their own weakness instead of passing the blame to someone who cannot change the appearance God gave her."

Eva stumbled to a halt. "You . . . you think I'm beautiful?"

"Don't go changing the subject on me, Evangeline Hamilton." Logan shook his finger at her, aiming for a little distraction of his own. Her looking at him all shy and hopeful like that was making his own weakness abundantly clear. "I'm not done taking you to task for all that hiding."

She nibbled her lip and glanced away, then resumed her strolling pace.

Logan sensed the truth lurking behind the silence, yet he

didn't want to press her too hard. So he just walked beside her. Steady. Patient. Supportive.

He might not verbally press her, but he wasn't about to change the subject, either. Few people could let quiet stretch for long unchallenged. They had a little over two miles left. He could wait.

Before they'd traveled a hundred yards, Eva inhaled and broke the silence.

"Several years ago, a man visited from another town—a man of some importance, I assumed, by the way everyone treated him with deference. A revival preacher, someone told me later. He was asked to lead a prayer during the service." She slipped her hand free of his arm, but Logan refused to let her withdraw from him. He reached out and clasped her hand, lacing his fingers through hers and holding tight. She glanced up at him, questions burning in those lovely eyes of hers.

Logan smiled in encouragement. "What happened with this man?"

Eva turned to focus on a spot farther down the road. "He approached the pulpit, his leather Bible clasped firmly in his hands. He scanned the crowd, his face harsh and judgmental, as if ready to call down fire and brimstone on anyone who dared fidget or yawn on his watch."

So many details. Which meant there was a lot of emotion attached to them. They'd lodged in her mind and not given in when time tried to siphon them out.

"He had just invited the congregation to bow their heads," she continued, "when his attention reached the back pew—reached me. His eyes flew wide, then narrowed in accusation. He clutched his Bible to his chest like a shield and pointed a bony finger at me. 'Demon child,' he said. 'How dare you defile the house of the Lord? Begone!'"

Outrage fired Logan's veins, stealing his ability to speak or even move. He halted abruptly, snapping Eva around and leaving Shamgar to bump his chest against the back of Logan's shoulder. The only thing that kept the imminent eruption inside him from blasting free was the sad little smile curving Eva's lips.

"You should have seen Zach." She shook her head and even managed a small chuckle. "He was halfway down the aisle, ready to physically remove the old man from the pulpit and the building itself, when four men leapt from their pews to restrain him."

Logan would have cleared his path.

"Mr. Clem managed to smooth things over, got the man's son to escort him back to his seat, then publicly apologized to me and our family."

Not before the damage had been done. What on earth would lead a man of God to say something so vile?

"Charlotte told me later that the old preacher's mind had been slipping for some time. The family had tried to hide his deficiencies, but after the episode in Pecan Gap, they forced him to retire and kept him at home, where his outbursts would cause less harm. It's sad, really, if you think about it. After all those years of godly service bringing lost souls to Christ, he didn't deserve to have the good forgotten simply because he misspoke while in a confused state."

Didn't deserve . . . ? Logan gaped at her. How did she forgive so easily? Confused or not, that man had hurt her with his cruel words, yet she felt pity for him. Compassion. Sure, Jesus taught his followers to love their enemies, but Logan didn't think anyone actually *did* so. Tolerate them, maybe. Refraining from actual violence against them seemed loving enough to his way of thinking. But Eva? She took things to a different level, one he'd thought only existed in sermons and books. Not in real life.

Yet the truth of it lay written on her beautiful face. She'd forgiven that old man. Completely. A shadow of leftover hurt and embarrassment might cast an occasional pall over her, but it didn't define her. Didn't control her.

An uncomfortable sensation jabbed at Logan's chest, but he tamped it down. Eva was still speaking. He needed to focus on her, not wear out his brain analyzing his own motives.

"It took several weeks and a dozen or so visits from the Clems before I felt up to returning to services," she admitted with a sheepish glance his way, as if afraid he would think less of her for being human. "Zach threatened never to darken the doors again, but he wasn't about to let me go without him, so we reclaimed our pew a couple months later."

"And you started hiding your eyes to keep some other closed-minded dolt from sticking his foot in his mouth?"

She twisted from side-to-side, her skirt swishing against the edge of his trousers. "Something like that." She sighed, and the swishing slowed. "I wish I could say that I keep my eyes hidden to promote orderly worship and to ensure I don't inadvertently cause a brother to stumble. But in truth, I do it because it's easier. If I hide my eyes, I don't have to see how others react to me."

Logan released Shamgar's lead line and cupped the side of Eva's face in his hand. "If you hide your eyes, you'll never teach them to accept you." His thumb stroked the softness of her cheek. "Let them see you, Eva. The real you. The brave, cheerful wood sprite who spreads joy wherever she goes. Once they do, the surface differences will fade from their notice."

He leaned forward, his gaze shifting to her mouth. The urge to kiss her was so strong, he nearly forgot they were standing in the middle of a road where anyone could happen by. Thankfully, a jangle of harness from somewhere ahead of them jerked him back to reality.

He lifted his head, searching for the wagon that must be near. But nothing was on the road.

"I heard it, too," Eva said, her brow crinkling as she scanned the area. "Maybe off the road?" She slid her hand from his and walked to the north edge. "Oh, there. I see. A wagon down by the river." She pointed at a small path that veered from the main road to a low spot along the river's edge.

Logan came alongside her and squinted into the distance. "Someone having a picnic perhaps? That fellow seems to be carrying a rolled up blanket or carpet or something." The distance was too great for him to make out any details, but something felt off. The man's movements were lumbering, labored. Even a heavy carpet shouldn't cause that much difficulty.

Before he could share the puzzle of it with Eva, she bolted down the road toward the river.

"Eva!" He ran after her and caught her before she could get up to full speed. He spun her around to face him, and the distraught look in her eyes immediately set his senses on alert. "What is it?"

"That's no picnic. It's murder!"

Evangeline struggled against Logan's grip. She didn't have time to explain. She had to get down to the river before it was too late.

It wouldn't be the first time someone had decided to rid themselves of an unwanted animal in such a vile manner. The stream off the main river wasn't deep, but an animal wrapped in a pillowcase or sheet wouldn't stand a chance. It would drown in a matter of minutes. And that infernal path led right to the stream, making it all too easy to drive up to the water's edge and dump the defenseless creature, just like that horrid man was doing right now.

"You don't understand!" She dragged Logan a few steps toward the river. "I have to stop him."

"Eva." He gave her arm a sharp tug. One she couldn't ignore. She looked up at his face.

"We have a horse."

Shamgar! Of course. That would be so much faster.

Evangeline immediately ceased struggling and spun back toward the horse. "Give me a leg up," she ordered as she swept past him.

Logan, bless his heart, didn't argue. Just did what she asked, waiting only long enough for her to grip the horn before clasping her foot and hoisting her into the saddle. Collecting the lead line, he jabbed his own foot into the stirrup and swung up behind her, his arms coming around her on either side, his warm chest pressing against her back.

Too bad she didn't have time to enjoy the closeness, but a life hung in the balance. So she grabbed a handful of mane, leaned forward, and urged Logan to hurry.

Logan nudged Shamgar into a canter and left the road to cut cross-country, closing the gap faster than she could have hoped. Even so, the man at the wagon had already lugged his load to the water's edge and dropped it.

"Stop!" Evangeline shouted.

The man jerked around, still too far away to recognize. All she could see was a gray hat, blue shirt, and brown trousers. Half the men in the county dressed the same.

She turned in the saddle. "Faster, Logan."

He answered with a flick of the reins and a sharp, "Yah" to Shamgar, who gamely picked up the pace.

They closed the gap, but the farther they traveled away from the road, the rougher the terrain became. Their progress slowed. Evangeline's heart pounded. *Please, Lord. Please let us get there in time.*

The man lodged a boot under the wrapped animal and rolled it deeper into the water before abandoning the helpless creature and making a run for his wagon. Evangeline's eyes never left the long bundle of charcoal-colored wool that darkened as water soaked through the fabric. It sank deeper into the stream while the hard-hearted fiend responsible drove off in the opposite direction.

It was a large creature. Heavy enough to sink in the river silt. Maybe a dog stretched out, or a goat. Animals crippled by predators or old age and ones no longer useful to their owners were the usual targets. But no animal deserved such cruel treatment. They were God's creation, too. They deserved kindness. Dignity.

Rising tears blurred her vision. She batted them away, letting the wind dry them on her cheeks.

By the time they reached the river's edge, the offender's wagon had disappeared around the bend, yet Evangeline was more concerned about the victim than the villain. The moment Logan slowed Shamgar, she tried to lift her leg over the horse's neck to dismount, but her skirts hindered her movement.

"Easy," Logan murmured in her ear. "I'll get you down."

And he did. With admirable haste. He dismounted in a smooth motion and immediately set his hands on her waist to lift her from the saddle.

"Help me," Evangeline cried as she broke free of his gentle hold and ran toward the sinking bundle.

She plunged into the knee-deep water, unconcerned about how her Sunday dress would fare. The current tugged at her petticoats and skirt. Mud oozed over her shoes and stockings as she neared the edge of the nearly black blanket.

Squatting down, she hooked an arm around the end of the bundle closest to her. Cold water splashed her front, plastering the light blue muslin against her chest and sending a shiver through her. She ignored it, gritted her teeth, and lifted with all her might.

Instead of grabbing the other end, Logan bent down and stabbed his arms into the water beneath the middle of the bundle. With a loud grunt, he raised the entire mass out of the river.

Water sluiced off the blanket, pattering the stream's surface. Evangeline continued to support her end as she circled around into deeper water in order to allow Logan to turn and wade back to shore.

Cords stood out along his neck, and his face reddened, attesting to the extreme effort he was exerting. Her own sodden skirts dragged at her. The soaked wool of the charcoal blanket must have doubled the weight of whatever was wrapped inside. And that *whatever* was limp and still, not struggling for freedom, which made Evangeline's heart ache with dread.

As soon as Logan reached the bank, he dropped to his knees, and together they laid the bedraggled bundle on the ground. Evangeline hunted for a blanket edge, desperate to free the poor creature trapped inside. Finally she found a corner and seized it. She lurched to her feet, yanked on the fabric, and grabbed for more. Logan helped, and as soon as he added his strength, the bundle unrolled, flopping the occupant over three times before finally releasing its hold.

Evangeline gasped. "Dear God."

It was a woman. Face down. Dark hair tangled. Black dress twisted around thin limbs. Unmoving.

Logan immediately rolled her onto her back. Evangeline crouched over her, placing her ear next to the young woman's face.

"I don't think she's breathing." She lifted her head to peer at Logan, praying he would know what to do. The woman's skin was unnaturally pale.

"Loosen her collar," Logan snapped, the shock in his eyes hardening into a determination that shored up Evangeline's flagging confidence.

She fumbled with the tiny buttons at the woman's throat while Logan moved to straddle her. Evangeline frowned. "What are you—?"

"Gotta get the water out of her lungs." He placed his palms, fingers angled outward, above the woman's waist and thrust upward toward her ribs in a sharp motion.

The woman rocked but remained unconscious. His face grim, Logan tried again. And again.

Tears scalded Evangeline's cold cheeks. *Please, Lord. Please.* She held the woman's hand, not knowing what else to do. Cold, wet fingers lay lifeless in her palm. She squeezed them, tried to warm them.

Logan raised up on his knees and thrust again. Harder.

Water spewed from the woman's mouth. Evangeline grabbed for her face, turning her head as she sputtered. Logan jumped off and rolled the woman to her side, giving her a few solid whacks on the back to help clear her lungs.

The woman coughed. Choked. Breathed.

Thank you, God!

"It's all right. You're safe." Evangeline combed the girl's matted dark hair away from her face. "No one's going to hurt you. You're with friends."

Glazed green eyes blinked in the sun as if trying to adjust to the light. When they finally focused on Evangeline's face, on her *eyes*, the girl screamed. She shook her head back and forth and grunted like a terrified animal, then tore free of Evangeline's gentle hold and scrambled backward. She tried to stand, but her feet tangled in the blanket. Coughs wracked her as she pushed up onto all fours. She collapsed, her arms too weak from her near drowning to support her weight, so she curled onto her side, drew up her knees, and ducked her head. A mewling sound emerged as she started to rock.

Logan met Evangeline's gaze. "Do you think she suffers from idiocy?"

"I don't know." Such an impairment might explain her irrational reaction just now, but in her heart, Evangeline knew the truth. Her eyes had spooked the girl. She probably thought she'd escaped one terror only to find herself in the clutches of a river witch.

Evangeline ignored the pinpricks of hurt jabbing her heart and focused on the half-drowned girl in front of her. The girl's mental abilities or lack thereof were immaterial. As were her superstitions about mismatched eyes. She deserved to be safe.

Evangeline slowly lowered to a crouch in front of the woman. "All I know for certain is that she's terrified. She needs our patience and kindness."

Keeping her movements steady and measured, Evangeline gently laid her hand on the girl's shoulder. The woman flinched and her mewling cut off, but she didn't uncurl or look up.

"I'm a friend," Evangeline said, her voice low and even. "You're safe. He won't hurt you anymore."

For long minutes, the woman just lay there, curled into a ball. Not moving. Not speaking. Evangeline didn't move, either. She kept her hand on the girl's shoulder, letting her get used to her presence. Letting her learn that she meant no harm.

Logan hunkered down opposite them, watching. He never grew impatient. Never suggested they pack the girl up and leave. He never said a word. Just watched. Until the wind picked up and the girl started shivering. Then he quietly rose to his feet, stripped out of his jacket, and tenderly laid it over her shaking form.

The sleeves were damp from the stream, but the majority of the fabric must have carried his warmth, for the moment he draped it over her curled back, the shivers slowed and a tiny sigh escaped her.

Evangeline smiled her thanks at him, his actions confirming what her heart already knew to be true: Logan was a good man. A kind man. He carried secrets, but he had a core of decency that could not be denied.

Turning back to the woman huddled before her, Evangeline slid her hand out from under the coat and attempted stroking the woman's hair again. As she lifted a section of dripping dark hair and moved it to the far side of the girl's neck, her chin came around. The girl unfolded just enough to meet Evangeline's gaze. She jerked away from Evangeline's touch, obviously still frightened, but she didn't try to run this time. Evangeline counted that as progress. Refusing to be offended by the girl's behavior, she offered her friendliest smile.

"You're safe," Evangeline repeated, hoping the young woman had calmed enough to understand her this time. "We just want to help you."

The girl twisted, looking at Logan. He touched the brim of his hat and dipped his head. "Ma'am."

"Do you have family nearby?" Evangeline touched the girl's shoulder. She spun her head back around but made no attempt to answer Evangeline's question. "Is there somewhere we can take you? Someplace you'll be safe?"

"You don't recognize her?" Logan asked.

Evangeline shook her head. "No. Maybe she's from Ben Franklin." She turned back to the girl. "Is that where you're from? Ben Franklin? Do you want us to take you there?"

The girl launched to her feet, Logan's coat sliding to the ground as she shook her head adamantly.

"All right," Evangeline soothed, holding her hands out in front of her as she rose from her crouched position. "We won't take you to Ben Franklin. What about Pecan Gap? Do you know anyone there?"

The woman shook her head even harder, then started backing away. Her eyes darted from Logan to Evangeline to Shamgar.

Did she think to steal their horse?

Logan must have thought so, for he gave a short whistle, and Shamgar trotted over to stand beside him. The woman sagged in defeat, and tears streamed down her face.

Evangeline's heart broke. This poor girl needed help. Needed a friend. Needed dry clothes, for pity's sake. And Evangeline had the means to give her all three.

"Well, you obviously don't want to go to town, so I'll just have to take you home with me." She marched up to the girl and held out her hand. "I'm Evangeline Hamilton." She pointed eastward. "I live about two miles down this road with my brothers, Zach and Seth. We can protect you from whoever did this. Our place is quiet and out of the way. We hardly ever get visitors, so you don't have to worry about anyone coming around looking for you. Logan's our neighbor." Evangeline nodded her head toward him. "He can help protect you, too."

The woman nibbled her bottom lip. She was obviously terrified and didn't know who to trust. But what option did she have? Two well-meaning strangers who'd rescued her from drowning had to weigh more favorably than setting off on her own with no food, no money, and no protection. Even if one of them had demon eyes.

"You can stay as long as you like and leave whenever you wish," Evangeline promised, still holding out her hand. "Please. Come home with me."

Ever so slowly, the girl extended a trembling hand and grasped Evangeline's.

Evangeline beamed her approval as she squeezed the girl's fingers tightly in welcome. "Oh, I'm so glad! You won't regret it, I promise. You're actually doing me a favor, you know," she rambled as she bent to retrieve Logan's coat and laid it back on the girl's shoulders. "I've been the only female at the house for ages. My brothers are great men, don't get me wrong, but I can't exactly share sisterly confidences with them, now can I?" Evangeline wrapped her arm around the girl, who was a couple inches shorter, and gently steered her toward Shamgar. The girl kept her eyes glued to Evangeline's face as they walked, as if she couldn't trust her without watching her every move. "You'll be my first friend to stay over!" Evangeline was determined to make this traumatized girl feel safe and give her a healthy dose of hope. One couldn't survive darkness without hope. Evangeline knew that firsthand. "We're going to be the best of friends. You'll see."

The girl's eyes seemed to glaze over a bit as she stumbled along in Evangeline's enthusiastic wake. But by the time they reached the horse, her tears had ceased and a touch of light had entered her eyes.

Evangeline turned to Logan. "Would you mind giving us a leg up?"

He had an odd look on his face. Nervous, almost. But that didn't make sense. He had nothing to be anxious about.

"I don't think she'll make the walk, Logan," Evangeline said in a hushed tone when he didn't immediately step forward to help them mount. "But I don't want her to feel alone, so I thought I would ride with her. That doesn't leave much room for you, I'm afraid."

He shook off his stupor and immediately moved to cup his hands for her to use as a step. "Of course. I'll lead Shamgar while the two of you ride." He glanced at the girl's back as she petted his horse, then lowered his voice as he turned to Evangeline. "You sure we shouldn't take her to town? We should notify the law or . . . or at least find someone who knows her."

"Pecan Gap doesn't have a marshal. We'd have to send to Cooper for the sheriff, and you saw how scared she was at the thought of going to town." Evangeline gave him her sternest glare. "She's coming home with me, Logan. And that's the end of the matter."

"Home," he muttered as his gaze dipped away from hers. "Right."

CHAPTER

13

Logan put one foot in front of the other until they reached the homestead. It was all he could manage. He felt as if *he* were the one trapped in a blanket. Suffocating. Drowning. Seeing his old house from a distance was one thing. Being close enough to touch the walls that had once been his home . . . he'd thought he was prepared. Obviously he was wrong.

He led Shamgar past the barn, telling himself to focus on the house in front of him, but his gaze darted sideways against his will. The barn door stood open, and in a flash, Logan was sixteen again, coming upon his father's lifeless body, his mother's good tablecloth draped over all but one side of his sire's face. Bile rose in Logan's throat. His steps faltered. But he righted himself, tightening his hold on Shamgar's lead line as if it were his tether to sanity. Forcing his feet to keep moving, he jerked his attention back to the house.

"Zach!" Eva's shout effectively snapped Logan's mind back to the present. "Seth! We need your help."

Before her sentence was even fully uttered, Hamilton threw

open the door and bounded outside, fists clenched, jaw set. He zeroed in on Logan. "What did you do?" he growled, advancing.

Logan lifted his chin but held his ground.

"He saved this poor girl's life, Zacharias," Eva said. "That's what he did." Logan swore he could hear her roll her eyes. Her exasperation made him grin, which only darkened Hamilton's features further. A nice bonus. "Quit your posturing and come help me with our guest."

"Guest?" Hamilton's head zipped around as he faced his sister with a look halfway between incredulity and horror. "What do you mean, *guest*?"

Logan couldn't help but be a little gratified that he wasn't the only one having his life turned upside down by the fierce little sprite glaring down at them all from atop her commandeered steed.

"Oh, for pity's sake. Does no one around here have an ounce of hospitality in their tiny male brains?" Eva glared at Hamilton, then grumbled something under her breath as she slid off Shamgar's back. "Seth. Thank heavens." The blond Hamilton brother approached Shamgar cautiously, his gaze darting between his sister and the woman still atop the horse who appeared to be trying to fold in on herself. "My new friend needs help, and Zach doesn't seem to be up to the task."

Hamilton made a sound of protest, but Eva turned her back on him and addressed Seth instead.

"Be careful," Eva warned in a quiet tone. "She's been through a horrible ordeal and needs a hot bath, dry clothes, and a good meal."

"Here, miss," Seth said, his voice low and gentle as he extended his arms to her. "Let me help you down."

His brother's acceptance of the woman seemed to snap Hamilton out of his shock-induced stupor. "I'll put extra water on the stove," he grumbled as he shot one last glare at Logan before stomping back toward the house, "but don't think we won't be discussing this."

Eva didn't bat an eye. She lifted her chin and glared at his retreating back. "After supper," she said. She turned to Logan. "And we'd love to have *you* join us for the meal."

"What?" Hamilton halted, spun to glare at Logan, then turned his attention to his sister and shook his head adamantly.

Eva, however, just kept smiling, undeterred. "It's an insufficient thank-you for your heroics today, but I hope you'll join us. Seth's Sunday pot roast is delicious, and there's always plenty to go around."

Knowing Hamilton wanted nothing more than to send him packing made accepting Eva's offer that much sweeter. With a bow of his head and the sizzle of Hamilton's searing glare boring through his chest, Logan fingered the brim of his hat. "Much obliged, Miss Evangeline. I'd be honored to share your table."

"Excellent." Her eyes danced with mischief, and Logan loved the feeling of comradery springing up between them.

Eva stepped aside as Seth collected the injured woman from atop the horse. When he settled her into his arms to carry her to the house, she made a grab for Eva's hand, and all teasing vanished from Eva's face. She cast a quick glance at Logan, begging him to understand.

He nodded. "I can find my way around," he assured her. "I'll tend to Shamgar, you tend to her."

Her eyes warmed with gratitude, and his chest warmed with something else altogether. Something dangerous. Something that could derail his plans.

Logan clicked to Shamgar and set off for the barn. Time to remember why he was here.

Seth set the young woman on her feet once they reached Evangeline's room. "I'll bring in the tub," he said, "and some extra blankets. The poor gal is shivering something fierce."

Evangeline met her brother's concerned gaze. "Thank you."

Once he left, she extricated her hand from the woman's grip and bustled over to the wardrobe to retrieve two clean skirts and shirtwaists. After laying them on the bed, she turned to face the woman, who hadn't moved. Pointing to first one skirt and then the other, she asked, "Would you like the brown or the red?"

The girl pointed to herself, her eyebrows arching upward.

"Yes." Evangeline touched her arm lightly, careful not to make any sudden moves. Then she looked the girl up and down and pretended to give the inane fashion decision serious contemplation. "The red, I think. No more blacks and grays for you." She shivered, recalling the charcoal blanket dragging her down. Then a thought occurred. "Oh, unless you're in mourning." She eyed the soggy black dress plastered to the woman's body. "I probably have something darker if—"

The woman shook her head and pointed to the red skirt.

Evangeline grinned. "Red it is." She set the gored skirt off to one side and laid the matching calico shirtwaist on top of it. Sprigs of dark red flowers dotted the pleated tan bodice and puffed sleeves. "This will look lovely on you. All that dark hair of yours. I think I have a red ribbon somewhere, too." She crossed to her dresser and fetched dry underclothes for both of them from the drawer, then pulled a ribbon from the basket that sat on top.

"I've got the tub," Seth called from the doorway, the large copper bathing tub stretching his arms wide.

"Wonderful." Evangeline tossed the underthings onto the

bed and stepped past her guest to help her brother situate the tub along the interior wall in its usual place. She pulled two blankets out of the basin along with the toweling Seth had added and set them on the chair she kept by her writing desk.

Ten minutes later, Zach had filled the bath with water from the kitchen pump along with a pail from the stove's reservoir and two steaming kettles. Evangeline plunged her arm in to test the temperature. Her skin was chilled enough that the sudden warmth was a tad uncomfortable, but not unbearable. Just what a shivering female needed to regain her equilibrium.

With the men gone and the door closed, Evangeline reached for her guest and clasped her hands. "The water's warm. I'll help you out of this sodden dress and let you soak for a while. Then I can wash your hair and help you comb out the tangles. Would you like that?"

The girl's eyes misted, but she nodded, and Evangeline smiled. Heaven knew this poor dear had been through enough hardship for one day. A little pampering was definitely in order.

As Evangeline helped peel away the black dress and aided her guest out of her frayed petticoat and threadbare chemise, she fought to hide her rising anger. Bruises. All over the girl's body. Purple marks in the shape of fingers along her upper arm. Shadowy contusions on her belly. Thin red marks on her back as if she'd been struck by a switch or a cane.

No wonder she hadn't struggled when that beast had carted her to the water's edge. She'd been beaten into submission. Probably into unconsciousness. Evangeline would have to take care with washing her hair. The girl had probably been knocked on the head before being rolled into that awful blanket.

Evangeline sniffed quietly and blinked away the tears that threatened to spill down her cheeks. The girl didn't need pity right now. She needed hope. So Evangeline took her by the elbow, gave her a nod that promised a lending of strength until the girl could recover her own, and helped her into the bath.

Logan kicked the toe of his boot against the fence post and leaned his forearms along the top rail. What was he doing? For the first time in years, he was back on his father's property, the barn and the house both at his disposal. The girl they'd pulled from the river made a perfect distraction. He should be searching for something he could use against Hamilton, some type of leverage to force him to the gaming table.

Instead, Logan was leaning over the rail of a pigpen, watching a boar named Hezekiah wallow in a slimy mud puddle and worrying about the welfare of a woman he didn't even know. Not to mention obsessing over the woman he *did* know.

He hadn't been able to stomach the barn for more than a few minutes. He'd loosened Shamgar's girth, rubbed him down a bit, and walked him over to the trough by the well so he could drink his fill. Then Logan had turned his back on the mausoleum that masqueraded as a harmless shelter for animals and trudged in the opposite direction.

He'd needed to escape the darkness of his memories, to find relief from the vise tightening around his chest, the growing pressure making it hard to breathe. When he'd spotted the pig, he'd immediately crossed the yard to the pen and leaned over the fence rail. Not because porcine rapport was particularly comforting in and of itself, but the bristle-haired creature snorting in the corner brought a much fairer companion to mind, one who could siphon sunlight through the darkest cloud. And if ever he'd needed a dose of sunlight, it was now.

"I understand you and Hezzy have a history."

Logan straightened and twisted his neck to cock a wry grin

at Seth. He supposed he should be thankful the younger Hamilton brother had been the one assigned to quiz-the-suitor duty. After his brief stint in the barn, Logan didn't think he was up for a confrontation with Zacharias.

"Well, I did try to shoot him when we first met," Logan said, tipping his chin toward Eva's pet, "but your sister insisted I spare him." He leaned his weight on the fence after Seth rested his back against the wooden slats. "I thought maybe if I hung out with him, he'd grow on me."

"Hasn't worked for me yet." Seth crossed his arms over his chest, his pale blue eyes scanning Logan's face. "But the strategy is sound enough."

Logan raised a brow. "Trying it on me?"

"Yep."

Logan chuckled at the honesty. "Am I growing on you yet?"

Seth shrugged. "Too soon to tell. But be warned . . ." He straightened away from the fence, his arms still crossed and his eyes anything but teasing. "We've been dealing with Evie's penchant for bringing charity cases home for years. We know how to protect her." He nodded toward the boar who was giving his back a good scratch against a post. "Pulled Hezzy's cutters out before they grew long enough to inflict any damage." Seth dipped his chin, his gaze lowering to Logan's waistband before lifting back to his eyes.

Logan tapped the brim of his hat in acknowledgment of the brotherly threat. "I'll keep that in mind."

"Good."

They fell silent. Seth turned and braced a boot on the bottom rail of the fence as they both stared at the pig neither of them liked. 'Course, they didn't much care for each other at the moment, either.

"So how's the girl?" Logan said, finally breaking the silence.

"Under Evie's wing." Seth lifted his face toward the sun, as if he, too, thought of Eva as a bright spot in a dark world. "Best place for her right now."

"Agreed. Your sister can raise a person's spirits better than anyone I've ever met."

"Spoken like someone who's spent significant time in her company." Seth shifted to face Logan, his bland expression doing nothing to disguise his pointed interest.

Logan inwardly scolded himself for the misplay. The compliment to Eva had risen unbidden and slid off his tongue without thought. He'd played a card that should have been kept hidden in his hand. She had him off his game.

Seth eyed him with raised brows. "Exactly how much time have the two of you spent together, *neighbor?*"

Logan did his best to downplay his interactions with Eva. "We've met a few times out and about. She was kind enough to help me decide on the best place to build my cabin."

Seth looked far from appeased. "She told *us* you weren't planning on staying. That you'd only bought the property as an investment."

"That's true." Logan didn't blink as he met Seth's stare, doing his best to project the aura of a man who had nothing to hide. "But your sister convinced me that I might have more interest from buyers if the property was improved upon." He shrugged. "I don't have any compelling appointments elsewhere, so I opted to follow her suggestion. I've got an area cleared and plan to start framing out the walls this week."

"Does your hanging around have anything to do with your intentions toward Evie? You caused quite a stir after church this morning, you know. If you plan to entertain yourself with her company while you're working on your land, then head on to greener pastures once you find a buyer, I'd advise against it. Evie doesn't deserve to have her emotions trifled with, especially in full view of the town. My brother and I would take exception to such treatment."

"As you should." Logan pushed away from the fence, his jaw tightening. "Look, I know you want to protect your sister, and I respect that. But she and I have only known each other for a week or so. It's too early for me to declare any specific intentions. What I can assure you is that I hold Evangeline in the highest regard. She's a rare woman. Kindhearted. Funny. Yet not afraid to chew you up one side and down the other if needed." A grin tugged at the corner of his mouth as he looked toward the house. "I'm drawn to her."

The gentle breeze that had been swirling around them suddenly kicked up, gusting hard enough to flap Logan's damp trouser legs. Yard dust pelted his face and stung his eyes. He turned his back to the gust only to find Seth's eyes widening in alarm. Wracking coughs beset Eva's brother out of the blue, harsh rasps that refused to let up. He yanked the top of his shirt over his mouth and nose and spun toward the house. He only made it halfway to the porch before he bent double and stumbled to a halt. One hand held the shirt in place while the other pressed against his chest as he gasped for breath. He sounded like he was dying.

Logan rushed to Seth's side as pieces of what Eva had told him about her brother's lung condition flooded his brain. "Here, let me help you." He grabbed Seth's left arm and dragged him toward the house. They had to get out of this wind.

Seth didn't fight him, but he didn't do much to help, either. Finally Logan stopped, hoisted Seth's left arm across his shoulders, and grabbed him around the waist. "Hamilton!" he yelled as he struggled to keep Seth upright. "Get out here!"

Zacharias threw open the door and took one scowling look at Logan before his eyebrows shot upward. He sprinted down the porch steps. In a heartbeat, he reached their side and had Seth's other arm around his neck. Together, they dragged Seth up to the porch and into the kitchen. Hamilton kicked the door closed behind them, then helped Logan sit Seth in a chair near the stove.

"Slow and steady, Seth. Remember the exercises." Hamilton spoke in a remarkably calm tone, given the panic raging through Logan's veins. "Slow and steady." Yet Hamilton was anything but calm. He turned to Logan, worry lines etched into his forehead. "Grab a towel and dampen it. Then pour some coffee."

After issuing that brusque order, he turned back to his brother, stripped the coat from Seth's back, and flung it over to the corner by the front door. Then he yanked down Seth's suspenders and started on his shirt.

Logan spotted a dish towel by the dry sink and dashed over to collect it, the sound of Seth's wheezing urging him forward. He worked the pump handle until a trickle of water poured over the cloth. He squeezed out the excess and ran it back to the table.

"Here," he said as he dropped the cloth next to where Seth sat.

Hamilton pushed the dishes that had been set out for lunch toward the middle of the table and picked up the cloth. He wiped it over his brother's face in a long, smooth stroke. Cleaning away the dust? Must have been, for he cleaned Seth's neck and hands as well after he tossed the shirt to the same corner as the coat, leaving his brother in nothing but his trousers, undershirt, and drooping suspenders.

"Coffee!" Hamilton snapped, and Logan jolted back into action.

He opened cupboard doors until he found a mug, then snagged the coffeepot from the back burner of the stove. A stove he recognized from when his mother had stood in front of it. Pushing aside the memories, he concentrated on pouring the dark brown liquid into the cup and carrying it over to the table. Just as he set it down, the sound of a door opening somewhere close by brought his head around.

"Here's what's left of the second kettle," Eva said, rushing into the kitchen with a porcelain washbasin in hand. She brushed past Logan without a glance and set the steamy bowl in front of Seth. "I heard the commotion."

Hamilton gently bent his brother's face over the basin. He didn't urge him to inhale, interestingly enough, just told him to feel the warmth of the steam. To close his eyes and relax.

He was good. Diffusing the panic instead of adding to it. His deep voice murmured a soft, steady cadence, like a drummer urging a soldier to march in step with his timing.

Seth's hand trembled as he reached for the coffee. Eva helped him grasp the cup and bring it to his lips. He might not have been able to draw a full breath, but he could chug coffee as if his life depended on it. Although, from what Eva had told him, it very well might.

A movement in the doorway caught Logan's peripheral vision. He turned and spotted the woman they'd pulled from the river. She was clean, her dark hair combed and braided, the ends tied with a red ribbon that matched the red skirt she wore. Her frightened gaze darted from one person to the next until Logan intercepted it. Then she latched on to his face, her light green eyes begging for an explanation.

He stepped closer to her and spoke in a low voice. "He has asthma." Then he recalled her probable mental deficiency and thumped a hand onto his chest to try to help her understand. "He has weak lungs. The dust hurt him."

The girl darted her attention to the threesome huddled at the table, then back to Logan, demanding more details.

Maybe she wasn't as deficient as he'd thought. She certainly knew how to communicate with her face. Even a non-poker player could have interpreted that signal.

"He'll be all right," Logan assured her, hoping he wasn't lying. Hamilton and Eva seemed well-practiced with their treatment regimen, so surely that meant Seth had survived attacks like this before. "He just needs to calm his lungs down, so they can work properly."

As if compelled to help somehow, the woman sidestepped Logan and strode for the stove. She found the towel he had used to protect his hand from the hot coffeepot and put it to use herself, refilling Seth's mug. Then she sat in the chair directly across from him, folded her hands, bowed her head, and started praying. At least that was what Logan assumed she was doing. Her eyes were closed, her mouth was moving, but she made no sound.

Logan followed her to the table, braced his hands on one of the chair backs, and bowed his own head. It seemed like the right thing to do, though he felt a little awkward praying with someone when he couldn't hear the words. He figured he could guess the sentiment, though.

Help his lungs work, Lord.

Not the most eloquent of prayers, but he figured it would get the job done. What else needed to be said? Logan opened his eyes. Apparently the river gal could come up with a few more requests. Her lips were still running a mile a minute. Logan turned back toward the Hamiltons, his heart clutching at the distress lining Eva's face. An amendment to his petition rose from his rusty spirit.

Eva's lost enough in her life. She doesn't need to lose another brother. Please spare him.

Ironic, really, that he should be praying on behalf of a Hamilton while standing in the very kitchen they had stolen from him. Yet he didn't regret it. How could he, when Eva glanced over at him with gratitude shining in her eyes? Besides, he didn't wish true hardship on these people. Just justice for his father and restitution for his mother.

Seth drank the second cup of coffee. When he plunked the cup down on the table, the girl sitting across from him opened her eyes. They stared at each other, their eyes locked as if nothing else existed in the room. Seth's wheezing lessened, and his bent spine slowly straightened.

Whether it was the coffee, the prayers, or the calming effect of a mysterious young woman sitting across the table, Seth's breathing gradually eased. As did the tension clawing at everyone in the room.

All five of them sat in the silence for a handful of minutes, listening to Seth's slow, even breaths as if they were the finely tuned notes of some fancy orchestra.

"Well," Eva said, finally breaking the silence, her smile brave yet wobbling slightly, "I'll see to getting dinner on the table."

Seth's face reddened as he pushed away from the table. "I'll, uh, get a fresh shirt." He glanced over at the girl, who rose from her chair as well. "Sorry about all the excitement. I hope the pot roast didn't dry out."

"Even if it did, it'll still be better than the canned beans and jerky I thought I'd be eating today." Logan chuckled, earning a small grin from Seth as he turned and stepped away from the table.

"Zach," Eva called, "why don't you and Logan empty the bathing tub while we womenfolk put the finishing touches on dinner?"

Logan's gaze slammed into Hamilton's. The other man looked as loath to agree as Logan felt.

"I can handle it," Hamilton grumbled. "Logan here's a guest. He should . . . take a load off in the parlor or something."

Logan frowned. He wasn't about to be painted as some kind

of shirker in front of Eva. "I'm not really the parlor-sitting type," he said, his jaw clenching in preparation for an argument. "Might as well put me to work while I'm here."

Hamilton's eyes narrowed. "I said I can handle it."

Logan narrowed his right back. "*I* said I'd be glad to help."

Hamilton advanced a step. Logan followed suit.

Until a dish towel flew into his face, jerking his head backward as he made a clumsy grab for the fluttering fabric. "What—?" He glanced toward the projectile's source.

Eva stood at the stove, one hand on her hip, her eyes—both the brown *and* the blue—rolling in exasperation. She jabbed a thumb toward the interior doorway. "First room on the left, Logan. See if you two can manage to dispose of the tub without sloshing water all over the place. Might be a tall order with your egos constantly dueling, but I have faith in you." She sweetened the scolding with a smile that promised favor to the knight who fulfilled her quest, and suddenly, obtaining her pleasure outweighed maintaining his pride.

Logan lobbed the towel back to her and grinned. "Yes, ma'am."

He eyed Hamilton warily as he strode over to the hooks on the far wall of the kitchen and hung up the hat he'd been too flustered to remove during the chaos of Seth's attack.

Proving once again that he was soft where his sister was concerned, Hamilton let out a beleaguered sigh as he scooped up the porcelain washbasin Eva had brought out and marched toward her room. "Well, come on, then," he groused, even though Logan was already on his heels.

But when they reached Eva's doorway, Logan hesitated, memories assailing him with unexpected force.

His room. She was using his old room.

The furniture was different. His bed and small bureau had

been packed up with the rest of their belongings when he and his mother left, but the walls stood in the same place, the window faced the same direction, and the floorboard. . . . Logan took a single step into the room and purposely pressed the toe of his boot against the third wooden plank. Yep. It still creaked. He'd always been careful to avoid that board when he'd snuck to the kitchen for a late night snack.

"I thought you said you wanted to help." Hamilton's aggravated tone snapped Logan's attention back to the present. Hamilton dumped the leftover water from the basin into the half-filled tub, then dropped it onto the nearby washstand.

Logan gave a sharp nod. "I did."

"Well, quit gawkin' at my sister's things and pick up your end of the tub."

"Got it." Logan bent and gripped the handle with his right hand.

He hadn't really been paying much attention to Eva's things, but now that Hamilton mentioned it, he couldn't help noticing everything from the wrinkled coverlet on the bed to the open wardrobe with its colorful assortment of feminine garb to the dresser top with its brushes and ribbons and hairpins. She'd made it her own.

For the first time, the thought of taking it away from her seemed wrong.

"Whenever you're ready, Your Majesty." Hamilton glared up at Logan from his hunkered position gripping the tub's other handle.

Logan returned the glare as he heaved upward and started backing out through the doorway behind him.

Taking away Eva's home might feel wrong, but taking it away from Zacharias Hamilton still felt incredibly right.

CHAPTER
15

Evangeline smiled as she handed the last of the washed dishes to her female companion to dry. She really needed to figure out the young woman's name. She'd intended to quiz her in private while she combed the tangles from her hair after the bath, but the girl just stared at her lap while Evangeline worked out the knots, making no response to any of Evangeline's queries. Then Seth's asthma attack hit, and priorities shifted.

The girl wasn't a stranger to hard work. In fact, she'd jumped up to help before Evangeline could do more than tie her apron strings. She knew her way around a stove, too. The pan gravy she'd made had saved the pot roast and corn bread from being far too dry. The roast had overcooked after the broth evaporated, and the corn bread had sat too long in the warming oven. Not that anyone complained. Seth breathing normally again was worth tough beef and overbrowned potatoes any day.

That attack had been a bad one. The first one he'd had in months, and the most severe in over a year. Usually Seth took every possible precaution to avoid anything that could seize his lungs, but he must have been distracted by their extra guests.

Thank heavens Logan had been around to yell for Zach and help Seth into the house.

Of course, Seth probably wouldn't have been outside in the first place if he hadn't seen it as his responsibility to harass Logan. But that wasn't Logan's fault. Boneheaded brothers tended to fall prey to overprotective urges. There was no controlling it.

"I think it's time for a family discussion," Zach announced the instant the last dry dish left the girl's hand to clink softly atop the stack of clean plates.

Evangeline swallowed her sigh. Speaking of overprotective urges. . . . She was going to have to do some fancy talking to get Zach to agree to let her new friend stay here.

The girl beside her didn't react to Zach's announcement, but then, she didn't know Zach. Which was probably good. He could be rather intimidating.

Logan piped up next. "I think I'll hang around for that." He pushed his kitchen chair slightly away from the table and stretched out his long legs, getting comfortable. Apparently Zach's intimidation didn't work on Logan.

Case in point: when Zach scowled at him, Logan just grinned and took another swig of his coffee.

"You ain't family, Logan."

He shrugged. "Neither is the girl. But I figure she'll be staying, since she doesn't have anywhere else to go. Besides, the meeting's going to be about her situation, right?" He crossed his arms. "I pulled her from the river. Gives me a right to have a say in her welfare."

A muscle twitched in Zach's jaw.

Evangeline touched the girl's arm and led her back to the table, glaring at Zach as she went. Keeping her voice low—as if that would make a difference—she settled in the chair next to

Logan and reached over to touch her brother's elbow. "Someone tried to kill her, Zach. The more people we have looking out for her, the better."

"Someone tried to *kill* her?" Zach slammed his palms on the table and came half out of his seat. His voice rose to a near shout. So much for delicacy. "All you said was that Logan fished her from the river. You didn't say anything about someone trying to kill her."

The girl shrank back, leaning as far away from Zach as she could. Seth gently took her hand. Her head swiveled toward him, and she started to jerk her hand away, but then she met his gaze and something changed. She calmed.

"Easy, Zach," Seth warned. "You're scaring her."

Zach blew out a breath and lowered himself back into his chair at the head of the table. He ran his hand through his hair and visibly worked to control his temper.

Her eldest brother had always been quick to pull the trigger when danger threatened his family, but he could also be a meticulous, thoughtful planner. He'd been her rock for years. Solid. Reliable. She had faith in him to do the right thing. Shoot, just figuring out what the right thing was in this crazy situation would be a significant accomplishment.

Finally, Zach glanced toward her and Logan. "Start at the beginning."

Evangeline shared a look with Logan on her left. He nodded. Then she glanced to her right to smile encouragingly at her new friend before turning back to Zach.

"Logan and I spotted a wagon down by the river as we were walking home. A man was struggling to carry something rolled in a large blanket. I feared he intended to dispose of an animal of some kind." Why was her mouth suddenly going dry and her voice quavering? These were her brothers; she could tell them anything. Yet she felt ridiculously close to tears all of a sudden.

All the terror and outrage she'd experienced when she'd first realized what had happened seemed to rise again to torment her. And what must the young woman next to her be feeling? To hear her near death described in a dry recitation of events.

Logan must have sensed her unease, for he shifted in his seat and stretched his right arm across the top of her chair back. He didn't actually touch her, yet his show of support and increased closeness infused her with a much needed dose of fortitude.

"I couldn't let that man hurt one of God's creatures without trying to stop him," she continued, steadier now, "so Logan took me up on his horse, and we raced down to the river, shouting at him to stop."

Zach's gaze flicked over to the second female at the table, then returned to rest on Evangeline. "I take it he didn't have a dog wrapped in that blanket."

Evangeline shook her head.

Bracing his right elbow on the edge of the table, Zach leaned forward. "Did you recognize him?"

"No. He drove off in his wagon before we got close enough to see any facial features. And by then, I was too focused on saving whatever he had shoved into the river to pay him much heed."

"Not too tall," Logan broke in. "Maybe five foot ten. Bulky build, but judging by his difficulty with the load he carried, I'd say the bulk was from something other than muscle. Dark hair. Tanned skin. Gray hat with a black band. Blue shirt. Brown trousers. Buckboard had a spring-mounted seat. Weathered wood. No paint or trim. Team consisted of one gray about fourteen hands, speckled haunches, dark mane and tail; and a black, closer to fifteen hands with white socks on both hind legs."

Evangeline stared at Logan as he rattled off his list of obser-
vations. He had the catalog skills of a scientist! How had he
seen so much? All she remembered was the gray hat. Yet Logan
had absorbed details like wet paint grabbing dust from the air,
sucking them in until they solidified in his brain. Amazing.

And incredibly attractive.

She couldn't help but lean a little closer to him. Handsome.
Heroic. Handy in a crisis. And brilliant to boot. Her heart was
in serious danger.

But that danger was nothing compared to what the young
lady beside her had faced.

Zach nodded a grudging thanks to Logan, then turned his
attention to their other guest. He kept his voice gentle and calm,
like he had when he'd helped Seth with his breathing. "Who
tried to hurt you, miss?"

She immediately ducked her head and shook it from side
to side.

"You don't know, or you don't want to tell me?"

She made no response. Not even a shrug. Almost as if . . .

Evangeline pondered a moment, then slowly rose from the
table. Logan's hand slid away from its resting place on her chair
as he turned to watch her. He raised a brow in question, but
she gave him a quick smile of reassurance and continued on.
She moved behind the table to the stove, where the large, metal
roasting pan sat, filled midway with soapy water to soak the
baked-on grit.

As Seth rubbed the girl's hand and promised protection, Evangeline carried the pan to the dry sink and poured the dirty water
into the empty washtub. Zach asked the girl a second time about
the man who had dumped her in the river, and again she made
no response.

Evangeline walked back to the stove, then a few steps past.

Zach and Seth paid her no mind, their attention focused on the girl. Logan, on the other hand, caught her eye, his intrigued expression posing more questions.

He'd have his answers soon enough. And so would she.

When Evangeline was in position, directly behind the young woman, she lifted the roasting pan shoulder high and dropped it.

The crash was so loud when it hit the floor that all three men jumped. Even Logan. The girl startled, too, but a hair slower than the rest.

"For pity's sake, Evie!" Zach yelled.

She was pretty sure he was glaring at her, but she didn't look his way to confirm. She kept her gaze locked on the woman who was turning in her chair to see what had happened.

Evangeline bent to retrieve the pan, then mouthed an apology to the woman. *I'm sorry. I hope I didn't scare you too badly.* She gave the words no actual voice, but it didn't matter. Her new friend somehow read them in the shape of her lips. The girl smiled and shook her head as if to say everything was fine.

"You can't hear me, can you?" Evangeline asked.

The girl's eyes widened in horror, and she jumped from her seat, knocking her chair sideways in the process.

"It's all right." Worried that the girl would try to bolt, Evangeline dropped the roasting pan again and held up her empty hands in a placating manner. "I'm still your friend." She slowed her words down and spoke in a louder voice. Then, realizing how silly speaking louder was, she grinned at herself and resumed her normal tone. She added a few hand motions, thinking they might aid communication. "You must be so smart," she said, pointing to her head. "To figure out what people are saying without being able to hear." She tapped her ear then pressed her palms to her own chest. "I'm so impressed."

Tears glistened in the girl's eyes. "I'm broken," she said,

her voice a little muddy, the ends of her words indistinct, yet Evangeline understood them. Understood but didn't accept. She couldn't allow this amazing woman to believe herself inferior.

Pointing one finger to her blue eye, then moving it to her brown one, Evangeline said, "So am I." Then she gestured to the others in the room. "We all are."

The young woman turned to look at each person around the table. First to Seth—no doubt remembering his asthma attack—then to Zach, and finally to Logan. Each of the men nodded as she glanced his way, confirming that they, too, recognized their own imperfections and flaws.

Logan nodded to the girl, but he also raised his eyes and speared Evangeline with a piercing look, as if he were trying to communicate a message. Something important. Something about flaws and imperfections, perhaps? She longed to delve and explore, yet even as her pulse sped at the lure of unraveling a piece of the mystery surrounding her new neighbor, she forced down the desire. Logan's secrets would have to wait. She had more pressing matters at hand.

Drawing the girl's attention back to herself by stepping close and touching her shoulder, Evangeline spoke the words on her heart. "People might try to hide their broken places and pretend to be whole, but the truth is that we all have failings. That is why we need each other." She gestured to Seth and Zach. "My brothers make me stronger. They shore up my broken places with their love and support. And I do the same for them." She reached for the girl's hands and clasped them firmly. "Let us do the same for you. Please. We can help you. We can be your family."

The girl's arms trembled. Her chin quivered. Her focus darted to each occupant of the room, uncertainty and hope vying for supremacy in her eyes. Then she turned back to Evangeline, straightened her spine, and with a nod of her head, chose hope.

CHAPTER

16

The woman was amazing. Well, both of them, really. After all, it wasn't every day a man encountered a deaf person who could speak and understand what was spoken to her. Yet it wasn't the girl from the river who astounded Logan. It was Eva.

We're all broken, she had declared. Without shame. Wanting only to bond with a frightened girl who feared her secret would cause her to be cast out.

Who did that?

Society trained its members to hide their defects from an early age. Self-preservation demanded it. It was why he angled his hat to cover the scar slashing across his left eye. Why he concealed his last name. Why he bluffed in poker when he held weak cards. To be successful, one required an edge on the competition, even one built solely on perception.

Eva, on the other hand, forfeited her edge without hesitation. Despite her ingrained insecurity about her eyes and a history of outsiders devaluing her because of them, she openly professed her brokenness and offered it as a gift to a stranger.

Not only that, but she offered home and family, too.

Logan rubbed a hand against an odd tightness suddenly pressing against the inside of his chest, one that felt uncomfortably like envy. Would Eva be as accepting of *his* flaws and secrets when he finally revealed them, or was her generosity reserved only for those in immediate need?

Why did he care so much? It wasn't like he wanted to be fostered into the Hamilton family. They were the enemy. Or at least *one* of them was the enemy. He couldn't paint Eva with that brush, not even to protect himself from the doubts and inconvenient longings that cropped up with alarming regularity while in her company.

She couldn't have been more than twelve when her brother stole Logan's home. Too young to be culpable, too innocent to recognize the sin that had been committed. She'd probably never questioned how her brother had provided their little ragtag family with a home and security. Logan couldn't hold her accountable for her brother's actions.

Yet neither would he absolve her brother of guilt for her sake. Logan had family, too. A mother who depended on him. One who hadn't been the same since the day she found her husband dead, which would never have occurred had Zacharias Hamilton not cheated Rufus Fowler out of his land.

"You got something you want to say, Logan?" The low, rumbling voice of his nemesis snatched him from his thoughts.

Logan jerked his gaze right, accusatory words clawing at his throat for release. However, the man beside him looked merely curious, not antagonistic. Logan bit his tongue.

Hamilton raised a brow. "Your face went dark all of a sudden. Do you have concerns about the girl staying with us? See any threats she might pose to Evie?"

The girl from the river. Right. Logan gave himself a mental shake. *Focus, man.* With his gambling background, Hamilton could probably read posture and expression as well as Logan. He needed to tread carefully.

Scrambling to come up with a sufficiently dark alternative thought to explain his lapse, Logan glanced at the females, who were clasping hands in silent solidarity. Fortunately—or unfortunately, as the case might be—coming up with a substitute worry was all too easy.

Pitching his voice to match Hamilton's quiet timbre, Logan murmured, "It all depends on how determined that fella is to see this girl dead. If he just wanted to rid himself of her, he might not care where she ends up. But if he needed her dead for some other reason, he might come after her. Though I doubt he has any better idea of who we are than we have of him. She should be safe here for the time being."

"The thought occurred to me as well." Hamilton pushed to his feet and gestured for the ladies to resume their seats at the table. "Why don't we start with something easy," he said as the two females settled themselves. He lowered himself back into his chair, then leaned his forearms on the table as he peered at the girl from the river. "What's your name?"

The girl darted a glance at Eva, who gave her an encouraging nod, then turned back to Hamilton. She hesitated, though, looking down at her hands folded on the table in front of her. She nibbled her bottom lip as if weighing her options. After a moment of mental calisthenics, she straightened her shoulders and lifted her chin.

"Christie Gilliam."

Hamilton dipped his head. "Pleasure to make your acquaintance, Miss Gilliam." He pressed a hand to his chest. "I'm Zach Hamilton." He stretched his arm out to grab Seth's shoulder. "My brother, Seth." He nodded toward Eva. "Our sister, Evangeline, and our, uh, neighbor, Logan."

Logan ignored the less than enthusiastic introduction and smiled at Christie.

Her pale green eyes met his. "Thank you for saving my life."

Uncomfortable with her gratitude, he shrugged. "I just pulled you out of the water. Eva's the one who realized you were in danger. She's the one who deserves your thanks."

Christie reached for Eva's hand. "Thank you."

"I'm glad we reached you in time." Eva held her gaze. "Who was it, Christie? Who tried to drown you?"

The girl's chin tilted downward again, and her teeth emerged to bite the corner of her lip. "I don't know. Not for sure."

But she suspected someone. Logan frowned. Who? And why didn't she want to name him?

"I was hit from behind," she explained. "It's the last thing I remember before waking up on the riverbank. I never saw my attacker."

"Were you at home when it happened?" Seth asked.

Christie didn't respond. Eva squeezed her hand to get her attention, then nodded toward her brother. Seth repeated his question.

"No." Christie shook her head. "I was walking home from town after making a delivery for my stepfather."

Seth leaned forward to place himself directly in her line of sight. "Which town? Ben Franklin?"

She nodded. "Yes."

"Were you carrying money?" Zach probed after wagging a finger at her to get her attention.

"Some."

Logan shook his head. "Robbery doesn't make sense. A thief might bash her on the head and take her coin, but if she never saw him, there'd be no reason to kill her."

"I agree," Eva said, sending waves of satisfaction rolling

through Logan. Waves that should have been nothing more substantial than pond ripples, since they were simply talking through possible scenarios. No true sides were being drawn. Yet having her agree with him in front of her brother on anything seemed to trigger ocean-level crests.

He wanted her on his side. Always.

"And it doesn't explain the bruises," she added.

Logan's attention jerked to Christie's face. He didn't see any discolored marks. "What bruises?"

Christie's face reddened, and she ducked away from his regard.

Ah. So the bruises were in places not usually seen when clothed. Eva must have noticed them during the young woman's bath.

Eva touched Christie's arm. "I'm sorry. I didn't mean to embarrass you. But someone has hurt you. That same person could be the one who threw you into the river."

"My stepfather is not the patient sort, but I don't think he would go so far," Christie said. "He's lazy. And cowardly. Without me to run his deliveries, he'd have to do it himself."

"Are your deliveries that toilsome?" Seth scanned her slender frame, no doubt drawing the same conclusion Logan had—that any task managed by a woman of such slight build couldn't be that difficult for a man to take over.

A derisive smile twisted her mouth. "It isn't so much the work as the risk he wants to avoid."

Seth raised a brow. "What, exactly, do you deliver?"

"Moonshine." Christie drooped a bit at the admission, as if waiting for her new friends to change their minds about her welcome. "My stepfather's a bootlegger."

A low whistle escaped Logan's lips. Her stepfather's choice of occupation opened up a world of unsavory possibilities. With Delta County being dry, a man of low character could make a tidy sum stilling corn into whiskey. Most bootlegging operations were too small for local law to bother chasing down, so the risk was minimal. In fact, it wasn't unheard of for a lawman to accept a jug or two under the table in payment for turning a blind eye. And while most customers were harmless citizens with a thirst for the occasional strong drink, prominent clientele would have more to lose should it be discovered that they were willfully breaking the law.

"Your stepfather's taint is not on you." Eva was getting that stubborn look again, that feisty *I'll-defend-you-to-the-bitter-end-even-if-you-won't-defend-yourself* look that Logan couldn't help but admire. She might be a bleeding heart, but she was a warrior, too. A warrior unafraid to surround herself with soldiers who were broken, weak, and scarred as she charged into battle against whatever foe stood in their way.

Christie shook her head. "But I participated. I made his deliveries. Collected his money. Ate food he provided. Wore clothes he supplied by preying on the weakness of others."

"Did you have a choice?" Eva pressed. "Did you ever try to say no?"

Logan recognized immediately where Eva was headed. The bruises. The girl had been battered into submission. Forced to do what was necessary to survive. She didn't need the added burden of guilt by association if she'd not been a willing partner.

Christie shrugged. "I tried to refuse a few times in the beginning, but it only made him angry. My mother had made the deliveries before me, but she died two years ago when I was sixteen. With her gone, Earl demanded I take over the family responsibility. I tried to act like I didn't understand. Mama had never told him I was deaf. She thought it would be safer for me if Earl thought I was just slow. That way he'd want nothing to do with me. It worked for a while. You see, I didn't lose my hearing until I had scarlet fever when I was ten, the same fever that took my Pa. I was top of my class in school before the fever." Pride flashed in her eyes before they dimmed once again.

"Unfortunately, Pa had run up a bunch of debts before he passed. Earl offered to pay those debts if Mama wed him. She didn't particularly care for Earl, but she feared being taken to a poor farm, where paupers were housed with petty criminals and the mentally ill. So she chose the lesser of two evils. I hid my books away, swallowed my pride, and pretended to be less than I was, at least around Earl. But I was determined not to become the idiot he thought me to be.

"So I closed myself up in my room with Mama's hand mirror and practiced mouthing words in front of the glass for hours, learning the shapes of certain letters and sounds. When he was away, I dug out my favorite books and mouthed sentences from *Black Beauty* and *Heidi* until I memorized all the basic shapes. Then I practiced wherever we went, staring at shopkeepers as they assisted Mama with her purchases, the old men who stood around jawing outside the livery, other children when they invited me to play. It became a game.

"Until Mama died and left me alone with Earl." Christie glanced down at her hands and started picking at the cuff of her right sleeve. "If I couldn't figure out what he wanted fast enough, he'd hit me. Call me foul names. Throw things. He wore a beard, so it was hard to read what he said. Without Mama there to help, I made a lot of mistakes."

Logan ran a hand over his face, the bristles of his recently trimmed beard rubbing against his palm. He could feel the smoothness of his lips at the edge of his mustache, so she'd probably been able to read him well enough, but if a man let his beard grow long and scraggly, his lips would be almost completely obscured. What an untenable position for a young woman to find herself in. Cards stacked against her with only a bluff and her wits to see her through.

"Over the last year or so, things got easier," she said, her chin lifting once again. "I got better at guessing what he wanted before he asked, and he's dumbed things down so much now that instructions are rarely needed. Earl ties different colored ribbons around the jug handles, and I match them to the colors in the hidden compartments where I leave the moonshine. Inside a hollowed-out stump with a streak of blue paint across the top, behind a bush at the back of a red barn, another beneath a green wagon seat, and so on. I make deliveries on Sundays while all the God-fearing folk are at church, out of the way. Of course, some of those God-fearing folk leave money in the hidey-holes, too."

Zach's chair creaked as he shifted his weight. "And you were making deliveries this morning when the attacker struck?"

Christie's forehead crinkled. "Sorry. I didn't catch that."

Zach repeated his question, slowing it down. "Were you making deliveries when you were attacked?"

She nodded. "Yes."

Logan stroked a hand over his beard, making sure it lay as flat as possible before he voiced the thought that had been niggling at him for the past thirty minutes. He motioned with his hand to gain her attention. "What was different about today? Did something go wrong? Did you see something you weren't supposed to see?"

The young woman cocked her head to the side, and her hands stilled. "I don't think so. I delivered the jugs and collected the payments as I always do. One customer left a slender book instead of cash, but this isn't uncommon. If people are short on ready funds, they often leave something else in barter. If Earl is unsatisfied, he takes it up with the customer later. My job is just to bring home whatever is left for me. So I took the volume, stuck it in my burlap sack, and went about my business." She scratched the edge of her nose. "The attack didn't come until twenty minutes later, when I was halfway home."

Logan's poker instincts flared. She was bluffing. The super-fluous details. The guarded posture. The hand to the face. She wasn't telling them the whole truth. The question was . . . why?

CHAPTER

17

It didn't take long for Christie to find her niche at the Hamilton homestead. She was so determined to earn her keep that she'd cut Evangeline's household chores in half. A circumstance that afforded Evangeline more time for afternoon exercise—which just happened to involve long walks through the countryside. Countryside shared with a particular neighbor who made her heart flutter in the most delicious way whenever he smiled at her. Or looked at her, for that matter. And if he happened to touch her—well, actual palpitations had been known to occur.

Who knew having a sister would bring so many benefits beyond simple female companionship? Not only did Christie free Evangeline to pursue more intriguing interests than dusting shelves and weeding gardens, but she kept Seth distracted. Evangeline grinned as she and Hezekiah navigated a shallow ravine at the border of Logan's property. Seth hounded her a lot less these days about where she was going and what she planned to do while she was out. She'd like to think he was finally treating her like an adult and trusting her judgment, but Evangeline suspected that he placed fewer barriers to her leaving because it meant fewer barriers to him spending time alone with Christie.

The two had grown close over the last three weeks.

It was really quite sweet. Christie seemed to share a bond with Seth that went beyond even what she and Evangeline shared as women. She probably saw Seth as a kindred spirit—someone who had been dealt a handicap yet sought to control it instead of letting it control him, just as she did.

Christie went out of her way to dust every nook and cranny in the house on Seth's behalf, exceeding even Evangeline's tight standards. Who knew dust collected atop doorframes? Evangeline couldn't see that high, let alone think to dust there. Christie always made sure the coffeepot was filled and warm as well, and joined Seth for fish every day. He had taken to bringing home two or three fish instead of his usual one. How the girl stomached eating catfish and crappie every day was a marvel Evangeline had yet to fathom. However, she *could* understand the desire to share a meal with a man she found attractive. The small basket containing corn bread muffins and a jar of honey currently dangling from the crook of her arm attested to that truth.

She whistled to Hezzy, who had stopped to root at the base of an oak tree, then continued down the thin path her many visits had worn into the ground on the way to Logan's cabin. A cheerful tune absently danced through her mind, and she hummed the melody, matching her strides to the bouncing rhythm. The basket of goodies swung in time to her song as the framed-out cabin came into view.

It was such a nice cabin. Cozy. Homey. One she couldn't stop imagining belonged to her. Easy to do when the craftsman regularly asked for her opinions and had basically been building it to her specifications.

Speaking of which, where was he? Usually she heard hammering or sawing before she made it this close to the site. She heard nothing now beyond a mockingbird chirping somewhere overhead and Hezzy snorting a few yards behind. Evangeline craned her neck, her humming temporarily fading as she scanned the vicinity for a familiar male form. No black hat bobbing between wooden slats. No handsome bearded jaw or intriguing gray eyes in evidence anywhere.

"Hello!" she called. "Logan?"

No answer. Unless one counted the mockingbird's mimic.

Well, shoot. She'd missed him somehow. Evangeline's pace grew sluggish, but she pushed on the rest of the way. She might as well see what progress he'd made since yesterday. Maybe she'd even take tea in the kitchen. She had no tea—or table for that matter—but she had cakes and honey. What more did a girl really need? All right, she had hoped to have more handsome company than a muddy-nosed swine, but surely she could make do and manage a perfectly lovely outing all on her own. Just think—with the spaces between the studs, the view would be unmatched. Perhaps a mite breezy, but she'd not complain. There was no one around to impress with fetching hair anyway. Not that there was much fetching left in her hair after traipsing through the countryside for half an hour.

Evangeline approached what would eventually be the front door and sauntered into the house. She started in the front parlor, took a shortcut into the first bedroom by ducking through the wall, then meandered into the hall, across to the second bedroom, and up into the kitchen.

Nothing had changed since yesterday. No new boards had been added to the back wall where he'd been working. The horizontal siding still only reached her waist. Logan's toolbox hadn't moved, either.

She lowered her basket to the floor next to it then knelt and ran her finger over the smooth wooden handle of the hammer that lay atop the other tools. He'd held these in his hands, toiled with them, built this very structure with them. The hammer and level. The wood plane and saw. So masculine. Strong. Purposeful. Like the man who owned them.

A man she'd wanted to spend the afternoon with. Too bad that didn't seem to be an option at the moment. Evangeline let out a sigh. It bothered her more than it should that Logan had left without informing her of his plans, but that was his prerogative. She had no true claim on him. At least not yet.

That thought drew a grin. With new energy zinging through her, she spun in a quick little circle, watching as her skirt twirled out at her ankles like an upside-down trumpet flower. The afternoon was filled with possibilities, just like her future. She simply had to be bold enough to explore them. Maybe she'd go down to the creek that Logan had shown her, take her shoes and stockings off, and wade in the cool water. A perfect activity for a hot summer day. She could even give Hezzy a bath. She glanced down at her butter-yellow skirt. Perhaps not. She'd just laundered this skirt.

Evangeline stood and crossed the room, heading for what would be the back door. At the halfway point, the clicking of her heels dulled to a hollow echo. She glanced down at a thin rectangle outlined in the floorboards. The root cellar. Logan had never really shown it to her, the hole being too dark to see into without a lantern. Maybe *this* was what he'd been working on. He might have just run into town for some additional supplies.

Evangeline jabbed two fingers into the hole at the end of the trapdoor and lifted. It opened easily. She laid it all the way back against the floor and spied a rope tied near the hinges. Usually ropes were attached opposite the hinges so the person climbing down could pull the door shut once inside should there be a storm or some kind of attack. Yet this rope was fastened so close to the hinges that there would be no leverage to close the door. Logan was too meticulous to make that kind of mistake, so it must serve a different purpose.

She crouched down and peered into the dark hole. It smelled of damp earth. The sun angled down from the west and highlighted a small area inside. There wasn't much to see, mostly just different shades of dark.

Wait. There, pushed back from the opening. Was that Logan's duster? She'd seen him in the long black coat a time or two, especially when he was coming back from town, but in the heat of summer, it wasn't the most practical garment. He must have decided to store it in the cellar. Sensible. It would be safe from anyone who happened upon his homestead while he was away.

What else did he keep hidden down there? Evangeline bit her lip, then shot a glance around her in all directions. Her pulse thrummed in her veins. She really shouldn't. Snooping through another person's belongings was a violation of their trust. Their privacy.

But what if she could learn something about Logan—something that shed light on his true purpose for being here? With all their conversations over the last weeks, he still hadn't trusted her with his last name. And as much as she didn't want to let that omission bother her, it did. He was hiding something from her. Something that surely tied into the justice he sought for his father.

What if he had something dangerous planned? Something that could lead to him getting hurt? She knew next to nothing about what went on in saloons, but she'd heard tales of card games ending in gunfights. Of knives and fists inflicting deadly damage.

Another thought struck her. Why had Logan chosen this particular piece of land to invest in when he first came to town? She'd not thought to question it before, but after spending time with him, she couldn't help but wonder—had it been coincidence or strategy? Did his plan for vengeance somehow involve her family? Logan and Zach butted heads every time they came within ten feet of each other. She'd attributed it to Zach's antagonism toward a potential suitor, but what if there was something more to it?

An unwanted heaviness settled in her belly. Logan was a good man, her heart argued. He rescued women from boars and rivers, he aided men in the throes of asthma attacks, he laughed and teased and never once stared derisively at her unconventional eyes. Yet he harbored secrets and plotted revenge. For it *was* revenge, no matter how much he dressed it up in the wrappings of justice. Didn't she have an obligation to do whatever it took to protect Zach and Seth? They'd done so much to protect her over the years, some of which was probably as morally questionable as it was necessary. She could do no less.

She didn't want to abuse Logan's trust. She cared for him, she truly did. Yet if there was even the slightest chance that his intentions toward her family were less than honorable. . . .

Evangeline stiffened her shoulders. Zach and Seth came first. They had to. As much as she liked Logan, he wasn't family. Until he was—was it crazy to wish for a future with him while she actively betrayed him?—her allegiance belonged to her brothers.

Taking hold of the rope whose tether now made sense, Evangeline lowered herself into the cellar. Well, it was more falling than lowering, seeing as how the rope slid through her hands the instant her full weight left the floor above. She managed to slow her descent enough not to lose all dignity by splatting on her rear, but the stinging in her hands made her reconsider the wisdom of this hastily crafted plan.

Oh, well. Now that she was here, she might as well see the deed done.

Shaking her scraped hands to alleviate the sting, she moved to where Logan's duster lay and quickly rifled through his pockets. Nothing. Well, some might count the thirty-five dollars in cash stuffed in the outer right pocket as something, but Evangeline wasn't interested in money. Information was the only currency she sought.

Just to make sure she hadn't missed anything in the folds, she stood up, held the duster by the shoulder seams, and gave it a good, snapping shake. Nothing fluttered free. Sighing, she folded the coat back up and bent to drop it neatly into place. But before she released her grip, a sunbeam shimmered off something metal just a few inches deeper into the cellar. Setting the duster aside, she stepped forward and hunkered down again, extending her hands to feel her way around until she touched a leather pouch with a metal buckle. She grabbed it and dragged it toward the tepid pool of light beneath the overhead door.

His saddlebags. Her fingers trembled as she reached for the buckle.

"Sorry, Logan," she murmured, the concession not doing much to dull the guilt riding her conscience.

Her fingers trembled, causing her to fumble the buckle, but she didn't falter. She kept after it until the saddlebag was unfastened. *For my brothers.*

She reached into the first pouch and dragged out the contents. Clean shirt. Trousers. Comb. A small pouch of coins that she didn't bother to count. She shoved her hand back in and worked her fingers into every seam of the leather, but except for caking an unpleasant layer of grime under her nails, she gained nothing from her hunt.

She turned her attention to the second saddlebag, the thinner of the two. She found matches, jerky, and two more bags of coins. Exactly how much money did Logan carry around, anyway? Losing heart, she reached in a final time. Something crinkled. Something smooth, like paper.

Stomach tightening, Evangeline sucked in a breath and wrenched her treasure out of the bag. A letter. She held the envelope up to what little light filtered down and squinted to make out the address. To Logan Fowler from the Delta County Land Office in Cooper.

Fowler. Satisfaction shot through her. She'd uncovered one of his secrets. His name. Logan Fowler. It was a good name. Strong. Capable. And just the tiniest bit familiar. Why was it familiar?

Evangeline shrugged off the question. She could ponder that later. Right now, she needed to see what was inside the envelope before the man it belonged to returned.

Once she had the letter free, she unfolded the single page and angled it toward the light.

Dear Mr. Fowler,

I am pleased to inform you that the land you inquired about is available. The forty acres immediately northeast of Zacharias Hamilton's property can be purchased at the Delta County Land Office at your convenience. Please have any necessary financing arranged with your bank before you present yourself to the land agent.

Sincerely,

R. W. Downing

Evangeline lifted her head even as her stomach sank. Mere chance hadn't brought her new neighbor into her life. Somehow he'd known who Zach was and had plotted to place himself in her brother's path. For what purpose? Zach hadn't even seemed to recognize him the few times they'd met.

Her shoulders sagged, suddenly feeling too heavy to hold erect. She couldn't let Logan hurt Zach. Yet she couldn't believe the man she was falling in love with would want to. Logan knew how much her brothers meant to her. How beholden she felt toward them. How dedicated the Hamiltons were to one another.

There had to be another explanation.

She glanced again at the letter. It was dated more than four months ago. Maybe things had changed since then. Maybe now that Logan had gotten to know her, to know Zach and Seth, he'd set aside his plan, whatever it had been. Maybe he truly intended to live in this cozy little cabin. To marry her and be permanent neighbors with her family. It was possible.

Heavy clicks on the floorboards overhead threw her into a panic. She shoved the letter back into its envelope, pushed it into the pouch, and dumped the rest of Logan's belongings in on top of it. The buckle refused to yield to her shaking fingers, so she tossed the damning evidence away from her as the clicking grew closer.

She turned her face toward the opening and pasted on a bright smile. A face peered down at her. Dark. Hairy. An enormous nose.

Snort.

Evangeline clutched at her chest. "Mercy, Hezekiah. You gave me a start."

Her pet just stared at her, as if chastising his mistress for putting herself somewhere she did not belong. Well, she wasn't the only one.

"Shoo!" Evangeline waved the boar off. "You know you're not supposed to be in the house."

She swore she saw the pig shrug before he lumbered off, his hooves clicking on the floorboards. Insolent critter.

Evangeline rubbed the back of her hand across her brow to clear away the perspiration that had gathered there. She supposed she ought to climb out of this hole before getting caught for real. After taking a minute to tidy Logan's second saddlebag and fasten it properly, she inhaled a deep breath, grabbed hold of the rope, and pulled.

Her arms tightened, her torso lifted. The opening was only a few feet above her. Her neck strained. It shouldn't be too hard to climb out. Her legs kicked through the air. Well, unless one happened to have rope burns on her hands and embarrassingly little upper-body strength.

She dropped to the ground and cradled her sore hands.

Evangeline blew out a self-castigating breath as she crossed her arms and examined the thoroughly escape-proof cellar.

She was stuck. Apparently she had more in common with those foolish dime-novel heroines than she'd thought.

CHAPTER

18

Logan gathered his solitaire cards from the ground and gave them a vigorous shuffle. Tension radiated up his forearms as he repeated the familiar motion twice more. His quarry should've been here by now. Logan glared up at a sun well past its zenith.

He'd expected to be home by now, sharing his discoveries with Eva. Basking in her awe of his investigative prowess. Or at least listening to her praise his mediocre carpentry skills at the cabin and enjoying whatever snack she'd chosen to tantalize him with that afternoon. Instead, he was stuck outside Ben Franklin, waiting for a lazy bootlegger to get around to making his delivery.

Seated beneath the low-hanging branches of an ancient oak, Logan was hidden from the path that wound toward the school building and the all-important outhouse at the back. An outhouse with lovely purple flowers on the door, no doubt painted by some overzealous schoolgirl. Yet the purple would make it easy coding for the system Miss Gilliam had described.

Logan dealt out another hand of cards, his eighth. He was down, two games to five, and losing didn't help his mood any.

He glanced at the empty path and scowled. *Bring the whiskey, already. I've got better places to be and better company to keep.*

School had let out an hour ago. The kids had tromped off. The schoolmaster had followed about thirty minutes later, getting into a smart black buggy and driving back toward town. He looked like he could have benefited from the exercise of walking the half mile, but his balding, hatless pate would have suffered without the protection of the buggy's shaded top.

Logan picked up the ace of hearts he'd just turned over and set it aside. He moved the two of hearts to that new pile and flipped over the card beneath it to find the king of clubs. He frowned at the five cards stacked beneath the king, unable to move until the man on top got out of the way. And the king couldn't get out of the way until a fresh path opened up, just as Logan couldn't move until the bootlegger appeared. He could only guess what the bootlegger was waiting on. Christmas, probably.

A grunt rumbled in his chest as he flipped over the next card. Waiting needled his nerves, especially when the prize was within sight. He'd spent the last two and a half weeks working the tables and cozying up to the Ben Franklin locals at the Seven Ponies Saloon, preparing for the perfect moment to broach the subject of moonshine stills. That opportunity had finally presented itself last night.

He'd purposely lost a tidy sum to a braggart named Bellows, who loudly crowed over his victory, earning the disdain of the rest of the men at the table. Logan carefully exploited this contempt as he commiserated with the losers. A comment bemoaning the lack of strong drink available to wash away the pain of losing to such a sore winner was all it took to finagle an invitation to a jug party out behind the livery.

The livery owner—the second-highest loser for the night—

had disappeared into the stable, then emerged with a jug labeled with a brown ribbon. Once uncorked, the jug was passed around, each man taking a swig. Logan blended with the rest, though he didn't take more than the smallest of sips each time his turn came round. Had to keep his wits about him, after all.

When the party started to break up amid hearty belches and back-slapping, Logan tossed out an inquiry about how to acquire a jug of his own to take back to Pecan Gap. The livery owner, now in jolly good spirits, slapped Logan on the back and vowed to acquire a jug for his new friend. He collected an exorbitant price, no doubt pocketing a commission from the deal, then instructed Logan to take a room at the hotel for the night and wait for a message to be delivered.

The message hadn't arrived until nearly noon, when a nondescript piece of paper was slipped under the door. The hotel clerk had known nothing about who delivered it, or at least nothing he was willing to admit. Jack Simmons, the liveryman, was the most likely culprit. Whoever it was, he'd kept the note brief. All that had been written on the paper was a time and location.

5 o'clock

Privy behind school

Logan had taken up his position at two o'clock, thirty minutes before class let out. The bootlegger would want to be long gone before the stated delivery time to avoid detection, yet not so early as to risk being noticed by schoolchildren walking home. Therefore, Logan had extrapolated that he'd make an appearance around four, which had come and gone—Logan dug out his pocket watch and flipped open the lid—thirty-five minutes ago.

Had he been swindled? Logan snapped the watch closed and stuffed it back into the inner pocket of his coat. The gambler outmaneuvered by a bunch of skunk-drunk yokels? Surely not. His fingers flexed, making the playing card edges dig into his palm. If no one showed in the next hour, he was going to drop by the livery and demand a refund.

Even as that thought crystalized in his mind, a man with a burlap sack slung over one shoulder emerged from the woods north of the schoolhouse.

Logan forfeited his solitaire game, gathered his cards, and stashed them in a pocket. Slowly, he rose from his seated position into a crouch and peered beneath the low-hanging branches.

This man looked taller than the one by the river. Thinner, too. And he limped slightly on his left leg. The man at the river had lumbered about, but he'd seemed equally unsteady on both legs while he'd struggled with Miss Gilliam. Tan hat instead of gray. Dark trousers and sloppy cotton shirt too nondescript to be helpful. No wagon to compare, either.

When the man reached the outhouse, he swung the sack off his right shoulder with a visible wince. He rubbed the sore joint and lifted his arm in a slow circle to stretch the muscles before opening the privy door and dragging his sack inside.

An injury, perhaps? From carrying a woman's weight down to the river?

Logan didn't think so. The man at the river had carried Miss Gilliam in front of him, which would be more likely to cause back spasms than a shoulder injury. Considering the amount of gray in this man's scruffy beard, rheumatism was a more likely explanation. If getting around was difficult for him, it would explain why he'd been relying on his womenfolk to handle his deliveries.

Logan couldn't say with absolute certainty, but he'd lay good odds that Miss Gilliam had been correct. Her stepfather had not been the one trying to kill her.

Still, he was a despicable creature. Logan's upper lip twitched in disgust when Earl exited the outhouse after several minutes, stretching his fallen suspenders back over his shoulders and refastening the buttons on his trousers.

Really? He'd relieved himself in the very location where a paying customer was set to retrieve his goods? Not that a privy smelled particularly pleasant at any time, especially during the summer, but leaving a fresh deposit minutes before a collection couldn't be good for business. Though, Logan had to admit that it gave him an excuse for being there, should anyone happen to see him.

Logan grimaced and held his position, waiting for his distributor to head back the way he'd come.

Only he didn't. Instead, he let himself into the schoolhouse through the back door.

What was he up to? Logan shifted, itching to take a closer look, but he dared not leave his cover. This hand wasn't over yet. He'd keep his cards close to his vest a little longer.

Less than a minute later, the firm sound of a door closing announced Earl's departure out the front. Whatever he'd been doing, it hadn't taken long.

Too curious to let it go, Logan took a quick peek at his watch. A little early, but he could make it work.

Abandoning his post, he ran as quietly as possible through the woods, circling back toward town. As slowly as Earl moved, outdistancing him wouldn't be a problem. Staying hidden presented more of a challenge, but Logan kept to the trees as long as possible before slowing his pace and sauntering out to the road.

Keeping his stride loose-limbed and casual, Logan swung his arms and whistled an improvised tune to disguise his slightly labored breathing as he rounded the bend that would bring him into Earl's path. Sure enough, halfway into the turn, the bootlegger limped into sight.

"Howdy." Logan lifted his hat in greeting as he examined Earl.

Nothing seemed to have changed. No bulging pockets. No new items in his hand. Just the burlap sack. A sack that should have been empty yet remained flung over his shoulder.

Earl lifted his free hand to give a cursory tap to his hat brim and grunted something that could've been a greeting. Could've been a loud stomach growl, too. Hard to tell, even with two good ears. No wonder Miss Gilliam had so much trouble interpreting her stepfather's communication.

Logan pointed his hat in the direction he was walking. "The schoolhouse down thisaway?"

"Yep." Earl kept his head down.

Humorous, really, his weak attempts to remain anonymous. No sense making him nervous, though, so Logan slapped his hat back on his head and grinned like a simpleton. "Thanks!"

As Earl limped past, Logan turned, making a show of waving as he watched the older man go by. Something small and rectangular sat in the bottom of the sack. It could have been in there earlier with the jug and Logan just hadn't noticed it from the greater distance, but his gut told him Earl had picked it up during his short tour of the schoolhouse.

Had Jack Simmons stashed the payment in a book and left it in the classroom? Possibly. But why not simply pocket the banknotes and leave the book behind? Something didn't add up.

"Good day to ya," Logan called, channeling Eva's cheerful spirit as he backpedaled down the road.

Earl never turned, just raised a hand in silent farewell. Not even a grunt this time.

Logan let him go and kept his sedate pace all the way back

to the schoolhouse. Once there, however, he accelerated his timetable. In the span of twenty minutes he'd collected the odiferous moonshine, buried it in a shallow grave beneath the oak tree he'd used for surveillance, and fetched Shamgar from the shady spot down by the stream a quarter mile from the schoolyard.

After mounting, Logan urged Shamgar into a canter. If he hurried, he might still make it back in time to pay a call on Eva before suppertime.

But when he rode onto the Hamilton homestead—odd that he'd started thinking of his father's property in those terms— the chaos that met him pushed all thoughts of supper from his mind. Hezekiah was snorting and running between his pen and the back door. Zacharias was strapping on a gun belt, and Seth was arguing with a deaf woman about his asthma not stopping him from doing what must be done.

The one person Logan didn't see was Eva.

The knot in his stomach hardened into a stone.

CHAPTER

19

Logan trotted Shamgar straight to the back porch. "What's happened?"

Zacharias speared him with a glare. "What are you doing here? You're supposed to be with Evie." He spat the accusation like a shotgun spewing birdshot, and the pellets hit their mark. Every word stung the hide around Logan's heart. Fear seeped in through the quickly widening holes.

"What do you mean I'm supposed to be with her? I haven't seen her since yesterday." He eyed Seth striding down the porch steps, his furrowed brow only increasing Logan's worry. "I stayed the night in Ben Franklin."

Seth approached Shamgar but maintained about a foot or two of buffer between himself and the horse, no doubt avoiding the heavy layer of trail grit on both the gelding and its rider. Logan made a point to minimize his movements to prevent stirring the dust.

"Did Evangeline know you were in Ben Franklin?" Seth queried.

Logan shook his head. "No. I hadn't planned to extend my

stay, but something came up." He glanced at the porch, where Miss Gilliam stood, wringing her hands in her apron, then looked back at Seth.

The younger Hamilton brother seemed to catch his meaning. He raised a brow and snuck a peek over his shoulder at the pretty brunette. He wanted to ask for details, Logan could feel it, but the urgency of Eva's disappearance took precedence over Miss Gilliam's situation.

Zacharias marched toward them. "If Evie didn't know Logan was gone, we can still start the search at his place." He tossed a box of .38 caliber cartridges to his brother, who snatched them out of the air with one hand, the rattle of the metal slugs raising the hair on the back of Logan's neck. "Grab some rope and a couple lanterns," he ordered as he set off for the barn. "Hopefully we'll find her before dark, but I don't want to waste time fetching lamps if we haven't."

Logan's grip tightened on Shamgar's reins, and the horse sidestepped. "How long has she been gone?" he demanded of Seth as he forced his grip to relax.

"A few hours." Seth followed his brother toward the barn, and Logan nudged Shamgar to keep pace. "I got a little nervous when she didn't return in time to help with supper, but when Hezzy showed up without her, we knew something was wrong." Seth paused at the barn entrance and met Logan's eyes. "She never lets that pig roam around unsupervised. Too afraid some hunter will turn him into ham steaks."

"I know," Logan muttered, recalling the first time they'd met. She'd been so spirited in defense of her pet, so vibrant, so . . . alive. If she'd been hurt because he was off playing detective . . . No. He wouldn't think that way. He had to stay focused on finding her. On protecting her. "She's smart," he said, more to himself than to Seth. "And she's got grit. She'll be all right."

Please, Lord, let her be all right.

Seth said nothing in response, and his silence ate at Logan's confidence. This was taking too long. Eva was out there somewhere, and she needed him.

Logan reined Shamgar around. "I'm heading out."

"Wait!"

He hesitated at Seth's shout, even as instinct insisted he wait for no man. Tugging Shamgar around, he glared impatiently at Seth.

"Where's your cabin?" Seth asked.

"Northeast of the creek that runs along the back of your property line. Eva usually cuts through on foot, but if you want horses, there's a small path about a quarter mile up the road. I'll tie a handkerchief to a tree limb so you don't miss it, but I can't wait any longer."

"Go." Seth waved him off. "Find my sister."

"I will."

Logan kicked Shamgar into a canter, his whole heart throbbing with the weight of that vow. He *would* find her. No other outcome was acceptable.

He raced Shamgar down the road, yanking his handkerchief from his pocket as he went. Not sparing the time to dismount, he drew his horse to a halt at the turnoff, leaned forward in the saddle, and tied two corners of the cotton square to a branch of the blackjack oak that served as his landmark. Then he resumed his pace, pushing Shamgar as fast as he dared over the uneven terrain.

As soon as the clearing came into view, Logan started shouting Eva's name. He leapt from the saddle before Shamgar had fully stopped and ran toward the cabin.

"Eva?" He bounded across the threshold, his gaze jousting through the framed walls, desperate to take in the entire interior at once. No skirts or lovely auburn hair in sight. "Eva!"

"Here!"

Thank you, Lord!

Logan took his first full breath since he'd arrived at the Hamilton place. "Where?" he called. "Where are you?" She'd sounded far away yet near at the same time.

"In the cellar."

The cellar? He jerked his attention downward and finally noticed the gaping hole in the floor. Good gravy. In his haste, he could have tumbled right down on top of her. Lurching forward, he dropped to his knees and peered over the edge.

"Are you hurt?"

"No." Her beautiful face tipped back to look at him, her magnificent eyes glowing bright with gratitude and . . . guilt? That couldn't be right. His senses must be skewed from all the blood pumping through his overwrought veins. He'd nearly missed the gaping cellar door, after all. Yet unease niggled at him, refusing to be dismissed.

He shook the unsettling feeling away and smiled in relief. Eva was unharmed. That was what mattered.

Logan motioned for her to scoot back. "I'm coming down," he said. "Make room."

She obeyed, and Logan grabbed the rope and lowered himself into the cellar. Halfway down, his duster caught his eye. It was folded more neatly than he usually managed, and it completely covered the saddlebags he'd stored beneath.

His gut clenched. Maybe she *did* have something to feel guilty about.

Masking his suspicions, he kept his expression neutral as his feet connected with the dirt floor. Then he spun to face Eva.

"Oh, Logan!" She rushed him. Her chest collided with his ribs; her arms snapped around his waist. Then her eyes squeezed closed, and she pressed her cheek to the hollow below his shoulder. "I should never have come down here. I wanted to explore, but that was a mistake."

A mistake because she trapped herself, or because she regretted snooping?

Then she shuddered, and he no longer cared about her reason. She was here, in his arms, and upset.

"I tried to climb the rope, but my hands were too sore, and then it was just so dark and . . . and lonely." She glanced up at him, moisture glistening in her eyes. "Even Hezzy left me." Her lower lip trembled, but she bit it and hid her face from him again. "I'm not usually such a weakling. Afraid of the dark." She made a scoffing sound. "But I was down here so long, and I started worrying that something awful had happened to you, that you weren't coming back." Her already tight grip contracted even further. "I'm just so glad you're here."

Suddenly that was all that mattered. That he was there with her. His heart chugged like a speeding locomotive, not yet recovered from the scare of losing her. Her body trembled with residual fear from being trapped in a dark, unfinished cellar. Thoughts of bootleggers and Hamiltons and family responsibilities fell away, allowing feelings to take over.

Feelings of belonging. Desire. Rightness.

Logan ceased thinking altogether. His palms pressed into Eva's back and slowly moved upward to the space between her shoulder blades, then higher to the delicate line of her neck. She felt so good in his arms. His jaw rubbed against the side of her head. She lifted her face, the filtered light lending a sparkle to her eyes. His hands automatically came forward to cup her cheeks.

She inhaled, and his breath faltered. Her lips parted. Logan's thumbs caressed her face, his eyes locked on her mouth. Nothing else existed. Only Eva. Only the two of them together.

Her lashes lowered, severing his control like the plunge of a

guillotine. He crushed his lips to hers. So sweet. So perfect. So
. . . *Eva.* She lifted up on tiptoes to return his kiss with abandon,
infusing him with her essence. Joy. Light. Effervescence. He
wanted it all. Wanted her. Triumph surged through him when
she gripped the back of his coat and tugged him closer, as if
she feared he'd try to escape.

Never. She belonged with him.

Logan's fingers tunneled into the hair at Eva's nape as he
deepened their kiss, her soft, moaning hums heating his blood.

A dull thudding echoed around them, and it took a long,
disoriented moment for Logan to realize that it wasn't stem-
ming from the blood pounding through his veins. It came from
hoofbeats. Outside.

"Logan!" Zacharias Hamilton's booming voice cracked
through the air.

Eva jumped and wrenched herself from Logan's arms. Her
wide, innocent eyes blinked, as if she couldn't quite absorb
what had just happened between them. Not that he could blame
her. He might not be as innocent as she was, but he was just
as stunned by the effect of that kiss. He balled his hands into
fists, both to keep from reaching for her again and to still their
shaking.

"Evie! Where are you?" Seth's voice carried the same panic
that had coursed through Logan not ten minutes earlier.

"In the cellar," Logan called. "She's all right." He cleared
his throat and forced his mind to more practical matters. He
turned to Eva. "Let me see your hands."

She held them out, and he cupped them gently with his own.
He frowned at the angry red abrasions. The skin had even torn
in a few places on her right hand. He clenched his jaw. He was
building a ladder. Tomorrow.

He reached for his handkerchief, intending to bandage her

hand and protect it from the roughness of the rope, but his empty trouser pocket had nothing to offer. The white cotton square he usually carried was flapping in the breeze, tied to the tree branch by the road.

Plan B. The cellar ceiling was only about eight feet high. He could lift her out. She wouldn't have to touch the rope at all.

He put a hand on Eva's waist and drew her close.

"Logan." She arched away from him. "My brothers are coming."

He grinned. "Where is your mind, Miss Hamilton?" he teased. "I'm only trying to get you out of here without further injuring your hands."

"Oh."

Was that disappointment in her voice? He sure hoped so. Heaven knew he'd much rather be pulling her into his arms for another private embrace than handing her into her brothers' keeping. Had he known he would find her unhurt in the privacy of his cellar, he never would have given the Hamiltons directions to his cabin.

Hurried footsteps on the floor above told him he was out of time.

He moved behind Eva and placed both hands on her waist. "When I count to three, jump." He bounced a bit with her, giving her the rhythm as they bent their knees in time. "One." He widened his stance. "Two." He tightened his grip on her waist. "Three!"

She leapt. He lifted. Bending deep at the knees, he hoisted her onto his right shoulder, then pushed up with his legs until he had straightened to his full height.

He blew out a breath as he stepped closer to the edge of the opening, making sure her position was steady when she reached up to the men crouching at the cellar entrance.

"Careful with her hands," Logan ordered. "They're torn up from the rope."

Zacharias and Seth immediately adjusted, clasping her forearms, one brother on each arm. In an instant, her weight lifted from Logan's shoulder, and she disappeared from view.

Not liking the feeling of having her stripped away from him, even if it was for her own good, he immediately grabbed hold of the rope and climbed out. Yet being on equal footing didn't bring him into their circle. The brothers peppered her with questions and wrapped her hands with *their* handkerchiefs while she assured them she was fine and asked about Hezekiah.

She didn't look at Logan. Not once. Filling him with questions of his own.

Did she regret their kiss, or was she just trying to keep her brothers from guessing what had transpired before their arrival?

He glanced into the cellar as he folded the trap door shut. Or maybe she'd figured out who he really was.

The twinge in his chest intensified into a full-on throb.

CHAPTER

20

"Are you sure you're all right? You gave us quite a scare." Christie paused in applying salve to the torn places on Evangeline's right palm in order to watch her new friend's face.

Evangeline smiled and nodded. "Yes. I'm fine. Nothing but a few scrapes and some wounded pride." She rolled her eyes. "It was my own fault for sticking my nose where it didn't belong." She touched Christie's knee with her left hand. "I'm sorry I worried everyone."

The two girls had secreted themselves in their room, Evangeline having declared that she needed to wash up and change after her ordeal, and Christie insisting she could handle the minor doctoring required without male oversight.

Christie dabbed a final bit of salve on the padded area beneath Evangeline's thumb. The touch stung, even with her careful ministrations. Evangeline winced but forced her hand to remain still until Christie had finished.

"I've never seen Seth so worked up," Christie said as she wrapped a linen bandage around Evangeline's hand. "I feared his lungs would seize."

Evangeline's heart warmed at the young woman's concern for her brother. Maybe in time, she and Christie would be sisters in truth. Wouldn't that be marvelous? Christie and Seth living here, she and Logan living across the way. She just needed to find a lady for Zach in order to complete the perfect fairy tale.

After Christie tied off the bandage and glanced up, Evangeline smiled and sidled closer to her on the edge of the bed. "I'm glad you're looking out for him. He doesn't like to be mothered, but it doesn't hurt to have someone ready to fight on his behalf should the need arise."

Red colored Christie's cheeks. "You're right about the mothering. He got mulish when I suggested he leave the searching to Zach." She nibbled her bottom lip as if debating whether or not to speak further, then bravely met Evangeline's eyes. "I might have said something about him not doing you any good if he fell ill along the way," she confessed. "He didn't take too kindly to that."

Evangeline chuckled. "No, I don't suppose he did." She leaned close and nudged Christie's shoulder, careful to keep her lips in full view. "A man's pride does tend to be a mite touchy. I've learned never to cast doubt on their abilities. Haranguing them over their pigheadedness, however, is perfectly acceptable."

Christie laughed, and Evangeline joined in. Mercy, but she loved having a sister. Another woman to confide in was such a blessing. And speaking of confidences . . .

Evangeline darted a glance toward the door, ensuring it was closed.

Christie's brow furrowed. "What is it?"

Evangeline felt her own cheeks warm as she struggled to meet Christie's gaze. Keeping her voice so low it would be impossible for anyone to hear—and thanking the Lord for a friend who didn't require any volume at all—Evangeline let the secret she'd been carrying inside all evening finally burst free.

"Logan kissed me," she mouthed, barely more than a whisper giving life to the words.

Christie's green eyes widened before crinkling joyfully as her gaping mouth curved into an excited smile. She bounced the mattress with her enthusiasm as she clasped Evangeline's unbandaged hand. "Was it wonderful?"

Evangeline grinned and nodded. "I've never been kissed before," she admitted, "so I don't have anything to compare it to, but I don't know how it could have been any better." Once again she felt Logan's strong arms circle her waist, the light touch of his fingers in her hair, the way her whole body hummed with excitement as his lips pressed against hers.

Oh, dear. It occurred to her that she might have actually hummed *out loud*. So much for impressing him with her sophistication.

Though, if memory served, Logan hadn't seemed particularly distracted by her random noises. His focus had been quite extraordinary, under the circumstances.

Evangeline grabbed a small book off her bedside table and fanned her face. Goodness. Was Seth warming dinner with a bonfire out there? She swore the temperature in this room had just increased ten degrees.

"I've never been kissed, either," Christie confided, leaning her head close. Evangeline set the book aside. "Never wanted to be. Not by any of the men who came around the house looking for Earl."

She glanced toward the door. She didn't say anything, but she didn't really have to. Evangeline could read the longing on her face. The new men in her life were nothing like the old ones. Especially a particular fellow with blond hair, blue eyes, and a penchant for cooking. Not to mention reading. Evangeline had lost count of how many times she'd come home in the afternoon to find Christie and Seth sitting quietly together in the parlor, each with a book in hand. Lately, they'd even been spotted sharing the settee.

Evangeline squeezed Christie's hand to regain her attention. "If it's the *right* man, a kiss can make your heart sing."

"Is that what happened with you and Logan?" Christie grinned shyly. "Did your heart sing?"

"Oh, yes." Evangeline turned sheepish. "So much so that I fear I sang aloud, too. I'm praying he didn't notice."

Christie giggled. "I've seen the way Logan looks at you. You could sing the contents of an entire hymnal, and I don't think he would care."

Evangeline ducked her head, but she couldn't stop the pleased smile stretching wide across her face. Was Christie right? Had Logan come to care for her enough over the last few weeks to overlook her idiosyncrasies?

Or more importantly, her snooping?

A knock on the door scattered her thoughts.

"Supper's ready, ladies," Seth announced.

Evangeline released Christie's hand and pushed to her feet. "Be right there."

Christie caught on immediately and stood. She crossed to the mirror above Evangeline's bureau to check her hair and smooth her bodice a final time before following Evangeline to the kitchen.

When they entered the room, Seth's eyes immediately found Christie, even though his gaze had to dodge around his sister to find his intended target. Only when Zach's gruff voice broke the silence to ask if Evangeline was feeling better did Seth's attention shift guiltily to his sister.

"Yes, Evie. How are the hands?" he asked as he jerked into motion after having frozen mid-ladle when the girls had entered.

Well, when *Christie* had entered. He dipped the ladle into the stockpot on the stove and dished out a healthy portion of vegetable soup into a bowl.

Evangeline grinned as she moved to the table. "Much better, thank you. Christie has a gentle touch."

The ladle slipped from Seth's hand and banged against the side of the pot. Evangeline stifled a giggle.

"Here, let me help." Christie glided over to the stove and retrieved the next bowl from the pile stacked on the cabinet beside Seth. His neck reddened, but he quickly shifted sideways to make room for her.

Evangeline turned to share a teasing grin with Zach only to find him scowling. She rounded the table and slid her left arm through his right.

"What has you so out of sorts? I think it's nice to see the two of them getting along so well."

His scowl softened, but his eyes glowed with an intensity that made her stomach cramp with foreboding. "You know I've only ever wanted you and Seth to be happy, right?"

"Of course." She peered into his face, distressed by the shadows in his eyes. "What are you trying to tell me, Zach?"

He let out a breath and glanced toward the window. "Nothing, I just . . ." He pulled his arm from her loose hold and stepped closer to the table, grasping the back of the chair in front of him. His knuckles whitened. "Things are changin' around here, is all." He pitched his voice low to ensure it didn't carry farther than Evangeline's ears. "And I want to make sure they're changin' for the better."

Always the protector. Zach might try to hide his big heart behind growls and scowls and curmudgeonly antics, but it drove every decision he made and every action he took, whether he'd admit it or not.

Evangeline slid her arm back through his and laid her head on his sturdy shoulder. "I hate to break it to you, big brother, but Seth and I aren't kids anymore. We don't need you to protect us from the world and all the possible problems it might send our way. You've taught us how to stand on our own. Perhaps it's time you let us do that."

He stiffened and didn't respond for a long minute. Worried she'd somehow hurt his feelings, Evangeline lifted her head and peered at his face. But before she could ask him anything, he released the chair back and straightened away from her.

"You might be right."

At the hiss of boiling water, Logan wadded a bandana in his hand and moved the coffeepot from the rack atop the campfire. He pulled the lid open, dumped a heaping scoop of coffee grounds into the steaming water, swirled it around a bit to stir, then set it aside to brew. Next he collected the cast iron skillet he'd layered with bacon slices earlier and moved it onto the fire. Bacon, a tin of beans, and coffee. A man's meal. Rustic. Rugged. And bland as could be.

Thank heavens he'd found the corn bread muffins and honey Eva had left behind when her brothers snatched her away. He'd already eaten two. Only extreme self-discipline had allowed him to set the remaining two aside until after he'd cooked up his rations for the night. But he knew they were there. He could hear them calling to him from the basket, begging to be devoured. But he'd waited this long; he could wait a little longer. He'd use one to soak up the bacon grease and crumble it into the beans. Then he'd slather the last one with honey and savor it for dessert.

Logan swallowed the saliva pooling in his mouth and used a fork to turn the bacon. The grease sizzled and popped, and a droplet jumped from the pan onto his wrist. He jerked his arm back and rubbed the scalded spot against his pants.

Eva wasn't even here, and he was *still* off his game.

He'd lost count of how many times he'd relived the kiss they'd shared in the cellar. The feel of her in his arms. The sweetness of her lips. Not even the honey could compare.

Yet there was bitter to go with the sweet. She'd found the letter from the land office. Had seen his full name. Could even now be sharing what she'd learned with her brothers.

Logan reached for the coffeepot, gave it another swirling stir, then turned the bacon. For seven years he'd been working toward finding justice for his family. Promises made to his mother might never be fulfilled because he'd let himself get distracted by a pretty face and sunny disposition.

His gaze drifted from the bright orange of the fire to the gray outline of his cabin. *His* cabin? Ha! It was hers. All hers. The layout, the design, even the stupid ladder to the cellar he'd spent the last two hours installing instead of eating supper like a normal person. The entire thing was for her.

Everywhere he looked, he recalled her delight, from the first day when he'd cleared the foundation and she'd danced around, building imaginary porches and parlors. Porches and parlors he'd constructed into reality. The wooden studs seemed to have absorbed her warmth, her joyous nature, because every room conjured a memory of her smile. So much so that he found himself lingering within the unfinished walls at the end of the day in order to feel closer to her. To ease the loneliness in his soul. He'd even set up his bedroll in the front room and fell asleep each night dreaming of her beside him.

Logan's jaw clenched as he pulled the skillet from the fire. He opened the coffeepot and added a dash of cold water from his canteen to settle the grounds.

That was what he needed. To settle. To focus on the business of serving up justice before the woman under his skin served him up to her brothers on a silver platter.

Snatching a strip of bacon, he shoved half the length into his mouth and chewed as if the act could somehow banish Eva from his mind. It didn't work, of course, because the salty bacon drippings reminded him of her corn muffins. Before he knew what he was about, he had the bread crumbled into the pan and spooned into his mouth. He was a sorry case, all right.

Then Shamgar nickered and accomplished what Logan had been helpless to do all evening—focus his mind.

Hooves plodded against earth, leather creaked, and a lantern bobbed in the dinge of twilight. Somewhat blinded by the fire, Logan stepped out of its glow and into the darker recesses of the unfinished cabin. Slowly, he slid his pistol from the holster at his side and took aim at the approaching horse and rider. The glare of the lantern masked the rider's identity, but Logan could think of only one man with reason to challenge him tonight.

"If that's you, Hamilton," he shouted, "you better declare yourself before my trigger finger gets twitchy."

CHAPTER

21

"Easy, Logan. It's just me."

"Seth?" Not the Hamilton Logan had expected. He lowered his weapon and stepped out of the shadows. "What are you doing here? It's near dark." A terrifying thought jabbed his brain. "Is it Eva?" He surged forward, his long strides consuming the distance between him and his visitor. His heart pounded. "Was she hurt worse than we thought?"

Seth batted away his concern with a wave of his hand. "Evie's fine."

Thank heaven. Logan's pulse calmed, and his pace slowed as he reached Seth.

"She and Christie turned in early." The wind shifted, and some of the smoke from Logan's campfire wafted over. Seth lifted a hand to his mouth and coughed. "Christie's the reason"— *cough*—"I'm here."

Logan took the reins of Seth's horse. "There's a path behind the house that leads to a creek. Head that way while I tend your horse and douse the fire." The last thing he needed was for Eva's brother to die of a lung seizure on his watch.

Seth managed a nod between coughs and swung down to the ground. "Thanks."

Logan led the roan gelding over to where Shamgar was tethered, then rescued his coffeepot and skillet before kicking dirt onto his cook fire. He considered dumping the contents of his canteen on the coals, but he'd need to reignite the fire after his guest departed. Having a few embers banked beneath the sand would save time.

He shoved two more bites of bacon-bean-muffin crumble into his mouth, then downed a healthy swig of water from the canteen before striding toward the creek. Halfway there, he stopped, turned, and jogged back to his campsite. Coffee. Seth had downed the stuff as if it were a magical healing elixir the day his asthma attack hit at the homestead. Drinking some now couldn't hurt. Logan snagged the pot and his tin cup and resumed his march to the creek.

He found Seth crouching at the edge of the water, scooping a handful up to his mouth.

"I brought coffee," Logan said.

Seth turned, his eyes going straight to the pot. He pushed to his feet. "Great. Thanks."

Logan filled the tin cup nearly to the brim, then handed it over with a warning. "It's fresh."

Seth nodded but still brought it straight to his mouth and downed a swallow that must have scalded his tongue and throat. Logan winced in sympathy as Seth's jaw tensed and the tendons stood out from his neck. But he went back for seconds and thirds before slowing down.

After the fourth swig, he inhaled a slow, deep breath. When no coughing or wheezing ensued, he lowered the cup to a more relaxed position and focused on Logan.

"What did you learn in Ben Franklin?" Seth demanded. "About Christie?"

Wow. He must really be sweet on the girl. He hadn't been able to go a full four hours before tracking Logan down and quizzing him about that vague reference he'd made earlier.

Logan grinned. "You've got it bad, don't you?"

Seth raised a brow. "Almost as bad as you."

That sobered him up. Truth had a tendency to do that to a fellow. Logan's smile slid from his face as he eyed his companion. "I'm afraid I don't have much to tell. Not yet, anyway."

"But you've got something, and something's more than what I've got." Seth blew out a breath, plunked his coffee cup atop a tall, flat rock, then paced down to the creek's edge and back. "Whoever tried to kill Christie is still out there. For all I know, he's plotting a second attempt. And I'm trapped inside a box, powerless to do anything to help her beyond keeping her in the box with me. That's no way to win a war, holing up and waiting for the enemy to charge. Shoot, I don't even know who my enemy is! He could walk right up to the front door, and I wouldn't know it was him until it was too late."

Logan kicked at a loose stone with the toe of his boot. "I don't know who he is either, but I know who he ain't."

Seth stopped mid-pace and whipped his head around. "Who?"

"Her stepfather. Earl."

Seth frowned. "Explain."

Logan launched the stone into the creek with a swing of his leg, then set the coffeepot on the same knee-high rock holding Seth's cup. "I've been worried about the girl, too," he began.

"Her name's Christie."

Logan held up a hand in apology. "Right. Christie." Seth's scowl didn't lighten much at Logan's use of Miss Gilliam's given name. Sheesh. Logan was starting to see the family resemblance after all. When riled, all three Hamiltons glowered with identical ferocity. "I pulled her from the river, remember? I've got a stake in her well-being, too."

"Just tell me what happened in Ben Franklin."

"Something about Miss Gilliam's explanation of what happened that day never sat right with me. I don't think she lied about anything," Logan hurried to assure Seth when his brows started dipping into a deep V, "but I think she knows more than she let on. So I decided to do some digging on my own. Subtle digging, of course. Didn't want to alert anyone of her whereabouts or my connection to her. I focused on the one lead I already had—whiskey."

Seth's eyes glittered. "You tracked down the bootlegger."

Logan nodded. "Spent a couple weeks chumming with the locals at the Seven Ponies until I managed to get myself invited to a jug party behind the livery. The jug they passed around had a brown ribbon tied through the finger hole."

Seth crossed his arms and gave a grunt of understanding. Color-coded jugs were Earl's calling card.

Glossing over his hours of poker playing—no need to reveal his skill in that arena just yet—Logan filled Seth in on the rest of the pertinent details. "I mentioned I'd be interested in procuring a jug of my own. The livery owner took my money and arranged a pickup for the next afternoon. Hence my overnight stay."

"And . . . ?"

"And I staked out the meeting place and waited for the deliveryman to show."

Seth uncrossed his arms. "How do you know it was Earl? He could have hired someone else to make the run."

Logan shook his head. "Don't think so. He matched Miss Gilliam's description. Bushy beard, older, lazy demeanor, carried a burlap sack to hide the whiskey. It was Earl. And he isn't the man I saw at the river. Of that, I'm positive."

"So we're no closer to unraveling who wanted her dead." Seth snatched up his coffee cup and downed the remainder of the brew before slamming the tin vessel back onto the rock.

"Maybe not."

Seth peered at Logan expectantly, a tiny spark of hope lighting his eyes.

"You've spoken to her more than I have, but she gave me the impression that she didn't go out much. That Earl kept her under his thumb most of the time."

Seth nodded. "Christie's never mentioned any friends, but that doesn't surprise me. Ben Franklin's not her home. She moved there after her mother married Earl. To keep her deafness secret from her stepfather, she would've had to hide it from the townsfolk as well and make everyone believe she's a simpleton. These last few weeks have been the first days in years that she's been free to be herself." He gripped the back of his neck. "I can't stand to think about what her life must have been like before. I've watched her devour books as if she's starving for knowledge, and she can discuss the most complicated ideology like a trained scholar. Not to mention total a column of numbers in her head faster than I can manage with pencil and paper. She's brilliant. Going back to that life, being trapped in that lie again—it would destroy her. But she can't hide away forever, either. I won't let her trade one prison for another. She deserves to live a rich, full life. And she can't do that if the man who tried to kill her is free to try again."

"Well, she needs to stay hidden awhile longer. There are handbills posted in the Seven Ponies about a missing girl. Someone's looking for her. Might be Earl, might be the man who tried to drown her. Can't be sure which. Posters say to report information to the town marshal. His is the only name on the flier."

Seth frowned. "If the man who attacked her went back to check the river, he'd find her gone. He wouldn't know for sure she wasn't dead, but he'd have plenty of reason to suspect she survived. If he's the type to tie up loose ends, he'll want to discover what happened to her."

"Exactly. So we need to stay ahead of the game." Logan paced toward the stream, then pivoted and strode back with purpose. "We need to probe Christie for more information. Details about exactly where she was and what she did prior to her attack." He moved closer to Seth and put a hand on the other man's shoulder. "She trusts you. She'll open up to you."

Seth wagged his head and shrugged off Logan's hand. "I can't just interrogate her without giving her context," he groused. "I'll have to tell her about your investigation. Explain that we want to help her."

Logan stiffened. "I don't know if that's wise. What if she balks? She might get angry about our interference and clam up. Or worse—leave."

Seth froze, that last threat hitting the mark. He turned slowly, his eyes sad, his face haggard, but his jaw was as firm as the rocks lining the creek bed. "I can't let my fear of losing her keep me from doing the right thing." The quiet timbre of his voice heightened the conviction of his words. "Secrets create distance. Just look at Christie's life before. No friends. No close relationships with anyone. All because of the secrets she kept. I won't perpetuate that cycle with her. I care about her too much not to be honest with her about everything." He looked away when he said that last word. *Everything.* He had other hidden truths he was now willing to bring to light. Because he didn't want anything to impede the closeness he was building with Miss Gilliam.

A situation uncomfortably similar to Logan's own relationship with Eva. Maybe her finding that letter in the cellar was a good thing. A chance for him to come clean. To test her trust, her loyalty. Seth was man enough to take the risk. Logan could do no less. Only his risk was infinitely greater, for he wasn't simply *hunting* a threat, he *was* the threat.

But that was a problem for tomorrow.

"I think the key to uncovering the man who tried to kill Miss Gilliam lies in the book she found," Logan said.

Seth's brow crinkled. "Book?"

"Yes. Remember she said that the only thing different about her deliveries that day was that someone left a book instead of money in exchange for the moonshine."

A thoughtful look crossed Seth's face as he bent to retrieve the coffee cup and poured himself another serving. "You think the book is the key because it was the only thing out of the ordinary that day? Seems like a bit of a stretch."

"Not when another book made a suspicious appearance today after Earl delivered my whiskey."

The coffeepot clattered unsteadily back onto the rock. Seth straightened. "Another book?"

Logan nodded. "After Earl dropped off the jug in the schoolhouse privy, he didn't just leave. He walked through the empty schoolhouse, and when he emerged, his burlap sack had something slender and rectangular inside."

"A book."

"Yep." Logan propped his foot on the table rock and leaned forward, bracing his forearm across his thigh. "Two books in suspicious circumstances can't be a coincidence. You need to find out where she picked up the book. Was it at the schoolhouse? What does she know about the local schoolmaster? He was dressed much more formally than the man I saw at the river, and he had a fancy black buggy instead of a beat-up buckboard, but his build was similar. Bulky. Overweight."

Logan closed his eyes, trying to recall details about the horse hitched to the buggy. It had been black, but had there been white socks like the animal pulling the wagon at the river? He hadn't considered the possibility until just now. He'd been focused more on matching the man than the animals.

He growled in frustration. "I can't recall enough details to match the horse pulling the buggy to the team hitched to the wagon. It was black, like the second horse, but that's all I remember." He jerked upright. "I should have paid closer attention."

Seth frowned. "I thought Earl was alone at the school. Was the teacher there, too?"

"No." Logan waved a dismissive hand in the air, still disgruntled with himself for missing such a vital detail. "I spied him more than an hour earlier when he left the schoolhouse."

"Then you couldn't have known there was a reason to suspect him."

Logan fisted his hands. "It's my job to notice details! All of them."

Seth raised a brow. "You a lawman or something?"

That surprised a laugh out of him. "No." He shook his head and grabbed hold of his rioting emotions. *Don't get sloppy now, partner. Play it cool.* "Just a businessman. I have an easier time closing deals when I pick up on nuances my competitors miss. Hence my habit of collecting details."

Seth stared a little longer than Logan would have preferred, but eventually he let it go. "So I'll ask Christie about the book and about the schoolmaster. Anything else?"

Logan shrugged. "Start with that, then follow your instincts."

"That what you do?"

"Usually."

Only with Eva, his instincts seemed to be running in such varied directions, it was hard to know which path to follow.

I can't let my fear of losing her keep me from doing the right thing. Seth's words jumped back into the forefront of Logan's mind. Challenging. Prompting.

Maybe the time for secrets had passed.

CHAPTER

22

"I'm heading out for a walk," Evangeline called to Seth as she dashed through the kitchen toward the back door.

Christie had taken a book to the parlor just a few minutes ago, so Evangeline figured her brother wouldn't care if she ducked out earlier than usual. She'd flown through her chores this morning, an odd mixture of guilt and anticipation urging her on.

She needed to confess to her snooping and apologize to Logan. Then quiz him about what she'd discovered. And yes, she supposed those two agendas were at odds with each other, but that was where she found herself. Sorry she'd acted without permission, yet not sorry she'd uncovered a new facet of the man who was slowly making himself at home in her heart. A man who just might kiss her again if he forgave her breach of trust.

As she imagined Logan's strong arms sliding around her waist, Evangeline's feet floated over the wooden floorboards, her mind bobbing above in a dreamy haze.

"Wait, Evie." Seth skittered through the kitchen doorway and obliterated her lovely mist. "Don't go yet."

She frowned. "Why not?"

Was he trying to keep her away from Logan? Because he had absolutely no right. She should have known he'd try to pull some ridiculous big brother overprotective nonsense after she got herself stuck in the cellar yesterday. Well, he could demand all he wanted, but she was a grown woman, fully of age, independent—

"Something's happened with Christie's situation."

Her indignation evaporated.

She released the doorknob and hurried toward him. "What? When? Does Zach know?"

Seth nodded. "I filled him in last night."

Evangeline's brow scrunched. "Last night?"

"After I paid Logan a visit."

"You went out to Logan's cabin? Alone?" Evangeline stumbled and had to grab the table edge for support.

Seth wasn't a hermit. He traveled to church once a week and occasionally went to town for supplies, but he rarely went anywhere by himself. She or Zach usually found an excuse to accompany him. Just in case.

"I'm not an invalid, Evie. I can take a ride in the evening should I wish."

"Of course you can." She pulled an exasperated face, knowing better than to show anything that could be construed as pity. "I'd no more try to dictate your comings and goings than I would let you dictate mine." A little reminder about her own autonomy never hurt, either. "I'm just surprised, is all. I didn't think you and Logan were all that friendly."

"We're not." And judging by the grumpy look on his face, he wasn't terribly interested in changing that status.

Well, tough turnips. He and Zach would just have to get used to Logan being part of the family, because she fully intended to keep him.

If he'd have her, of course.

Which he would, right? An honorable man didn't kiss a woman unless he had intentions.

"I got wind of Logan's investigations on Christie's behalf in Ben Franklin," Seth said, effectively banishing her romantic doubts and focusing her attention where it belonged—on her friend. "I decided to ask him some questions."

Logan had been searching for Christie's attacker? Why hadn't he told her? Then again, he hadn't told her his last name either, so she shouldn't be surprised by his secrecy. That didn't keep her heart from aching about it, though, as she followed Seth down the hall to the parlor.

Not that she didn't have her own secrets, she supposed. If one were to split hairs, Logan didn't know her last name, either. Not her real, born-into-it, last name. And she hadn't yet confessed to her snooping, so that was another secret in her cache.

Why beholdest thou the mote that is in thy brother's eye, but considerest not the beam that is in thine own eye? Thou hypocrite, first cast out the beam out of thine own eye; and then shalt thou see clearly to cast out the mote out of thy brother's eye.

Evangeline pressed her lips into a tight line as she took a seat on the settee. The problem with memorizing scripture was that it rose up to prod her conscience at the most inconvenient times. Nothing like having Jesus call her a hypocrite to slap down her indignation over Logan's infractions.

"You both look so grim," Christie said, her voice shaking slightly. "Have I done something wrong?"

"No."

"Absolutely not."

Christie's face turned side to side and her forehead crinkled as she tried to take in Evangeline and Seth's synchronous denials from her position in the chair across from the sofa.

Seth scooted to the edge of the cushion, leaned forward, and reached for Christie's hand. Her gaze locked on his. Slowly, she extended her hand and fit it into his.

"We want you to be safe," Seth said as he rubbed his thumb over the back of Christie's hand. "And to help you."

"You *are* helping me." Christie dodged a look to Evangeline before turning back to Seth. "You've opened your home, taken me in." She glanced down at her lap then forced her chin back up. "You haven't looked down on me because of my deafness or my connection to moonshiners." Her lashes blinked rapidly, and Evangeline felt her own eyes moisten in sympathy. "I owe you my very life."

"I'm glad you feel that way." Seth smiled at her, but the effort didn't seem to comfort Christie.

The poor girl squirmed in her seat, obviously sensing the growing tension. Evangeline felt it too and gripped her hands together in her lap.

Seth rested his elbows on his knees as he brought his free hand around to cover the top of Christie's. Her delicate hand was now fully encased in both of his. "I want to ask you a few questions about the day you were attacked."

She frowned. "Why? I've already told you everything."

"Not everything."

Christie stiffened at Seth's gentle indictment.

Evangeline sat a little straighter. It took every ounce of self-control not to interrupt with her own questions, but she was just here to be informed and to offer moral support to whichever adopted sibling needed it most.

"Tell me about the book you collected." Seth's eyes held apologies even as his jaw firmed into a determined line.

Christie tugged her hand free of Seth's hold and leaned away from him. "It was just a book."

Seth didn't straighten. He left his hands dangling in front of him, bridged off his knees, as if begging her to reconnect. "But you read it, didn't you?"

Evangeline wished Christie could hear the tenderness in his tone. If so, she'd recognize how torn he was, how much he cared about her, how much he wanted to help.

"I've seen how you are with books," he teased. "You can't resist peeking between the covers."

Christie bit her lip and turned her face away, refusing to answer or even continue the conversation. But she hadn't left the room. She wanted to stay, yet something was scaring her. What?

Seth slid off the settee and knelt on the floor. Like a gentle predator, he pursued her, crouching at the side of her chair. He stroked her cheek, his fingertips trailing her hairline before softly turning her face back toward his.

Evangeline's breath caught at the shimmer of tears in her friend's eyes. Her heart demanded she go to Christie to offer what comfort she could, but her head recognized that Seth was the one she needed right now.

Christie's chin trembled. "You don't understand."

"Then tell me," Seth said. "Let me help you."

She bit her lip and looked at the ceiling.

Seth stroked her cheek, bringing her attention back to his face. "Who left the book for you?" he urged. "The schoolmaster?"

Christie reared back.

Schoolmaster? Evangeline frowned. From Ben Franklin? Was this what Logan had been investigating?

"Tell me, sweetheart." Seth captured Christie's hand. "Please. We can help you."

She shook her head. "It's too dangerous. If he finds out you know his secret . . ." She bit her lip. "He might try to hurt you, too. Or Evie. I can't let that happen."

"There's no way for him to know what you've told us," Seth said. "He doesn't even know where you are."

Christie pressed her lips closed, unconvinced.

Seth planted himself directly in front of her chair and focused in on her. Evangeline knew that look. The one that wrangled the truth out of her no matter how determined she was to hold on to a secret. Christie didn't stand a chance.

"All right," Seth said, his tone sharper. Christie might not be able to hear the difference, but she must have sensed it in his posture or facial expression, for her eyes widened, and she grasped the chair arms for support. "Let's say he does find out where you've been staying and who you've been staying with. What's to keep him from assuming you already told us everything? He couldn't afford to take that risk. So whether you tell us or not, the threat is the same. The only difference is that if you tell us what you know, we have more ammunition for fighting him."

Christie's shoulders slumped. "Yes," she whispered. "The book was Mr. Benson's."

"And did you read it?"

She ducked her head and nodded.

When she looked up again, Seth asked, "Where were you when you read it? Could Benson have seen you?"

"I don't know. I waited until I was halfway home, in the cover of some trees, before I opened it. Usually Benson attends church, putting on a righteous show for the parents of his students, so I thought it would be safe." A fierce look entered her eyes. She leaned forward, and her hands slapped down over his wrists, her fingers latching into place. "I had to take the risk, Seth." Her knuckles whitened as her grip on his arms tightened. "Earl always keeps the ledgers locked in a metal box under his bed. This was the first time I'd been trusted with transporting one of them. I couldn't waste the opportunity."

"So Earl and Benson are partners."

Evangeline recognized the intense expression on her brother's face. He was pondering, fitting things together, discerning patterns, and plotting likelihoods, just like he did when researching a new investment opportunity.

Evangeline was still trying to make sense of the ledgers and why Christie was so keen to read them, while Seth had already jumped to what they signified. No wonder their family had enjoyed increased financial security over the last five years. He was always two steps ahead.

"Not true partners," Christie qualified. "Mr. Benson has his own barter system set up with Earl. He gets one free jug of moonshine a week in exchange for tallying the accounts. Earl gives him supply receipts and order lists, and Mr. Benson organizes everything into tidy ledger rows."

Seth's brows scrunched together. "I don't understand. Why would you care about the ledgers?"

"Because they don't just encompass the moonshine accounts," Christie intoned as if it were the most scandalous secret. "They include the household accounts as well."

Seth shook his head. "I still don't under—"

"I'm trying to find my baby brother," Christie blurted.

Evangeline nearly toppled the settee as she grabbed the sofa arm and jerked forward. "What?"

Christie must have caught the movement in her peripheral vision, for she glanced away from Seth and met Evangeline's gaze. "My mother had a child before she died. A little boy. Archie." Her voice cracked, and she stopped to take a couple breaths before continuing. "I haven't seen him for two years.

When Mama died, Archie was only a year old, not even fully weaned. Earl didn't want to be bothered with a baby and didn't trust me to tend him, so he sent him away. To a sister, I think, but I can't be sure. Earl just took Archie away one day and returned without him. Stole my brother from me and told me to forget him. As if I ever would."

Christie turned back to Seth. "What if Earl's sister is as cruel as he is? I can't bear the thought of that sweet little boy suffering. He's only three. I don't want him under Earl's control, either, but if I could learn his location, I could run away from Earl and track him down. That's why I needed to examine the ledger. Earl has to be sending money somewhere for Archie's upkeep. If I could find an address or even a bank name, I would have a place to start."

Seth bent his neck and dropped a soft kiss on one of the hands gripping his wrists. Then he lifted his face and met Christie's dewy gaze. "We'll find him, Christie. I swear to you. Whatever it takes, we'll find him."

A small sob escaped Christie's chest, and an empathetic tear rolled down Evangeline's cheek. Memories of Hamilton besieged her as determination filled her breast. Christie's brother was still alive. He could be found, restored to her. Evangeline would do whatever she could to make that happen.

"Thank you." Christie folded over onto Seth, fitting her cheek next to his. "Thank you. Thank you. Thank you."

Evangeline stood, thinking to grant them some privacy, but Seth stopped her with a look. Gently, he pulled his head away from Christie's and helped her to her feet. She released her grip on his wrists, and he wrapped his arm around her waist.

"I have one more question for you, Christie," he said.

She sniffed a bit, then nodded.

"Why would Benson attack you if you were just looking at Earl's ledgers? That makes no sense to me."

Christie's face hardened. "Because he didn't leave me Earl's ledger. He accidentally left one of his own."

Evangeline met her brother's puzzled look, then both of them turned back to Christie.

"The scoundrel's embezzling money from the school board."

CHAPTER

23

Logan stood in front of the door he'd barged through as a kid and shuffled his feet. Then pulled off his hat. Then cleared his throat.

For pity's sake, man. Just knock on the door. It's not as if you're asking her to marry you or anything. You're simply paying a call.

At her home. With at least one brother in residence. The other, thankfully, was out working the sorghum. Logan had checked. Still, this was the first time he'd called at the Hamilton homestead of his own volition. Technically he'd attempted a call last night, but he'd never actually dismounted from his horse in all the excitement surrounding Eva's disappearance, so that didn't count. He hadn't had time to get nervous.

Staring at the back door with a covey of flushed quail flailing about in his gut, Logan couldn't help wishing for some other emergency to sweep in and save him. He much preferred having her on *his* turf, away from her brothers, but he'd grown impatient waiting for her to show up at his place today. And really, waiting was for cowards. What kind of man forced his woman to do all the courtship work? Men were the hunters, the pursuers. Seth and Zacharias were aware of his presence, so there was no point in hiding any longer. Time to lay claim to his woman, to make his intent clear.

An intent that had only become clear to him last night. Oh, it had been sneaking up on him for a while. It wasn't like he hadn't seen it coming. He just hadn't expected it to *whoosh* down on him like a twister, knocking his feet out from under him and banging his limp carcass against rocks and trees until finally spitting him out at the feet of truth.

He was in love with her. If he lost her . . . well, it would hurt a heck of a lot more than that twister ride.

"Ya gonna stand there all day or actually thump knuckles to wood?"

Logan lurched sideways, his hat nearly falling through his fingers as his heart rammed his rib cage. "Hamilton!"

Good gravy. He hadn't even heard him approach. His nemesis stood not five feet behind him, just off the porch—smirking. So much for Logan's keen observation skills.

"I didn't hear you come up," Logan said.

Was it possible for a smirk to get smirkier? If so, Zacharias Hamilton had mastered the maneuver. "Countin' the grain lines in the wood?"

He was hilarious, too.

Logan shrugged. "Everyone's got a hobby."

Was that a flare of warmth in Hamilton's steely eyes? Heaven help them if they actually started liking each other.

Not that it would stop Logan from doing what must be done, but burgeoning respect between them could make the final show-down less of an ordeal for Eva—something he found mattered more to him with each passing day.

"Well, if you're willing to forfeit your counting, you can follow me inside." Hamilton pointed to something up on the roof. "Seth called me in, so I imagine something interestin' developed during his conversation with Christie."

Logan craned his head back to view the roof. A small blue flag undulated gently in the breeze. Something else he'd failed to notice. Of course, he'd ridden in from the opposite side, but still—his pride was taking significant hits today.

"We rigged a pulley between the window of Seth's room and the chimney years back so he could signal if he ever needed help. Red is raised in an emergency. Blue just means come when you can."

Clever.

Logan tucked his chin back into place and turned to regard the man who'd stolen his father's home and life. Gall didn't surge up his throat to choke him as it had the first time he'd spotted Hamilton on his father's property. Nor did hatred throb in his veins. A dull, resentful ache still permeated his chest, but even that was more a glowing ember of old hurt than the blazing fire of justice that had fueled him for so long.

He was going soft. And what was worse, he couldn't seem to dredge up more than a twinge of outrage over that sorry state of affairs.

"So I take it Seth told you about his little foray into my camp last night?"

"Yep." Hamilton climbed the porch steps, but instead of brushing past Logan and throwing open the door, he paused and held out his hand. "I misjudged you. What you're doin' for Christie . . . it's a good thing."

Logan stared at the proffered hand, stunned. If Hamilton knew his true intentions, that hand would be balled into a fist, swinging for Logan's jaw.

Yet he couldn't just ignore the gesture. So he slowly fit his palm to Hamilton's, forcing his face to remain bland as his stomach churned. The contact was blessedly brief, neither of them wanting to prolong the awkwardness, but shaking hands with the enemy still rattled him.

His enemy had become an ally. Miss Gilliam needed assistance, and it seemed Seth wasn't the only Hamilton brother invested in her well-being.

Hamilton yanked the door wide and marched into the kitchen. "You comin'?"

Logan followed, taking a moment to close the door behind him. His mama had scolded him so many times about leaving that door open, he swore her voice lingered on the very walls as part of the glue that held the decorative paper in place. She'd probably fuss about his boots, too, though he'd ensured they carried no mud when he dismounted earlier.

It wasn't his mother's voice he heard echoing down the hall, however, but Eva's.

"We have to report this to the marshal in Ben Franklin."

"No!" That from Miss Gilliam. "You don't understand. They think I'm feeble-minded. They won't believe my word against his. Not without proof. He dines with the mayor and his wife every other Saturday, heads the missionary committee at church, and lets the Populists use the schoolhouse for political meetings. He's the town's favored son. I'm just the bootlegger's idiot stepdaughter."

Logan caught the last half of that speech in person as he stepped inside the parlor. Seth stood beside the overwrought Miss Gilliam, a supportive hand on her shoulder, while Eva stood in front of a small sofa, a mulish look on her face.

"Then we go to the sheriff in Cooper," Eva insisted. "Benson's a criminal. You won't be safe until he's behind bars."

Logan moved past Zacharias and approached Eva from the

side. "But if she reveals herself without proof," he intoned softly, "she'll be in more danger than ever."

Eva's gaze jerked toward him. "Logan? Where did you come from?"

"Found him counting lines in the wood grain of the back door," Zacharias supplied helpfully.

Eva frowned. "What?"

Logan shot Hamilton a glare. "Ignore him." He turned back to Eva. "Did Christie remember something about the school-master?" He glanced toward Seth to include him in the question.

"You were right about the book," Seth explained. "It was a ledger. Benson apparently helps Earl with his bookkeeping. Only instead of leaving one of Earl's ledgers for Christie to retrieve, he accidentally left one of his own. One that showed the creative accounting methods he's using to pocket school board funds."

"See? He's a criminal." Eva, bless her innocent heart. She probably thought all lawmen were honest and chivalrous and would do everything in their power to protect a female in trouble.

Logan knew different. As did Seth and Zacharias, judging by the matching scowls on their faces. Even an honest lawman couldn't do anything without proof. The ledger was gone, no doubt retrieved by Benson when he attacked Miss Gilliam, and if she never saw her attacker, she couldn't level a charge of assault against him.

Logan couldn't testify that Benson was the man he saw dump her in the river, either. They'd been too far away to identify him with certainty. All he could say was that the men were of the same height and build. Maybe if they found the wagon or matched the horses to ones Benson owned, but even that would be circumstantial. And judging by the shiny black buggy the schoolmaster drove, he'd probably borrowed the rickety wagon Logan had seen. Most likely from Earl.

Logan cupped Eva's shoulder and waited for her to turn her vivid, adorably mismatched eyes on him. "The sheriff can't arrest a man with no proof of wrongdoing. And if Miss Gilliam comes out of hiding to accuse Benson"—he eyed Seth—"he'll know where she's been staying and who's been helping her." He rubbed Eva's arm, trying to soothe both her and himself at the thought he was about to voice. "Not only would Miss Gilliam be in greater danger, but so would you and your brothers."

Eva looked at him, defiant even in the face of defeat. Man, but he loved her spunk. "We can't sit back and do nothing, Logan."

He smiled at her, thankful for the chance to be her hero once more before tumbling off his knightly steed into the mud. "I'm not the do-nothing kind, sweetheart."

A snort echoed behind him, but Logan didn't care, not when hope lit Eva's face and her eyes glowed with absolute confidence in him. He savored that look for a heart-stopping moment, knowing it would probably be the last time he saw such unwavering faith, at least for a while, then thrust it aside to get back to business.

"I said we couldn't go to the sheriff without proof. So what do you say we get some?"

Evangeline's heart nearly burst from the sudden onslaught of love gushing through her. Love . . . and fear. Logan looked so capable, standing there with that cocky smile and loose-limbed stance. Yet as much as she wanted Christie to be free of the man bent on hurting her, she didn't like the idea of Logan taking all the danger upon himself.

A masculine throat cleared at the back of the room. "I'll help."

Zach. Of course. Evangeline shot a thankful smile across

the room to her eldest brother. Zach might act like a lone wolf, but he was a protector by nature. He'd never stand idly by and let a woman be persecuted if there were something he could do to prevent it.

"Me, too," she immediately volunteered, crossing her arms over her chest and jutting out her chin to let Logan know she'd not be relegated to the sidelines. "What can I do?"

Logan's jaw tensed. "You can stay as far away from Mr. Benson as possible."

And there he went, relegating her to the sidelines. He better think twice about that snap judgment before she—

"Please!" Christie raised her hands to her head as if grasping for purchase in a windstorm. "Everyone's speaking too fast. I can't keep up."

Evangeline glared a warning at Logan that their discussion of her involvement was *not* over, then moved in front of Christie. "I'm sorry," she said. "That was rude of us."

"I don't care about rude," Christie responded, her voice agitated. "I care about understanding what you plan to do." She stepped away from Seth and marched over to Logan. "You want to go after the ledger, don't you?"

Logan tossed his hat onto the settee. "Yep. I think I know where he keeps the logbooks stashed, at least the ones containing Earl's accounts. And if he mixed his ledger up with Earl's on the day you retrieved it, it follows that he must keep them both in the same general vicinity."

"But wouldn't the mix-up cause him to change that pattern?" Christie asked. "You could be searching in the wrong place."

Logan shrugged. "Possibly. But we won't know until we look, will we?"

Seth crossed to Christie's side, and Evangeline followed. Zach joined the group as well so that they all stood in a circle.

Seth took Christie's hand and squeezed it. "How often does Earl have Benson check his accounts?"

"Every two weeks."

"Then we have some time." Seth cast Logan a meaningful glance. "If Earl collected his ledger from Benson yesterday, that gives us a dozen days to strategize."

Logan frowned. "Why do we have to wait for Earl's ledger to come back into Benson's possession? Benson's account book is the one we care about."

"Discrediting Benson and getting him behind bars where he can't hurt Christie is the main objective. But it's not the only one." Seth brought the back of Christie's hand up to his lips and laid a gentle kiss on it. "I have a young boy to find."

Christie's eyes filled with tears as she bit her trembling lower lip. Evangeline patted her friend's back, her own eyes misting.

"If we go after Benson's ledger now, we'll spook Earl and lose our chance to get our hands on the information we need from *his* account book. We need to make our move when both ledgers are in Benson's possession. Two birds, one stone."

Logan's forehead scrunched, making the scar across his left eye more pronounced. "What does a kid have to do with anything?"

Evangeline touched his arm. "I'll explain later. The two of us need to talk anyway."

She ignored the raised eyebrows of the two other men in the room, concerned only with the man to her left. The man whose gray eyes had just clouded with . . . dread.

Suddenly, outmaneuvering a murderous schoolmaster seemed far less worrisome than cracking open her heart to her inscrutable neighbor.

CHAPTER

24

"Let's go out the front," Evangeline said, steering Logan out of the parlor and finally escaping the weight of her brothers' stares.

Thankfully, neither Seth nor Zach had said anything, but the warning glances they'd shot her way hadn't helped her rioting pulse. She could hear their admonitions to be careful ringing through her brain as if they'd shouted them aloud.

Being careful only got a gal so far. Sometimes she had to take a few risks to get what she wanted. And she wanted Logan— every complicated, secretive, heroic piece of him.

When he held the door open for her, she bustled through, then bounced up onto her tiptoes and leaned over the porch railing to pick the perfectly ripe peach she'd spotted between the branches earlier that morning. The tree was nearly done producing, but one luscious gift hung high, half hidden in the leaves.

Evangeline plucked it from the stem, wiped it gently on her bodice, then turned and presented it to Logan with a smile. "For you."

All right, *yes*, she was trying to sweeten him up. She remembered how much he'd enjoyed the canned peaches she brought him in that first basket of goodies. Surely a fresh peach would be equally pleasing.

She needed him as pleased with her as possible before she owned up to her treachery.

Logan's eyes met hers as he accepted the peach from her hand. His calloused fingertips brushed the back of her hand, and Evangeline's breath caught. There was no dread in his expression now—only heat, appreciation, and a connection so intense, she wanted to wrap around him like a wisteria vine grabbing hold of a mighty oak.

Slowly, Logan pulled a knife from the sheath at his waist. Looking down, he ran the blade around the outer edge of the peach. Juice dripped from the ripe fruit, and the air thickened with its sweet scent. He wiped the blade on his trousers, slipped it back into its place on his belt, then cupped both sides of the peach and twisted gently until the halves came apart.

"Share with me?" He held out the half without the pit.

Evangeline took the fruit from him, her fingers lingering over the roughened feel of his hand before sliding down to the fuzzy peach skin.

Mercy. When had eating a piece of fruit become such an intimate activity? Warmth flushed her cheeks, and she had to duck away from the intensity in his gray eyes. She raised the peach to her lips, hoping to find relief in the mundane process of eating, but when she took a bite, a small rivulet of juice ran down from the corner of her mouth, further fueling her embarrassment.

Until the back of Logan's finger gently brushed it away. Her gaze flew to his face, but he wasn't looking at her eyes. He was staring at her mouth. Hungrily. Rather like he had in the cellar right before he kissed her. Her pulse thrummed, and her breathing shallowed. Heavens, she wanted him to kiss her again.

But not here. Not where Seth or Zach could see, should one of them happen by a window or decide to stroll out the front door. An all-too-likely possibility, given their interfering natures.

Instead of raising up on her toes and lifting her mouth to Logan's as instinct demanded, she twirled around and scrambled down the front porch steps.

"There's a pretty place down by the pond," she called over her shoulder. She tried to smile invitingly, but she couldn't quite manage the lighthearted gesture with all the strong emotions rioting through her midsection. "We could sit and talk."

The lines of his face hardened just a bit, and his eyes cooled. The change was subtle, but Evangeline felt it pierce her chest.

He quirked a grin as if nothing of import had just been smothered, and jogged down the three stairs to join her. "Sure." He sank his teeth into his peach half. He didn't give her a chance to enjoy the sight, though, for he strode past her as if he knew exactly where they were going, effectively nailing the coffin lid shut on a moment that had brimmed with life and promise just heartbeats earlier.

It was for the best—or at least that was what Evangeline told herself as she traipsed after Logan while he made his way toward the smokehouse. Again, as if he knew exactly where the pond was located.

Her brow furrowed. She slowed her steps just enough to allow him to stay in the lead.

She'd never shown him her pond. She'd described it to him, might have even mentioned its general location, but not with enough detail for him to have formulated an internal map. Yet he marched west past the smokehouse as if the star of Bethlehem were igniting the sky and marking their destination.

When he ducked between the twin pecan trees that provided

shade for the handful of large rocks at the pond's south edge, Evangeline knew it couldn't be coincidence. He'd led her directly to the only natural seating around the pond's perimeter.

Pausing between the trees, she braced one hand against the trunk closest to her. "You've been here before."

He stopped, his back still toward her. The sound of a heavy sigh met her ears a moment before he turned to face her.

"You're right. I have." He glanced in the direction of the house, his features so somber that Evangeline's chest ached. "I grew up here."

"What?" She shook her head, the action, unfortunately, doing nothing to shake the scattered pieces of what she knew of him into a picture that made any sense. "I don't under—"

"Come," he said, reaching out a hand. "I'll explain everything. I promise."

She slid her hand into his, the connection still warm, still comforting. Whatever he had to tell her, it couldn't be too bad. Not when he touched her with such tenderness. In fact, she should be excited, she told herself as she let him lead her to the worn boulder where she used to sit and watch her snapping turtle. Logan was finally going to reveal his secrets. That meant he trusted her. Cared about her. Wanted to remove any barriers between them. That was a good thing, right?

Logan released her hand so she could sweep her skirts beneath her and take a seat on the stone. There wasn't really room for him to sit beside her, but he stayed close, leaning a hip against the boulder.

Then he bent at the waist, picked up a pebble, and tossed it into the pond, sending ripples over the placid surface. The sight created an oddly unsettled feeling inside her. Not knowing what to do, yet not wanting to jabber about inanities when they both stood on the brink of a conversation that could dictate the direction of their future, Evangeline stuffed her mouth with another bite of peach.

Logan smiled, his eyes a little sad as he tilted his head toward the piece of fruit in her hand. "My mother would be glad to know her tree is producing so well."

Evangeline swallowed in a rush and wiped the back of her hand across her lips. "*Her* tree?"

"Mm-hmm." He glanced away and lifted his own peach up for inspection, yet his eyes didn't seem to focus on it. "She pestered my father for months about planting fruit trees around the house. Peaches. Apples. Pears. He'd grumble that they didn't have the money for such frivolous things. She'd insist he wouldn't consider them frivolous when she put up preserves and pear butter and baked fresh apple pie. It took nearly a year, but Pop finally brought a pair of saplings home and planted them, one on either side of the front porch. She babied those trees like they were her children. Watering. Weeding. Covering them with a sheet to protect them from frost and snow." Logan shook his head. "I think leaving those trees behind was harder on her than leaving Pop's grave." He met Evangeline's gaze. "She knew his fate, after all. But she had no way of knowing what would become of her trees. Thank you for taking care of them for her."

Evangeline's head swam. Logan's mother had planted their peach trees. Nurtured them. Ensured their survival so the Hamiltons could enjoy their bounty.

With those peaches, Evangeline had paid Charlotte Clem for cooking lessons. With those peaches, she'd baked pies, put up jam and the syrupy preserves Zach loved to spread on his flapjacks every Sunday morning. With those peaches, she'd just tried to woo a man into a forgiving mood. A man more deeply imbedded in her family's history than she could have ever fathomed.

"This was your home?" Why did that idea have such difficulty penetrating her mind? Logic grasped the concept, but she struggled to make sense of its emotional ramifications.

Logan nodded. "Yes." He bobbed his chin toward the house. "I helped my father build the house you live in. The barn that stables your horses." He swept his arm in a broad gesture. "I've explored every inch of this land. I know the best fishing holes. The best places to snare a rabbit. The best climbing trees." Memories lit his eyes, fond boyhood memories, and for a moment his countenance lightened. But when he turned his face back to her, shadows clouded his eyes once more. "Do you remember the day I told you about my father? About why I hate gambling so much?"

The sweet taste of peach juice soured in Evangeline's mouth. Her stomach cramped as trepidation twisted her insides. Thickness clogged her throat and blocked the words trying to exit. She managed a shaky nod instead.

Oh, yes. She remembered the heart-wrenching story of his father taking his own life. Leaving his wife and son destitute and alone. All because he hadn't had the sense to cut his losses at the poker table. He'd raised the stakes higher than he could afford, and his family had paid the price.

How could a father do such a thing? Risk his family's livelihood on the turn of a card. It was irresponsible. Foolish. But even that paled in comparison to what followed. Evangeline ached for the man who'd been broken by the consequences he'd brought upon himself, even as she bristled with indignation at the selfishness of leaving his wife and child alone to clean up the mess he'd created.

No wonder Logan so passionately sought to restore what had been lost. He'd been thrust into the role of provider while just a boy. A boy who mourned his father and no doubt wanted things to go back to the way they were.

So much pressure. The burden of responsibility. She'd seen the weight of that mantle on Zach's shoulders for years. He'd carried so much from such a young age. Providing for them the best he could, doing whatever it took to ensure their survival, and keeping whatever darkness he encountered along the way deep inside himself so it wouldn't taint her or Seth.

Logan and Zach shared a history that should never be forced on a child.

Shared a history . . .

Her heart plummeted to her stomach. Oh, merciful heavens. They *shared* a history.

"I see you're putting the pieces together," Logan said, his voice tinged with regret.

The peach fell from her suddenly numb fingers and landed in the dirt at her feet.

Zach had won their home in a card game. She recalled the night he came home with that deed in his hand. He'd woken her up and showed her the paper. He'd been so happy, so proud. He'd promised she'd never have to sleep in a ratty hotel room or abandoned barn ever again. That they could make a place that would be safe for Seth. They would finally have a home.

She'd been so excited, she'd not slept a single wink the rest of the night. A real home!

Never once had she considered that their gain meant someone else's loss. Neither did she understand why Zach's enthusiasm soured a few days later. Why he put away his favorite deck of cards—the only thing he had from his father—and never touched them again. He never spoke of what happened. Never offered explanations. Just put his head down and worked to build the home they all wanted.

The home that should have been Logan's.

She couldn't meet Logan's eyes. Could barely form the words

that had to be said. "Zach is the one who beat your father in poker that night, isn't he?"

Logan gently took hold of her chin and turned her face until her eyes met his. "No, Eva. Zach didn't win that night. He cheated."

She pulled away from Logan's touch and violently wagged her head from side to side. "No! He would *never*—"

"He did." A muscle in his jaw twitched. "He cheated. Stole my father's property and stole my father's life."

The animosity in his voice slapped her across the face. Tears pooled in her eyes.

Logan was mistaken. He *had* to be. Zach would never have done something so dishonorable. He was a good man. He worked hard. Selflessly. Did whatever it took to take care of their family.

Whatever it took.

Dear Lord. It couldn't be true. Could it?

CHAPTER

25

Logan watched the color drain from Eva's face. He clamped his jaw shut and kicked his boot heel against the boulder behind him hard enough to bang his ankle. He hated destroying her illusions, but he'd vowed there'd be no more secrets between them, and he aimed to see it through, no matter how distasteful the task.

Too bad blackening Zacharias's name would eventually lead to blackening his own. At least in her eyes.

His pulse ratcheted up a level, and he swallowed despite the sudden dryness coating his tongue. He might as well spill the rest before she recovered from the shock enough to slap him for slandering her do-no-wrong brother and run back to the house.

"My full name is Logan Fowler," he said as he studied her reaction. "My father was Rufus Fowler, a name you might recognize from the land deed, if you've ever seen it."

A spark of recognition lit her eyes, and he knew she had.

"I knew that name sounded familiar. I just couldn't place it," she mumbled, and Logan nodded, startling her into meeting his gaze. She bit her lip, her cheeks flushing, but her eyes didn't dodge away. "I looked in your saddlebags when I was trapped in the cellar. I found the letter from the land office. Found your name."

He smiled. She was so honest. So pure of heart. He could see the guilt weighing on her over an indiscretion so small, he would have barely blinked at it. Somewhere in the last seven years, the gauge on his conscience had lost its sensitivity. Maybe if she stayed with him after all this was over, she could help him repair the damage.

If she stayed.

He brushed back a strand of hair the breeze had blown across her cheek. "I know."

She look down at her feet. "Are you angry?"

He lifted her chin with a finger and waited for her to reveal her glorious, vivid, purely Eva eyes. "No. I'm not angry. I understand what drove you to do it." He stroked her chin with the pad of his thumb. "I just hope you can understand what is driving me as well, and offer the same forgiveness."

Her eyebrows flattened into downward arrows. "You came to hurt Zach, didn't you? I remember what you said about seeking recompense from the man who took your father's land. That's why you *invested* in the property next to ours, isn't it? You were scouting us out, looking for ways to hurt us in return for how we hurt you."

"No, Eva. I'd *never* hurt you." He hurled his peach over the entire pond, anger and fear lending strength to his arm. He planted himself in front of her and cupped her face in both of his hands, ensuring she looked at him. "I don't even want to hurt your brother. Not really. I just want a chance to win back what was stolen from us, to restore what my mother lost."

She pulled away from his hold, her eyes flashing blue and brown fire. "Win? As in a poker game? Zach would never agree to that. He hasn't touched a deck of cards in years. Besides, the land isn't the same as it was seven years ago. We've worked it, improved it, added a cash crop. You wouldn't just be taking back what was lost, you'd be taking what we've built as well. Which would make you as much of a thief as you claim Zach to be."

She rose to her feet, her arms stiff at her sides. "It wasn't Zach who forced your father to wager something he couldn't afford to lose. He did that all on his own. Zach would never make such a wager, so you'd have to force his hand somehow." Her eyes narrowed. "At gunpoint? By holding me hostage?"

"Of course not!" Logan's mind spun at her accusations. How could she think he would do such a thing?

"You've been deluding yourself all these years, Logan. It's not justice you seek." She raised her hands to his chest and shoved. "It's revenge."

He allowed her to push him back, but he wasn't about to let her leave. He charged after her. "What your brother did was wrong, Eva. He cheated a man out of his home. Turned a family out on the streets. Justice demands he pay a price for that sin."

She spun around to face him. "And what of your father's sin? Does justice demand that we pay for that as well? Because that's what we'd be doing. It wasn't Zach's job to talk your father out of wagering his property. It was your father's job never to put it on the table in the first place. It was your father's job to provide a new life for you and your mother, but he chose to abandon you instead. And as much as I hate the pain his choice cost you, I can't let you blame Zach for decisions your father made."

"Do you think I don't know my old man was a fool?" Tension radiated through Logan's neck and back. As if he wasn't fully aware of his sire's crimes. It was *she* who didn't understand the depth of her brother's treachery. Logan widened his stance and dug his heels into the earth. "My father had no business wagering our home. You're right about that. But it wasn't his wager that destroyed him. It was your brother's cheating."

Eva crossed her arms and jutted out her chin. "Zach is *not* a cheat. He's worked hard for every penny he's ever earned." Her eyes glared with challenge. "And from an even younger age than you."

Logan crossed *his* arms, mocking her stance as he raised a brow. "I'm sorry to break it to you, sweetheart, but your brother's not the hero you'd like to think him. He's a survivor. A scrapper. Life dealt him a worthless hand, so he bluffed and manipulated and cheated his way through until the cards got better. Some might consider that heroic, but I can't. Not when my widowed mother is slowly being torn apart by a grief he caused."

Something flickered in her eyes. Uncertainty? It was hard to tell, because as fast as it appeared, it vanished again beneath resurging flames of indignation. "Do you have proof?" she demanded. "Proof that he cheated?"

"My father told me what happened—"

"Oh, your father told you, did he?" She scoffed as if *he* were the naïve one. "And he would certainly have no reason to lie, to blame another for his own faults." She slashed her hand through the air. "Of course he'd tell the son who adored him that the loss was not his fault, that the winner had cheated. I might not be an experienced gambler like you are, but I would wager my entire savings right now that players who lose big at the tables are quick to cry foul, to claim the person who bested them had cheated. How else are they to salvage their pride? You've probably been on the receiving end of such an accusation yourself."

Logan's jaw tightened, but he was unable to deny her words. "That's beside the point."

She slapped her arms against her sides. "It's *precisely* the point."

Taking a moment to inhale before he said something he'd regret, Logan relaxed his stance, let go of his defensiveness, and just shared his heart with her.

"My old man played cards every Saturday night. Usually for pots of less than a hundred dollars, but every once in a while, he'd find a group interested in deeper play."

Eva's face remained set in stiff lines, but she didn't interrupt him, which meant she was probably listening. He'd count that as a win for the moment.

"He was good, Eva. Had a mind for numbers. Could keep track of all the cards in the deck and calculate the probabilities of what would turn up next. The only time he wagered his deed was when he was certain he held the winning hand."

"He'd done this *before*?" She sounded horrified, and frankly, he couldn't blame her.

His father had been reckless. He won more often than he lost, bringing home jewelry for Mama and fine leather boots for Logan, but there were also times when Mama had to sell her jewelry and Logan ran around barefoot. Uncertainty hung over their household like an ever-present storm cloud. They never knew if it would bring a gentle restorative rain or pounding hail that destroyed everything in its path. Logan would never subject his family to such a thing. As soon as he made things right with Hamilton, he'd put away the cards for good.

"He held four kings that night. The only thing that would beat him was a stack of aces or a straight flush. He'd discarded an ace earlier, so he knew that possibility was gone, and he'd seen enough middle cards from each suit during play to negate the likelihood of a straight. Yet when your brother called his bet by offering up his gun, saddle, and horse, he miraculously turned over the three through seven of clubs. An impossible run, unless the deck had been stacked."

Like a jousting knight of old, Logan held tight to his lance, not giving an inch. He had to unseat Eva's brother from the pedestal she'd placed him on. She wouldn't thank him for it now, but if he was to have any chance of winning her heart in the end, she had to recognize that Hamilton's armor was just as dented and tarnished as Logan's.

"Your brother dealt that hand, Eva," he said, wielding the sharpest weapons in his arsenal. "Controlled the cards. Probably even fed my father the kings to induce a large bid. He manipulated play from the start so that he could dictate the outcome. Without a care for who it might hurt, your brother shredded my father with ruthless precision. All for a house and a piece of land."

"A house that probably saved Seth's life." She threw out the rejoinder like a seaman tossing a bucket of water overboard from a ship already half sunk. The boat was going down, but she wasn't yet willing to admit defeat. Her legs trembled, and this time when she crossed her arms over her midsection, there was no anger in the motion, only a bid for comfort, as if her insides had suddenly gone cold.

Logan's heart twisted, and he stepped forward, wanting to hold her, to ease her pain somehow, even though he'd been the one to cause it.

She stumbled backward away from him, something wild entering her eyes. "Have I been a means to an end all this time? A tool for you to use against Zach? To manipulate him into a corner as some way to even the score?"

"No, Eva." He advanced and took her arms in his hands. He couldn't let her think that, not even for a moment. But he couldn't lie to her, either, not if he wanted a solid foundation to build a future upon. "Not all this time."

"But some of the time?" Eyes that had started to soften in relief hardened again with suspicion.

Logan sighed. "I'm tired of secrets between us, Eva. I want honesty, even when the truth is less than palatable. Don't you want that, too?"

She pressed her lips together, stared at him for a long, searching moment, then gave a shaky nod.

"When I first met you," Logan said as he rubbed her arms, "logic dictated that I keep you at a distance. Lower my risk of exposure." A smile curved his lips as he remembered their first meeting. "But you were so different from what I expected. Different from any woman I'd ever met. Feisty. Cheerful. And with a generosity of spirit that stirred a craving inside me. A craving for sunshine.

"So I started rationalizing. Telling myself that being friendly with you would give me an advantage. That I could mine you for information and later use it against your brother." His hands stilled as he silently pleaded with her to hear the truth in his words. "The more time I spent with you, the less I thought about my plans for justice. I started making new plans centered on you. On a future free of plots and schemes. A future where we shared that cabin I've been building." He reached for her face and stroked her cheek with his thumb. "I love you, Eva."

Her eyes misted, the brown one pooling a little more deeply than the blue. "I've had the same dreams," she admitted, and his heart tripped. "But I won't abandon my family. Not even for you."

He shook his head. "I'm not asking you to."

"Of course you are." There was no accusation in her words, only sadness. "You want me to choose you over Zach. To stand by your side and watch you destroy him." A tear fell from that brown eye, moistening the pad of Logan's thumb. "Don't you see that by hurting him, you're hurting me?"

What could he say to that? She was right, and he could do nothing except push through and hope that with time she'd forgive him.

"Please," she entreated. "Just let this quest of yours go." Her chin wobbled as she tilted her head back to meet his gaze more completely. "For me?"

He wanted to. So badly that he physically ached. This was the woman he loved begging him. His knees nearly gave way from the force of his desire to please her.

But another woman's image rose in his mind. A woman with graying hair who withdrew inside herself more and more each day. A woman he'd loved his entire life. One he'd sacrifice anything to protect.

Even his future.

His hand slid slowly from Eva's face, and her tiny moan echoed between them. A sword cleaved his heart as he stepped away.

"I . . . I can't."

CHAPTER

26

Evangeline fisted her hands in her skirt, desperately grasping the fabric to find purchase against the flash flood that had just knocked her sideways and threatened to drag her under.

He *couldn't*?

More like he *wouldn't*. She pressed her lips together in a tight line. He wouldn't choose love over vengeance. Wouldn't release the past in order to build a future.

"You have to understand," Logan began. His face, usually so stoic, was a picture of torment. Lines etched his forehead. His eyes pleaded. But she didn't want to hear what he had to say.

"No." Evangeline shook her head. "No, I *don't* have to understand. I can't. A man who says he loves me shouldn't seek to harm my family."

"And a woman who cares for me shouldn't automatically assume me a villain because I dare to speak the truth about her brother."

"A truth that has yet to be determined," she countered even as her conscience pricked. She *had* been quick to cast Logan in the role of villain. But only because he was being so unreasonable.

He took another backward step, his head hanging low. "Whether you believe it or not, Eva, I do love you. But I love my mother, too. I vowed to get justice for her. It's the only way I know to heal her pain."

"*This* will heal her pain?" Did he really believe that? Lord help him. "Have you even asked your mother what she wants?" Evangeline's voice rose. She had to make him see the fallacy of this ridiculous plan. Only then could they salvage their future. "Do you think she wants to come back to this house, to the barn where she found your father's body? To relive that horror? Or do you expect a piece of paper showing ownership will bring her out of her depression?"

He withdrew another step, and worst of all, he closed his face from her. His eyes went flat. His forehead smoothed. All hint of feeling vanished from his features.

Maybe she'd pressed too hard. But what choice did she have? She was losing him to a tragedy that happened seven years ago.

She released her skirt and grabbed his hand. "Vengeance doesn't heal pain, Logan. *Love* heals pain. That's why God tells us to leave the vengeance to him and instead focus on loving each other, including our enemies."

He pulled away from her touch. Rejection slashed through her heart like a scythe hacking through sorghum at harvest time.

She dropped her hand to her side, but her heart wasn't ready to forfeit its position. "Where is the love in what you're doing?" she murmured.

Where is the love in leaving me?

Logan gave no answer, just kept backing away until he reached the pair of pecan trees that guarded the pond. Then, with a swiftness that dripped lemon juice into every scrape inflicted by this conversation, he turned his back and left.

Her feet stumbled after him on instinct, but when she reached the trees, she braced her palms against the rough bark and held herself back. Going after him would do no good. She'd chosen Zach; Logan had chosen his mother. They had no middle ground.

Her arms trembled. Then her knees started quaking. Then her bottom lip quivered as her entire being gave way to grief. Unable to hold herself erect, she slid to the ground as the tears she'd been holding at bay streamed forth unchecked.

She'd thought Logan was different. That he'd seen past her crazy eyes and ragtag family to the person beneath. But loving her hadn't been enough.

Twisting to brace her hunched spine against a tree trunk, she drew up her knees and buried her face in her arms. If you loved someone, you weren't supposed to leave. Not ever. Not unless death forced your hand.

Fuzzy, faded images of her parents and brother flittered through Evangeline's mind. Why did everyone leave? Was she cursed? Destined to be alone?

"Evie? That you?"

Evangeline's head shot up at Zach's voice. She scrubbed the tears from her cheeks. Good grief. How was a girl supposed to wallow in her brokenhearted misery if her brothers wouldn't leave her be?

She wiped her sleeve against her runny nose. Yes, complaining about not being left alone while she was bemoaning her lonely state was a ludicrous contradiction, but that was how she felt. Ludicrous. And lonely.

Now her eyes were pooling again. *Get ahold of yourself, Evie.*

"Just saw Logan ride off. Thought we were going to strategize—" Zach's tone sharpened. "What happened?" It was a demand, not a question. "Did that bounder hurt you?" Harsh, choppy steps brought him to her side in a rush.

His hands closed around her elbows, and he hefted her to her feet like a sack of potatoes. She intended to bluff, to insist she was fine and simply wanted some time alone—Zach had never been one to hang around when feminine emotions ran amok, after all, gladly delegating that role to Seth—but as soon as her oldest brother's arms came around her middle to steady her as she tried to stand, Evangeline's intentions crumpled. Giving up all pretense, she clasped the front of Zach's shirt, pressed her face to his chest, and sobbed.

To his credit, Zach didn't say a word. Just held her as she wept, giving her back an awkward pat every now and again. After all the wrong things she'd had to listen to Logan say, having a man keep his mouth shut and hold her went a long way toward soothing the raw places inside.

When her crying finally subsided, she lifted her head and surveyed the damage she'd done to Zach's shirt. "Sorry," she mumbled, feeling sheepish all of a sudden.

Zach dug in his trouser pocket and extracted a handkerchief. He shoved it at her, which was his version of being sweet. Just because there was a glazed, panicked look in his eyes didn't mean he didn't sincerely want to help.

In truth, seeing the evidence that he wished he was anywhere else, doing any*thing* else—probably including picking cotton— while he stayed steadfastly by her side, lifted her spirits.

Love stayed. Even when things became messy and unpleasant, love stayed.

Evangeline wiped her eyes, blew her nose, then smiled up at her big brother. "I love you, Zach."

He grunted, which was Zach-speak for *I love you, too.* "Want me to shoot him for you?"

Evangeline burst into laughter. "No." She swatted one of his arms as he crossed them in his don't-mess-with-me-or-mine stance.

"'Cause I will, if he got out of line with you."

"He didn't," she assured him. "Just bruised my heart, is all. I suspect it'll heal eventually."

"Well, if it don't, my offer stands."

She grinned and nudged him with her shoulder. "Thanks."

Oh, Zach. Tough, curmudgeonly, wonderful Zach. God had blessed her well when he placed her in Zach's path. But what would happen when Logan carried out his plans? Her smile cratered. Zach might appear rugged and imperturbable on the surface, but deep wounds plagued him on the inside, wounds that would be reopened and prodded none-too-gently when Logan leveled his accusations.

She had to warn him, prepare him for what was coming. "Zach, there's something you should know."

A sour taste filled her mouth. *Ignore it. Your loyalty belongs to family, not to handsome, kind, heroic neighbors with hidden agendas.*

Kind. Heroic. Logan *was* those things. In the heat of their argument, she had forgotten the good he had done. The way he stood up for her when the town looked down their noses. The way he rescued Christie—continued rescuing her, as a matter of fact. He'd taken on the task of finding her attacker single-handedly. A task that had nothing to do with his revenge plot and everything to do with his innate sense of justice.

"Evie?" Zach's voice interrupted her mental pretzel-making.

She cleared her throat and set her shoulders in a militant line. "It's about Logan. And the real reason he came here."

Zach looked at her expectantly.

Evangeline sucked in a quick, shallow breath and spilled what she knew. "His last name is Fowler. You won this land off his father in a poker game, and he intends to force you into a new game with him so he can win it back."

The color drained from Zach's face, and he staggered sideways. His arms came uncrossed, as if they no longer possessed the will to hold themselves together.

"Zach?" Alarmed, Evangeline reached for him. She clasped his arm, but his flat expression didn't flicker. It was as if he hadn't even registered her touch.

"He said you cheated, but I told him you would never do such a thing," Evangeline said, trying to convince her brother that she believed in him and not in Logan's wild tale. "You're honest and hardworking. Dependable and honorable. It was his father who was in the wrong. He wagered something he couldn't afford to lose, then blamed someone else for his loss and cried foul when it was too late. I know that. But Logan kept insisting otherwise. Telling me I was naïve."

"You are," Zach croaked, finally looking at her.

She flinched. Her heart thumped in slow, hard beats. "What?"

"Naïve," he said. A muscle in his jaw ticked. "And I did everything in my power to keep you that way. To protect you from the ugly side of life." His Adam's apple bobbed as he swallowed, the motion strangely exaggerated. "You'd lost enough. You didn't need to lose your innocence as well, your gift for seeing the best in people." He paused, a thickness entering his voice. "For seeing the best in me."

"What . . ." The word emerged as barely more than a whisper. She lifted a hand to her throat and tried again. "What are you saying?"

Color rushed back into Zach's face. Red, angry color. He drew himself up to his full height and glowered at her. Belligerent. Defiant. "I'm saying Logan's right. I cheated. Cheated brilliantly, as a matter of fact. Beat the cardsharp at his own game."

Evangeline shook her head, unable to believe what he was

saying. Yet her action only seemed to fuel his determination to shatter her stubborn illusions.

"All your clamor about being a woman grown and not wanting to be sheltered—well, here's some unsheltered reality for you. Life stinks. It's hard. It's not fair. And if you want to survive, you gotta grab whatever you can and not look back.

"I worked, yes," he said, "but I stole, too. Stole, cheated, fought—whatever it took to fill your bellies and keep a roof over your heads. So yes, when I saw a chance to get a real house and acreage that could support us for the long term, I snatched it." He thrust his arm in front of him and grabbed at the air with a fist. "And what's more," he declared, "I don't regret it. Not any of it."

Zach stormed off, and Evangeline reached for the nearest pecan tree to steady herself.

Dear Lord. It was true. All of it. Every horrid detail.

Except that last bit. Her brother might claim to have no regrets over his actions, but the agony in his tortured gaze proved otherwise.

CHAPTER

27

Logan urged Shamgar to greater speed, blurring past the cutoff that would have taken him home. The last place he wanted to be was at his cabin, where every room reminded him of *her*.

Why did she have to be so stubborn? So closed-minded? Did the time they'd spent together mean nothing to her? He'd told he loved her. Did she think those words came cheap? They'd been wrenched from his heart. He'd exposed his soft underbelly, and she'd kicked him. Called him a liar. A thief. Accused him of seeking revenge when what he sought was justice. Demanded he abandon his quest to heal his mother's pain without even considering the role her brother had played in the wounding.

Shamgar's hooves pounded the road with the same force that Logan's anger pounded through his veins. Harder. Faster. He leaned over his mount's neck and raced, sensing that if he allowed his pace to slow, the pain would catch him from behind.

Betrayal. Rejection. His.

Hers.

For that was what he'd seen in Eva's eyes when he'd refused to forfeit his plans. When he'd chosen his mother over her.

Gritting his teeth, Logan sat up in the saddle and gently eased back on the reins, slowing Shamgar to a walk.

"Sorry, old boy," he murmured.

Sorry to you, too, Eva. For everything. For using her to gain information on Zacharias. For destroying her illusions. For asking her to choose.

He never should have gotten involved with her in the first place. He should have kept his distance. Kept his heart locked away in his chest where it belonged. Then his resolve wouldn't be weakening. His mind wouldn't be fixated on the way she'd looked as she pleaded with him to let the matter go, the tears that had glimmered when his refusal stole the last vestiges of hope from her expression.

Maybe he *was* a thief.

A farm wagon approached from the opposite direction, and Logan guided Shamgar to the right side of the road, taking stock of his whereabouts for the first time.

Good gravy. He was nearly to Ben Franklin. He'd pushed Shamgar harder than he'd realized.

He tipped his hat to the farmer and grinned as if he were simply out for an afternoon stroll, but the moment the wagon rolled past, the fake smile fell away.

"Let's get you to the livery," he said, leaning forward in the saddle to pat the chestnut's neck. "You deserve a good rubdown, some water, maybe even a feed bag of oats for putting up with me. What do you say?" The last thing Logan needed was a second coat of guilt painted onto his still-wet conscience. He might not be able to smooth things over with Eva just yet, but by thunder, he could make things up to his horse.

Logan counted at least five men lounging about the livery by the time he trotted into Ben Franklin. Kids draped themselves over the paddock fence, trying to coax a horse or two near enough to pet. Women bustled along the boardwalk across the way, shopping and visiting and whatever else town females did in the afternoons. The hum of a distant sawmill added a buzz to the air that didn't quite drown out the yipping dog that had decided to dance around Shamgar's hooves.

As if Logan's head didn't already pound enough.

He ignored the ache throbbing behind his temples and dismounted. Shamgar deserved some pampering. No yappy dog was going to dissuade him.

"Little early in the day for you, ain't it, Logan?" Jack Simmons stepped out of the shade of the livery to greet him. A pair of graybeards playing checkers on a board balanced atop an old pickle barrel paused their game to stare.

"Didn't come for cards this time," Logan said, forcing a smile he didn't feel. "Just out for a ride. Pushed Shamgar a bit harder than I intended. Thought I'd give him a good rubdown and maybe a few oats if you've got some to spare."

"Don't have any to spare, but I got some to sell." The livery owner smirked as the old men guffawed. "Though it sounds like *you* might be the one needing the extra treat. Of the two of you, you're the one looking like you been put through the wringer, not yer horse. That chestnut'll be right as rain after a little water and a good brushing, but you, my friend, look like you could use another dose of that liquid refreshment I procured for you."

Chuckles broke out around them. Apparently the men who frequented the livery in the afternoon were well acquainted with Jack's moonshine connections.

"Sounds like quite a jovial gathering," a more cultured voice said from behind Logan.

"Howdy, Lawrence." Jack nodded a greeting to the newcomer. "Checkin' on that bench spring you ordered for yer buggy?"

Logan pivoted, a polite smile in place. A smile that nearly

curdled when he caught sight of the man behind him. Bald pate. Heavy build. Familiar black suit. The schoolmaster.

"Indeed," Benson said. "I hoped to have the repair completed before my trip tomorrow."

Trip? Logan's interest piqued. If he knew for sure the teacher would be away, he could search the schoolhouse ahead of time. They'd still have to wait for the second ledger to come into play, but knowing the hiding place of the first would simplify matters a great deal.

"Where're ya headed?" Logan kept his voice nonchalant.

Benson raised a folded white handkerchief to his forehead and dabbed at the moisture glistening there. "Down to Cooper for the weekend. I'm meeting with some investors. We hope to gain sufficient funds to purchase new schoolbooks for next term. The children will be out for the harvest in another month, and I want to be able to promise them there will be new books when they return this winter. Our current materials are sadly outdated."

So he'd be gone the next two days. Good.

Logan fiddled with Shamgar's bridle strap. "You're the school-master, then?"

Benson offered a reserved smile while something intelligent and guarded flashed in his eyes, like a cardsharp who suspected a skilled player had just entered the game. "That I am." He held out his hand. "Lawrence Benson. And you are?"

"Logan Fowler." No need to keep his surname hidden any longer. Holding it back would only cause suspicion.

Jack pounded Logan's shoulder blade as he invited himself into the conversation. "Logan's from Pecan Gap. Comes by every few nights for a game of cards."

Wishing he could muzzle the chatty liveryman, Logan re-strained the glare itching to burn a hole in Jack's forehead and shrugged. "The Gap's a little too tame for my taste. I prefer the entertainment in these parts."

"Yeah, he's taken a real *shine* to us."

One of the graybeards at the checkers table snickered. "Good one, Jack."

Logan bit back a retort. He was seriously regretting striking up a friendship with this yahoo.

"Well, Ben Franklin certainly has more to offer an enterprising young man like yourself than Pecan Gap." Benson sold the town as if he were the mayor. "And speaking of enterprising . . ." He nodded toward Shamgar. "You wouldn't be interested in selling that animal, would you? We don't see too many beasts of his size in Delta County."

Jack Simmons raised a brow. "I, uh, think this might be a bit too much horse for you, Lawrence." The livery owner had lost his irreverent humor, hesitating over making his recommendation as if worried about the teacher taking offense. Miss Gilliam had been right. Benson had clout in this town.

The rotund man chuckled off the warning with a wave of his handkerchief. "I'm not asking for *myself*, Mr. Simmons. Mercy! How ridiculous would that be? I'm sure I couldn't even mount the creature. I won't be trading in my buggy any time soon."

Jack grinned, obviously relieved that no offense had been taken.

"No, it's my nephew I'm thinking of. The boy's nearly as tall as Mr. Fowler here, and he loves to race." Benson leaned forward and winked at Logan. "I spied you on the road earlier. Running like the very wind, you were."

Logan kept his mien pleasant despite the fact that this weasel watching him while he'd been too caught up in his own head to notice churned his stomach. Benson must've been traveling on the crossroad that led from the schoolhouse. Logan had been so stirred up over his conversation with Eva that he'd paid little attention to his surroundings until that farmer had passed him.

"Shamgar's a real goer, all right," Logan said. He gave his gelding a pat. "But he's not for sale."

"That's a shame. I would have been the boy's favorite uncle for certain." Benson shrugged and stuffed his handkerchief back into his coat pocket. "Can't blame a fellow for trying."

Not unless his trying involved drowning a young woman. Logan could blame him all day for that. But of course, he kept that accusation to himself.

"You have a good eye for horseflesh, sir." Logan tugged the brim of his hat. "I'll take your offer as a compliment."

"As it was intended." Benson smiled, then turned to the liveryman. "Now, Simmons, how about that bench spring?"

"I'll get right on it," Jack said. "Should have it to you by the end of the day."

As Jack followed the teacher out to where he'd parked his buggy, Logan took the initiative to lead Shamgar to a back stall. Away from the teasing. The noise. The need to pretend.

In the dim recesses of the stable, Logan inhaled to settle his nerves and his mind. The familiar aromas of hay, manure, and horse liniment filled his nostrils as the voices faded. He moved to unbuckle Shamgar's cinch and eyed the schoolmaster over the horse's back. Benson was leaving, speaking to each fellow as he went, even going so far as to raise a hand in farewell to Logan, his gaze finding him at the back of the livery as if he'd been fully aware of his location the entire time.

A shiver snaked down Logan's nape, but he grinned and raised a hand in return.

That was not someone Logan would choose to sit across from at the poker table. Too calculated and ruthless. Even if Logan hadn't been aware of Christie Gilliam's story, Benson's bearing and mannerisms proclaimed his traits. This was not a man you crossed.

He probably had the best behaved students in the county.

But it was his intent toward Miss Gilliam that caused Logan the most concern. Pleasing his pupils' parents would keep the schoolmaster in check in the classroom, but Earl hadn't seemed particularly distraught about his stepdaughter's disappearance. The only scuttlebutt Logan had picked up the last two weeks over poker games was a comment or two about the idiot girl who had finally run off. No one seemed surprised by the news. Some figured she had tired of dodging the backside of Earl's hand, while others speculated she'd wandered into the woods and was too dull to find her way home. The marshal's fliers were the only evidence that anyone harbored a concern for her whereabouts, and those could have been posted as easily at Benson's behest as Earl's. If Benson was behind them, that meant no one would notice, or even care, if the girl never returned.

Logan really needed to discuss the situation with Seth. Fine-tune the plan. Nail down the specifics. If Seth would even give him the time of day once Eva revealed Logan's true agenda.

Logan sighed and lifted Shamgar's head from the water barrel. "Not too much, now." He distracted his horse by slipping his bridle off to give him a break from the bit. "We don't want you cramping. Enough things have gone wrong today already."

Eva. Were things really over between them, or was there hope for reconciliation? Logan grimaced as he hefted the saddle from Shamgar's back.

Lord, I don't want things to be over. She means too much to me. But I'm stuck. Gaining justice for my mother means hurting Eva's family, and letting go of my quest means hurting my own family. What am I supposed to do?

No answer spoke to him from the rafters as he slid off the

saddle blanket and started rubbing the gelding down with an old towel. Instead, pieces of his conversation with Eva came zinging back to land like mosquitoes on his skin. Pricking and stinging and leaving an itch he couldn't quite scratch.

Have you asked your mother what she wants?

Logan grabbed the back of his neck. So what if he hadn't asked her outright? She was so withdrawn, she barely spoke to him at all. She'd just stared out the window of his aunt's house and knitted baby blankets for the poor box at church. He'd even bought her an apple tree sapling with some of his first winnings, hoping she would perk up and find purpose in gardening again, but she'd made him return it. Said she had no use for it.

He wanted his mother back. The woman who smiled at him and nurtured fruit trees and scolded him for bringing muddy shoes into the house. He'd thought restoring what had been lost to her would restore what had been lost to him.

Vengeance doesn't heal pain, Logan. Love heals pain.

But it didn't. He loved his mother. He'd shown it in a hundred different ways, yet she still clung to her grief. To her despair. Where was the healing in that?

Where is the love in what you are doing?

"I don't know!"

Shamgar tossed his head and craned his neck around with a scold in his eyes for interrupting his nap and massage. Logan grabbed a currycomb and worked through the chestnut's coat, but his mind refused to settle.

That was the problem. He didn't know. Didn't know how to help his mother. Didn't know how to keep Eva in his life. Didn't even know how to leave this town without looking like a complete imbecile for riding here in the first place.

"There is a way which seemeth right unto a man, but the

end thereof are the ways of death." The proverb, spoken in his mother's voice, echoed in his mind.

"Remember this, Logan," she had said as the two of them walked hand-in-hand to the stagecoach after visiting his father's grave for the last time. "Your father never took this verse to heart. I don't want you making the same mistake."

Why was that memory suddenly popping into his head? He hadn't thought of that conversation in . . . well, not since it happened. To be honest, he'd been too angry to think about anything beyond making the man who'd cheated his father pay.

Making him pay . . .

The currycomb dropped from Logan's hand and thudded to the floor. The livery walls faded. Even Shamgar ceased to exist as the curtain veiling Logan's heart finally fell away.

All this time, he'd convinced himself he sought justice. That his quest was righteous. A noble sacrifice that he'd dedicated seven years of his life to achieving. The wrong would be made right.

All this time, he'd lied to himself.

Deep inside, he was still that angry boy who wanted to make someone pay.

Dear Lord. Logan staggered backward until his spine pressed into the wall behind him. Eva was right. He was seeking revenge.

He raised a trembling hand to his face and rubbed at eyes that suddenly itched. His jaw clenched, and he banged his head against the wood planks supporting him, disgusted by the ugliness inside him. The anger. The hurt. The thirst to inflict pain.

"*Thou shalt not avenge, nor bear any grudge against the children of thy people, but thou shalt love thy neighbor as thyself: I am the Lord.*"

The verse rammed into Logan's gut like a sucker punch. "*I*

am the Lord." Those last four words left no room for arguing. For diverting blame. For rationalizing.

"Vengeance is mine; I will repay, saith the Lord."

Logan sank down the length of the wall, his hands covering his face. Covering his shame. His heart throbbed as truth chiseled away its petrified outer layer. How had he ignored this voice for so long? Had his heart really become so hard?

"He that hath ears to hear, let him hear."

The chisel dug into another layer. Breaking him. Bleeding him.

"I hear you." The whispered acknowledgment fell from Logan's lips like a prayer. "I hear you."

CHAPTER

28

"Logan?" Jack Simmons's irritating voice shattered the holiness of the moment. "Ya get lost back there?"

Logan scrambled to his feet, rubbed the moisture from his eyes, and dragged his hat forward to hide the evidence of his encounter with the Almighty. His heart was too raw, and Jack was too flippant. Better to hide until he could find some privacy to chew over what had just happened.

"There you are," Jack said as he approached the last stall. "I brought you a feed bag if'n you still want it. Two bits."

Logan nodded and dug a quarter out of his trouser pocket. "Thanks." He accepted the bag without meeting Jack's gaze. "I'll be done here in a few."

"No rush." Jack patted Shamgar's hindquarters. "You gonna stick around for some cards at the Seven Ponies later tonight? That braggart Bellows can't wear his hat no more with how fat his head's swole up since he raked in those winnings from you the other night. He needs someone to shrink him back down to size."

Logan slipped the feed bag over Shamgar's nose and fit the strap behind his ears. "Not tonight. Got some unfinished business back at my place."

"That business got something to do with a female?"

Logan's head whipped around.

Jack chuckled. "Don't look so shocked. There's only one thing that gets a man worked up enough to race his horse to a lather when there's no prize money at the end of the line—a woman."

"Yeah, well, this particular female is worth the exercise." Logan settled the saddle blanket back into place. Shamgar had rested enough, and Logan was more than ready to be away from the nosy liveryman.

"Got it that bad, do ya? No wonder yer turning us down for poker. The little woman's got her reformin' hooks in ya already." Jack shook his head. "Pity." He grabbed the saddle from where it straddled the half wall on the far side of Shamgar, then came around to swing it up onto the gelding's back. "Just remember, you know where to come for *medication* when she ties your guts in a knot. Guaranteed to unravel what ails ya and erase troubles from the mind."

"And create a few dozen more," Logan grumbled beneath his breath.

Jack must have heard, for he chuckled as he sauntered down the center aisle toward the front of the livery.

Logan patted Shamgar's neck. "Time to get out of here, old boy." He had changes to make. A life path to renavigate.

He had to get right with God before he could get right with Eva.

He removed the feed bag, cinched the saddle, and placed the bit back in Shamgar's mouth. Then, without more than a wave to Jack and the rest of the gathering, he led his horse away from the livery and back to the road. Back toward Eva and the Hamiltons.

When Ben Franklin lay a handful of miles behind him, Logan slowed Shamgar to a walk and returned his thoughts to where they'd been before Jack had interrupted.

"I screwed up." Not the most elegant prayer ever uttered, but he figured it needed to be said. "Sorry, Lord." And he was. Down to his bones.

He ached with remorse. With self-derision. He'd listened to the serpent, just like Eve had so long ago in that garden. He'd chosen to ignore the Lord's instructions and instead focused on the message that matched what he wanted to hear. *You're not seeking revenge. You're seeking justice. An eye for an eye. It's your right.*

How conveniently he'd forgotten Jesus's teaching of turning the other cheek, of doing good to those who persecute.

"I need to make this right, Lord. With the Hamiltons. With Eva. But what do I do about Mama?" His throat clogged at the thought of his mother alone in her room, closing herself off from the world.

Seek ye first the kingdom of God, and his righteousness; and all these things shall be added unto you.

The words of Jesus echoed in his mind, a pointed reminder that it was Logan's job to live for God, and God's job to take care of the rest. Letting go didn't come easy, not where his mama was concerned, but all his efforts to fix the situation thus far had failed. Time to bring in the big guns, the ones he should have engaged from the start.

"Help her, Lord." Logan squinted against the sun as his face lifted heavenward. "I don't know how." His fingers tightened on the reins. "Heal her heart, and show me how to be the son she needs."

An idea whispered into his heart. He should write to his mother and apologize for being so consumed with his selfish schemes that he'd left her alone and neglected. Eva had recognized his mistake from the very start, and like a blockhead, he'd waved off her concerns as if she didn't know what she was talking about.

He had a lot to atone for. With his mother. With the Hamiltons. With Eva.

His head brimming with thoughts of letters, apologies, and reparations, Logan clicked his tongue at Shamgar to increase their pace. Yet when they turned down the lane to his unfinished cabin, all higher-plane thoughts narrowed to the sharpened point of the physical.

Someone had been in his yard. The sawhorses he'd set up by the lumber pile were missing.

Logan moved the reins to his left hand and reached for his revolver with his right. His knees tensed, sending Shamgar's ears pricking forward at attention.

He scanned the area. Nothing else seemed amiss. He turned his attention to the cabin, and his gut tightened. A dark shadow loomed in the kitchen. Not moving, just . . . waiting.

Logan dismounted, careful to keep his gaze as well as his gun trained on the doorway. Still no movement inside. He jogged closer, until the shadow took shape.

A man. Definitely a man. Seated.

Odd, since Logan had no furniture.

"Who's there?" he called.

"Holster your weapon, Fowler. This ain't that kind of ambush."

But it *was* an ambush. Zacharias Hamilton was waiting for him. In possession of Logan's full name and his intentions, as well.

Logan lowered his revolver and straightened his stance. The moment he'd been planning for seven years was upon him, and instead of satisfaction and triumph, he felt only dread and regret.

Fitting his revolver into its holster, Logan breached the threshold.

Zacharias Hamilton sat on a crude stool fashioned from a log from Logan's woodpile. The missing sawhorses supported four wooden planks from his lumber stores to create a tabletop, and a matching log stool of dubious height sat close to the door, waiting expectantly for Logan to join the tableau.

"I understand you want to challenge me to a game. High stakes." Hamilton's face showed no emotion beyond a sardonic confidence designed to inspire the opposite effect in his opponent. He thumped a knuckle against the top of a thin leather pouch sitting on the table to his right. "I brought the deed."

Logan shook his head. "Put it away. We won't be playing."

Hamilton raised a brow. "I thought that was your endgame."

"It was, but not anymore." Logan stared his nemesis straight in the eye. "I forgive you."

He hadn't known what to expect from Hamilton after uttering those words, but it sure as shooting wasn't for him to leap from his stool like a wolf out for blood.

"You *forgive* me? No. That's not how this works." Hamilton advanced around the table. "You initiated this game when you came to Pecan Gap, when you courted my *sister* as a way to get close to me."

Logan's jaw clenched. "Leave Eva out of this."

Hamilton jabbed a finger at Logan's face. "*You're* the one who brought her into it. The one who broke her heart and left her crying in your wake."

Logan's gut twisted at the image Hamilton painted. Eva,

cheeks stained with tears he'd caused, her heart aching, the wings of her beautiful spirit clipped and sore. "I never wanted to hurt her," he murmured through a clogged throat. "I love her."

"Well, I love her too, and unlike you, everything I do and have ever done is to protect her. To provide for her." Hamilton curled his hand into a fist and, with deliberate slowness, lowered it to his side. "Yes, I cheated your father out of his land. And I'd do it again to provide a permanent shelter for an asthmatic kid who was so thin you could see the outline of his bones through his skin and a little girl who prayed for a real home every night in her bedtime prayers."

A growl rumbled in Hamilton's throat as he pivoted away from Logan and stalked to his side of the table. "I'm sorry you and your ma lost your home," he admitted, his back turned as he braced his hand against the framed wall studs, "but I ain't sorry Seth and Evie found theirs." He dropped his hand and turned to face Logan. He picked up a small, rectangular case from the center of the table and tossed it to land faceup in front of Logan. Two initials were tooled into the russet leather.

"J.M.?"

Hamilton's face gave little away. "Jedidiah Mitchell."

Logan's brows shot up. "The riverboat gambler?" Mitchell was a legend. Even in Texas, people knew of him. Just as young hotheads with pistols sought to make a name for themselves by challenging experienced gunslingers to duels, young cardsharps sought to establish their expertise by taking down legends like Jedidiah Mitchell at the tables. At least they had, until a poor loser back-shot him in an alley in New Orleans.

"My father."

Logan met Hamilton's eyes.

"Those are his cards. The only thing of his I have left. I haven't touched them since . . . well, since the game I played with

Rufus." Hamilton glanced away, leaving the horror of Rufus Fowler's suicide unspoken. "Until today. You deserve a chance to win back what your father lost, and I deserve the chance to prove I can keep it without tarnishing what honor I have left by cheating."

"I'm not going to play you," Logan stated. "Not today. Not ever."

Hamilton frowned. "But Evie said—"

"Eva said a lot of things, many of which crawled under my skin and took root this afternoon." Logan widened his stance and forced his voice to ring with a confidence he wanted to feel but couldn't entirely claim. "I've changed my mind. I'm letting the past go."

"Because of Evie?"

Logan shrugged. "Partially. But mostly because it's the right thing to do."

Hamilton's face hardened. "Deal the cards, Fowler."

"No. I don't want the game anymore."

"But I do." Hamilton regained his seat and snatched up the card case. His fingers trembled as he extracted the playing cards and started to shuffle, the cards moving choppily at first, then smoothing out as he repeated the motion and regained his flow. "I need to."

To banish Rufus Fowler's ghost. He didn't say the words, but Logan could see the truth in his eyes. Hamilton was haunted and grasping at straws to escape the past, just as Logan had been.

Should he play? Not for revenge, but to help Eva's brother exorcise his demons? It seemed like the right thing to do. But then, his barometer on righteousness had been less than accurate lately.

"Sit!" Hamilton demanded.

At sea in his own mind, Logan sat. Cards appeared in front

of him. He picked them up and stared blankly at the red and black markings. Coins hit the plank table, clattering against the wood. Logan blinked.

"Ante up, Fowler. Time to put the past to bed once and for all."

CHAPTER

29

Evangeline mashed the potatoes with excessive force. And why not? She could work out her frustration over Logan's obstinance and produce silky smooth potatoes at the same time. Benefits all around.

Brushing a droopy strand of hair from her forehead with the back of her wrist, she exhaled in what would have been dramatic fashion had anyone been in the room to appreciate her woebegone fervor. Not that she wanted an audience. She'd pointedly avoided both of her brothers all afternoon. Seth was busy encouraging Christie, and Zach . . . well, those wounds were too fresh to prod just yet.

He'd cheated. Without apology. And stolen and lied and who knew what else, all in the name of providing for her and Seth. It made her feel dirty. Undeserving. She shouldn't be standing in this kitchen making dinner; Logan's mother should be. Zach never should have stooped so low, no matter how great their need.

But he had. And a man had died. Not at Zach's hand, but still—sin had consequences, and these had been steep. A family ruined, and Zach? She'd seen the agony he tried to hide. He suffered, too. It was all a huge mess, and as much as she wanted to rail at Zach for not being the idealized hero she'd thought him, she couldn't despise him. In fact, deep down, she ached for him, for the guilt eating away at his soul. He'd made a mistake. Many mistakes. But so had Logan. So had she. No human had ever escaped that fate.

Except one. And that divine exception was the only one who could take all their wrongs and create something right.

I don't know what's going to happen between those two, Lord, but please keep them from hurting each other. Or from doing something they'll both regret.

Logan.

Evangeline set aside the masher and gazed out the window, as if wishing for him could make him materialize. He might not have been willing to let go of his vengeance, but Evangeline wasn't quite ready to let go of him. After cooling her heels on a long walk with Hezzy—in the *opposite* direction from Logan's property—she'd calmed and examined the situation from a slightly more objective position.

Logan had said he loved her, and she believed him. She loved him as well, even with his destructive agenda. He hadn't challenged Zach to that awful game yet, so she had time. Logan was worth fighting for. Their future was worth fighting for. She wouldn't give up while hope remained, no matter how thin the thread, so she'd prayed with all her soul. Prayed for the Lord to soften Logan's heart, to speak truth into his life in a way that could not be ignored.

She'd prayed for her brother, too. For Zach to find healing from the scars he'd carried for so many years, and for her to forgive his mistakes and not hold them against him.

She was still working on that forgiveness. For both the men

she loved. Hence the silky potatoes. Potatoes that needed to be in the warming oven.

Evangeline snapped out of her thoughts and set the bowl of potatoes next to the ham she'd sliced earlier. Green beans with a few ham chunks thrown in for flavor simmered on a back burner. Yeast rolls sat in a towel-covered basket on the table, butter crock alongside. Dishes were laid out. Utensils in place. Everything was ready.

Except for the folks who were supposed to eat.

The last she'd seen Seth, he was in the parlor with Christie, learning all he could about the schoolmaster, her stepfather, and her baby brother. Evangeline had wanted to listen, to distract herself with someone else's problems, but the two of them had been cozied up together on the sofa, their conversation low and intent. She'd felt awkward about interrupting, so she'd turned her attention to the kitchen. And good thing she had. Seth was so involved with Christie, she doubted he was even aware of the time.

Evangeline strolled down the hall and waltzed into the parlor. Only to have her feet freeze to the ground while her jaw fell unhinged.

Seth had Christie wrapped in an amorous embrace, the two of them kissing with impressive enthusiasm.

Heat rushed to Evangeline's cheeks, and she ducked her head. Good heavens. Her dinner announcement could wait.

She started to back out of the room, wishing herself invisible. If someone had walked in on her and Logan while they'd been embracing, she would have been mortified. She couldn't do that to Christie. She'd probably find the wherewithal to tease Seth about it later, but not now. This was a private moment, one she had no business witnessing. Especially since seeing their shared intimacy highlighted all the bruised places on her sore heart.

She missed the doorway, and her heel knocked into the hutch that stood against the wall. The knickknacks inside rattled, and Seth's head came up. Fierce blue eyes ready to do battle zeroed in on her.

Sorry, she mouthed, hoping Christie hadn't been alerted. "Dinner's, um, ready."

He gave a small, disgruntled nod, then turned his full attention back to the woman in his arms.

Evangeline pivoted and navigated her way safely through the doorway without jostling any other random furniture items along the way.

She was happy for her brother. Seth deserved to find love, as did Christie. They were perfect for each other.

Just as she and Logan were perfect for each other. She set her jaw. They *were*. They'd just hit a bump in the road, that was all. Logan would come to his senses. She'd help him. Maybe she'd even go visit his mother, have a nice long chat with her, see what she could do to help the two of them reconcile.

She'd been praying for Mrs. Fowler every night in her evening prayers, just as she'd told Logan she would do when they first met. The poor woman had been through such horrible heartbreak and loss—a loss Evangeline could relate to all too well. Her parents. Her home. Her brother, Hamilton. She'd not leave Mrs. Fowler to battle that pain on her own. Neither would she abandon Logan.

Or Zach.

Evangeline's forehead scrunched. Her neck craned back toward the boys' bedroom door, which she'd just passed in the hall. Open. She backtracked two paces. Empty. Usually Zach had come in from the fields by now, as he seemed to tell time with his stomach. Yet he wasn't here.

She strode through the kitchen and out the back door.

"Zach!" she yelled, aiming her voice toward the barn, since she saw no sign of him in the yard. "Supper's ready!"

"He's not here."

Seth's voice behind her startled her. She spun to face him, and his unusually ruddy complexion made her smile.

Her smile made him scowl. "Said he had some business to attend to. Told us not to wait supper on him."

She glanced over his shoulder but saw no hint of Christie.

Seth rubbed the back of his neck. "She wanted to freshen up a bit before dinner."

Evangeline's grin widened. "I imagine so." A tiny giggle escaped.

"Not a word, Evie. Understand? I won't have her embarrassed."

"Don't worry. I'll save all my teasing for you." She stepped back into the house and closed the door. "What kind of business did Zach have?"

"He was going to see Logan. Not about Benson, though. Something else."

Something else? Evangeline's heart squeezed.

No. No, no, no!

She pushed Seth aside and ran to the room her brothers shared. With a tiny leap over the pile of dirty laundry at the end of the first bed, she rushed to the small chest of drawers that belonged to Zach and scanned the surface.

Comb. A random button that needed to be reattached to a shirt. A book on hog husbandry. And a conspicuously dust-free rectangle at the far edge of the dresser top.

"They're gone." She sagged onto the bed, deflated.

"What's gone?" Seth leaned in through the doorway.

"The cards." Which meant the deed was probably missing, too.

Oh, Zach. Why? I need more time.

"Cards? Oh." Seth's voice deepened. "I'd hoped he'd given that up for good."

"He had." Evangeline stiffened and jumped up from the bed. "He *has*. I'll see to it. I'll stop them before anything gets out of hand." She vaulted over the clothes again and tried to sidle past her brother, but this time Seth grabbed her arms.

"Whoa, sis. What are you talking about? What's going on with Logan and Zach?"

"There's no time to explain." She tore free of his hold. "I'll tell you everything when I get back."

She nearly ran over Christie in the hallway in her rush to get outside. She wouldn't bother with a horse. She could get there faster overland, anyway. Evangeline threw open the door and ran down the porch steps.

If only Zach had waited for Logan to make the first move. But that wasn't his way. He was the take-charge type who dictated situations instead of reacting after someone else initiated. Only this time, his taking charge might have just killed her future.

No one would escape this idiotic game of theirs unscathed. Couldn't they see that?

"Evie! Wait!"

Evangeline slowed slightly alongside Hezzy's pen and glanced over her shoulder. Christie was running down the steps after her, concern etched into her face.

A loud crack pierced the air.

Christie's eyes widened in shock a heartbeat before she crumpled to the ground.

"Christie!" Evangeline screamed and sprinted to her friend's side. She fell to the dirt, sheltering Christie with her body as her brain tried to process what had just happened.

Someone was shooting at them. From where? She peeked behind her but saw nothing.

Then Seth roared out of the house, rifle in hand. "Get her into the house," he ordered, his eyes harder than she'd ever seen them as he jammed the rifle butt against his shoulder. He strode forward into the yard, away from cover, planting himself squarely between the women and whoever meant them harm. "Move!"

Evangeline startled out of her shock and grabbed Christie's arms. The girl whimpered. Only then did Evangeline notice the blood soaking her right sleeve.

But Christie was tough. She met Evangeline's eyes with purpose as she scrambled to a sitting position. "Help me." She grimaced but reached out with her good arm. "Seth won't take cover until we're inside."

She was right. Not that Evangeline had any desire to dally. Draping Christie's left arm around her shoulders, then wrapping an arm around her friend's waist, Evangeline hefted them both to their feet. They dashed lopsidedly back to the porch and into the kitchen.

"We're in!" Evangeline yelled to Seth.

He backed toward the house, scanning the yard, the buildings, any cover that could be concealing a gunman.

No further shots echoed.

Seth gained the porch, but before ducking inside, he aimed the muzzle of his rifle at the sky and fired three quick shots.

If Zach was within earshot, he'd come running.

Evangeline had wanted to bring her brother home, but not like this. Not with Christie paying the price.

CHAPTER

30

Logan stared at the cards he'd been dealt. Three kings, a strong hand. His fingers itched to sort his cards. His mind buzzed with strategy. His heart pulsed with excitement, with the thrill of the challenge. But his soul? His soul whispered, *no*.

With a pang of regret for the royalty being sacrificed, Logan grimaced and laid the cards facedown on the plank table. "I'm not going to play, Hamilton." He eyed the man across from him. "Or should I call you Mitchell?"

Hamilton's jaw stiffened. "I don't care what you call me," he ground out, his lips barely moving, "so long as you pick up those cards."

Logan sighed. "Look. This is my fault." He leaned back and shook his head. "My ill-advised quest to reclaim a past that can't be restored. I never should have started down this path. You were wrong to cheat. My father was wrong to wager our land. And I was wrong to harbor revenge in my heart. There's plenty of blame to go around, and no card game is going to put any of it to rights."

Something flickered in Hamilton's eyes as he slowly lowered

his cards to the table. "I *need* it put to rights." The hoarse whisper was barely intelligible, but Logan pieced it together, and something resembling empathy stirred in his chest.

"I know what you mean." Logan met the gaze of his nemesis and felt a kinship with him for the first time. The same ghost haunted them both. "That's what has been driving me for seven long years. *Needing* to put things right. But this isn't the way. I see that now."

Logan blew out a breath as he contemplated what else he could possibly say. Then an idea materialized as if from vapor, slowly taking shape until he saw the story he needed to tell. Both for himself and for the man sitting across from him.

"When my dad came home from the card game that night, he ranted and raved about the man who cheated him, vowing he'd bring you up on charges for theft or fraud or whatever he could make stick. But the next day, when he took his righteous indignation to town to complain to the marshal, the lawman wouldn't give him the time of day. None of the men who were there that night would back my father's story, yet several were willing to testify that Rufus Fowler had been known to use his deed to lure men into deep play and then run off with their hard-earned coin. They were more than happy to see him reap some of what he had sown.

"That was what turned my father's anger to despair—the realization that he had brought disaster upon himself." Logan examined the memory with fresh perspective. "When he came home from town, he couldn't look Mother in the eye. He barely spoke except to bark at me to leave him alone so he could think. The guilt must've worn on him. He'd always had a mercurial temperament, and when he sulked, he'd fall into deep melancholy. I suppose the depth overwhelmed him this time, and he failed to pull himself out."

"Why're you tellin' me this?" Hamilton's ashy face was drawn in tortured lines.

Logan leaned forward. "Because I want you to know that my father's death wasn't your fault." He might have believed exactly the opposite for the last seven years, but that didn't make it truth. "He made his own choices."

Hamilton wagged his head. "He might have chosen to stampede off a cliff, but I'm the one who put the burr under his saddle. If I hadn't rigged the—"

A distant sound, sharp yet faint, echoed behind his words. Logan swiveled toward the door.

"Was that a gunshot?" Hamilton asked.

Logan pushed to his feet and stepped into the open air beyond the cabin doorway. "Don't know."

Hamilton followed, both men silent.

One minute passed. Then another.

Insects buzzed. A breeze rustled the tree leaves. Nothing out of the ordinary.

Then it came—three shots in quick succession. Muffled, but definitely from the west.

Eva!

Hamilton bolted past him, making a run on foot. Logan sprinted for Shamgar, thanking God his horse was still saddled and ready.

Please let her be all right. If anything happened to Eva . . . Logan clenched his jaw and mounted.

"Yah!" He swiped his heels across Shamgar's flanks and leaned forward in the stirrups. *Focus on getting to her*, he ordered himself. He'd deal with whatever he found when he got there.

Shamgar slowed slightly as they neared the junction to the main road, and Logan leaned left into the turn. As he did, another shot rang out, this one much closer. So close, in fact, that a telltale whistle tickled Logan's ear as a bullet whizzed by his head.

He lunged more deeply to the side, using Shamgar as a shield even as he urged the gelding to a greater pace. The ex-cavalry horse responded, surging forward as a second shot cracked the air.

Logan twisted his neck, trying to peer behind him for any clue to his assailant's identity, but he saw nothing. Just brush and dirt and Shamgar's rump. He dared not rise up any higher, even to spy the culprit. He needed the cover. If he could get to the bend in the road a few yards ahead, he'd be out of the gun's sights.

A third shot exploded, and a slight sting arced along Logan's right side. He hissed at the pain, even as he thanked God it had just been a crease. The shooter might not be terribly proficient at hitting a moving target, but even Shamgar couldn't protect Logan's back if the shooter found the right angle.

Deciding speed was more important than the shrinking cover his current position afforded, Logan pushed against the left stirrup and returned to a more natural riding position.

"Come on, old boy," he urged, focused on the quickly approaching bend. Hunching down to make himself as small a target as possible, he raced for safety.

A fourth shot rang out. Logan flinched, but no pain slammed into him, and Shamgar didn't stumble. In the next moment, he was around the bend, safe as long as the shooter didn't give chase—an unlikely development, since his attacker had been shooting from the cover of scrub brush, which was too short to conceal a man on horseback.

As Logan relaxed his posture, his mind ran the odds of this incident being a coincidence. Odds that long didn't warrant consideration. There was only one explanation for shots being fired both at the Hamilton homestead and at him.

Benson had recognized him. Or, more accurately, his horse. He had been unusually interested in Shamgar this afternoon. The pieces clicked into place. Benson had spied Logan galloping on the road, just as he must have seen him and Eva racing down to the river on Shamgar's back the day they rescued Christie.

If Benson had beaten a straight path at a quick pace from the livery in Ben Franklin to Pecan Gap, he could have asked about Logan in town. Ascertained where he lived. What girl he'd been courting. Where *she* lived.

A rescued female would be much more likely to take sanctuary with the family of another female, after all, than with a bachelor in an unfinished cabin. With the slow pace Logan and Shamgar had set on the way home, Benson would have had ample time to set up an attack.

Unfortunately, while they could show he had opportunity and motive, they had no actual proof unless Seth or one of the girls had spotted him. And now that Benson knew where the women resided, their plan to wait on the ledger had to be retooled. They no longer had the luxury of time. Or anonymity.

As he steered Shamgar off the main road and down the lane that led to Eva's house, a scrap of red fabric above the roof caught his eye as it flapped in the wind. The signal for an emergency.

A vise tightened around Logan's gut. Not that he hadn't already concluded the first shot he and Zacharias heard had originated here, but the removal of all doubt churned his stomach.

Logan galloped Shamgar straight into the Hamiltons' yard without slowing. Seth would probably have a gun trained on anyone approaching, but Logan trusted him not to shoot.

"Eva!"

Was she all right? *Please let her be all right.*

He cut hard to the right to slow Shamgar, then dismounted from the left before his trusty mount could fully halt. His boots slammed into the ground. Reverberations shot up his legs as he quick-stepped to keep his balance.

"Eva!"

The door cracked open, and the face he loved peered out. "Logan. Hurry!" Her arm emerged, frantically waving him closer. "Get inside. There's a crazed gunman out there somewhere."

He pounded up the steps. "I know," he said as she flung the door wide to grant him entrance. "He took a few shots at me on the road."

She gasped. "Are you hurt?"

"No." The pinch in his side didn't count. He slammed the door closed behind him then grabbed her arms. "Are you?" He scanned her body from head to toe with a critical eye. Disheveled and dirty she might be, but all her pieces were where they belonged, thank the Lord.

Though there was one addition he hadn't expected. A rifle. *She* was the one standing guard? Where was Seth?

Her lower lip trembled as she nodded. "I'm fine. But Christie . . ." A sob caught in her throat as if she'd been holding it in too long. "Oh, Logan. Someone shot her!"

He reached for her, and she came with no hesitation. The rifle fell from her hand to clatter onto the floor as she dove into his embrace. Slender arms wrapped around his waist, stinging his sore side, but he didn't care. She was back in his arms, her beautiful face burrowing into his chest.

All the unresolved issues between them vanished as he held her to him, stroking her back and laying kisses on her hair. This was where he belonged. With her. Forever.

Footsteps pounded outside. Logan thrust Eva behind him and snatched his revolver from its holster. The scrape of metal on wood told him she'd retrieved her rifle and stood ready to meet whatever trouble was headed their way.

Logan eased the door open. "That you, Hamilton?" he called.

"Stand aside, Fowler!" Zacharias Hamilton barreled up the steps at full steam, as if intending to stampede his way inside, regardless of who or what stood in his way.

Logan pulled the door wide and shifted backward to ensure Hamilton didn't trample his sister in his haste.

Zacharias careened to a halt, his heavy breathing filling the tense stillness of the room. His gaze immediately found Eva's. "You all right?"

She nodded.

"Where's Seth?" He scanned the kitchen, his urgency only slightly ameliorated by the evidence of Eva's well-being.

"In my room, tending to Christie. She was the only one hurt. I . . ." Eva's bottom lip quivered, but she pressed her mouth closed and willed it into submission. "I'm not sure how badly. I had to stay out here and keep watch."

Logan holstered his revolver, then reached for the rifle she held. His eyes met hers. "Go to her. Zach and I can manage out here."

Relief and gratitude warmed her eyes, but a hint of uncertainty flared as well when she glanced at her brother then back to him.

Logan winked at her. "We'll behave. I promise."

She hesitated only a moment, then bounced up on tiptoes to place a kiss on his cheek. "I love you," she whispered before dashing off to the room that had once been his.

She loved him. He stared after her, stunned. How could she love him when she still believed he intended to harm her brother?

He hadn't had the chance to tell her about his change of heart. Yet she said she loved him. Now. In spite of everything he'd told her.

His heart swelled to near painful proportions. He didn't deserve a woman like her—one determined to see the best in him, to *bring out* the best in him. He didn't deserve her, but he'd fight to his very last breath to keep her.

And considering the threat closing in on them, he might have to do just that.

Logan turned to Hamilton, who was winded but hiding it well. He grabbed a napkin from the table and ran it over his forehead and face to clear away the sweat.

"Whoever took a shot at Miss Gilliam took a handful of shots at me as well," Logan said casually as he pulled out a chair and took a seat. "From a spot along the road about half a mile northwest. I think it's safe to assume this particular attack is finished for the moment. The schoolmaster's probably halfway to Ben Franklin by now."

"So you think it was Benson."

Logan pivoted at Seth's voice. The other Hamilton walked into the room, his face grim.

"How's the girl?" Zacharias asked.

Seth blew out a heavy breath. "Christie's fine. The bullet took a chunk out of her right arm, but we got the bleeding stopped. She might need a couple stitches though, so if you really think the coast is clear, I'd like to drive her to town and get the doc to take a look."

Logan pushed up to his feet. "I'll ride with you, help keep an eye out."

"I'll do it," Zacharias insisted. "The girl's living under my roof. She's my responsibility."

Logan glared at him. "You've got another girl living under

your roof, and unless you prefer that I stay here alone with her, you'd best rethink your stance. Even though I doubt Benson still poses an immediate threat, there's no way I'll risk Eva's safety by leaving her here alone."

"He's right." Seth crossed the room to stand between his brother and Logan. "In fact, I think we should all go."

"What?" The question emerged from Logan and Zacharias with perfect synchronicity. Zacharias scowled at Logan as if affronted by the harmony. Logan grinned. Nice to know they could agree on *something* from time to time.

"If the shooter was Benson," Seth said, oblivious to the tension between the other two occupants of the room, "then he knows where Christie is. Which means she's no longer safe here. After we visit the doc, we can stop by the church and ask the Clems to take Christie and Evangeline in for a few days. Harder to ambush them if they're in town. Too many witnesses."

Logan nodded. "And with the girls out of harm's way, we can take the offensive."

Zacharias crossed his arms over his chest. "Any idea how we're gonna do that when we still ain't got any proof that Benson's the one behind this?"

"Think of it like a poker game," Logan said, giving Zacharias a look he knew the other man would comprehend. "Our opponent's getting impatient. Taking chances. Telegraphing his next moves. But he still thinks he's smarter than us. So we use that overconfidence against him. Change up our game play. Do the unexpected."

A slow smile creased Zacharias Hamilton's face, and Logan decided that having this man as an ally was much preferable to facing him as an opponent.

CHAPTER

31

"Why didn't you tell me you were hurt?" Evangeline's belly clenched at the sight of the red welt on Logan's right side. The doctor's wife was smearing it with a healthy layer of salve.

The sneak had waited for her to leave to set up their lodging with Mrs. Clem before seeking out medical attention. On purpose, no doubt. Hiding his injury from her. Not wanting her to worry.

Well, if the two of them were going to share a future, they had to share their worries as well. Evangeline lifted her chin. If Mrs. Clem hadn't already been in conversation with Miss Abingdon, the Sunday school teacher, Evangeline would probably still be at the parsonage, trapped by the talkative preacher's wife. Completely unaware of her man's injury. Unacceptable.

Logan twisted his head to look at her. "It's just a scratch, Eva. Nothing to get worked up about."

"Worked up?" Evangeline stomped closer. "Logan Fowler, you have yet to see me worked up."

"I'll, uh, let you two converse in private." The doctor's wife closed the salve tin, and with twitching lips and dancing eyes, exited the examination room.

Logan turned to face her as he lowered his shirt back into place. Slowly enough to make sure he didn't bump that *scratch*. Slowly enough to give her a lovely view of strong muscles that carried not an inch of excess paunchiness.

"Look, Eva . . ." The shirt fabric fell into place, obscuring the last bit of exposed skin.

Oh, right. She was perturbed with him. She stiffened her spine and marched straight to the table where he perched. Muscled torso or not, she had a bone to pick.

"No more secrets." She jabbed her finger into the hollow of his left shoulder. "Isn't that what you said?"

He raised a wary brow. "Yes . . ."

"Well, that includes injuries and scrapes and *scratches*." She jabbed him again, but he was ready for the attack this time and grabbed her finger.

She jerked backward, but he held tight, tugging her closer until only the thinnest sliver of air separated them. She drew in a breath, shrinking the buffer even further.

His gaze pinned her in place with a heat that made her toes tingle. Slowly, he released her finger and placed both hands at her waist. "I'm fine, Eva." He was so close, so warm, so blessedly alive.

She ducked her head, suddenly shy. "I know. I just . . . I don't want you to hide things from me." She forced her attention back to his face. "Even little things."

"Little things, huh?" He grinned at her. "Like the fact that I know your brother's last name isn't Hamilton, but Mitchell, and that he's the son of one of the most famous riverboat gamblers of all time?"

Her heart pounded. "He told you?" Zach never shared that

secret with anyone. She wouldn't know it herself if she hadn't quizzed him about the monogram on his card case a few years ago. Even then, all he'd given her was the name—Jedidiah Mitchell. It had been Seth who'd explained the significance.

"Yep. It came up when I refused to play cards with him."

Everything in her stilled. "You . . . *refused?*" Hope fluttered so fiercely in her belly, her knees took to trembling.

Thankfully, Logan held on tight—steadying her, supporting her. His lips curved into a self-deprecating grin. "Let's just say the Good Lord got my attention and jabbed my conscience with a red-hot poker."

Evangeline tried unsuccessfully to subdue a smile. "Sounds painful."

"Yep. But effective." He lifted a hand from her waist and stroked her cheek with the back of his fingers. "You were right, Eva. About all of it. In fact, once we get everyone settled tonight, I'm going to write my mother a long letter to explain my change of heart and ask what I can do to help her. I'll throw a few apologies in there . . . tell her about you."

Heat flooded Evangeline's cheeks. She glanced away. "Me?"

He cupped her face and gently tilted her eyes up to meet his. "When a man meets the girl he wants to spend the rest of his life with, his mama needs to know about it, don't you think?" The intensity of his regard stole her breath.

Just that morning, she'd believed she'd lost him forever. She'd grieved, prayed, then set her mind to fixing things, but it seemed there was nothing left to fix. God in his goodness had done the mending for her, responding to her petitions with a swiftness she'd never experienced. It left her a mite dizzy, truth be told.

"Do you mean it?" Her whispered words were barely audible, but it was the best she could manage with a blanket of awe mummifying her.

Logan smiled with such sweetness, she swore she could taste the sugar on her own tongue. "Did *you* mean it when you said you loved me?" he asked.

She nodded. "With all my heart."

His smile brightened, his gray eyes twinkling like polished silver. "Then that settles it," he announced with a slap to his thigh. "Time to hang up my gambling boots, finish our cabin, and get to work making a more reputable living. I was thinking cattle. Or we could clear the land and try our hand at cotton. What do you think?"

Our cabin. It was as if he had peeked inside her heart, seen her dreams, and then set himself the task of making them all come true.

"I might even shave off this hairy mess," he said, since she hadn't yet found the wherewithal to string any intelligible words together. He rubbed the beard that camouflaged the bottom of his face. "It gets mighty itchy in the summer." He made a comically pained expression. "And since I don't have to intimidate saloon folk anymore, I don't really need it."

Finding her balance—and a touch of boldness—Evangeline projected a ponderous mien as she took hold of his face and turned it from side to side. "Hmm. I suppose kissing *would* be easier without all this scruff in the way."

Logan's eyes widened. "Tonight." He sat up straighter on the examination table. "I'll shave it off tonight."

She laughed softly, then leaned in and touched her lips to his. Not a deep kiss, just a light touch, a promise of love and belonging. Her lashes flickered closed as she savored the soft joining. Drawing back slightly, she ended the kiss but lingered nearby. Her lips hovered above his, almost touching. The memory of the kiss was so vivid, it was as if they *were* touching. Her breath mixed with his. Her pulse thrummed.

Then the door opened.

Dropping her hands from Logan's face, Evangeline lurched backward. Logan didn't let her go far, however, keeping hold of her with the one hand still at her waist.

"If you're done mauling my sister," Zach said, his scowl firmly in place, though his words didn't carry their usual heat, "we got some plans to work out."

Logan waggled his eyebrows. "I believe your sister was the one doing the mauling. Not that I'm complaining."

"Logan!" she scolded under her breath, mortified.

Zach grunted. "If you and that scratch of yours can walk, we're supposed to meet Seth and Christie at the parsonage."

Logan stretched his long legs down from the examination table and gained his feet. His gray eyes lost their teasing light. "We'll be right there."

Zach nodded once, then pivoted and left the room with the same abruptness with which he'd arrived.

Logan held out his hand to her, and she clasped it. "Ready?"

"Ready." Because as much as she wanted to bask in her love for this man and revel in happy dreams of their future together, she couldn't ignore the danger that threatened both him and the young woman they'd rescued.

Dreams would keep. Reality wouldn't.

When darkness finally fell that night, Evangeline climbed beneath the covers next to Christie in Charlotte Clem's guest room, fully expecting to fall unconscious the moment her head hit the pillow. This had to have been the longest day of her life. Her heart felt like it had been thrown around like a child on a twenty-foot seesaw—exhilarating highs followed by crashing lows, only to repeat with new joys and terrifying fears. It left her light-headed, off-balance, and a tiny bit nauseated.

Evangeline rolled onto her side and drew her knees up to her belly, breathing through her nose to help her stomach settle. She should be deliriously happy after Logan's change of heart and declaration of intentions—this very moment he could be writing about her to his mother!—but the uncertainty of what lay in store for them over the next few days ate away at her serenity.

"Do you think their plan will work?"

It seemed she wasn't the only one unsettled.

Evangeline stretched an arm across the bedside table, turned up the lamp, then rolled over to face Christie. "Having second thoughts?"

The girl nibbled her bottom lip. "Yes," she finally admitted, "but not about trying to find the ledgers. Mr. Benson's trip to Cooper offers the best opportunity to search the schoolhouse. I just wish Seth wasn't the one doing the searching."

"Well, it's less dangerous than tracking Benson's movements in Cooper." The queasiness in Evangeline's stomach intensified. "Benson has never seen Zach, so that gives him a layer of anonymity, but Logan? They've been face-to-face. Even if Logan shaves and alters his clothing with the items he borrowed from Seth, there's no hiding that scar on his face. If Benson gets a glimpse of that, he'll recognize Logan at once. The snake already took a handful of shots at him on the road today. I don't want to tempt a repeat performance."

Christie's face tightened. "So our men risk their lives while we hide away."

Evangeline reached for her friend's hand. "I know," she said as she squeezed Christie's fingers. "I hate it, too. But you're Benson's main target. We have to keep you out of play until the men get him backed into a corner. Once we have the evidence we need, you can testify before the judge and put Benson away for good. Until then, we wait."

Christie tugged her hand free of Evangeline's hold. "I'm tired of waiting." She pushed up on one arm, her features fierce in the shadowy lamplight. "I'm tired of everyone trying to protect me. My mother, passing me off as an imbecile. Seth hiding me away when I should be helping."

Her hand balled into a fist and smacked the mattress between them. "When that bullet hit me today, it brought several things into sharp focus. I haven't been living, I've been surviving. And I refuse to be a victim anymore. Hiding my deafness. Hiding my location. Hiding my feelings." Her eyes sizzled with green fire. "I care about your brother, Evie. A lot. And I intend to stand by his side, even in danger. He shouldn't be at that schoolhouse alone. If someone comes along and catches him digging through school property, he'll be arrested. Or worse, he'll become Benson's next target.

"I brought this trouble upon your family, and I'm not going to hide away while Logan and your brothers fight my battles for me. Stay here if you like, but I'm going to Ben Franklin tomorrow. I'm going to stand watch and do all I can to ensure Seth's safety." She drew in a breath, her voice wavering slightly. "And that's not all."

What more could there be?

"Since I don't have to worry about facing the consequences of Earl's anger anymore, it's time I quit dawdling and go after my stepfather's ledger. With deliveries on Sunday, he'll be out at the still all day tomorrow. I know where he keeps the lockbox under his bed. I'll break it open somehow—take the wood ax to it if I have to."

Good heavens, Christie was turning into a veritable warrior. Evangeline glanced down at the sheet and pressed her lips together. Far be it from her to quench a fellow female's fire, but . . . "Perhaps we shouldn't tackle this all at once." She held Christie's eyes. "Let's deal with Benson first, then we can go after your brother." Seth would never allow Christie to help. Not when her life was in danger. Better to temper her expectations now than have them trampled tomorrow. "Seth promised to help you find your brother, remember? He won't go back on his word. You just have to be patient."

"But Archie could be suffering!" Tears sprang to Christie's eyes. "I could have died today, and no one would have been left to protect him, to care for him. What if the worst happens, and our plans tomorrow fail? What if—?" Her voice choked a little. "What if Benson manages to kill me? What happens to Archie then?"

Evangeline swallowed, her own throat growing thick with the threat of tears.

Was that what had gone through Hamilton's mind while he lay dying on the floor of that derailed train so many years ago? Had he known Zach would take care of his little sister, or had he spent his last moments fretting over Evangeline's future?

"He needs me, Eva." Christie's voice softened to a near whisper. "If he was *your* brother, what would *you* do?"

CHAPTER

32

Logan checked the note he'd scribbled last night to confirm they'd found the right shop, then stuffed the scrap of paper back into his shirt pocket. "This is the bookseller Christie recalled seeing multiple times in Benson's ledger."

Zacharias mounted the boardwalk in front of the shop. The placard read: *Baldwin's Books & Stationery.* "All right, then. Let's go have a chat with Mr. Baldwin."

Logan glanced behind him before following. An unnecessary move, since Benson had to be at least an hour behind them, yet he couldn't help himself. He was antsier than a greenhorn at the poker table with his last chip in the pot.

He and Zacharias had risen at dawn, ridden to the outskirts of Ben Franklin, and watched for Benson's black buggy. As soon as they confirmed the schoolmaster was at the reins and heading for Cooper as planned, they retrieved their mounts and rode cross-country toward the Delta County seat. They shaved off a good four miles from the twelve-mile trek by going overland instead of following the roads. Add to that the average pace of a buggy being much less than a man riding horseback, and they should have gained a substantial lead.

As an extra precaution, they'd paid for stalls at the livery to keep their mounts out of sight. Logan had even shaved his beard and switched out his black duster and Stetson for a blue plaid cotton shirt and floppy tan farmer's hat he'd borrowed from Seth. Their identities were well and truly hidden.

So why did his gut twist every time he looked over his shoulder?

Shoving aside the uneasy feeling, he snagged the edge of the shop door before it closed in his face and caught up to Zach at the counter.

A friendly fellow with a tidy black suit, spectacles, and pomaded hair parted down the middle stepped down from a ladder attached to a large bookcase on the left side of the store and hustled forward to greet them.

"Morning, gentlemen. What can I help you with this fine day?"

As agreed, Logan allowed Zach to take the lead, going so far as to turn his head away from the shopkeeper as he pretended to peruse the portable writing desks and pen sets on display in the glass case that ran the length of the counter. Best to be as forgettable as possible in case the bookseller happened to mention their visit to Benson later in the day. A nondescript, quiet fellow would draw less notice than the man conducting business, and since Benson had never met Zach, any description the shopkeeper might offer would ring no bells.

"Looking for school books. Readers and the like," Zach said.

"You've come to the right place, sir." The clerk shuffled over to the shelves near the front door and pulled four different volumes from a low shelf, then hurried back to lay them upon the counter for inspection. "I have primers, readers, and arithmetic books, as well as geography and science texts on hand and can order anything else you might need. Is this for private use, or are you shopping for a school setting? I supply all the schools in Delta County, I'm pleased to say, and even into Commerce and Sulphur Springs. Can't beat my prices or selection."

"I'm glad to hear that," Zach said, "'cause I'm needing a goodly supply, but my funds are on the short side." He surreptitiously glanced around the store, then turned back to Baldwin. "I heard from a confidential source that you were the man to see if one needed a special deal."

Baldwin reddened and laughed nervously as he started straightening the perfectly tidy shelf next to his elbow. "I have been known to help out a friend from time to time, but I'm afraid this is a business, not a charity organization. Who, uh, recommended me to you?"

Zach crossed his arms over his chest and straightened his posture. "I ain't askin' for charity, mister. I know a fellow in Ben Franklin who tells me their kids seem to be getting by on a tight budget. I'm just asking for similar consideration."

Playing a hunch that Benson was running some kind of shell game with the school board's funds, Logan and Zach had opted to bluff with deuces instead of kings.

Baldwin stiffened, and his face pinched. "The Ben Franklin School Board is made up of a bunch of empty-headed fluff-mongers, if you ask me. They place more importance on community beautification than the education of their children. It's shameful." A gossipy look entered his eyes. He lowered his voice. "Why, I have it on good authority that they squander their budget on items like an engraved school bell, indoor paint, and *flowers,* of all things, wanting the place to look nice for the various social events that occur there. All this while they scrimp on the very items necessary for education. Flowers over books? Outrageous!"

Baldwin adjusted his spectacles and marched to the far side of the counter, lifted a box from somewhere behind the display case, and set it on the countertop. "Thankfully, the schoolmaster at Ben Franklin cares more about nurturing the minds of his students than beautifying the town. These are books I've set aside for him. Secondhand, but in good condition. Even so, he wouldn't be able to afford the quantity he needs without the land speculation money."

Logan met Zach's gaze.

"Land speculation?" Zach masked his surprise as he turned his attention back to the shopkeeper.

Baldwin nodded. "About five years ago, Lawrence invited myself and two other gentlemen here in Cooper to join him in an investment group."

Logan slipped the scrap of paper out of his shirt pocket and scanned the notations beneath the bookshop name. PB, AG, HC—each of those initials had been listed in the ledger. PB must be Baldwin, first name Paul or Phillip or something. Christie hadn't known what they meant, but now they had context. An investment group.

"All of us have modest incomes," Baldwin continued, "yet Lawrence had the clever idea of pooling our resources and using the funds to invest in properties likely to draw the interest of the railroads. We made a tidy profit last year with some acreage around Greenville."

"Sounds like a savvy play," Zach flattered.

"It's worked well so far." The shopkeeper winked, then grew more serious. "Lawrence is the real mastermind. He manages all the details for us."

And most likely cheats Baldwin and the other investors as much as he cheats the school board, Logan thought as he picked up a composition booklet from a nearby shelf and fanned the pages.

"He even came up with the idea of tithing our gains." The shopkeeper idly straightened the schoolbooks in the box so they all stood in tidy columns.

"Tithing?" Zach leaned an elbow on the counter. "Like giving to the church?"

"Precisely." Baldwin smiled. "Before divvying up the profits, he sets aside ten percent and places it in a special account here in Cooper. Whenever one of us wishes to donate to a charitable cause, we submit our request to the group, and if all agree, the funds are withdrawn. Lawrence submitted his pupils, and we've been giving to them on a regular basis. Each time he purchases books from me, I write up two receipts. One for the stingy amount the school board is willing to pay, and the second for the true price, including the tithing money. That way Lawrence can keep an accurate accounting."

Or an *inaccurate* accounting. Logan clenched his jaw as Benson's scheme crystalized in his mind. Baldwin gave the schoolmaster two receipts—one for, say, $200 that didn't include the tithing money, and one for $400 to show the actual total cost for the books, with each man in the investment group basically donating $50 from their tithing account to make up the difference. Baldwin expected his partner to turn in the $200 receipt to the Ben Franklin School Board and use the second receipt for personal record keeping. But if Benson turned in the $400 receipt and received reimbursement for the higher amount from the school board, that would mean he donated $50 from his tithing money but made $200 from the school board, netting him $150. His partners received nothing from their $50 donation beyond the satisfaction of helping needy schoolchildren, never realizing they were actually helping Benson line his pockets.

A hundred or so dollars here and there would certainly

add up, but it didn't seem a sum worth killing over. Unless the crooked schoolmaster was also skimming money from his investment pool.

Use money siphoned from the school board to invest in land speculation, use the tithing money to perpetuate the con, then cheat his partners from their share of the profits. Give each investor enough profit to satisfy, make them believe they have equal say in what is done with the tithing funds to enhance their illusion of control, all while making off with the lion's share of the earnings.

It was quite cunning.

And quite illegal.

How much did Benson keep for himself? Fifty percent? Sixty? *That* might be an amount worth killing over.

Mr. Baldwin's obvious prejudice against bureaucracy in school governance made him an easy target to manipulate. The other partners would be equally gullible. Yet if those men ever discovered they'd been duped, they'd bring Benson up on charges in a heartbeat.

"I don't guess you have any more of them secondhand books sitting around, do you?" Zach wisely steered the conversation back to neutral waters. Pressing Baldwin for details now would only rouse suspicions. "Sounds like that's the price I'm needing."

"I'm afraid all of these volumes are reserved for the children in Ben Franklin." Baldwin removed the box from the counter and lowered it out of sight. He fell silent for a moment, then brightened. "I do have some older editions of McGuffeys that I was planning to mark down. I can give those to you at a discount. There's only about five copies, but it would be a place to start. Oh, and some of the Ray's Arithmetic series I received in my latest shipment arrived damaged. I can give you those for the cost of the postage it would take to return them. There are only four of those, and they're all Volume I, I'm afraid, but they're yours if you want them."

Yes, this kind man with a heart for children would be livid if he discovered Benson's perfidy. Not only was Benson short-changing his pupils, he was profiting from their shortfall.

"I'll take them," Zach said. "Thanks. Oh, and do you have a price sheet for your newer schoolbooks? It might help to show a list to our school board, so they have a better idea of the cost of materials."

"Absolutely." Baldwin reached beneath the counter and extracted a printed flier. "I work one of these up every year when the new books come in. Yours isn't the only organization to request such information." He placed the handbill on the counter and pushed it toward Zach. "I have those books in the back. Let me go wrap them up for you."

Zach nodded, and as soon as Baldwin disappeared, Logan approached.

"Benson's got them all bamboozled," Logan said in a low voice.

Zach scanned the handbill. "Not sure this will be enough to cast doubt on him, but maybe it will get a few board members to start asking questions. Crooks like Benson are smooth as silk on the surface, but their veneer is thin. Start poking at it, and it will tear."

"If we can couple what we've learned from Baldwin with what's in the ledger, we might even get the law to take an interest."

Zach frowned. "That's if Seth found the book. Benson might have moved it out of the schoolhouse."

The one part of their plan that could easily go awry. They were banking on Benson's arrogance. But if he'd gotten nervous and moved the incriminating ledger, all they'd have was a price list and an unsubstantiated theory.

Logan turned to face the front windows, scanning the growing number of people out and about. One in particular—a boy of about twelve or thirteen—appeared to be headed toward the bookshop.

"We might have to visit Greenville and dig up some property sales numbers," Logan said as he angled his face away from the door that was opening. "Show them to Baldwin to see if they match the return on his investment. My guess is that they won't."

The bell above the shop door jangled, and the lanky youth bounded inside. Logan turned his back to the boy and pretended interest in a box of ivory writing paper.

Mr. Baldwin emerged from the back of his shop, a stack of thin books under one arm with a length of brown wrapping paper and twine dangling from the opposite hand. He smiled at the boy as he set his items on the counter.

"Billy. Good to see you. What brings you in today?"

The boy glanced at Zach, then gave him a wide berth as he made his way to the counter. "Got a telegram for ya."

"Ah." Baldwin accepted the folded message, then opened the till and gave the boy a coin. "Thank you for your timely delivery."

Billy snatched the coin, tugged on his cap, and made for the door.

"Give my best to your mother," Baldwin called after him.

A wave was all the response he received as the boy hotfooted it out the door and down the street.

Zach picked up one of the arithmetic books and started examining the slight damage around the binding, giving Baldwin the chance to read his telegram.

"Oh, dear."

Zach glanced up. "Not bad news, I hope."

"I'm not sure," Baldwin said. "Lawrence, the man I told you about? He was supposed to meet with me and the others later this morning, but he wired to say he's not coming. A situation arose that demanded his immediate attention. I do hope it's not one of the children."

Zach jerked his gaze to Logan. The panic surging in Logan's breast reflected in Hamilton's eyes.

Seth was walking into a trap.

CHAPTER

33

Evangeline hunkered beneath the branches of a low-hanging oak behind the schoolhouse, scouring the landscape for any sign of movement. Christie sat poised across the way, watching the road, barely visible behind a clump of juniper near the front of the building. They'd followed Seth without his knowledge, deeming it wiser to avoid the argument that was sure to result if they informed him of their intentions. Evangeline only felt a little guilty. Seth and Zach had been protecting her for years. It seemed right to return the favor.

Her one hesitation centered on exposing Christie. Yet her friend had been determined to lend her aid whether or not Evangeline joined in, which left Evangeline with little choice. She couldn't exactly tie the woman to the bedpost to keep her from leaving. Not that Evangeline hadn't briefly considered the idea. At least this way, she could watch out not only for Seth but for her friend as well.

I know you see everything, Lord. Help us to see, too. To keep those we love safe.

No sooner had the prayer lifted from her heart than a motion caught her eye. Christie. Waving and pointing.

Evangeline crooked her neck around to view the road from the east. A man on horseback approached. A stout fellow dressed in black. The schoolmaster? It couldn't be. He had left town this morning. Logan and Zach would have returned to the house to warn Seth not to search the school if he hadn't.

Heart pounding, Evangeline crept out from under the branches. How Lawrence Benson had come to be here didn't matter. All that mattered was getting Seth out of the building before he was discovered.

With Christie's frantic gestures urging her to hurry, Evangeline sprinted across the open yard to the back of the schoolhouse, keeping her body hunched to make herself as small as possible, not wanting to draw the attention of the man on the road.

She reached the door and eased it open a few inches. "Seth!" If it was possible to yell and whisper at the same time, that was what Evangeline did. "Benson's coming. We have to go. Now!"

"Evie?" A very angry-looking Seth yanked the door inward. "You're not supposed to be here."

She glared at him. "Lecture me later." She grabbed his arm. "Let's go."

Thankfully, her brother was an intelligent sort and settled for a severe scowl that warned of castigation to come as he allowed her to drag him outside. He pulled free of her grip and clicked the door closed behind them, then took the lead, clasping her hand and dashing north into the more wooded area.

As they passed the privy, Christie darted out to meet them. "This way," she urged. "There's a path that leads to my old house. I'll show you."

Seth jerked Evangeline's arm to keep them behind the young

woman leading their escape. "You brought *Christie*? How could you?" The betrayal and stark fear in her brother's eyes shredded her heart.

"This was *her* idea, Seth. She was worried about you and determined to come with or without me. Would you prefer I let her come alone?"

He had no answer. Just made a frustrated rumbling in his throat and pushed her ahead of him on the path while he took up the rear. Evangeline hiked up her skirts and ran. They could hash out who was to blame later.

Christie bounded through the wooded area like a doe, following a path only she could see. Evangeline stayed close, her breaths growing labored. Yet it was the sound of her brother wheezing behind her that spurred her to greater speed. When they hit a small clearing, she surged forward, overtaking her friend and drawing her to a halt.

"What are you doing?" Christie tried to pull away. "We're almost there."

"Seth." The single word was all that was needed.

Christie gasped and pivoted.

Seth, pale yet fierce, stumbled to a halt behind them. "I'm fine," he ground out between wheezes. "Keep going."

Christie wrapped an arm around him to support him.

He shrugged her off. "I said I'm fine. Go!"

She flinched at his jerky motion, but obeyed. As she moved past Evangeline, she leaned close. "Will he be all right?"

Evangeline nodded. "He can speak, so it's not too bad. If the house is close, he should make it."

Christie glanced once more at Seth, then resumed her flight, albeit at a slower pace. Evangeline jogged after her, keeping her ears tuned to her brother's breathing. The rasping sounds grew deeper, heavier, but his footsteps kept pace. She thanked God for his provision and continued moving. The only thing Seth hated more than his asthma was having people treat him like an invalid because of it. He wouldn't take kindly to her checking over her shoulder to make sure he was all right. However, when the house they sought finally came into view, everything inside her sagged with relief.

Christie rushed to the door, opened it and checked inside, then waved the rest of them over. Evangeline scurried forward and held the door for Seth. Christie left her to manage the door, murmuring about getting some coffee on before darting deeper into the house.

Once Seth was inside and the door closed, he hunched forward, braced his hands on his knees, and closed his eyes. Evangeline recognized the posture. He was trying to calm his breathing before his lungs seized. She rubbed his back, his shoulders, trying to help the clenched muscles relax.

"Christie's making coffee," she reassured him. "You'll have some soon." She inhaled and exhaled long, semi-steady breaths of her own, a challenge when she was winded as well. Zach often modeled deep breathing with Seth when he was in distress, so she tried to do the same.

As Seth struggled to draw a full breath, he reached for his gun belt and drew his revolver from its holster. He shoved it at her, his eyes opening long enough to meet hers with imploring urgency. "In case . . . Earl . . . comes home."

Evangeline accepted the weapon without argument, tucking it in the waistband of her skirt at the small of her back. "Christie said he should be out at the still all day, prepping for tomorrow's deliveries."

Seth managed a nod, but his eyes slid closed once again as he fought for air.

Christie rushed back into the small, ramshackle room that

served as both parlor and bedchamber, judging by the pallet in the far corner. "I have water on to boil and ran beans through the hand mill." She looked at Seth, then back to Evangeline. "Can you add the grounds once the water boils? I need to grab that box we discussed earlier."

"Of course."

Christie's eyes never left Seth as she crossed the room to the closed door that stood behind a lopsided chair with faded yellow upholstery. She paused, bit her lip, then pivoted abruptly and opened the door, slipping into the room beyond.

Seth remained in the center of the room, slouched, eyes closed, all his energy focused on inhaling and exhaling. The wheezing had eased slightly, praise God, so Evangeline left him long enough to finish making the concoction that would aid his recovery.

The hiss of water coming to a boil drew her to the stove, past the filth of food scraps and dirty dishes piled in the dry sink. Crinkling her nose, she tried not to breathe too deeply as she located the coffee mill on the counter along with a large tablespoon that appeared to have been given a quick wipe instead of a much needed scrub. Oh, well. It would get the job done, and right now, speed was more valuable than cleanliness.

Bunching up skirt fabric in her hand to protect against the heat, she tipped open the lid of the dented tin coffeepot. Steam spewed out, but when it cleared, she saw a full boil. Taking it off the heat, she heaped in enough grounds to make several strong portions, stirred, then set it aside to brew.

Cringing a bit, she pushed back the grease-spotted curtain of the only window in the room. Bits of broken machinery and tools littered the yard. A chicken coop sloping dangerously to one side stood to the left, a tired-looking wagon to the—wait. The wagon.

Evangeline honed in on the vehicle. Buckboard. Weathered

wood. Spring-mounted seat. No paint or trim. It was *the* wagon. The one that had carted Christie's unconscious body to the river's edge. The one driven by the would-be killer.

Here. On this property. It had to belong to Earl.

Could Logan have been mistaken? Could Earl, *not* the schoolmaster, have been the one trying to kill Christie?

The curtain fell from Evangeline's suddenly trembling fingers. The gun she'd shoved into the waistband of her skirt pressed into her spine. She should have tried harder to convince Christie to wait in town. Coming here was a mistake. They might be standing in the lair of the very man who wanted her dead.

Unwilling to wait any longer on the coffee, Evangeline found a bucket of drinking water by the back door and used the ladle to bring a dipperful to the coffeepot. She opened the lid, wet her fingers, and sprinkled the cool water into the brew, waiting a few seconds for the grounds to sink before filling the mug Christie had left on the small kitchen table. The burn marks and knife cuts littering the table's surface demonstrated a level of negligence and violence that only heightened Evangeline's worries.

Carrying the hot drink, she hurried back to the main room, approached her brother, and gently touched his shoulder. "Here, Seth. Drink."

Slowly, he straightened, reaching for the mug as he unfolded. He staggered over to the faded yellow armchair and sat, bringing the coffee cup to his mouth.

"I saw the wagon," she blurted, needing to tell someone of her discovery.

Seth took a healthy swig of the hot brew, but his gaze zeroed in on hers from above the mug's rim.

"From the kitchen window," she said, turning to point to the room she had just vacated. "It's here. The one Christie's attacker used to cart her to the river. Do you think—?"

The front door slammed open and banged against the inner wall. "I knew you'd come crawling back here, gal. Been watchin' for ya." Earl limped through the door, spittle spraying his unruly beard under the force of his words. "Ungrateful wretch. Leaving me to do your work. You'll feel the back of my hand before you fill your belly with any of my . . ." His words faded, and his brow crinkled. He squinted at Evangeline. "You're not Christie."

Evangeline willed her hands to cease their trembling as she reached for the revolver. "No," she said as she pulled the gun from behind her back. She pointed it at Earl and cocked the hammer. "But I'm a friend of hers, and I won't let you or anyone else hurt her ever again." Behind her, she heard Seth stand.

Earl's eyes widened at the sight of the gun, then narrowed as he discounted the woman wielding it. "You're tresspassin'." He took a step forward and gestured viciously back toward the door. "Get out!"

Seth stepped forward, jaw set, nostrils flared. No one would think he was still recovering from an asthma attack, not when he looked that mean. Pride and confidence in her brother steadied Evangeline's hand.

Earl's attention swung to Seth. He halted his advance but not his bluster. "You, too," he demanded. "Out!"

"No, Earl," a quiet voice said from behind Evangeline. "We aren't leaving until I get what I came for."

Earl staggered back a step. "Christie. You're . . . you're talkin'." His Adam's apple plunged up and down as he gaped. "But I thought . . . I thought . . ."

She advanced into the room, chin high. "You thought I was an imbecile. I know. But I'm not. I'm deaf. That's all, just deaf. My mind is as strong as yours. Stronger."

Earl glowered. "Why, you disrespectful little—"

Seth shifted into his path. "I'd watch what you say if I were you, mister."

Shaking his head and muttering something Evangeline couldn't understand, Christie's stepfather retreated.

"Where's Archie?" Christie's voice grew stronger as she faced down her tormentor. "I want him, Earl. Want to raise him, take care of him. You owe my mother—you owe *me*—that much."

"I don't owe you nothin', you ungrateful—" His attention caught on the lockbox in Christie's hands. "Oh, I see how it is. You came to rob me." He gestured to the room at large. "Thieves, the lot of you. Breaking into a man's house, stealing his valuables. I'll bring you all up on charges."

Evangeline squared her shoulders. "Not before we bring you up on charges of our own. Attempted murder, for starters."

"What the devil you talkin' about, woman? I ain't never kilt nobody."

"Not for lack of trying." Evangeline advanced a step. "I saw the buckboard in your yard. The very same buckboard I witnessed at the river the day someone tried to drown your stepdaughter. She was wrapped in a blanket as if she were some kind of animal. Dumped. Shoved under the water with the kick of a man's boot. That man deserves to rot in prison."

"Well, it weren't me!" Earl roared. "I might have smacked her around a time or two, but I never tried to kill her. What would be the sense in that? I need her to make my deliveries. My bum leg can't handle the mileage."

"Then someone used your wagon," Evangeline pressed.

"But no one's driven that thing since . . ." Earl's eyes narrowed to slits. "Why, that slimy snake! Sabotagin' my business. I'm gonna chop Benson down at the knees for this."

Evangeline's stomach flip-flopped. The evidence they needed to prosecute Benson. Right here. Growling and stomping about like a riled bear. Earl was the key. He could testify against the schoolmaster. And judging by his demeanor, he'd be more than willing.

She looked at Seth, understanding and agreement passing between them. Seth moved forward, intent on taming the bear, but before he could get within reach, a loud explosion boomed, shaking the walls of the cabin.

Earl yelped. "My still!"

Without warning, and moving much faster than a man with a gimpy leg should be able, he sprinted out the door.

With a roll of his eyes, Seth downed the last of his coffee, traded his mug for Evangeline's revolver, and gave chase.

CHAPTER

34

Logan urged Shamgar into a full gallop as they hit a patch of flatland. The eight-mile trek to Cooper that had taken a little over an hour on the way in needed to be cut in half. Even then, they might be too late to help Seth. All they could do was pray. And ride like a gale-force wind.

Shamgar responded well to his rider's demands. The ex-cavalry mount had been trained for long-distance speed. Hamilton's mount, on the other hand, struggled to keep up.

They hit a rugged section of terrain, forcing the pace to slow as they picked their way over eroded ground and miniature arroyos. Logan turned in his saddle to judge Hamilton's progress. He had fallen well behind. His horse was heavily lathered, its head drooping.

"Go on," Hamilton shouted to him. "If I push Jack much more, I'll risk running him into the ground."

"You sure?" It felt wrong to leave him behind.

Hamilton's gaze met his, and even across the distance that separated them, Logan could feel his intensity. "Help my brother."

The words cut through every barrier remaining between the two men. *This* Logan understood. This drive to protect one's family. To rescue those who depended on him. He for his mother, Hamilton for his adoptive siblings.

"I will." The vow echoed in the air. Firm. Resolute.

Logan set his jaw, faced forward, and touched his heels to Shamgar's flanks. "Time to run, old boy. Seth needs the cavalry."

Together they raced over hills and through trees—a regiment of one.

Gradually, the landmarks became more familiar. They were closing in on Ben Franklin. Maybe a little under two miles—

Boom!

The sound of distant cannon fire concussed the air. Shamgar didn't so much as flinch, but Logan jerked his head up so quickly, he nearly unseated himself.

What on earth?

Slowing Shamgar just enough to take stock of his surroundings, Logan searched the horizon for any clue as to what had transpired. It hadn't really been cannon fire, he knew, but something had definitely exploded.

There. A trail of smoke barely visible above the trees. North to northwest. Near the Ben Franklin schoolhouse.

His pulse thumping as loudly in his ears as Shamgar's hooves, Logan leaned over his horse's back and surged forward, praying for Seth with every stride.

"Wait!" Christie cried as the man who had the answers she sought ran away from her. She darted over to Evangeline and grabbed her arm. "We have to go after them!"

Evangeline didn't waste time arguing. Seth wasn't in any condition to chase down Earl on his own. He needed more time to recover before exerting himself again. "Let me grab the rest of the coffee first. Seth might need it."

Christie nodded. "I'll stash the lockbox back under the bed. I know where Earl keeps the still, so we won't be far behind."

Coffeepot in one hand and mug in the other, Evangeline ran as smoothly as she could, keeping her arm upraised and the pot's spout aimed away from her body in case any liquid sloshed out. Christie kept pace with her, though Evangeline didn't really need her guidance. The thick gray smoke billowing to the east pointed the way like an Old Testament pillar of cloud. Yet this cloud was far from holy. Even from a distance, she could smell the caustic odor of burnt corn mash.

Seth would never be able to breathe in there.

She had to get to him and take over the role of protector, whether he liked it or not. Just like when she'd warned him in the schoolhouse about Benson—dear heavens! Benson!

Evangeline threw her mug arm out across Christie's stomach. The young woman exhaled a muffled *oomph* and stumbled to a halt.

"What is it?"

"A trap." Evangeline peered ahead, into air thick with smoke. Smoke that would obscure the man who wished her friend dead. She scanned the area around them and spotted a stand of pecan trees. "There. Come on."

Not taking the time to explain, Evangeline herded Christie like a recalcitrant ewe toward the grove, getting behind her and pushing her shoulder against the young woman's back.

Once behind the trees, Evangeline set down the coffee supplies and took her friend by the arms. "Benson wants you dead. We know he's here. We saw him. There's a good chance he saw us as well. He's probably the one who blew the still, hoping to draw us out. Lying in wait just like he did at the homestead."

Christie's green eyes flashed with panic. "Seth!"

"I'll go after him, but you've got to stay here. Hidden. It's the only way." Christie shook her head, but Evangeline tightened her grip on the young woman's arms, unwilling to let her think with anything other than cold logic. "Benson's not after me or Seth. But if you go in there, he'll get exactly what he's been wanting—another chance to kill you with no witnesses."

"But Seth—"

"I'll send him to you," Evangeline interrupted. "Be ready with the coffee. If he's in that smoke, his lungs will be seizing. He needs to know exactly where to find you. I'll tell him to look for this copse of trees. Once he's here, get that coffee into him, then get him as far from the smoke as possible. Can you do that?"

Christie stiffened her shoulders and nodded.

"Good. Be watching."

Without the coffee paraphernalia to slow her down, Evangeline flew down the well-trodden path into the woods. The deeper she went, the more smoke she encountered. What started as a slight haze quickly darkened and obscured every loping step she took.

Then she heard the sound she most dreaded. Hacking, uncontrollable coughs. She spied Seth's tan shirt through the trees and raced for him. He stood bent in half, a handkerchief tied around his face, a hand clutched to his chest.

"Seth!" She ran to him and wrapped her arms around his middle, trying to move him back the way she had just come. "You have to get out of this smoke."

"Earl . . . couldn't . . . follow . . ." His body shuddered as coughs wracked him.

"Don't worry about Earl. I'll go after him."

He shook his head. "No. Too . . . dangerous . . . Benson . . ."

"Benson wants Christie, and she's alone by a stand of pecans a hundred yards back. Go to her, Seth." If she'd managed to get Christie to stay put by convincing her it would help Seth, the reverse ought to work as well. "She's the one in danger, not me."

He tilted his head and gave her the look that said he knew exactly what she was trying to do. Obviously, he had much more practice divining her machinations than Christie did, but he couldn't deny that she spoke the truth, even if it was an incomplete version.

"You're not doing anyone any good here, Seth." If cajoling didn't get him moving, maybe harsh truth would. "The smoke's too thick for you to follow Earl, and your lungs are too weak to stay here, even if your hard head doesn't want to admit it." Another set of coughs quaked through him as if to make her point for her. She raised a brow at him. "Go to Christie. Watch over her. Clear your lungs. Trust me. I'll stay hidden and use the smoke to my advantage. I won't interfere with anything. I'll just keep an eye on Earl." She set a hand on his arm. "We need him, Seth. He can testify against Benson."

Seth was stubborn, but he wasn't stupid. With a tight nod, he straightened, his hand going to the buckle of his gun belt. "Here," he rasped as he shoved the heavy accessory at her. She reached for it, but he hesitated in letting it go. "Stay . . . safe."

"I will," she vowed, the love and concern in her brother's face making her eyes itch more than the haze of smoke. She took the belt and strapped it around her waist, the holster hanging low over her hip. On impulse, she clutched Seth in a quick, fierce hug, then gave his shoulder a little shove. "Go."

Her heart surged in thankfulness when he turned and staggered into a jog that took him away from the smoke.

Evangeline ratcheted up her skirt and yanked at the petticoat beneath. Her hems were always ragged, thanks to her regular jaunts with Hezzy, so it took little time to find a tear she could exploit. Using both hands, she yanked a large section of cotton free from the lower ruffle, then tied the material around her nose and mouth. Inhaling what would be her last gulp of halfway decent air, she squared her shoulders and forged deeper into the thicket.

Within minutes, Earl's angry voice rasped through the trees. "You destroyed my still! I'll see you hang!"

"Moonshining's illegal, friend." Another voice. Benson? "I'm doing the community a favor."

Evangeline slowed to a near halt and skirted away from the path, moving from tree to tree, looking for a safe vantage point from which to watch the confrontation. She squeezed between the trunks of two oaks growing practically on top of each other and squinted into the smoke. Her eyes, raw and stinging, watered. She brushed at them impatiently with the back of her hand. Just then, a breeze blew, clearing a path for her to see. Secreting her body behind the larger of the twin oaks, she peered around the trunk.

Earl stood with his back to her near a pile of rubble that looked to be a mess of barrel shards and copper tubing.

Another man stood across from him. A man in a black suit, with a shiny bald head.

And a shotgun.

"They'll thank me for ridding their town of an unwanted bootlegger," the man in the suit argued in a smooth, cultured voice. Calm. Confident. Controlled. Not even the smoke seemed to affect him. "You're the criminal here. Not me."

Earl limped forward, ducked his head to cough and spit something vile upon the ground, then advanced again. "I reckon they'll see things differently when they learn you tried to kill my stepdaughter."

Silence, thick as the smoke billowing up from the splatter of sour mash, filled the air.

Earl pressed his advantage. "She can talk. Betcha didn't know that, did ya? Told me what ya done. How you used my wagon to cart her down to the river. My own wagon."

Evangeline cringed. *Stop talking!* The fool was giving too much away. He was going to endanger Christie even more with his bravado.

Earl continued ranting, too worked up by the destruction around him to consider the consequences. "You're a bold one, Benson. Too bold. I *will* see ya hang."

"I don't think so."

In a blink, the schoolmaster jerked the shotgun he carried up to his shoulder and pulled the trigger. Earl grabbed his belly and fell to the ground.

Evangeline jumped at the booming sound of the shot and gasped at the sight of Earl crumpling to the ground. Smoke filled her lungs at the violent inhale, and coughs immediately followed. She lunged behind the oak, pressing her hand tight against her mouth to muffle the sound.

"Who's there?" Benson snapped.

Tears stung her eyes as she tried with all her might to keep her coughs inside. An impossible task. One escaped. Then another.

Pressing her lips together to try to hold in the coughs, she pulled Seth's revolver from its holster and clutched it in front of her with both hands.

Footsteps crunching against scorched earth mixed with Earl's moans and curses.

"That you, Miss Christie?" Benson's voice. Closer. "You've caused me no end of trouble, my dear."

More steps.

Should she run? Stay hidden? *God above, what do I do?*

CHAPTER

35

Logan stopped at the schoolhouse long enough to determine that Seth wasn't there, then immediately remounted and headed in the direction of the smoke. The same direction Earl had come from the day he delivered that jug of bootleg whiskey.

Hurry, his gut urged. *Faster!*

Bending over Shamgar's neck, Logan pushed the horse to a gallop. He approached a small, rundown cabin and slowed. "Hello, in the house!"

No one answered.

"Seth?" he shouted as he turned Shamgar around in a tight circle.

Go! That inner voice demanded obedience, and Logan responded without questioning. He pointed Shamger in the direction of the smoke and gave him his head.

After riding a short distance, a movement to his left drew his eye. A woman. Arms overhead, waving. He squinted into the thin haze. Christie?

His heart plummeted. If Christie was out here, that meant . . .

"Eva!" He reined Shamgar in and jumped from the saddle

before the horse had a chance to halt. "Where is she?" he yelled at the deaf woman. "Where's Eva?"

"Come," she said, grabbing his arm and tugging him toward a copse of pecan trees. "You have to help. He's too heavy for me."

He? Logan didn't care about any *he*. He needed to find Eva.

Then he saw Seth, lips slightly blue, body hunkered against a tree trunk, a sick wheezing sound echoing in the air.

"I need to get him away from the smoke, but he's too weak to walk." Christie's voice cracked. "Please."

Eva would never forgive him if he walked away from her brother. Shoot, he wouldn't forgive himself. Logan bent, grabbed Seth's arm, and stretched it around his shoulder. Seth was barely conscious. Logan took hold of his middle and lifted. His thighs and back strained under the weight, but with an extended grunt, he got him up, then dragged him toward Shamgar.

He caught Christie's eye. "Hold the horse's head still." Shamgar wouldn't shy, but the girl looked desperate to help.

Seth roused enough to grab the horn and swing his leg awkwardly over the saddle. But before Logan could turn to give Christie a leg up too, Seth grabbed Logan's wrist.

"Evie . . . in woods . . . gunshot . . . Benson . . ."

Logan's blood turned to ice. He wanted to throw Seth off Shamgar's back and race into the trees, but that wasn't an option. Not with Seth at death's door.

Logan stared him in his bloodshot eyes and gave his solemn vow. "I'll find her."

Seth's hand fell away.

Logan spun to lift Christie up behind Seth. The sooner he got them away, the sooner he could go after Eva.

"How far to the still?" he demanded of the young woman when she looked at him to collect the reins he held out to her.

She wrapped her arms around Seth's slumped torso and

gathered the leather straps around her fingers. "No more than a hundred yards straight into the thicket." She nodded her chin in the direction.

Logan slid the rifle from the saddle boot, then turned Shamgar toward the clearer air back toward the cabin he'd passed. With a smack to the horse's rump, he sent Seth and his lady off, then sprinted straight for the woods and the heart of the smoke.

Evangeline cocked her revolver with a quivering thumb, pointed the barrel to the sky, and slowly leaned toward the opening between the twin oaks, keeping her belly as close to the tree as possible. She couldn't risk running without first pinpointing where her hunter stood. His occasional coughs told her he was somewhere to her right, but she didn't know how close.

She slid sideways a hair farther, until her right eye cleared the trunk, then jerked back. Dear heavens! He stood less than ten yards from her. Running was out of the question.

But hiding would do her no good, either. Eventually, he'd wander close enough to discover her location.

That left only one option. Brazen it out.

Inhaling a deep breath would only wreak further havoc on her lungs, so she had to settle for a quick closing of her eyes instead as she reached deep into her gut to find her courage. *Lord, help me.*

Then, with bleary eyes and burning lungs, she stepped through the narrow opening between the twin oaks and pointed her weapon straight at the schoolmaster's chest. "Stop!"

The command would have been much more satisfying had it not exited her mouth as a wimpy rasp. Thankfully, her body bluffed better than her voice, for her hands were steady and her legs held firm.

Benson didn't jump or startle. He simply turned to face her . . . and smiled. "Ah, Miss Hamilton. Aren't you the plucky one?"

"Toss your shotgun on the ground!" That order had a little more gumption in it. She even made a gesture with the barrel of her revolver to indicate where he should throw his weapon.

"I don't think so."

He'd made that same reply to Earl a heartbeat before he'd shot him. Evangeline swallowed and narrowed her eyes. "Now!" she blustered. She couldn't let him think her weak.

But it seemed he'd already made up his mind about that, for he called her bluff, shaking his head as he lifted his weapon an inch higher. "You won't shoot me. You don't have the stomach for it."

Was he right? Probably. Her gut was churning even now at the thought. But she couldn't let him win. He'd just shoot her and go after Christie.

She pulled the trigger. He actually jumped this time. Satisfaction surged in her chest when his weapon dropped back to its original position near his waist.

"That's your one and only warning," she growled through her petticoat kerchief like a real bandit as she adjusted her aim back to his torso. "Now, drop your gun."

Unfortunately, the schoolmaster didn't follow the script and start quivering in his boots. Instead, he smirked that superior, condescending smirk of his and said, "No."

Of course he said *no*. He hadn't blinked an eye over shooting Earl in the belly, either.

The shotgun started a slow crawl back toward Benson's shoulder. "You won't shoot me," he mocked.

Her finger hovered over the trigger, ready but frozen. Oh, mercy. He was right. She couldn't do it. Couldn't shoot a man.

He grinned in triumph as he set the stock to his shoulder. "Your heart's not hard enough."

"Mine is!" a male voice boomed.

Evangeline dove for the ground, and a shot rang out behind her.

Benson yelped and took off at a run.

"Eva!" Footsteps pounded the ground. Then all at once Logan knelt beside her, wrapping his strong hands around her shoulders. "Are you all right?" His beautiful gray eyes searched her face.

Heavens, but she wanted to curl up against his chest and let him hold her until her nerves settled and her heart ceased trying to jump out of her rib cage. But she couldn't. Not when there was so much at stake.

She sat up and yanked the makeshift kerchief from her mouth. "I'm fine. Go after him." She pushed at his arm. "He shot Earl. If you catch him, we can take him before a judge. I saw it happen."

Logan glanced in the direction Benson had run, then back at her, clearly torn.

"Go!" She pulled away from him and stood on her own feet. The smoke was lifting, making it easier to see and breathe.

Still, Logan hesitated. "What about Earl?" The fallen man's moans had grown weaker, but they could still be heard.

"Benson gutshot him." Evangeline started walking toward Christie's stepfather. "I'll do what I can for him, but I don't think he'll last much longer." She nodded in the direction the schoolmaster had scurried. "Go, Logan. Bring Benson to justice."

He held her gaze for a moment longer, then pivoted and sprinted after the fleeing man.

Evangeline hurried to Earl's side and dropped to her knees. Blood was everywhere. It pooled beneath him, oozing over his hands where he'd tried to plug up the holes. Unfortunately, Benson's buckshot had left too many for him to stopper.

He turned his face toward her, his eyes already glassy. "Take it," he rasped.

"What?" Evangeline looked around for an object of some kind, but saw nothing.

Nothing but blood. *Dear Lord.* She had to try to help him. Grabbing her skirt, she found a relatively clean spot and pressed it against a place at his side that seemed to be oozing more than the others, though there was so much blood, it was nearly impossible to tell where the actual wounds were located. Dizziness assailed her, but she shook it off. She had to focus. Had to help him.

He must be in so much pain. Tears dribbled from the corners of her eyes. Bright red blood stained her fingers. She stared at the color on her hands, and her stomach lurched. She'd known he would be bad off, but she hadn't been prepared for . . . *this.*

"Quit . . . fussin', girl." He lifted a hand and swatted weakly at hers. "Too late . . . for me. Take it," he said again. "Take it . . . to Christie."

Evangeline frowned. "Take what?"

Slowly, with a tight grimace and a low moan, Earl lifted a hand to his chest and grabbed onto something inside his shirt. "Key."

He yanked downward, but it wouldn't come free. He was too weak to break the leather thong tied around his neck. His eyes slid closed in defeat.

Evangeline barely knew this man and liked him even less, thanks to his treatment of Christie, yet even so, her heart went out to him. He was dying. She couldn't just ignore his struggles.

Clasping his hand, she eased the key from his grip. She slipped the thong off his neck, and when she laid his head gently back onto the ground, the lines around his eyes softened.

"Tell her . . . she was right." Earl captured Evangeline's gaze. "Her ma deserved better. *She* deserved better." His breathing started to gurgle slightly. "Archie's in Longview . . . with my sister. Took him in . . . for the money. Won't want him . . . if the payments . . . stop." A cough interrupted him, a choking cough full of blood-colored spittle.

Evangeline set the key aside and lifted his head, turning it so he wouldn't choke. When he calmed, his eyes found hers again.

"There's letters . . . in the lockbox. Ledgers, too. Benson's not as smart . . . as he thinks . . . he is. Take him . . . down."

Evangeline gave a sniff, and dipped her chin to rub her eye against her shoulder. "We will," she promised. "He'll not hurt Christie or anyone else ever again."

Earl's eyes slid closed. "Good," he murmured, the word slurred and hard to understand. "Needs to pay . . . for blowing up . . . my still."

His body went slack. His breathing stopped. Evangeline bent over him and wept for a life cut short by violence. Wept for her best friend, who'd just lost another family member, even if he was a despicable creature who seemed to care more about his still than his stepdaughter.

However, he wasn't entirely heartless. He'd given Evangeline the key that could lead Christie to her baby brother. Maybe there'd been some good in him all along, hiding deep beneath the scurrilous surface.

You know the truth of his heart, Lord. Evangeline touched a hand to his shoulder. *Have mercy on his soul.*

She collected the key Earl had given her with his dying breath and stood. After wiping the blood off her hands with the neckerchief she no longer needed, she dropped the soiled scrap of petticoat next to the dead man and stared in the direction Logan had gone.

Keep him safe, Lord. One fatality was enough for today.

She tucked the key into her pocket and started walking back to Earl's cabin, praying all the way that the Lord would see justice done.

CHAPTER

36

Logan jogged through the woods, ears tuned for footsteps and heavy breathing. The occasional cough fell like a breadcrumb, creating an audible path for him to follow, yet the farther they removed themselves from the smoke, the fewer coughs sounded.

Benson seemed to be heading south, but he jigged and jagged so often, it was difficult to determine his destination.

Logan stopped to listen for another breadcrumb, but nothing out of the ordinary met his ears. He looked southeast. Would Benson head for Ben Franklin and the townsfolk who would rally around him and make a confrontation difficult? He shifted his gaze southwest. Or would he return to the schoolhouse, gather what he could, and make a run for it? Logan blew out a breath. Or maybe the crafty devil had stashed a mount somewhere in the woods and had a completely different escape route planned. There was no way to know.

Figuring that he would hear a horse, Logan opted to head southwest. The schoolhouse offered immediate shelter and anonymity. If Benson went to town, there would be witnesses to report which way he had gone.

By the time Logan hit the clearing on the outskirts of the schoolyard, sweat ran down the sides of his face. The pudgy schoolmaster was spryer than Logan had given him credit for. Of course, a man's survival instincts provided remarkable fuel.

Recalling the shotgun, Logan dashed toward the cover of the outhouse. A shot fired, but not at him. At least he didn't think so. It sounded too muffled. Raising his own rifle into a ready position, he peered around the side of the privy.

The back door of the school flew open, and a black-suited, bald-pated ball of a man rolled heels over head down the rear steps and sprawled on the ground, his back slamming into the packed dirt. A dark, avenging angel followed him out. Face fierce, Zacharias Hamilton tossed away the weapon that Benson must have tried to use on him.

Hamilton strode forward. Benson whimpered and floundered like an upside-down stink beetle in a hopeless effort to get away. Hamilton grabbed him by the shirtfront with one hand and lifted the teacher's head and shoulders off the ground. He drew back his right fist but paused before throwing the punch.

"Where's my brother?" he growled.

Benson shook his head. "I don't know," he whined. The smug bully who'd not half an hour ago shot an old man and threatened a woman had turned into a whimpering weakling when confronted by a man he couldn't intimidate.

Hamilton's fist slammed into Benson's jaw. His head banged against the dirt, and he actually started crying.

"Where's my brother?" The question was a roar this time.

Logan grinned. One would think a schoolmaster would be smart enough to figure out what came next if he didn't give the correct answer. Yet all Benson did was cower, shaking his head as if that would dissuade the man above him.

Disgusted yet driven to speed things up, Logan stepped out

from behind the outhouse right as Hamilton drew back his arm to deliver another blow. "Seth's up at Earl's cabin."

Hamilton kept his grip on Benson's shirtfront, but his fist fell as he turned his head to regard Logan striding toward him.

"He's in a bad way," Logan said, knowing Eva's brother would care more about family than punishing the man at his feet. "The smoke did a number on him, but Christie's with him. Hopefully Eva will be too, pretty soon."

Logan had hated leaving her behind, alone with a dying man. She might have acted tough on the outside, shooing him away with common sense and a competent bearing, but he knew her sensitive heart would take a blow. It wasn't easy to watch a man die. His mother had never fully recovered from the experience.

Hamilton straightened, bringing Benson's upper body with him as if it weighed next to nothing. "Where's Evie?"

"With Earl." Logan jerked his chin toward the schoolmaster. "Benson shot him. She bore witness. And I bore witness to him trying to silence her like he did his ex-partner."

Hamilton's eyes narrowed to slits. His fist drew back and struck like lightning. Benson's head snapped back, and he lolled unconscious.

Logan stared at Benson as Hamilton dropped him into the dirt where he belonged. "Great. Now I'm gonna have to carry him to the marshal's office."

"I'll leave you my horse," Hamilton said, voice dry.

Logan shrugged. "Good enough."

"He needed my fist in his face."

"Yep," Logan agreed. "Wish I had an excuse to bestow a second helping."

Hamilton grunted. Logan took it as agreement.

"Seth?" Hamilton lifted his head to consider a landscape other than Benson.

"There's a path to the north there." Logan pointed just past the privy. "It'll take you straight to the house. I'll drop Benson off at the marshal's office, then notify the undertaker to bring a wagon out for Earl."

Hamilton reached for something inside his coat, then shoved two thin books at Logan. "Found Benson inside, pryin' up a floorboard when I got here. These were in the space beneath."

Logan stared at the ledgers, his blood surging. The proof they needed.

"Testifyin' against him is all well and good," Hamilton said, "but a snake like Benson can twist words and popular opinion to suit his purposes. Proof in his own handwriting is harder to deny."

Logan tucked the thin volumes into the back of his waistband. "I'll make sure the marshal understands their significance." He glanced up at Hamilton. "Tell Eva I'll be back as soon as I can."

Hamilton nodded.

They still had rocks the size of boulders between them, but nothing impossible to navigate, given enough time and willpower. For Eva's sake, and perhaps even his own, Logan would clear the debris on his end and pray that Hamilton would do the same.

His former nemesis and future brother-in-law, if Logan got his way, took off at a jog, and Logan scowled down at the still unconscious schoolmaster.

"All right, Benson," he grumbled as he hunkered down and slung the man over his shoulder, "time to pay the piper."

Two hours later—who knew the marshal would make him write out his entire statement, or that the undertaker would have to be dragged away from the barbershop?—Logan finally made it back to where Earl's body lay. The marshal had more questions about what transpired, so he followed Logan to the cabin while the undertaker headed back to town. He interrogated each of the Hamiltons along with Miss Gilliam. Christie added another ledger to the pile of evidence collected. Apparently, Earl had kept his own record of barters, listing all the moonshine he had supplied the schoolmaster believed to be a pillar of morality in the community.

Thankfully, Seth had made a full recovery and was easily able to relate his version of events, but it was Eva's haunted recounting of Earl's murder that finally removed the last speck of doubt from the marshal's mind. By the time the lawman was ready to return to Ben Franklin, he'd worked up quite a temper and was ranting about calling an emergency city council meeting the moment he returned. Between the school board, Benson's investment group, and the hangman, there was no shortage of people who would be out for the man's blood.

Yet as satisfying as that was, Logan felt no closure. Not when heartache lingered in Eva's eyes. She'd been through a lot today, seen things no young woman should have to see. She put up a feisty front, assuring everyone she was fine, but Logan sensed the bruises on her spirit.

Eager to put this place behind them, everyone began to mount up. Christie and Seth rode double on one of Earl's wagon horses, Christie carrying the prized lockbox and a flour sack filled with what meager belongings she'd chosen to keep—two changes of clothes, a hairbrush, a Bible, and a photograph of her parents on their wedding day. Hamilton, sitting atop Jack, turned and raised an eyebrow at Logan.

"Go on ahead." Logan waved him on. "We'll meet you back at the house in a bit."

Hamilton scowled, opened his mouth as if to argue, then promptly shut it and gave a curt nod.

Trust and permission had been granted. Reluctantly, but granted nonetheless.

Logan held Hamilton's gaze, an unspoken pledge of honor passing between them, then watched as the three riders left.

Eva stood silent, petting Shamgar's neck. Head down. Shoulders slumped. Gently, he placed a hand at her waist and turned her to face him. She came without resisting, but her chin remained down, hiding her wonderful eyes from him.

"Eva," he pleaded, "look at me."

Her chin lifted first, then, gradually, her lashes. Her brown eye seemed vulnerable and sad, while her blue eye shimmered with uncertainty.

"Is it really over?" she whispered.

Logan tugged her close and reached a hand up to stroke her hair. "Yes, love. It's over. Christie's safe. Benson's behind bars. Everything's—"

She grabbed him so tightly, she squeezed off his words. With her face buried in his chest, her body shook with the force of her sobs. He wrapped both arms around her and laid his cheek against the top of her head. She'd been strong for so long. For Christie. For Seth. She'd even been strong for him, sending him after Benson while she dealt with Earl. He'd seen the body when he returned with the undertaker. A gruesome mess. How much worse must it have been while Earl was still alive?

His cheerful wood sprite had faced death three times today. With Seth. With Earl. Even on her own. It was no wonder her spirits had been depleted. It was a miracle she was still standing. She deserved to unload her burden, and the fact that she'd chosen him for the task over one of her brothers made his heart swell so full, if his ribs weren't there to cage it, it would surely have burst from his chest.

After several minutes, her grip loosened and her head lifted. She gave a little sniff and started to apologize, but he stopped her.

"No sorrys, darlin'. I'm here for you. Always."

A shaky smile curved her lips as her gaze met his. "I love you, Logan."

He closed his eyes and touched his lips to her forehead, lingering, savoring the closeness, thanking God for keeping her safe. The chilling image of Benson's shotgun aimed directly at her midsection would be burned into his brain for years.

"I love you, too," he said as his lips separated from her skin. "And I never want to let you go."

"That's good." Her smile grew steadier, her eyes reclaiming the teasing twinkle he so adored. "Because I don't plan on escaping any time soon."

As happy as that declaration made him, he had one of his own to make—one he hoped would lay a better foundation for their future than the slipshod work he'd done thus far.

"Eva, I have a favor to ask of you."

She must have noticed the seriousness of his tone, for she blinked and leaned back a little, choosing an angle better suited to examining his face. Yet no worry shone in her eyes, only trust.

Logan swallowed. No matter what he did from here on out, he'd never deserve this woman. But he'd do everything in his power to ensure she never regretted choosing to share her life with him.

"I need six months," he blurted before he lost his nerve. "Six months to finish the cabin, purchase a starter herd, and prove that I can provide for us without gambling." He blew out a breath, then dove in for the rest. "I need time to put things right with my mother," he rushed on, not quite able to meet her eyes, "which will take me away for extended periods. It's not ideal for courtin'." He dug at the ground with his boot heel.

"But it's important." Her words echoed verbatim the thought running through his mind, as if she'd peeked inside his skull and read it written there.

Logan found her eyes, and the utter acceptance gleaming in them melted away his last insecurity.

"Your mother is family, Logan. Taking care of her, loving her, is your God-given duty. All I ask is that you let me help. Bring me into your family just as I have brought you into mine."

Her plea so humbled him, he tugged her to his chest so she couldn't see the moisture gathering in his eyes. "You're already there, darlin'," he murmured, the words hitching only slightly over the emotion clogging his throat. "You're already there."

Epilogue

MARCH 1895

Evangeline held out her left hand to admire the new gold band residing on her third finger for what must have been the tenth time since Logan had placed it there an hour earlier. *Mrs. Logan Fowler.* Had there ever been a name so fine? For all the years she'd lived with a borrowed name, being gifted with a new one that bound her to a man who made her heart turn giddy little flips every time he smiled at her was a blessing that still hadn't fully sunk in to her brain.

Surely, Hamilton would approve. When Zach and Seth had both walked her down the aisle of the Pecan Gap church, she'd held her head high, making no effort to hide her eyes from the townsfolk. Hamilton had been right all those years ago. Her eyes were a gift from her parents, a way to remember them, and on her wedding day, she'd wanted all three of them near—Mama, Papa, and Hamilton. So she'd lifted her chin and marched forward on her brothers' arms, feeling *all* of her family surrounding her, bestowing their blessings and wishing her joy.

When she'd reached the front of the church and taken Logan's hand, his face alight with pride and love as he beheld his bride, she knew she'd never hide her eyes again. No doubt some people would still see her as an aberration instead of one of the Creator's more unique designs, but the small-mindedness of a few would no longer blanket her in shame. Not when her husband looked at her as if she were his every dream come to life.

"It's not going to get any shinier, you know." Christie's teasing voice brought a happy blush to Evangeline's cheeks as her sister-in-law entered the bedroom that Evangeline was vacating after nearly eight years.

She kept her arm aloft, looking up from the symbol of love on her finger only long enough to ensure the shape of her lips would be visible. "How long does it take for the wonder to wear off?"

Christie shrugged, lifted her left hand, and admired the ring on her own finger. "I don't know. Hasn't happened for me yet."

They laughed as Christie retrieved the small valise Evangeline had returned to fetch before she'd been caught up in the nostalgia of saying good-bye to her childhood and starting a new life as a married woman.

"Are you sad to leave?" Christie asked.

Evangeline shook her head, unable to stop a silly grin from overtaking her face as she thought about moving into the cabin Logan had crafted. "No. Especially since I know I can come visit any time I like."

"Of course. This will always be your home," Christie assured her.

"I'll always be welcome," Evangeline corrected, "but this is *your* home now. Yours and Seth's and Archie's."

Christie and Seth had married last Christmas. Zach had moved into the barn's tack room to give them the largest bedchamber, where Archie had slept on a miniature bed in the corner. Not exactly conducive to a newlywed couple's privacy. Seth had been more than eager to help Evangeline pack up her things last night, and if the box in the hall was any indication, he already had Archie's belongings ready to move into her space the moment she left.

He loved that boy, though, and Archie adored him. The little fellow followed Seth everywhere, especially down to the river. The fish stories those two could tell. They'd be catching whales by Easter.

"Mrs. Fowler," a deep voice boomed, "your husband is growing impatient."

Tiny pinpricks of excitement danced over Evangeline's neck at Logan's call. Heaven knew they'd both been growing impatient over the last few weeks. When he'd first asked her to give him six months to prove himself, she'd wanted to refuse. He hadn't needed to prove anything to her, after all, not since the moment he'd sacrificed his vengeance to make peace with her brother. Yet she'd sensed that he needed to prove something to himself, so she agreed to his terms, and the waiting period brought its own blessings. They'd developed a deep, soul-binding friendship that anchored their love in something more stable than mercurial passion. That friendship enriched her love for Logan and gave her confidence in the joy they would surely experience in the years to come.

Evangeline's thoughts must have shown on her face, for Christie grinned and gave her a little push toward the door. "Better not keep him waiting."

Evangeline looked over her shoulder. "How did you know?"

Christie laughed. "Who do you think sent me in here after you?"

"Mrs. Fowler," a different male voice called, "please inform Mrs. Jefferson that her husband grows equally impatient."

Evangeline smirked. "It seems Seth is eager to have his wife by his side as well."

Christie's cheeks turned pink, and Evangeline grinned.

Seth had reverted to his given surname at his marriage—Jefferson. Though all of their documents were signed with both last names, making Hamilton just as legal as Jefferson, Seth wished to pass on the name of his father to his own children someday. Perhaps even to Archie, should the boy wish it. He and Christie had decided to let him choose for himself which name he wished to carry once he was older.

"That man." Christie made a shooing motion with her hand even as her green eyes glowed with unfettered happiness. "I've only been gone for two minutes. You'd think it was *our* wedding night approaching, not yours."

With how quickly Seth had implemented the switch in sleeping arrangements, Evangeline imagined that was precisely what her brother was thinking. The faster he could send Evangeline and Logan on to their own cabin, the faster he could rid the homestead of the wedding guests and have the place to himself. She was pretty sure she'd overheard him scheming to have Uncle Zach invite Archie to camp out in the barn with him tonight, too.

Before Evangeline could tease her sister-in-law about that, though, the impatient men stormed the castle. Logan tossed the door wider than it already stood, strode in, and snatched Evangeline completely off her feet. She shrieked, then laughed and kicked her legs in weak protest.

"Come on, woman." The mock sternness of his face only increased her giggles. "We have a threshold to cross."

Evangeline wrapped her arms around his neck as he swished her sideways to allow Seth entrance. "Do you plan to carry me all the way to the cabin?"

Logan met her gaze, a roguish grin lighting his eyes. "Nope, just to the wagon. For now." He waggled his brows. "Once we get home, though, I plan to sweep you up again and not let you out of my arms until sometime tomorrow."

"Logan!" Evangeline swatted his shoulder as her cheeks burned, not that the scoundrel cared.

In fact, her unrepentant husband dipped his chin and captured her lips in a kiss that stole every thought of protest from her mind. By the time he finally pulled away, her fingers were thoroughly entangled in the hair at his nape, and her breathing had become embarrassingly ragged. The only thing that saved her from complete mortification was the fact that Seth was currently giving Christie the same treatment.

Her brother tugged her satchel from Christie's limp fingers and pushed it into the hand Logan had positioned beneath Evangeline's knees. Once the transfer was complete, Logan marched straight for the back door and out onto the porch.

A chorus of hoots, hollers, and whistles erupted. Evangeline hid her face against Logan's neck.

"Logan Everett Fowler," a cultured feminine voice scolded, "that's the future mother of my grandchildren you're man-handling."

"I've got a good hold on her, Mama," Logan called, removing any hope that he'd allow Evangeline to walk on her own two feet to the wagon. Then his clean-shaven jaw nudged her face up so he could look into her eyes. "And I'm never letting her go."

Her insides swirled and dipped like a ballroom full of waltzing troubadours. She no longer cared that they were making a spectacle for her neighbors and friends. All she cared about was the man she adored.

"I love you, Logan Fowler," she whispered for his ears alone.

His crooked smile made her pulse flutter. "I love *you*, Evangeline Pearson Hamilton Fowler. Forever."

He carried her down the porch steps, and everyone surrounded them to give their final well wishes as they made their way to the wagon. When they reached Logan's mother, though, he paused and bent down with Evangeline still in his arms to allow the small gray-haired woman with dancing eyes to kiss his cheek.

The change in Logan's mother had been remarkable. She had gone from a withdrawn, hopeless widow to a vibrant woman of renewed purpose and vitality. According to Logan's aunt, the change had started the day she received Logan's letter and solidified the first time Logan had introduced her to Evangeline.

It turned out her grief had not solely been due to the loss of her husband and home. The most acute portion had been reserved for the son she believed had followed his father's disastrous path. Once Logan convinced her he'd left that life behind, her sprits revived, and the baby blankets she had once knitted for the poor box were now piling up in a chest for the grandbabies she hoped would soon follow the wedding.

Evangeline reached a hand toward her mother-in-law. "Will you be all right, Mother? You know you're welcome to stay with us as long as you like."

"Nonsense, dear. I'll not be getting in the way of those grandbabies you promised me."

Heavens. Even Logan's *mother*? Evangeline doubted her cheeks would ever recover. They'd surely be stained bright red permanently.

Mrs. Fowler had avoided going inside any of the buildings of her former home. Not the house, nor the barn. The closest she'd come was to pat the trunks of the peach trees near the porch. She'd been staying with Logan until today and had accepted the Clems' hospitality for a final night before she left for her sister's house on the morrow.

"I'll expect letters, though." Mrs. Fowler's eyes narrowed. "*Detailed* letters. Regularly."

"Yes, ma'am."

Matilda Fowler turned her attention back to her son. "Go on, now." She released Evangeline's hand with a grin and waved them on. "Take your bride home."

"Don't have to tell me twice." Logan's long legs ate up the ground between the crowd and the waiting wagon.

Zach had the team hitched and waiting, and after Logan gently dropped Evangeline onto the bench seat, her brother approached. Logan moved to the horses' heads, checking harness Evangeline knew was perfectly in place.

A frown crinkling her brow, she turned to question her brother, only to find Zach's eyes tinged not with joy or teasing, but with something far heavier.

She reached a hand out to him. "What is it?"

He took her hand, looking down at their joined fingers. "I'm leaving Pecan Gap, Evie."

She reared back, heart thudding in alarm. "What? Why?"

"Logan's responsible for your welfare now. Seth's settled with Christie. You don't need me watching out for you anymore. It's time for me to set out on my own."

She tugged on his arm, trying to draw him closer, but his feet remained stubbornly rooted to the ground. "You're my brother, Zach. I'll *always* need you."

He finally lifted his eyes. "We're not kids, Evie. You and Seth have found the lives you've always wanted. Now it's time for me to do the same." His mouth twisted into a smile she didn't quite believe. "With Seth raising hogs now instead of crops, he can manage without me." He gazed over at the muddy pens where snorting hogs rooted around in the same ground that once supported sorghum stalks. "I hate farming, Evie. You know that. Crops, hogs, doesn't matter what kind. There's a fellow up north with a lumberyard who's looking for a partner to expand his operation. I'm meeting with him on Monday."

Dismay churned her belly. "So soon?"

"It's time."

Time for him to finally have the freedom he'd always craved. She remembered the tough kid with the chip on his shoulder who scared off all potential adoptive families so that he could create his own life instead of having one forced upon him. Yet one had been forced upon him anyhow. A life of instant parenthood, making him responsible for two orphans who depended on him for everything. A life that brought him back to the land, a living he despised, yet one he willingly took on to provide for his siblings.

It would be unfair of her to hold him back just because she would miss him. He deserved his chance at happiness, even if it meant she must revise her definition of happily ever after.

He was right. It was time.

"Promise me something?" she said.

Zach raised a brow, immediately suspicious. "What?"

"Don't cut yourself off from us." Evangeline squeezed his hand with all the pent-up grief and love this conversation inspired. "We're still your family. Always and forever. Follow your dream, Zach—heaven knows you deserve it—but share it with us. Write to us. Visit. Keep us involved. I've already lost one brother. I couldn't bear to lose another."

Zach cleared his throat and returned the tight grip on her hand. "I promise."

His low rasp brought tears to her eyes, but she blinked them away. Zach had never handled her softer emotions well.

344

"Then go with God, brother, and may he bless you as richly as he has me."

Zach gave a quick nod, then dropped her hand and stepped away from the wagon. As if the signal had been prearranged, Logan abandoned the horses and climbed into the driver's seat.

"Take good care of her, Fowler," Zach said.

Logan nodded. "I will."

Zach saluted with a touch to his hat brim, and Logan released the brake. The team plodded forward as the crowd behind them cheered.

Evangeline turned to wave, her smile bright until her gaze found Zach. To him she sent silent vows of support and encouragement. He might not be the heroic figure she'd once believed him to be, his knightly armor dented and tarnished from past mistakes and lingering repercussions, but he was her brother, and she loved him unequivocally.

Gradually, the house, her friends and family, and her worries for her brother faded from view, leaving her alone with her husband.

Logan covered her knee with his hand. "You all right? Zach told me about his plans this morning before the wedding."

She clasped his fingers. "I will be." She looked down the road as if looking into the future. "I'll miss him terribly, but he deserves his freedom."

"A man's plans don't always work out the way he expects." Logan's smile instantly reminded her of all they had gone through to get to where they were today. "Sometimes God throws a fork in the road at just the right time."

She grinned at her husband. "I just hope that stubborn brother of mine will be smart enough to see the road sign and follow it. He can be a mite set in his ways."

Logan caressed the outside of her knee with his thumb, and

Evangeline's pulse stuttered. "If the Lord sends your brother a road sign even half as spectacular as the one he sent me, Zach will see it."

Evangeline's stomach fluttered in pleasure. Such a glorious compliment deserved a reward. She stretched upward and kissed her husband straight on the mouth.

She intended the contact to be brief, but Logan took charge, dropping the reins and wrapping his arms around her. He drew her close and kissed her so deeply, she completely forgot where they were or what they were doing.

Until the wagon lurched to one side as the horses wandered off the road.

Logan released her and took up the reins, a chuckle rumbling in his throat. "You, Mrs. Fowler, just earned yourself a bumpy ride home." That roguish gleam danced in his eyes again as he snapped the traces and set the team off at a gallop.

Evangeline squealed as she grabbed the side rail with one hand and her bonnet with the other.

Her husband would always be a man of surprises, and who was she to complain? She rather liked him that way. She laughed into the wind as they raced by the trees, suddenly as eager as he was to discover where their next adventure would lead.

Christy Award finalist and winner of the ACFW Carol Award, HOLT Medallion, and Inspirational Reader's Choice Award, bestselling author **Karen Witemeyer** writes historical romances because she believes the world needs more happily-ever-afters. She is an avid cross-stitcher and shower singer, and she bakes a mean apple cobbler. Karen makes her home in Abilene, Texas, with her husband and three children.

To learn more about Karen and her books and to sign up for her free newsletter featuring special giveaways and behind-the-scenes information, please visit www.karenwitemeyer.com.

Sign Up for Karen's Newsletter!

Keep up to date with news on Karen's upcoming book releases and events by signing up for her email list at karenwitemeyer.com.

More from Karen Witemeyer

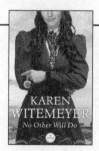

When the women's colony of Harper's Station is threatened, founder Emma Chandler is forced to admit she needs help. The only man she trusts enough to ask is Malachi Shaw, whose life she once saved. As Mal returns the favor, danger mounts—and so does the attraction between them.

No Other Will Do

You May Also Like . . .

In the aftermath of tragedy, Grace hopes to reclaim her nephew from the relatives who rejected her sister because of her class. Under an alias, she becomes her nephew's nanny to observe the formidable family up close. Unexpectedly, she begins to fall for the boy's guardian, who is promised to another. Can Grace protect her nephew . . . and her heart?

The Best of Intentions by Susan Anne Mason
CANADIAN CROSSINGS #1
susanannemason.com

Dr. Rosalind Werner is at the forefront of a groundbreaking new water technology—if only she can get support for her work. Nickolas Drake, Commissioner of Water for New York, is skeptical—and surprised by his reaction to Rosalind. While they fight against their own attraction, they stand on opposite sides of a battle that will impact thousands of lives.

A Daring Venture by Elizabeth Camden
elizabethcamden.com

Marianne Neumann became a placing agent with the Children's Aid Society with one goal: to find her lost sister. Her fellow agent, Andrew Brady, is a former schoolteacher with a way with children and a hidden past. As they team up placing orphans in homes in Illinois, they grow ever closer . . . until a shocking tragedy changes one of their lives forever.

Together Forever by Jody Hedlund
ORPHAN TRAIN #2
jodyhedlund.com

⧫ BETHANYHOUSE